THE WORLD OF THE GATEWAY

SPIRIT ASCENDANCY

SPIRIT
ASCENDANCY

Book 3 of The Gateway Trilogy

E.E. HOLMES

Lily Faire Publishing
Townsend, MA

www.lilyfairepublishing.com

ISBN 978-0-9895080-6-3 (Paperback edition)
ISBN 978-0-9895080-7-0 (Digital edition)

Publisher's note: This is a work of fiction. Names, characters, places and incidents are either the product of the author's imagination or are used fictitiously.

Cover design by James T. Egan of Bookfly Design LLC
Author photography by Cydney Scott Photography

For Myles, who lights every dark place, and scatters joy like rain.

"Fear no more the heat o' the sun,
Nor the furious winter's rages;
Thou thy worldly task hast done,
Home art gone, and ta'en thy wages:
Golden lads and girls all must,
As chimney-sweepers, come to dust.

Fear no more the frown o' the great;
Thou art past the tyrant's stroke;
Care no more to clothe and eat;
To thee the reed is as the oak:
The scepter, learning, physic, must
All follow this, and come to dust.

Fear no more the lightning flash,
Nor the all-dreaded thunder stone;
Fear not slander, censure rash;
Thou hast finished joy and moan:
All lovers young, all lovers must
Consign to thee, and come to dust.

No exorciser harm thee!
Nor no witchcraft charm thee!
Ghost unlaid forbear thee!
Nothing ill come near thee!
Quiet consummation have;
And renownèd be thy grave!"

—William Shakespeare
Cymbeline, Act IV Scene ii

CONTENTS

I

INTO HIDING

I STOOD ON THE ROLLING LAWNS OF FAIRHAVEN HALL. A warm, muggy breeze whipped my hair around my face. Ribbons of smoke rode on the air's currents, stinging my eyes. Before me, flames billowed around the castle, blackening its stone walls. Figures darted around the castle, thrown into sharp relief by the inferno's pulsing golden glow. Shrieks echoed in my ears: I shivered in the ashy warmth.

A small, cold hand slipped into mine and squeezed it tightly. I looked down. Mary, gazing out over the destruction, stood beside me.

"What have we done?" I asked.

"This was always going to be. It was etched in the pages before they were bound into the *Book of Téigh Anonn*. Like all those who try to flee from a prophecy, the Durupinen have run straight into its welcoming arms. The Prophecy was always waiting right here for them to arrive." Mary's voice—the voice of the Prophecy itself—was calm and sure.

I looked away from her and stared back at the flames. "So much destruction," I whispered.

"So much more to come," she replied.

I snapped my gaze back to her. "What did you say?"

"Wake up, Jess."

"What did you say?" I repeated. "What do you mean?"

Mary turned and stared at me with flames glowing in the sockets where her eyes should have been. "It's time to wake up, Jess," she said, in a voice very unlike her own. I knew that voice.

I pulled my hand away and felt a throbbing pulse of pain. I looked down in time to see my fingers crumble to ashes and float away on a gust of hot, smoky wind.

"Jess! Wake up!"

I opened my eyes and tried to focus my blurry vision. The dim interior of a car. The hum of an engine. Terrible pain in my hands and forearms. A figure beside me, shaking my shoulder gently.

"Jess, it's me. It's Finn. I let you sleep as long as I could, but you must wake up now."

As I met Finn's haggard expression, the terrible weight of the night's events came crashing on top of me again—events all more terrible than the nightmare I'd just left behind. Fairhaven Hall *was* burning, but it was burning at least fifty miles from here.

The fire was our doing: When Hannah had Called every spirit she could reach to attack the Durupinen Council, Fairhaven Hall had caught fire in the ensuing chaos. Hannah had only Called the spirits to enable our escape—an escape we desperately needed or else we would've been imprisoned in the dungeons for crimes we hadn't committed. Before we'd fled, the Durupinen had revealed to us their most ancient and feared Prophecy; this Prophecy, the Council believed, foretold our being the mythic twins who would bring about the rise of our mortal enemies, the Necromancers, and ultimately the annihilation of the Durupinen. We had barely managed to flee in a stolen SUV that Savvy and Lucida had hotwired, and now we were...

"Where are we?" I asked. My voice came out in a hoarse croak.

"Is she awake?" came another, much softer voice. I turned my head and saw Hannah's anxious face mere inches from my own. "How are you feeling?" she asked me.

"Like I stuck my arms into a blazing fireplace." I lifted my heavily bandaged appendages gingerly from my lap and let my mouth fall open in mock horror. "Oh, right. I *did* stick my arms into a blazing fireplace."

Hannah attempted a weak smile, but I knew she was only doing it to humor me.

"Okay, but seriously, how do you feel?" she asked again.

"Seriously? Like I would gladly consume every painkiller on God's green Earth," I answered. "How do I look?"

"Awful, but a quick trip to the hairdresser and a wardrobe intervention would cure that real quick," said Milo, popping through the seat beside me.

"Didn't we leave you back in the inferno? Shucks, I meant to," I said.

"Shut your face, you love me," said Milo.

"Well, if we met on the playground I'd probably punch you, so yeah, it must be love," I said. Then I turned to Hannah again. "Where are we?"

"Just outside of London proper," Finn answered.

I looked more carefully around me. The car had stopped, although the engine was still running. We had pulled into a cobblestoned alley beside a grubby-looking pub. The front passenger-side door hung wide open, and I could see Savvy lounging against a brick wall and savoring a cigarette with obvious relish. Lucida, talking animatedly on her cell phone, paced back and forth in front of the SUV.

"What's going on? Why have we stopped?" I asked.

"Lucida said we need to switch vehicles. She's on the phone with someone who can help us do that, I guess," explained Hannah.

"Normally, the Caomhnóir would be able to track their own vehicles," Finn said. "But Lucida's disabled the system—they shouldn't have been able to follow us. Still, they'd only need to report their car stolen and we'd have the PC after us as well. We've got to get rid of this SUV quickly."

"But I thought you said no one at Fairhaven would ever go to the police?"

"Jess," Finn began, "you and Hannah may very well be the Prophecy incarnate—the very thing they're most frightened of. That's never happened before. And Marion now has control of the Council... that's never happened before, either. We can't anticipate anything they might do now."

I nodded at Finn, then glanced out the window to make sure Lucida was out of earshot. Turning to Hannah, I asked, "Can we really trust her to do this? I know she's your mentor, but there were an awful lot of people at Fairhaven that we should've been able to trust—they turned on us in a heartbeat."

Hannah had begun shaking her head even before I'd finished speaking. "I know you don't like her, Jess, but just because you two don't get along doesn't mean we can't trust her. Think about it. Why would she have gotten us out of there only to turn us back in? It wouldn't make any sense. And anyway, what choice do we have now?"

I shrugged. "None, I guess." I swallowed the rest of my argument, which wasn't much of an argument at all. Hannah was right: I didn't like Lucida, but we didn't have the luxury of picking and choosing our allies right now.

I watched as Lucida finished her conversation. She then opened the back of her phone and removed what looked like a SIM card; she dropped the card on the ground and crushed it firmly beneath her heel. Finally, she tossed the phone into a nearby trash can and walked back toward the car.

"Did you just throw away your cell phone?" Hannah asked in disbelief as Lucida opened the door.

"Indeed, I did," said Lucida, sliding back into the driver's seat and twisting around to face us. "Disposable mobiles—they can't be traced. Okay, my lovelies, new wheels are on the way, but we aren't going far. The best course is to get you lost in the city. It'll be far more difficult for them to find you there."

"Isn't that where they'll expect us to go?" I asked.

"Of course. But it will be much easier to hide you here, even if this is where they're looking," she explained.

"If you say so." I didn't have any strength to argue; the pain coursing through my arms was making it difficult to concentrate.

"Don't forget who you're talking to, love," Lucida said. "I'm the best Tracker Finvarra's got."

"Tracker?" I asked.

"That's right. I don't just sit around looking smashing, you know. No one in the Northern Clans can hold a candle to me for detection and investigative work. That's why they put me on the case to find our girl here," she said, punching Hannah lightly on the arm. Hannah grinned, although I did not. "Point is," she went on, "I know every method the Durupinen use to find people, so there's no one better to hide you until we get this all sorted."

Savvy, noticing the conversation, flicked her cigarette onto the sidewalk and hopped back into the car. "Right, what are we in for now?" she asked.

"Car's on the way," Lucida said. "First point of order, though, is to decide where to take you."

"Oh, I got any number of mates we can crash with," offered Savvy. "If you can get us to the East End, I can ring up—"

"Savannah, don't be thick," Lucida said harshly. "Rule number one: We can't go anywhere that any of you have ties. The Durupinen know you're from London, Savvy; your people are the first places they'll look. So that means no looking up any of your

4

mates or your family whilst we're here, right? As far as any of yours know, you're not in the city at all."

Savvy's confident smile crumpled, and she nodded. She'd obviously expected to be of some use now that we were back on her turf, and I could tell she was disappointed to be rendered so useless. In fact, if anything, she was a liability—we'd have to be careful not to run into anyone she knew.

"Right, then," said Lucida, turning away from us and running her hands through her hair. "Right, let me think a minute."

"I have an idea!" Hannah said, lighting up. "Jess knows someone in London we can stay with, don't you, Jess?"

That pulled me out of my pain-induced silence. "What? I do?"

Lucida waved her off dismissively. "Haven't I just said we can't use any connections here, in case the Durupinen—"

"But the Durupinen don't know about this connection. At least, they have no idea she's in London! No one does!" Hannah went on.

"No!" I cried, startling Hannah. "I'm not dragging her into this! She's been put in enough danger already, and I'm not going to—"

"Who are we talking about, now?" Lucida asked.

"No one," I said shortly. I shot an angry look at Hannah, who had the decency to look contrite, but she plowed on regardless.

"Her name is Annabelle Rabinski," she said before I could stop her. "She was on that ghost hunting team Jess worked with back home."

"I'm familiar with the name," Lucida replied. "And she's here? Why?"

"Because... well, because of what happened to Pierce," Hannah said quietly.

Just the mention of Pierce's name caused a pain nearly as severe as that in my hands to shoot through my heart.

"Yeah, Siobhán mentioned he'd snuffed it," Lucida said with her usual lack of tact. "But why does that mean she's come to London?"

Hannah hesitated and looked at me, clearly unsure of how to proceed. I sighed deeply as everyone in the car turned toward me. It was time to lay all the cards on the table. Lucida and Savvy hadn't been in the Grand Council Room. Even Finn only knew part of the story. We couldn't proceed until everyone knew everything.

I rallied myself through my pain. "It's because of the Necromancers," I said. "Everyone needs to know about this before we do anything else, especially you, Lucida, because if you're trying to protect us, then you need to know the Durupinen aren't the only ones who'll be looking for us. This situation is much more dangerous than anyone realizes."

No one spoke. No one moved. It was as though the very name of that ancient enemy had sucked all the air from the car, suspended us all in time.

"They've been looking for Hannah and me. They must've been onto me even before I knew about the Durupinen, because one of them joined Pierce's investigative team last spring. His name is Neil Caddigan. He poses as an academic paranormal researcher. He and the other Necromancers—I don't know how many of them there are—have been reorganizing in secret. He kidnapped Pierce and tortured him for information about me, and he's the one who followed us into the city last month and ran us off the road. Milo saw him and recognized the Necromancers' symbol on his shirt."

"Yeah, he had a silver pin on his collar," Milo confirmed. "An arch or something. Not very chic."

"The Necromancers are back?" Savvy whispered.

"Yes."

"But what would they want with you?"

"At first, I had no idea why they would've singled us out. But now I think it's because of the Prophecy. They knew about it, somehow, and must've figured out that Hannah and I might be the twins it foretold. They've been after us ever since. And you," I paused, locking eyes with Lucida in the rearview mirror, "don't look at all surprised by this news."

Lucida returned my gaze. Although she had remained silent, her face was far too grim, and her eyes reflected entirely too much understanding for any of this to have been news to her.

Hannah tore her eyes from me and trained them accusatorily on Lucida in the rearview. "Lucida, did you know about this? About the Necromancers?"

Lucida shook her cloud of hair back and let out a bitter bark of a laugh. "Those fools. Those bloody ignorant fools. I suppose you tried to tell the Council this, did you? And Finvarra, too?"

"Yes."

"And I suppose they just laughed in your face, did they? Told you the Necromancers were finished, and to shove off?"

"Something like that, yeah," I replied.

6

"So bloody typical," Lucida said, then sighed deeply. She turned all the way around in her seat and gave me a long, hard look. "Don't leap to the wrong conclusion. I don't know who this Caddigan bloke is and I had no idea he was after your professor, but I was the one Tracking you both. There was... evidence that someone else was looking for you, too."

I frowned. "What do you mean?"

"Like when we'd arrive at a location with a lead, right, it was sometimes obvious that someone else had already been there. Twice we thought we had a trail for Hannah, but then the records we needed would go missing—someone else had already gotten at them. The first few times, I thought it was your mum covering her tracks, but it kept happening even after she died. I alerted the Council, but they fully dismissed me. Marion actually implied that I simply wasn't trying hard enough." Lucida laughed again. "Please. Like that woman could Track her own arse without signposts and a map."

"But you never thought it was the Necromancers?" I asked.

"I can't pretend the thought didn't cross my mind," Lucida said. "But I never considered it a serious possibility. I knew someone was looking for you, and that whoever they were, they were damn good at it since they could beat me to the punch. I knew it had to be someone with deep pockets and excellent Tracking skills, but... the Necromancers?" She shook her head with a low whistle. "We've all grown up thinking of them as much more myth than reality, like ancient history. But then, what's that saying about forgetting history?"

"I don't remember the exact wording, but I'm pretty sure it ends with us all being doomed," I said flatly.

"Right then," Lucida said, and for the first time since I'd known her, her cool demeanor revealed an undercurrent of anxiousness. "Well, I've taken on quite the task trying to keep you tucked away, haven't I? Not sure I would've bothered if I'd known the Necromancers would be on my tail as well." She reached across to Hannah and punched her playfully on the arm. "What a pain in the arse mentee you've turned out to be, eh?"

Hannah smiled sadly but didn't respond.

"So this Annabelle is in the city? Think you can find her flat?" Lucida asked, refocusing on the business at hand.

"Yeah," I said. "I know it's somewhere in Southwark, close to the Tate Modern."

Lucida smirked. "You'll have to narrow it down a bit more than that, love, or you'll be searching for days."

"I wasn't planning on going door to door!" I said defensively. "Annabelle sent a spirit to find me at Fairhaven—he said he used to live in the flat right above hers. All we need to do is track down that ghost..."

Lucida's eyebrows contracted together. "She sent a ghost to you? How the hell did she do that? She's not a Durupinen, is she?"

"No, Annabelle's just sensitive to the spirits. It runs in her family," I said, keeping my answer brief—there was no time now for explaining her family's Romanian-Durupinen connection. "The point is, if you can get us over to Southwark, we should be able to find her."

"Right then," Lucida replied. "It's as good a plan as any at this point."

A bright beam of light cut through the interior of the SUV and flashed twice. In panic, we all spun around defensively, but Lucida merely waved her hand in acknowledgment as she cut the engine. "That's our car. Everyone out."

We all climbed out of the SUV as directed. A sleek black car, the sort that wealthy businesspeople were chauffeured around in, was purring quietly in the entrance to the alley. Between the dark of the pre-dawn and the car's tinted windows, it would've been impossible to see who had been driving it, but it didn't matter—whoever it was hadn't stuck around for a chat. By the time we reached the car, it was abandoned. The driver's side door hung open and the key was in the ignition, but no trace of the person who'd delivered it remained.

"Nice, eh?" Lucida said, stroking the car as if it were a beloved pet. "I usually request the convertible, but as we've no time for a top-down joyride..."

We all piled into the car, then rode in tense silence across the city and over the Thames. Even Milo stayed quiet. Finally, we pulled to a stop in the Tate Modern's gloomy shadow.

Lucida motioned for us to get out of the car, and we did so quietly. Then she turned to Hannah. "Be sure to use a Summoner—a Blind one—when you've settled in, to let me know where you are."

8

"Lucida, you know I've never really tried that before. What if it doesn't work?" asked Hannah.

"With the control you just showed over those spirits back there? Of course it will work," Lucida replied. "Just follow the Casting, you'll be fine."

"Okay... I'll try," Hannah said, although she looked terrified. "Good luck, Lucida."

"We're going to need as much luck as we can get. I've got to waltz back into Fairhaven like I've no idea of what's happened and hope they'll believe me when I play dumb. Fortunately, I'm rarely where I'm supposed to be, and I *do* have a handy habit of dropping off the grid... I'm quite famous for it. Here's hoping they'll think I've just been up to my usual shenanigans."

"Yeah, they were looking for you at the Council meeting. Even Finvarra wasn't surprised you blew it off," I offered.

"Excellent. My reputation precedes me. Here, take this." Lucida reached a hand down the front of her shirt and extracted a roll of money. She tossed it to Hannah, who caught it automatically. "Get some food and some clean clothes. Some painkillers and fresh dressings probably wouldn't go amiss either," she added, looking at me. "Once you've got what you need, don't leave that flat for anything if you can help it. Wait until you hear from me."

Without another word, Lucida peeled off down the street, tires squealing in protest.

"What's a Blind Summoner?" I asked Hannah.

"It's a way that Callers can use spirits to send messages. Lucida taught me how to do it in our mentoring sessions," she said, as she tore her eyes from the spot where Lucida had disappeared before shivering violently. "I mean... she demonstrated it last week, but I never had a chance to actually try it myself. I'll explain it better later."

"Yeah, that was freaky," said Milo. "Just make sure you never Blind Summon me."

Hannah looked at him tenderly. "I won't," she promised in a whisper. She turned back to me. "Let's find cover. I don't like being out here like this, with nowhere to go."

"Couldn't have said it better myself," said Finn. His eyes were darting around the darkened street, and his stance was tensed for confrontation. He turned to me and asked, "Who is this spirit and how do we find him?"

9

"His name is Lyle McElroy. You remember him... he was the spirit who came to find me in Keira's class, the one you expelled when you thought he was getting hostile."

"And making *you* very hostile in the process," Savvy added with a snort.

I cracked what was probably my first smile in a week. It felt strange on my face.

"Before you expelled him, Finn, Lyle told me he haunts his old apartment right above Annabelle's. He's attached to his old collections—whatever that means. If we can find Lyle, we'll have a better chance of finding Annabelle, too."

"But you don't know where the flat is?"

"Not exactly, no, but Annabelle told me it was only a few blocks from here. That should narrow it down."

Finn rolled his eyes. "Like Lucida said, we can't very well knock on the door of every flat within—"

"We don't need to," I said, cutting him short. "We have a Caller, remember?"

We all looked at Hannah, who seemed to shrink several inches under our gazes. "Isn't there some other way to find him?" she asked meekly.

I frowned. "Not unless we take Finn's suggestion and start knocking on doors. Why can't you just Call him?"

She didn't answer. Hannah just shrugged and lowered her eyes to the ground, where she watched her own foot kick around a pebble for a moment.

"What's going on, sweetness?" Milo asked her. Again, she didn't answer.

I knew what was holding my sister back. "Hannah," I said, and waited until she looked up. "You don't need to be afraid to Call. You've been doing it for years. What happened at Fairhaven, it wasn't your fault. If you hadn't used the spirits, we'd be locked in the dungeons right now—and then who knows what Marion might've convinced them to do to us. The fire was a complete accident; if anything, it was Marion's fault for forcing your hand."

Hannah bit her lip. Her eyes had filled with tears while I was talking.

"She's right," Finn said, with a very gentle voice—much gentler than I would have thought possible for him. "You gave Marion a choice. She could've let us go peacefully, like you asked, but she chose to face those spirits."

"But I couldn't stop," Hannah said, her voice choked with tears. "Once I started controlling them like that, once that energy was running through me, I couldn't..." Her voice trailed away, but she didn't need to finish. I'd seen the blind power take her over. I'd watched her become entranced by it, and even now I wondered what she might have done if we hadn't been there to stop her. But I couldn't think about that now; there was no time.

"But you *did* stop," I said firmly. "And anyway, we're not asking you to do anything like that. This is a simple Calling, like you've been doing perfectly safely for years. And we need it, Hannah. We may be miles from Fairhaven, but we're not safe yet."

"You can do it, sweetness," said Milo, slinking up beside her and laying the length of his cold, calming presence against her. "Jess is right; this isn't anything like at Fairhaven."

"You see?" I cried, gesturing to Milo and regretting it immediately as pain knifed through my arm. "Even Milo agrees with me! This is historic! Someone should note this for posterity. Finn, where's your usual stash of diaries? Get this down."

Finn scowled at me, but I didn't care. Hannah smiled in spite of herself and, at Milo's encouraging nudge, nodded her head. "You're right. Okay, I'll do it."

"Thank you," I told her.

"But before I do, we should split up," Hannah said.

Finn looked alarmed. "We should stick together," he countered.

"I know it feels safer to stay together, but that will only waste time," Hannah said, shaking her head. "We have two things we need to do—buy supplies and find Annabelle's flat. If we split up, we can get both done at the same time."

Finn raised his eyebrows, evidently impressed with the logic of this argument.

"Savvy, you know the area best," said Hannah, thrusting the roll of money into Savvy's hand. "Take this and get what we need. Bring Milo with you so we can stay in touch. With any luck, we'll find the flat before you've finished shopping, so we'll be able to tell you where to meet us."

"Blimey," said Savvy, thumbing through the bills with widened eyes. "There's got to be a thousand quid here, easy!"

"Try not to spend it all," I said. "That might have to last us a while."

Savvy checked her watch. "It's still hours before most of the shops open, so the clothes will have to wait. But I should be able to track down some food."

"And the painkillers," I said. "For the love of God, don't forget the painkillers."

"Some bandages and antiseptic, too," Finn added, with a wary glance at my arms.

"Right," agreed Savvy, putting the money into her own ample cleavage for safekeeping. She turned to Milo. "You ready to shop, mate?"

"Oh, honey, I was born ready." He turned and blew a kiss to Hannah. "You be careful, and call me if you need me."

"I will," Hannah said, smiling.

Milo and Savvy turned off into the darkness—one figure in shadow, one luminescent in its own dull light.

I watched them go until they slipped out of sight around the corner. Then I turned to Hannah. "Okay, then. Do your thing."

Hannah took a shuddery-but-deep breath, then closed her eyes to center herself. She was quiet for several moments as she searched. Finn, evidently tired of looking repeatedly over his shoulder, started to walk in a slow, deliberate circle around us to keep an eye on all possible angles.

"Sorry, there are a lot of ghosts in this city," Hannah murmured after a moment. "I feel like I'm looking for a needle in a haystack."

"That's okay, take your time," I coaxed her. "You're doing great."

Finn glared at me, and I shrugged defensively. Apparently, "take your time," wouldn't have been his chosen turn of phrase; I guess "hurry the hell up," would've been more to his liking.

"That might be him," Hannah said suddenly into the tense silence.

"You found him?" I asked. My pulse quickened, which only made the pain in my hands and arms worse.

"I'm not completely sure. He's… it feels like the right energy. And there's a really strong attachment to an apartment."

"Yeah, that fits," I said. "Annabelle said Lyle was obsessed with making sure his stuff didn't get thrown out."

"He's actually kind of hysterical about feeling my pull. I don't want to force him away from his apartment or he might freak out,"

Hannah said. She opened her eyes and looked at me. I tried to rearrange my expression so that it wasn't contorted in agony, but I wasn't quick enough.

"Look at you," she said. "I don't think you're up to any sort of Casting if we have to control him."

"I'm fine," I lied. "Anyway, maybe we don't need to bring him here. Can you follow his energy to wherever he's tied? We really just need to find the right place."

Hannah sagged with relief. "You're right. Okay great, let's go."

"Lead the way," Finn said. "I'll bring up the rear. Keep your eyes well peeled for anyone who looks too interested in what we're doing."

2

REFUGE

M Y PREVAILING THOUGHT as we made our way down the street was that we couldn't have looked more conspicuous if we'd tried: Me, staggering along under the combined influence of exhaustion and whatever drugs remained in my bloodstream; Hannah, stopping every few feet to refocus on Lyle; and Finn, with his hackles raised, periodically circling us like a jackal, poised against any and all attackers. The few people who saw us stared openly. By the time we had reached Lyle's run-down brick apartment building, I was sure there wasn't a single passerby who would've forgotten about us if someone questioned them.

"This is it," said Hannah, heaving a sigh of relief. "He's up there, apartment 6F."

We entered the building and began trudging up the stairs, but I had to stop and rest, panting and dizzy, on two different landings before we made it as far as the fifth floor.

"This would go more quickly if I carried you," Finn grumbled.

I'm not entirely sure what expression my face betrayed at this suggestion, but it caused both Finn and Hannah to step back in alarm. I staggered back to my feet and sprinted up the last flight of stairs without another word.

Finally, we stopped in front of the door of apartment 6F.

"What do we do now?" Hannah asked. "I mean, I could Call him out here, but that wouldn't help us get into the apartment. Plus, we can't be seen in the hallway talking to thin air."

"Too bad we sent Savvy shopping. I bet she knows how to pick locks," I wheezed.

"She's not the only one with that skill set," Finn muttered. He had already reached into his coat pocket and extracted a small set of metal tools.

"You're kidding me," I said. "You just happen to have a lock picking kit in your pocket?"

"Caomhnóir need to be prepared for anything," said Finn, working two of the instruments into the battered lock and jiggling them around.

"So what else do you have in that coat?" I asked. "Walkie-talkies? Explosives? One of those pens that doubles as a voice recorder, like James Bond?"

"Will you shut up and let me work?" Finn growled. His tone was gruff, even for him.

I decided that quick, undetected entry was higher on my priority list than snappy comebacks, so I did indeed—rather uncharacteristically—shut up. I looked at Hannah, who was glancing anxiously up and down the hallway while bouncing on the balls of her feet.

Finally, after what felt like a very long thirty seconds, the lock clicked and the door swung open. Finn reached his hand into the doorway and fumbled along the wall until he found the light switch and flicked it on.

My first thought was that we'd opened the door into a documentary about hoarders. Most of the room was buried under pile upon teetering pile of newspapers and magazines; they rose up like a recyclable city skyline. The walls were covered in shelves, and the shelves were crammed with all manner of dusty figurines, teacups, thimbles, and other knickknacks.

"What the bloody hell?" Finn muttered.

He took a cautious step forward, and we followed him in. He stood on tiptoe and brushed a layer of dust off the top of the nearest stack of newspapers.

"It's a copy of the *Daily Mail* with a cover story about the royal wedding," said Finn, as he examined the faded photo. "Looks like this whole mound is copies of the same issue."

I glanced at the pile nearest me. Beneath the film of filth, I could make out a large photograph of Prince William beaming toothily.

"Well, at least we know that no one's living here," Hannah said. "There's no way they've rented this place out again if it's in this state."

We ventured in a few more steps. The place smelled overwhelmingly of cat urine. I was suddenly terrified that we would shift one of those mountains of paper and find a kitten squashed and mummified under fifty pounds of backdated *HELLO!* magazines.

"Everything on this shelf is commemorative royal stuff," said Hannah, edging her way over to the nearest display. She gingerly lifted a bobblehead doll of Queen Elizabeth II. "What do you think all this junk is?"

"Junk? What do you mean, junk?" came a sudden, perturbed voice. Lyle materialized beside Hannah, who was so startled she nearly dropped the figurine she was holding. "And be careful with that! It's a collector's item! These are all collector's items, some of them very rare and worth a lot of money. I would appreciate it if you kept your hands off!"

"I'm sorry," Hannah said, hastily replacing the figurine beside a tea cozy bearing the royal crest.

"Well, you should be! What are you doing here anyw—" Lyle stopped short and stared at Hannah. "Wait, you heard me?"

"Yes, we can all hear you, Lyle," I said.

Lyle's head snapped up and he spotted me for the first time. "*You*? What are you doing in my flat? That pest of a friend of yours hasn't sent you to harass me again, has she?"

"No, I decided to come and harass you all on my own," I answered. "But speaking of Annabelle, have you seen her recently?"

"No, thank my lucky stars," Lyle grumbled. "I haven't seen her in at least a week. And I still don't understand why I'm seeing you, especially here in the middle of my—DON'T TOUCH THOSE!"

Finn, with his hand on the corner of another heap, froze.

"Those are very, very valuable historical documents!" Lyle cried, before vanishing and reappearing offensively close to Finn.

Finn caught my eye and very nearly smiled before answering. "Mate, I hate to break it to you, but this is just a stack of rubbishy old magazines. You'd be better off binning them."

Lyle became practically apoplectic with rage. "Binning them? Don't you see? Everyone else will have binned them, but I kept them! I preserved them for posterity! You don't understand the importance of this collection. It is, I am quite sure, the most complete collection of important royal memorabilia in all the city and, quite conceivably, the world. It's worth a fortune!"

"Lyle, we need to… um… stay here for a little while," I said.

Lyle stared at me. "What do you mean, stay here?"

"I mean we're in some trouble, and we need a place to lay low in the city while we figure out what to do next. And since no one is living here at the moment..."

Lyle drew himself up, clearly affronted. "Oh, and I suppose because I'm not technically alive, that means I'm not living here anymore?" He made air quotes at the word *alive*, as though his death were merely a matter of perspective rather than a medical fact.

I snorted, "Well actually, that's pretty much exactly what it means."

Finn made a tiny sound that could have meant anything, but I took to be a snicker.

"Well, I don't care a fig for your problems," Lyle spat. "The contents of this flat are mine, and I'm not leaving them unattended—especially with people who have no idea of their true worth!"

"Look, we don't want to throw your things away," I said, lying through my teeth. "But maybe we could just... move them to a more convenient area so we could, y'know, walk? Or sit on the furniture?" I gestured toward the nearby sofa, which was buried under four-foot-high stacks of boxed newspapers.

"No, no, no!" Lyle shrieked hysterically. His energy seemed to billow out from him; it caused the hair on my neck to rise as if electrostatic. "You can't move these things! You *can't* do that! I have a system, an organizational system. If you disturb the system, things won't be cataloged properly. The whole integrity of the collection could be compromised!"

We all carefully avoided looking at each other for fear of laughing. It couldn't have been more obvious that the contents of the apartment were worth more as kindling for a bonfire than as any sort of legitimate collection. But to Lyle, these stacks and knickknacks were important treasures.

There was still a lot I needed to learn about dealing with spirits, but one thing I *had* managed to learn at Fairhaven was that a spirit could be pretty set in its ways, even much more deeply than a living person. A living person was always changing, growing, aging, and adjusting to the world, but it was a lot more difficult to coax any kind of change out of a ghost. Siobhán explained that this was why so many spirits were known for repetitive behaviors—walking the same hallway, looking out the same window, wailing at the same time of night. And, the longer a soul was trapped in a repetitive state, the less mutable it became.

With a sigh, I accepted that there would be no convincing Lyle to move or get rid of his precious collection. Unfortunately, there was also no way we could hide out in his royally-themed death trap of an apartment. So that meant...

"You'll have to expel him," I muttered out of the corner of my mouth to Finn.

Finn nodded grimly, as though he'd heard the entire argument I'd just considered in my head. He waited until Lyle was busy chastising Hannah for replacing Her Majesty's bobblehead at the wrong angle, then muttered back, "He's so attached to this flat that expelling him may only keep him out for a few moments. We'll have to act quickly. Do you know how to put up Wards to keep him out for good?"

"Well, I've never actually done it, but Hannah's got the *Book of Téigh Anonn*, so we can try," I said. "If it doesn't hold, we'll just have to think of something else."

"It's the only chance we've got," Finn agreed.

Finn took a decisive step forward, which was impressive amid the labyrinth of crap, and began to murmur under his breath. His movement caught both Lyle and Hannah's attention.

"That's it, I want all of you out of here right now!" shouted Lyle, throwing Finn a panicked look. "I don't care what kind of trouble you're in, you're not going to desecrate my life's work with your ignorant—"

Whoosh. Before Lyle could put the final flourish on his insult, he flew backward through the nearest wall and out of sight, as though snagged by an imaginary fishing line.

"What just happened?" Hannah asked.

"Expelled him," said Finn firmly.

"We're just going to force him out of his own—"

"Do you have a better idea?" Finn barked. "He was never going to give the flat up voluntarily, and I'm not about to tiptoe around this drek like it's a museum display. He had to go. This is the only safe space we have in all of London."

Hannah opened her mouth to argue again, but then closed it and nodded. "You're right."

"I know I am. But he's going to get his bearings back in a few minutes, so you two had best set up the Wards. I'm going to try to shift some of this stuff so we can see what we're dealing with in the rest of this flat."

Finn stalked off through the heaps as Hannah and I set to work. My Casting skills were better than they were a month ago, but I was still essentially useless when it came to the more technical aspects of Castings. Fortunately, Hannah was a natural at all things Durupinen; within minutes she had chalked the appropriate runes onto the door and under the windows. Then we sealed the runes with wax from a Spirit Candle for extra protection while we both recited the Casting. Thankfully, although the Casting was in an ancient form of Gaelic, the words were not overly complex.

"Well, I think that should do it," Hannah said. "We're really lucky that we performed the Uncaging last night, or I probably wouldn't have had any of this stuff in my bag when we fled." She held up her ritual bag, into which she deposited her chalk, book, and candle stub.

"Yeah, lucky," I said, fighting a wave of nausea.

"You look like you're going to be sick," replied Hannah, looking at me properly for the first time since we'd begun the ritual.

"Yeah, I *do* feel sick. I think I just need to lie down and get some sleep." The possibility of real sleep was probably a pipe dream, though, because the pain in my arms was now building to a pulsing crescendo. I found myself wishing one of the magazine towers would tumble over and knock me unconscious, just to put me out of my misery.

"But first, what about Annabelle?" I asked. "Shouldn't we head downstairs and see if we can find her flat?"

Hannah shook her head. "Not at this hour. We'll scare the life out of her if we go banging on her door now. It can wait until the morning." She looked at her watch. "Well, I mean, a normal time of the morning. And besides, you need to sleep. The question is, is there anywhere in this junk heap where you can lie down?" Hannah asked, with a skeptical expression. She turned and called over her shoulder, "Finn?"

"Eh?" came Finn's muffled voice.

"Is there anywhere Jess can lie down and get some sleep? She's not looking too good."

Crash, crash, bang, shuffle.

"Bed's clear," he shouted. "First door on the left in the back hall."

Hannah led the way, picking through the treacherous hallway until we reached a small, dusty bedroom. The room was in the same state of disaster as the rest of the flat, except for about three feet of clear space surrounding the bed in the corner. I was too tired and in too much pain to spare more than a passing, whimpering thought about the cleanliness of the mattress before collapsing upon it.

Hannah perched herself on the edge of the bed next to me, gingerly shifting a newspaper aside with her foot. She closed her eyes for a moment; when she opened them again she said, "Milo and Savvy should be back soon. I told him where to find us."

"What about Lucida? Aren't you supposed to let her know where we are, too?"

Hannah bit her lip. "I've got to try using a Blind Summoner, but I can't do it in here because I need a spirit. Since we've Warded the place, I'll have to go outside and try from there. Actually, I should probably go do that now."

She stood up, which looked as if it required far more energy than it should have, and walked out of the bedroom. I still didn't really understand what Hannah was going to do, but I decided that a detailed explanation of Blind Summoners could wait until tomorrow. I looked over at Finn, who was now trying to clear a wider path into the dingy, adjacent bathroom.

"I haven't had a chance to thank you yet," I said.

He glanced up from his work with a look that was filled with half-confusion, half-hostility. "Thank me for what?"

I rolled my eyes. "For getting us out of there. For saving our lives."

"I didn't get us out of there. That was all your sister's doing," he said, looking away from me again and flicking a dismissive hand over his shoulder.

"It wasn't just her. You... they tried to dismiss you, but you wouldn't go. You stayed with me."

"I'm obligated to stay with you in any situation that I judge to be potentially dangerous," he said, as though quoting from a Caomhnóir handbook. "I was just doing my job."

"Damn it, Finn, I'm trying to thank you, but you're making it really difficult. Can't you just say 'You're welcome,' like a normal person?" I cried.

He paused with his hand clenched around a commemorative teacup as though he were deciding whether or not to chuck it at me. Instead, he tossed the cup into a nearby box; we both heard it break as it landed.

I gave up on further conversation and tried to grope past my pain into sleep. I couldn't be sure whether I'd actually managed to drift off entirely, but the next thing I heard was Hannah's voice.

"Well, it worked, thank goodness. Lucida sent the Summoner back, so I know she got the message."

"Anything else?" Finn asked.

"What do you mean, anything else?" replied Hannah.

"Did she send any news? About... anyone at Fairhaven?"

"No, she just sent the Summoner back. There was no reply."

"Oh," said Finn; I could hear the frustration packed into this one syllable.

Something clicked. My heart started to thump; I sat up quickly.

"Jess, what are you doing up? You're supposed to be sleeping," said Hannah, frowning with motherly concern.

I ignored the scolding. I was too busy lamenting about what an idiot I was. I had somehow completely forgotten that Olivia was Finn's sister, and that he'd left her behind at Fairhaven.

"Finn, I'm so sorry," I said.

"Sorry for what?" He had cleared off a nearby wing chair and was now stooping to unlace his boots.

"I didn't even think... your sister is back there," I said, barely able to coax my voice above a whisper.

Hannah grimaced, and I could tell that she'd forgotten, too. "I'm sorry, Finn. I should've asked in my Summoning. I was so focused on making sure that Lucida knew where to find us that I didn't even think to ask about anything else."

"Olivia's fine," he said. He pulled off one boot and flung it aside. "I saw her in the entrance hall when we were leaving. I'm sure she got out. And when Lucida comes back, I'm quite positive that's what she'll tell us."

Finn's tone practically dared me to contradict him. I didn't. I couldn't. The alternative was too horrible to consider. I laid back down in silence.

The terror and adrenaline of our escape had left little room in

22

my mind to dwell on the carnage we'd left behind at Fairhaven. But now that we were safe—at least for the moment—my fear and guilt bubbled up through the cracks in my resolve; I let it rise, choking me. What had there been for Lucida to return to? Was Fairhaven gone? Had they been able to contain the fire, or had the castle been reduced to a smoking, hollowed-out shell? I thought about all of the irreplaceable history that Fairhaven contained—the tapestries, the library, the archives, the relics. Although I hadn't grown up in the Durupinen culture, I could appreciate the importance of Durupinen history; not a single precious item could ever be replaced.

But far more terrible was the idea that our escape could have cost someone in that castle their life. The fire had swelled so quickly; was it foolish to hope everyone had made it out alive? I thought of Mackie, still weak from an attacking ghost; I thought of Celeste and Siobhán and Fiona, who we'd left fending off the spirits in the Council Room where the flames had begun. I thought of all my terrified classmates, huddled in their pajamas in the entrance hall, scattering like frightened birds at Finn's command to flee. Had they escaped? Could some of them have gone looking for friends or sisters and been trapped inside? I knew the answer, and it made nausea roil in my stomach. Suddenly, after feeling relieved at having Lucida gone, I ached for her to return with any news that might extinguish the new fire that my guilt had lit within me.

3

RETURN FROM THE BRINK

"**W**OW, SHE REALLY LOOKS BAD. Just... can you try to sit her up a bit?"

"Have you had a look under those bandages since we got here?"

"I'm afraid to take them off."

"Fair enough, but shouldn't we be re-dressing her arms or something?"

"I have no idea. I don't know the first thing about caring for burns."

"Jess? Can you sit up? You need to drink this... it'll help. I dissolved your pain meds in this water, so you can just drink it."

I felt a hand cradling the back of my head, and I struggled to obey its pressure to sit up. The cool rim of a glass was then pressed to my lips; the cold water began trickling down my chin before I could force my mouth to remember how to swallow. I spluttered and choked. The liquid was bitter and gritty in my mouth.

"She feels really warm. Does she feel warm to you?"

Several hands pressed themselves to my cheeks. Every one of them felt like ice.

"She's burning up. What should we do?"

"We'll keep an eye on her. Those meds should help with the fever, too."

"Hadn't we best take her to A & E, yeah?"

"Are you crazy? That's much too risky. They know she's injured. They'll be scouting every hospital, clinic, and doctor's office in London. We'd be caught for sure."

"But—"

"I said no!"

A few minutes later—or several hours later, or maybe even

several pain-racked centuries later—voices broke through to my consciousness again.

"We have no choice."

"But—"

"Look at her, Hannah! She has an infection, a serious one. Nothing is keeping that fever down. If we don't, she might—"

"Don't! Don't even say that!"

"Well then, listen to me!"

"But she'd never agree to it! You were in the Council Room—you know how she feels about this."

"This isn't quite the same thing—and she doesn't need to agree to it. She's in no state to make a decision! It's been three days. She's dying, do you understand me? She's dying, and we're going to lose her unless we do this. Now, are you going to set up the Circle, or do I need to do it for you?"

Dying. Who was dying? The word had silenced the room; I struggled to understand what it meant.

"No. No, I'll do it," someone said. My sister. It was my sister's voice.

I blacked out again. When I came to, the voices around me had warped into dim, muffled sounds. I couldn't reach past the strange, swimming feeling in my head to ask what they were talking about. In my pain, I couldn't remember where we were or what we were doing here. Who was talking? Why couldn't I see? I thought I might be moving, that someone might be touching me, or carrying me. Or I could be floating. Floating away. How nice it would be to float away.

I could hear chanting, and I wished the chants could be musical, like the songs my mother would sing. Someone took my hand, cradling it very gently, but their touch lit my burns on fire. I cried out.

The chanting grew louder, and a familiar feeling flooded through me—a feeling of conductivity, of something opening within me. My mind spun with images, thoughts, and feelings I couldn't control and didn't recognize as my own. Was I dying? Was I going crazy? Who was I?

As I grasped in the whirlwind for some sense of myself, the cloudiness and confusion slowly—very slowly—started to ebb away. My vision began to clear. I became aware of my body, which was lying on a musty-smelling floor. And even as my cognizance of the terrible pain in my arms sharpened, the pain itself began to dull—receding as though someone was draining it out of me. As the last dull throb of pain pulsed away, the tumult of images flickered to a halt. Something inside me thudded closed, leaving me breathless yet entirely myself.

"Jess? Can you hear me?"

I opened my eyes. I was still lying on the floor, and five anxious faces were staring down at me. Gingerly, I sat up and looked around. We were in Lyle's flat. The area rug had been shoved on top of a heap in the corner, and a Circle had been chalked onto the floorboards around me.

"What's happened?" I asked.

"How are you feeling?" asked Hannah. Her face was streaked with tears.

"She should be feeling bloody fabulous," Lucida said with a smug nod.

I considered this and realized that I did, indeed, feel pretty damn fantastic. I felt utterly refreshed, like I'd just woken up from the best nap of my life. My mind felt calm and sharp. I felt like I could've run a marathon or scaled a building. My body was pulsing with a boundless energy that was shooting through my legs, coursing through my arms.

My arms.

I held my hands and forearms up in front of my face and gasped out loud. My formerly ravaged skin was flawlessly smooth and polished; it glowed as if it had just been buffed.

"What... I don't understand! What happened to the burns?"

"Gone. Healed," Lucida answered.

"That's the most smashing thing I've ever seen," Savvy said, grabbing my hand to examine it for herself.

"But how? How did you do it?" I asked Lucida.

"I didn't do it," Lucida replied, smiling.

I looked at Hannah, who had dropped her eyes to the floor.

"Hannah?"

"We had no choice, Jess. I knew you wouldn't like it, but—"

"But what?"

"The Aura Flow," Hannah said, with a fair trace of guilt in her voice. "We used the Aura Flow from the Crossing to heal you."

"Aura Flow?" I asked blankly. Then my brain caught up. "Wait. Are you talking about Leeching?"

I looked from Hannah's guilty expression to Lucida's snide one, and in that moment felt my heart drop, leaden, somewhere into the pit of my stomach.

"Please, no. Please tell me you didn't!"

"Of course we did," Lucida said. "And before you start laying a guilt trip on your sister, you ought to know she just saved your life."

"You were really in trouble, mate," Savvy said quietly. "You should've seen your hands."

"Jess, it wasn't pretty," added Milo. His lack of attitude spoke volumes about how sick I'd truly been.

"Everything was infected," Hannah added. "Your fever wouldn't go down and you were completely delirious."

"But why didn't you just take me to a doctor?" I cried.

"And risk getting caught?"

"Yes! You should have taken the chance! Damn it, Hannah, Leeching is wrong and you know it!" I sprang to my feet, something I hadn't been able to do in more than three days; realizing this only made me angrier.

"Do get off your high horse there, love. This kind of situation is exactly why Leeching exists," Lucida said. "Using the energy to save your life isn't just about you. It's about preserving the entire Gateway for the spirits who need it in the future."

"You think I'm going to listen to *you*... a woman who uses ghosts like Botox?" I said, turning on her with a humorless laugh. "When have *you* ever cared whether a spirit made it all the way through to the other side, as long as you could smooth out a wrinkle or two?"

"Now, now, I think you're underestimating my natural good looks," said Lucida, pouting theatrically.

"And I think you're underestimating how pissed off I am right now! Leeching is Leeching—there's no such thing as 'using an Aura Flow' as far as I'm concerned," I shot back. I turned to Finn, who had retreated into a corner. "What about you? You're supposed to be protecting the Gateway, right? Aren't you always going on about your duty? How could you let them do this?"

Finn's face was wrapped in a mask of shadows in the room's semi-darkness; I couldn't see his expression well. But when he spoke his voice was brusque and harsh—much more so than usual.

"It was the best decision to protect the Gateway," he said. "It wasn't only about saving you. Were something to happen to you, your Gateway would close and the entire system would be out of balance again—just like when your mother invoked the Binding."

I longed to spew a diatribe at Finn, but something caught in my throat. I couldn't clearly separate what was holding me back from my anger in that moment, but it might've been the way Finn dismissed out of hand the idea that saving my life was reason enough to use the Aura Flow. I wouldn't really have expected anything less from him, but there was something about hearing it out loud that cut deeply.

"Great. That's just great," I said, ignoring the sting. "Well, I guess we'll just forget about any of the spirits that just Crossed over. Screw them, right? If they're trapped in the Aether, who cares? That's the cost of doing business." My sarcasm was so sharp it even surprised me.

A shimmer in the corner of my eye made me turn. Milo's mouth was hanging half-open, as though he were about to speak. But when he caught my eye, he snapped it shut again.

"You should just be glad you didn't get too close, Milo," I said as I sprung up and began looking around for my jacket. "Maybe you could've been sucked into the Aether. Not that Lucida would care!"

"Where are you going?" Hannah asked; her tone was still wounded and tearful.

"For a walk. I need to clear my head."

"It's not safe to be out, Jess," said Lucida. "Someone might—"

"Stop talking. Your logic isn't going to convince me of anything—not now, not ever," I snapped. I abandoned the search for my jacket and opted instead for a dramatic exit. If I froze my ass off, so be it.

As I descended the stairs, I began to feel a strange sort of claustrophobia close around me. I picked up speed, taking the last flight of stairs at a run and practically threw myself out the door and into the crisp London night. The fresh air hit my face like a cold ocean wave. It felt so good that I started to cry—and once I started sobbing, I couldn't stop. I took off blindly down the street, but I'd gone barely two blocks when I heard footsteps slapping on the pavement behind me.

I took a deep breath and hoped that whoever was behind me wasn't some Necromancer thug or a Caomhnóir come to track me down—I didn't' think I could handle Lucida being right about

29

something so soon. With my heart pounding in my chest, I turned around.

Finn was following me like an obnoxious guard dog. Ugh, I take it back, I'd rather be chased down by Necromancers.

"Leave me alone, Finn," I gasped over my shoulder.

"No."

"Just... go back to the flat."

"Not happening."

I ignored him and picked up my pace as I began retracing our route to the river. I stopped only when I reached the bank. I grasped onto the cold metal of the railing in my hands, looked out over the water, and inhaled the cool night air in thirsty gasps as if I'd just resurfaced after nearly drowning. I could hardly believe the contradiction between how terrible I felt emotionally and how great I felt physically. My guilt made me want to fling myself into the Thames... but I knew if I jumped into the river, I'd just be able to swim the entire length of it, probably without even getting winded.

Finn hung back, giving me space while I calmed myself and let the beauty of the city lights reflected in the water shine some perspective into me.

There was nothing I could do: The Leeching was done. My only chance to make things right was to use my renewed health to get us out of this mess and make sure my Gateway—and every spirit who Crossed through it from now on—was protected.

When I turned to head back to the flat, I listened for the steady slap of Finn's feet on the sidewalk behind me. When his footsteps fell into step with mine, they were much closer than I had expected.

"Jess, hold up a minute," he said.

Begrudgingly, I slowed down just enough for Finn to draw himself level to me.

"Look, I know why you're angry, but you might go a bit easier on your sister, alright?"

"Excuse me?"

"I'm not saying it was a good thing to do. We all know that Leeching is wrong. Or at least," he screwed up his face, "most of us do. But there really was no choice, and this wasn't Leeching, properly speaking. Either we used the Aura Flow, or we let you die... with Hannah watching."

"We could've gone to a—"

"No, we couldn't. Stop saying that. Do you really want to be dragged back to Fairhaven? Marion would have the lot of us thrown in the dungeons, or worse. But that's nothing compared to what'll happen if the Necromancers find us first... and I guarantee they'll be looking in all the same places."

I opened my mouth to argue, but my words had run dry. I didn't have a leg to stand on, and we both knew it.

"Don't punish Hannah for the only choice she could've made. You're all she has—and you only found each other a few months ago. Would you leave her here in this mess, without you? Hasn't she lost quite enough?"

I was stunned; how could Finn—who barely admitted he had feelings of his own—be the one to remind me of my love for my own sister, my own twin?

I shook my head as my eyes filled with fresh tears. There was just so much guilt, I couldn't contain it. Guilt about the destruction back at Fairhaven; guilt about the spirits used in the Aura Flow and now possibly trapped forever between worlds; guilt about the way I'd just treated Hannah for the unforgivable offense of saving my life. I would surely suffocate underneath the weight of it all.

I resisted the temptation to dissolve completely into my misery. Finn already looked horribly uncomfortable at the sight of my crying—as if I were doing something both utterly foreign and inherently distasteful. He looked ready to turn tail and run headlong from my unpredictable female hysteria at any second. So instead, I pulled myself together and walked back to the flat. Finn kept several paces behind me, presumably so I wouldn't start crying on him.

I pulled the flat's door shut behind me. There'd been no hint of Lyle anywhere outside the apartment—an ominous sign that I didn't want to consider the implications of. Inside, the flat was dark and quiet. Savvy was sprawled out asleep on the sofa, and Lucida had slunk off into the night from whence she'd come. In the half-light bleeding from the bedroom, I could see Hannah curled up against the headboard of Lyle's bed, with Milo right beside her. I heard Milo's quiet crooning as he comforted Hannah with words I couldn't make out.

I let Milo continue. If I tried to talk to Hannah now, when there was still so much anger running through my veins, I would only damage things further. Instead, I poked and prodded at Savvy until she grumbled and slid over enough for me to cram myself onto the couch beside her. Then I closed my eyes and let sleep dull the knife-sharp emotions still stabbing away at my insides.

4

HOSTAGE

A SOMBER, HEAD-HANGING SILENCE GREETED ME in Lyle's cramped kitchen the next morning. Ah, yes, my morning dose of crippling guilt.

"Hey, guys," I said, without meeting anyone's eye. Not that anyone was looking at me either; they were all averting their gazes in case I started screaming again.

A dull murmur of acknowledgment followed my greeting. Wow, had I really been that unreasonable, or were they ashamed of themselves too? It could have been both, I suppose, but I didn't want to have that conversation. Not anymore.

I'd barely had the chance to register where Hannah was sitting—with her knees curled up under her chin, a plate of buttered toast untouched in front of her—when Milo came flying forward. He blocked my way as I stepped toward Hannah; his expression was defensive and stormy.

"Back for another pound of flesh?" Milo spat.

"Calm down, Milo. I just want to apologize," I said.

Milo did not back down, but instead glared at me as though he suspected me of carrying a concealed weapon. "What's the matter? Heard she finally stopped crying?"

"Hannah, will you please call off your attack ghost? I'll behave, I promise."

"Milo, it's okay. Let her through," said Hannah.

I stepped around Milo, who didn't try to stop me but instead hissed, "One harsh word and I'll go poltergeist on your ass," in my ear.

Trying to ignore the threat, I dropped into the chair beside Hannah. I had barely opened my mouth when she cut me off. "You don't have to apologize, Jess. You are absolutely right, it was

33

a terrible thing to do. We should have taken our chances at the hospital or—"

"No, *you* were right," I said, doing my utmost to keep the bitterness out of my voice. "All you were trying to do was save my life, and I attacked you for it. It was a shitty way to behave, and I'm sorry. I wasn't mad at you, not really. I was just mad that Leeching was your only choice. But it really *was* the only choice, and I know it wasn't easy for you to make it."

"Jess," she broke in, "I want you to know... it wasn't a Leeching, not really. I Called every spirit I could reach. I asked for the strong ones to come, asked them to give you just a little of their energy as they Crossed. Lucida didn't want me to, she said the spirits were ours to use, but I knew you wouldn't want that. Every single spirit that Crossed offered you an ounce of strength. Of their own free will, Jess. Just a sip from each, voluntarily."

I was too shocked to speak; I had underestimated my sister. Taking any energy from the spirits was less than ideal, yes, but of course Hannah wasn't a Leech. How could I ever have thought that? I hung my head in shock and shame.

After a moment of pure speechlessness, I looked into Hannah's eyes and whispered the only words I could form. "Thank you. Thank you for saving my life."

Hannah flashed me a watery but genuine smile, and I jumped up and hugged her. I felt her freeze up at first, like a startled animal, but then she wound an arm around my neck and buried her face in my hair.

"Well, doesn't that warm the heart?" Savvy said, punching me lightly on the arm as Hannah and I broke apart. "Now that you're talking to us, how about some breakfast? You hungry? I can knock together something."

"That would be great, thanks." I hadn't thought about it at all, but as soon as Savvy suggested food, I realized that I was absolutely ravenous. I hadn't eaten in days.

"You might want to rethink that," Milo said, wrinkling his nose in disgust.

"And why's that?" I asked.

"Yeah, why's that" echoed Savvy, looking affronted.

"Because you shopped like a frat boy!" Milo cried.

"Oi. What do you mean?"

34

"I mean, this," Milo said, and he caused the nearest cabinet door to burst open. "Look at this!"

I walked over to get a closer look. Milo had a point; the shelves were crammed with sugary cereals, pre-packaged Danishes and croissants, and something called "digestive biscuits," which appeared to be a healthy-sounding name for chocolate dipped cookies.

"Wow, it's a portal to a junk food paradise!" I said, grinning.

"You should've seen her in the store," replied Milo, rolling his eyes. "It was like letting a six-year-old do the shopping."

"I was hungry and stressed, yeah? You shouldn't have set me loose in a shop like that! And what did you think I'd manage to turn up at four in the morning, a gourmet meal?"

"Yes, but now everyone has to eat your feelings!" Milo cried.

"Why do you care Milo?" I asked, plucking a Danish off the shelf and shutting the cabinet door again. "You don't even eat."

"Someone around here has to be an adult," said Milo, rolling his eyes again. "I'm your Spirit Guide. So sue me if I want you to eat healthy. Geez, is that a crime?"

"Oh give it a rest, will you?" Savvy moaned. "There's some fruit in there somewhere."

"Strawberry pastries are not fruit!" yelled Milo, stamping a foot that made no contact with the floor and therefore no sound.

"Okay, okay, Milo, chill out!" I said through a mouthful of pastry. "We'll go out later and buy some tofu burgers or something."

I sat down beside Finn, who had not so much as looked at me since I'd entered the kitchen. He was bent so low over one of his shabby black notebooks that his hair trailed along the page. He was scribbling with impressive speed, with what looked like a bacon sandwich clamped between his teeth.

"Did you get down that whole conversation, or would you like me to repeat any of it?" I asked him.

Finn looked up, scowling, then pulled the roll from his mouth. "I'm not writing down your—"

"I know that! My God, have you never even been introduced to the concept of humor?"

He frowned at me for another moment, and then shoved the rest of the sandwich in his mouth and bent again to write. "No," he mumbled through the bacon.

"How sad for you." I opened the cabinet again. "Wow, that's some seriously impressive junk food, though. The only other person I've ever met who ate that much garbage was Karen, and at least she had an excuse since she was working all the time. Her fridge was... Hey, wait!" My change in tone caught everyone's attention. "Karen! Someone needs to get in touch with Karen to warn her about—"

"Already done," pronounced Finn, talking over me.

"You... really?"

"Yes, really. It was right after you fell asleep, the first day we got here. Hannah called her on one of the disposable mobiles."

"Did she freak out?" I asked. I envisioned Karen with her phone glued to one hand and her other hand busy booking an international flight on her laptop. "You know she'd be out here in a heartbeat if she knew how much trouble we're really in."

"Actually, I think I managed to convince her that we'd be in more trouble if she came," Hannah explained. "She knows how the Durupinen work; they aren't above using her as bait, if necessary, to lure us back to Fairhaven—and of course the Necromancers will be watching every connection we left behind, too. She's not safe anymore."

"So what's she doing?"

"Going into hiding as soon as possible. She also said it would be a good idea for your friend Tia to do the same, so she's going to arrange it."

"This is a nightmare! It's ruining everyone's lives! What about Karen's job? And what will Tia have to do, drop out of St. Matt's? Leave the country? And it's all my fault," I cried, dropping my head into my hands.

"It'll be okay, Jess," cooed Hannah, laying a soothing hand on my arm. "The most important thing is for them to be safe. This will all blow over soon. Karen is a brilliant lawyer, she'll have no trouble finding another great job. And St. Matt's will still be there when it's safe for Tia to go back to classes. It's just temporary—and we'll all feel better knowing that they're out of harm's way, won't we?"

"I know, I know, but... it just sucks."

"Yeah, it does," she agreed.

Despite everything that had happened between us, I felt a sudden surge of affection for Karen: She had not merely remembered Tia, but was actively trying to help her. I picked my head up. "Does Karen think she can pull it off? What does she know about getting people into hiding?"

Hannah shrugged. "I don't know, but she sounded pretty confident. She said she had contacts she could use from her Federal cases. I told her to call Lucida, but she didn't want to do that. She didn't want to use anyone connected to the Durupinen, just in case."

I snorted. "Yeah, and she also hates Lucida. I'm sure Karen would want to avoid her help, regardless."

I looked around the table and registered for the first time that Lucida was missing. "So where's she slunk off to, anyway?"

I had asked the room at large, but it was again Hannah who answered. "She had to go back to Fairhaven."

"So you're telling me that there's *actually* a Fairhaven to go back to?" I asked. I'd been sure the castle would've been burned beyond recognition, or—as in dreams I kept having—just continued to burn endlessly without ever consuming itself, like a horrible, magic torch.

"Yes," Hannah said. "The Caomhnóir were able to contain the fire to the east wing. The Grand Council Room was destroyed, and the East Tower collapsed, but most of the castle is still standing."

"What happened when Lucida went back? Did they buy her story?"

"Yes, thank goodness," Hannah said with a clear note of relief. "She concocted some wild alibi, and they had no problem swallowing it."

"Where did she tell them she'd been?"

"Paris," said Savvy, grinning. "Said she'd hopped the Eurostar with some friends, and taken the Chunnel to Paris where she'd spent the night partying."

"Won't it be easy enough for them to check that story out? What if they find out she was lying?' I asked.

Finn shook his head. "They won't. She called in some favors and set up a false trail. She knows what she's doing."

"She's got proper flair, that one," Savvy said with a chuckle. "From what she said, it sounds like she's well acquainted with Paris nightlife, even if it was just a cover story this time. I'm making her take me along when she goes back. It sounds fierce."

"Samesies!" Milo piped up.

37

I ignored this. Clubbing was the last thing on my mind. "Did she say when she's coming back?"

"No," Finn grunted. "And we have to be well careful about contacting her now. She's the one who's heading up the search to Track us."

"You're kidding," I said, forgetting to chew the Danish in my mouth; I nearly choked.

"Nope. Marion put her in charge the minute she got back," said Hannah, shrugging. "It's not that surprising, though. Like Lucida said, she's the best Tracker they have."

"So Marion's okay, obviously, but what about everyone else? Did Lucida tell you if anyone got hurt or...?" I trailed off as my heart seemed to lodge itself into my throat and choked off the end of a question I was half-scared to know the answer to.

"I forgot you didn't know! You were out of it for so long," cried Hannah, shaking her head. "Everyone's okay. Or at least," she amended, "no one's dead."

Her face suddenly took on an expression of guilt that must surely have been mirroring my own; she didn't go on.

Without even looking up from his notebook, Finn picked up the thread. "Everyone made it out. Some are injured, of course."

"Olivia?"

"She's fine. So is Peyton."

"So do we know who's—"

"Fiona is in the hospital wing with some bad burns, along with quite a few others. Lucida didn't go into too much detail; she was a bit distracted by your teetering on the verge of death. But we know Seamus is in properly rough shape, and Bertie inhaled a good bit of smoke."

Savvy shook her head sadly. "Stupid prat. Never would've thought he had it in him, but he ran back into the castle when he couldn't find me. Two of the other Caomhnóir had to go in after him to pull him out, and he didn't go quietly. Sort of makes me feel sorry for behaving so badly. Mind you," she added, scowling defensively, "he *is* generally useless, I stick by that. I don't know what he thinks he could've done if he'd found me—I must outweigh him by over two stone. But still, it's nice to know he would've given it a go, eh?"

"That's his job," Finn said bluntly, as though it were understood that every Caomhnóir would run headlong into a burning building

38

to pluck his Gateway from the jaws of death. I tried to picture Finn doing the same thing for me, and realized with a pang of guilt that I didn't doubt for a moment that he would—no matter how much friction there was between us.

"Maybe, but it's not a job he's cut out for," Savvy said. "Still, he'll be alright. They all will, as soon as they open up the Gateway and do a bit of..."

She broke off, as a flush crept into her cheeks and stained them crimson. She didn't need to finish the sentence. We all knew how the Durupinen would deal with the injuries left by our escape, especially now that Marion was in charge. It wasn't a subject any of us wanted to discuss.

"Well, I'm just glad everyone's going to be alright," I said, steering the conversation away from dangerous waters. "Has Marion put out a bounty on our heads? The Durupinen's most wanted? A million pounds, dead or alive?"

Milo coughed. Savvy and Hannah exchanged a dark look.

"Oh, my God, I was kidding!" I cried. "Please don't tell me we've got a bounty on us!"

"She's offering a reward to whoever brings us in," Hannah said. "Not for all of us, actually. Just me."

"Why just you?" I asked.

"Don't be jealous," teased Hannah with the slightest of smiles.

I didn't think this was at all funny. I glared at Hannah and she went on quickly. "It's obvious, isn't it? It's the Prophecy. I'm the dangerous one as far as she's concerned."

"But what's the point of a bounty when the Caomhnóir and the Trackers are looking for us anyway? It's their job. They don't need some reward to motivate them."

"The bounty isn't for Marion's Northern Clans," said Finn, slapping the cover closed on his notebook and looking up at last. "You're right: They'll be hunting for us, reward or not. The bounty has been added to tempt us, not them. A common tactic."

"That doesn't make any sense," Milo said.

"It makes perfect sense. They know we're all together: If we all have a bounty on our heads, we're all in equal danger—we'll stick together. But if the bounty is on Hannah alone, there's a chance one of us will betray the others and turn her in."

"None of us would ever do that!" Milo asserted.

"People have done worse for less," answered Finn. "Marion is counting on it."

No one had any response to that. I crammed the rest of the pastry into my mouth and stood up. I was suddenly filled with a panicky sort of energy, a need to do something—anything—besides waiting around for the Necromancers or the Caomhnóir to come busting down our door.

"Did Lucida give us instructions? Where we should go? What we should do?" I asked.

Hannah nodded. "We're supposed to lay low and stay in the flat as much as we can. The idea is not to attract attention."

"That's it?" I asked.

"That's it."

I groaned and started to pace. The room, already depressingly small, seemed to close in on me instantly.

"And what about Annabelle? Does she know we're here?"

Everyone stared at me blankly. "We've not gone down for a visit yet, Jess," said Savvy.

"You haven't? I was out of it for three days and you never bothered to check if Annabelle was home?" I asked incredulously.

"She was in hiding even before all this. We couldn't just go down and bang on her door," Finn said. "Besides, you're the only one she knows, and you've been in no fit state."

Finn's logic was maddening but I knew he was right. "Well, I'm okay now, so what are we waiting for?"

Hannah bit her bottom lip fretfully. "I don't know, Jess. Lucida told us not to contact anyone. I'm not sure if she'd want us to—"

"Hannah, I'm not talking about making social calls to our new neighbors. Annabelle is hiding out from the Necromancers. She's the one who warned me about the possibility of them in the first place, and she's in almost as much danger as we are. She needs to know what's happened at Fairhaven or she'll be in even more danger."

"I agree with Jess," Finn said.

"Well, there's a first time for everything," I muttered. Only Milo heard me. He betrayed only the slightest of sniggers.

"This Annabelle is a liability if we don't warn her," Finn went on. "She could get careless and lead either the Necromancers or Marion right to us. If she's caught, we're as good as caught, too."

I ignored the fact that Finn clearly had no concern for

Annabelle's well-being and jumped in before anyone else could argue with him. "Exactly. So let's go down to her flat and see if we can find her. The sooner we tell her what's going on, the safer we'll all be."

No one voiced any objections, so I headed for the door.

"Hey!" Finn called after me. Both his voice and his expression turned immediately defensive, like a soldier on high alert. "You can't just go charging down there! What if the Necromancers have already found her? We need to be smart about this, Jess!"

I turned on my heel. I should have known it wouldn't be that easy.

Finn went into battle-command mode. "Milo, you float down there and have a proper look. If she's home, and alone, Jess and I will go down. If not, we monitor the flat and wait for her to return."

Milo rolled his eyes. "Not even a 'please.' So typical."

With his quip still hanging in the air, Milo sunk through the floor. Or rather, he tried to sink through the floor. He suddenly stopped, knee-deep in the floorboards, with a curious expression on his face.

"Huh? This is weird. I think I'm stuck."

"What's that?" Finn asked brusquely.

"This is as far as I can go," Milo explained.

Finn crossed the room and knelt beside him, then began examining the floor. "Are you quite sure?"

Milo's look was positively wilting; he wiggled and struggled for a moment as if caught in a tar pit. "Yes, I'm sure. Don't you think you'd be sure if you were stuck in a goddamn floor? There's a barrier, and I can't get through."

"What does it feel like?" Finn pressed.

"Like one of those Wards back at Fairhaven. It's like the air becomes thicker, then sort of sticky, and then just... solid." He struggled for a moment as he tried to push his way through, but then rose up again, pale from his efforts. "Yeah, I'm definitely not getting through that way."

Finn was still staring at the floor as though an explanation might be written on it somewhere. He began to run his hands over the boards.

"Could this be because we Warded the place when we first got here?" I asked.

"No, I don't think so," Hannah said. "Milo has been getting in and out with no problem for the last few days. It's just like at Fairhaven. As long as I'm with him, he can move back and forth across the Wards freely."

Finn stood up. "Does Annabelle have any connection to the Durupinen?"

"Yes," I said. "From Romania. Her family used to be a Clan Family, but their bloodline hasn't produced a complete Gateway in at least a couple of generations. But Annabelle's grandmother passed on their family history to her—Annabelle knew a lot about it. And I think she still has some connections to other Clan Families because she was able to find out where Fairhaven was."

"Do you think she'd know how to Ward her flat?" Finn asked.

"I have no idea. She definitely knows a lot about the spirits. She's not totally connected to them like the Durupinen are, but she can still sense ghosts and communicate with them on some level. She knew how to contact Lyle and send him to me with a message, remember? And when I was in the hospital at St. Matt's, she recited an Incantation or something over me. But I don't know if she can do Wards. She'd need a copy of the *Book of Téigh Anonn*, wouldn't she?"

"Ain't it possible her family still has one?" asked Savvy.

Again, I shrugged. "I'm not sure. She never mentioned it, but it's possible."

"Okay then, we stake it out," commanded Finn. "We'll take turns waiting for her to come in or out. Only then will we approach her. Oughtn't take too long."

We all looked at each other and agreed. It was as good a plan as any.

§

It was also the most boring plan in the history of plans.

A stakeout sounds much cooler than it is in real life, as anyone who's ever actually been on one can tell you. There's a mystique around the term, but really it's a glorified name for waiting around and doing absolutely nothing until you want to scream from the monotony.

Hour after hour we watched while hoping for a glimpse of Annabelle's wild hair. We watched from every possible vantage point—from a bench across the street with our hoodies pulled tightly around our heads; from under a nondescript black umbrella while sheltering in a doorway; even from the window of Lyle's apartment while trying not to look too conspicuous as we strained our necks into odd positions. For our own protection, Finn insisted that he be with Hannah and me on all of our shifts, so we couldn't even joke with Savvy or gossip idly with Milo to pass the time. Instead, we sat in tense silence, jumping every so often when Finn leapt up at yet another false alarm. With each passing hour, there was absolutely no change—not a twitch from behind the drawn curtains, not a flicker of a light. Nothing.

Finally, after two days—and Savvy's increasingly whiny complaints about her shifts—Finn gave up. He was halfway through his breakfast when he pushed his plate away and stood up.

"Hannah, can you bring Milo back from his post? It's time to try something else."

Hannah nodded, then closed her eyes for a moment. Milo materialized at once.

"About time!" Milo cried. "I was ready to scrap this plan yesterday. I legit thought I was going to die of boredom, but then I remembered I sort of covered that already."

Savvy imitated a rimshot while Hannah giggled. Milo took a little bow.

"We needed to give it a chance," Finn said a tad defensively. "But either she isn't using the flat anymore, or she hasn't left it in two days. Either way, we're not getting anywhere. Time to see if we can get in."

At this, Finn marched across the room to the window and threw it wide open.

"What are you doing?" I asked.

"We can't send Milo, so I'm checking it out myself," he said in a maddening tone that implied I was an idiot.

"Out the window? And what are you going to use to get down to Annabelle's window, your keen Spider-sense?"

Finn looked at me like I was insane. "Huh?"

"Oh my God, you really did grow up under a rock, didn't you?"

"I'm going to use the fire escape." He pointed out the window, through which I could see the rusty metal stairs.

"Oh. Good idea," I said flatly.

Finn hoisted himself out of the window in one smooth motion. Awkwardly, I followed him. Within a few seconds, Hannah and

Savvy had also crammed themselves out onto the rickety landing. We were all wearing the pajamas Savvy had bought for us: I'm sure we looked like we'd just lost a game of truth or dare at a slumber party.

"Did I say this was a group outing?" Finn growled as he pressed himself against the back of the fire escape to make room for us all. It was a good thing Milo didn't need a physical space on the landing—there was no way all five of us would've fit; he hovered, six stories up, next to us.

"I'm the only one who knows Annabelle. I have to go," I said, arms crossed. "Otherwise you're just a random perv trying to sneak into her flat."

"Right then, Jess should come. But the rest of you need to go back inside," Finn said begrudgingly.

"I'm not missing the fun! C'mon mate, I've been nothing but dead bored for days! Give a girl a break, can't you?" Savvy exclaimed.

"I'm not staying up there by myself if everyone else is going," Hannah said firmly.

The landing made an ominous creaking sound. "Fine, fine, just be careful," Finn said reluctantly while shaking his head. "And don't come in until I tell you the coast is clear." I could practically see a thought bubble form over his head with an exasperated "Women!" written inside.

We stood huddled on the fire escape in the early morning chill. This side of the building overlooked a narrow, dingy alley. The sun had not yet risen high enough in the sky for any real light to reach inside the alley; shadows clung to the brick walls and draped themselves over the trash cans below. A sliver of relative brightness cut across the end of the alley, where a bit of the sidewalk and a slice of the street were visible; cars, as well as the occasional pedestrian, passed by, but no one looked in our direction as Finn made his way down the fire escape.

Through the rusty slats under our feet, we watched in silence as Finn peered into Annabelle's window and tested the latch. "I can't see anyone," he announced. "The flat's empty."

"How do you know someone ain't in one of the other rooms?" asked Savvy.

"It's a studio," Finn explained. "There's just the one room, and the door to the loo is open. Unless she's hiding in the closet, she's not home."

"She's got to come back sometime," I said. "Let's just come back later."

But Finn wasn't listening. He fiddled for a moment with the window sash, and before we could object he had opened the window and was climbing through.

"What the bloody hell is he doing?" Savvy exclaimed.

"I don't know, but we'd better follow him," I replied. "Milo, go back inside and wait. You shouldn't go into Annabelle's flat until we know what Wards they're using."

"You know Wards don't affect me if I'm with my Bound Gateway. And I'm staying with my girl," Milo said defiantly.

"Jess has a point, Milo," said Hannah. "Please. I'll call you if I need you."

"Fine. But only for you, sweetness," Milo replied with a wink before disappearing.

I started down the metal steps to Annabelle's landing. Hannah and Savvy followed me. The fire escape trembled and screeched with every movement. It was a good thing Annabelle wasn't home... we certainly weren't going to sneak up on anyone like this.

"Finn, what are you doing down here?" I asked, calling into the apartment. As I climbed into the room I experienced a strange sensation, as if I were pushing my way through an invisible barrier.

Sure enough, when I turned to look back at the window, there were runes scrawled beneath it. The same was true all around the room. Annabelle had practically covered the walls in runes and other symbols. Some had been painted on with black paint; a half-dried can of it was abandoned in a corner. Others had been scratched into the flowery wallpaper with something sharp. The effect was creepy in the extreme.

"I don't recognize some of these symbols," said Hannah, examining the markings as she walked slowly along the wall. "They aren't usually used for Wards, at least none of the ones I've seen."

"Maybe she's put some other kinds of protective Castings on the place, too?" I asked.

"Maybe," Hannah said slowly, with a dubious tone. "But some of these don't even look like runes."

45

"What are we looking for?" I asked Finn as he poked his head into the tiny bathroom.

"Anything that might tell us where she's gone. Obviously."

"Well she can't have gone far," Savvy offered.

"What makes you say that?" Finn asked.

"Her keys and purse are still here, mate," said Savvy, pointing to a small table by the door. A brown leather purse was resting beside a small glass bowl containing her keys, cell phone, passport, and some spare change.

Finn joined Savvy by the door. "It's locked from the inside," he declared.

"There's still a cup of tea over here," said Hannah.

I crossed the room to the kitchenette. A nearly full cup of tea sat in its saucer with a spoon resting across its top. The teabag was still in it, obscured by a milky film that had formed over the top of the liquid. As I stared down at it, a sinking feeling crept into the pit of my stomach.

"This isn't right," I said. "Something is really wrong here."

"Can you feel it, too?" Hannah asked. "It's giving me a headache."

I opened my mouth to say that wasn't what I'd meant, but then closed it again. Hannah was right. Something in the air was pulsating. If I stood totally still, I could feel it tugging at me like a gentle undertow in an invisible sea.

"I feel it, too," Savvy said, her eyes closed in concentration.

Without really understanding how I was doing it, I focused on the pulling sensation, trying to find the source of it. My eyes came to rest on the far corner of the room, where a double bed stood neatly made with a patchwork quilt on top. Strangely, even in such a tiny room, I hadn't noticed the bed before; it had hidden itself, tucked away in the periphery of my vision, as though it were trying to stay out of sight. But now that I'd seen the bed, I couldn't take my eyes off of it. It was at once the most normal and most bizarre thing I'd ever seen.

"The bed," I said.

"What bed?" Hannah asked.

"That bed! In the corner, it's... don't you see the bed? Look exactly where you feel you don't want to look!"

But everyone was already staring at it, each face mystified; no one else had realized it was there until that moment. The bed sat before us, steeped in the strange, pulsating energy, and I didn't understand how we hadn't noticed it at first. But now that we'd discovered the bed, its presence was overpowering.

"It's... what's wrong with it?" Savvy whispered. She took a careful step forward with all the concentration of someone navigating through a minefield.

"I don't know, but don't touch it," Finn said. He threw a hand out to grab Savvy's outstretched arm, but she shook him off as she froze in her tracks. That's when I realized she had stopped moving forward and had instead begun panting.

"I can't touch it," Savvy said, her voice straining as if with physical effort. "I can't get any closer than this. You try it."

We all started moving toward the bed. Sure enough, at about three or four feet from the brass footboard, I found I couldn't approach any nearer. It wasn't that there was anything physical in the way, as far as I could see, but every time I entered the bed's immediate vicinity my heart began to pound and my palms began to sweat. I was overcome with crippling, debilitating fear: If I touched the bed, terrible things would happen. It reminded me of the Circle that had held us captive the night the Elemental had attacked us.

"It's a Casting," Finn announced. "Someone's put a Casting around the bed, to keep people away from it."

"It's working, then," Savvy said. "I'm terrified to get any closer to it, but don't ask me why, mate, because I really couldn't tell you."

"Listen," Hannah hissed suddenly. With a horrified expression on her face, she bent closer to the bed. "I can hear voices. Do you hear them?"

We all fell silent, trying to listen. I couldn't hear any voices, but there was something there—the faintest hint of a murmuring in the air.

"There are spirits here!" Hannah whispered. "I can feel their energy, but it's all sort of... blended together. It's like they aren't separate beings anymore."

"How can there be ghosts here? The place has been Warded," Finn said.

"I'm trying to understand what they're saying, but it's all jumbled," Hannah continued, ignoring Finn. "All of their thoughts and feelings are all mashed together, and they're masked behind something," she explained as she reached a hand out in front of her. Her fingertips probed tentatively at the air; her hand trembled in the nothingness.

"What's she on about?" Savvy asked. "I'm not picking up on anything, and if there's a ghost about, it usually makes itself pretty damn clear to me straight off."

"Me too," I said. "I can tell there's an energy here, but I wouldn't have thought it was a spirit, let alone more than one. But Hannah's hypersensitive. It's a Caller thing."

"Hannah, can you make out anything specific?" Finn asked. "Is there a message? Can you ask them what's happening?" He was prowling around the bed like a caged animal, nervously cracking his knuckles against his legs.

Hannah shook her head sharply. "I can't understand them. There's something very wrong with them."

Finn ran a nervous hand through his hair. "I don't know what to do. This is outside my training. I've never seen anything like this before."

With effort, I tore my eyes from the vacant mattress; something odd caught my eye. "What's that under the bed?" I crouched down on my hands and knees.

Savvy and Finn dropped to their knees as well. There was a very large and complicated drawing carved into the floorboards under the bed. It comprised numerous symbols, three concentric circles, and smears of something that looked horribly like…

"Blood," Finn whispered.

"Well, that's creepy, yeah?" Savvy breathed. "Do the Durupinen ever use blood in their Castings?"

"No," Finn said, attempting to inch closer to the bed; he then pulled back, wincing. "There's not a single Casting in the *Book of Téigh Anonn* that calls for blood, human or otherwise. And none of the more esoteric Castings use it either, as far as I know."

I fought back a sudden urge to vomit. "Do you really think that's human blood?"

"I have no idea," Finn said. "But I'd rather not find out. Come on, I'm getting you out of here."

"No!" I shouted. Finn shushed me, but I ignored him. "Something really horrible is happening here, and it has something to do with Annabelle. I'm not leaving until we figure it out!"

Surprisingly, Finn didn't argue, but leapt to his feet instead. He brushed off his hands and started to pace. "This is the Necromancers' work. It has to be. They've found her already."

"But what does it mean?" I cried in panic. "Where is she? What have they done to her?"

He didn't answer, and I hadn't expected him to. He knew no more than I did.

"Maybe we can get in touch with Lucida? She might know what this is if we describe it," said Finn, thinking out loud.

The situation was so grave that I didn't argue with the suggestion of asking for Lucida's help. Instead, I said, "Hannah, I know you're supposed to be careful about contacting her, but you need to send her one of those Blind Summoner things she taught you to do."

"She's here," Hannah said.

"Lucida's here?" I asked, looking around blankly.

"No. Your friend Annabelle. I think she's here," Hannah replied.

I peered around again. Finn and Savvy did the same, then both turned back to me with confused looks on their faces.

"Hannah, what are you—"

"There's more than ghost energy here," she said. Her eyes were closed again; she was concentrating intently.

"What do you mean?" I asked.

"I'm trying to find someone to Call," Hannah said. "The spirit energy is presenting itself, but since it's all muddled together I'm having trouble latching onto just one of them. But there's also an energy here that won't respond to my Calling, and it feels like living energy."

I looked back at the bed. The empty, still bed. It was absolutely empty, I could see that. And yet...

"How can you tell the difference?"

"Living energy has a different movement," explained Hannah, opening her eyes. "It's like the spirits shoot around, totally unrestricted, waiting to be plucked out of the air. But the energy of the living, their energy is trapped within their own bodies. Living energy, it's different... muffled... like they're bouncing around in little cages. I can feel that right now. It's hard to pick up on because it's hidden behind all of this confused spirit energy, but it's there."

"So you're saying that even though we can't see her, Annabelle is somehow here right now?" I asked. As I heard the question come out of my mouth, it sounded too absurd to be true—even after all the shit we'd seen since discovering we were Durupinen.

"She's hidden," Hannah said as her eyes widened in horror. "They've hidden her right here in plain sight!"

Savvy looked back at the bed with a dubious expression. "I know you're tuned into all this stuff, love, but I don't know about this one."

"I'm sure of it!" Hannah exclaimed. "They're using the spirits to hide her. I don't know how they're doing it, but I'm telling you she's here!"

I turned to Finn. "What do we do?"

In absolute bewilderment, Finn looked from me, to Hannah, to the bed. "I... I don't know. I still don't understand..."

I turned back to Hannah. "What do we do, Hannah? There's got to be something we can do."

She shook her head, looking desperately confused. "I can't say for sure. I only know what I'm sensing. But I think we need to find a way to get the rest of this spirit energy out of the way. We won't be able to get to her unless we do."

"You're sure you can't Call them away from the bed and over to you?"

Hannah shook her head. "I've been trying. I don't know what's been done to them, but they aren't individual spirits anymore. They won't—can't—respond to me."

"Finn, can you expel them?" I asked.

Finn closed his eyes and concentrated. We watched him in tense, expectant silence until his eyes snapped open once more. "It's no use. It's many spirits, like Hannah said, but they don't feel... right."

He pulled out his Casting bag. Within seconds, Finn had drawn a rough Circle around the bed, including himself within its boundary. "Stand back, all of you," he said. "I'm going to try this, but I have no idea what's likely to happen."

We backed as far away from the bed as the tiny flat would allow and stood—with our backs jammed against the kitchenette—waiting.

Finn closed his eyes and muttered his Casting. He raised his hands to his chest, preparing to complete the expulsion, but rather than thrusting them forward as he usually would, his hands began to shake. I could see the muscles spasming in his arms, his veins throbbing, his face screwed up in effort.

"Finn, what's happening?" I asked, my voice rising in fear.

Breathing heavily from his efforts, it was all he could do to shake his head slightly in response. He let his arms drop to his sides while he caught his breath. Then he raised both arms again and—with what seemed to be a Herculean effort—let out a guttural, wrenching shout while simultaneously pushing outwards with his hands, as if he were shoving aside a monstrous barrier.

Something inside the room expanded, like an invisible explosion. As the force made contact, a cacophony of voices began battering me. Before I could fully register what I was hearing, all three of us were knocked right off of our feet. I flung my hands up and clamped them over my ears, but it did no good; the voices were inside my own head, resonating against the inside of my skull. The only other time I could remember hearing so many souls in so much agony was the night my mother had died, when the spirits had come to me in a dream.

A moment later, the voices had faded to nothingness, their absence leaving a ringing in my ears and a devastating sorrow tucked into the hollow of my ribcage. I pulled my hands away from my ears and blinked a film of tears out of my eyes. Beside me, Savvy cowered with her hands still clutched over her head.

"What... the bloody... HELL was that?" Savvy gasped.

"I don't know, but I think it's gone." More tears clouded my eyes. I swiped them away and tried to focus on Hannah, who had sunk to the ground beside me.

"Hannah? Are you okay?" I asked.

But Hannah wasn't listening to me. She was staring, horrorstruck, in the direction of the bed. I followed her gaze: I cried out.

There, huddled into a ball, with her body covered in runes, was Annabelle. She was completely naked, and the bedclothes—which had looked smooth and undisturbed moments before—were crumpled beneath her. Scraps of bread littered the bed, and the pungent, stale stink of urine filled the air.

"Oh my God!" With my heart in my throat, I stumbled to my feet and ran to her. I reached the bed and sunk to my knees, sure that Annabelle was...

Finn was still sucking in air as if he'd just run a marathon, but he reached towards Annabelle, gently extracted her wrist from underneath her body, and felt for her pulse.

"She's alive," he announced.

Even as he said it, Annabelle moaned quietly, turning her head so that her face was visible beneath her wild tangle of hair. Her eyes were closed but her mouth, muttering words I couldn't hear, was working feverishly.

"What the hell have they done to her?" I asked, unable to keep the tremor out of my voice. "She's been here the whole time?"

Finn shook his head. "I'm not certain, but I think there was a wall of spirit energy surrounding the bed. They were using it to hide her in plain sight."

"Sav, can you find her a blanket or something to cover her up with?" I asked, trying vainly to shield Annabelle's nakedness with my hands. I could feel myself blushing for her; she was always so dignified, so put together.

Savvy staggered to her feet and ran to the closet at once, throwing it open and rummaging through the top shelf. She pulled down an afghan and tossed it to me.

Carefully, I tucked the blanket around Annabelle. Her eyelids began to flutter rapidly.

"We've got to get her out of here," Finn said. "But first, move back Jess."

"Why, what are you—"

"Just do it!" Finn commanded.

I moved back from the bed as he grabbed onto the footboard with both hands. With a mighty tug, he pulled the bed away from the wall and out of the Circle. The moment the bed broke through the Circle's boundary, Annabelle shot straight up into a sitting position, gasping for breath as though she'd just emerged from icy water.

"What... what are you...?" She looked around, clearly panicked. "Stay away from me! What do you want? Don't touch me! Don't you touch me!"

"Annabelle, it's okay, it's me!" I said, starting forward. But Annabelle screamed at the sudden movement and lashed at me with her hands as I approached.

"Annabelle, look at me! It's Jess! It's Jessica!"

As Annabelle took in my features, I watched the light of recognition flare in her eyes; the animal terror faded from her expression. Her hands grabbed desperately at my shirt as she broke into a torrent of tears. I wrapped my arms around her, then pulled the blanket more securely around her shoulders—shoulders which looked much frailer than I remembered.

"They found me. They found me, Jessica," she sobbed brokenly. "The Necromancers. And David. Oh, Jess, David is... he's..."

"I know," I said, fighting back my own tears at the thought of Pierce. "I know all about it. It's okay, just try to calm down. It will be okay. You're safe now."

But that wasn't true. We were all in terrible danger, even more so now that we'd broken the Necromancers' Casting. I looked beyond Annabelle's heaving shoulders to Finn, who had pulled his phone from his pocket and was snapping photo after photo of the Casting marks on the exposed floor.

"Lucida said no phones!" I exclaimed. "They can be traced, Finn!"

"This is another burner," said Finn, taking photos of the walls. "Lucida gave one to each of us while you were delirious. No one can trace this, and even if they tried, I'll have properly disposed of it before they have a chance to track us down."

"Why are you even taking those pictures?" I asked. "What good will it do now, when we've already gotten her out!"

"I want to look up these runes, and find out what this Casting is. We've just broken through a very powerful Casting without understanding its nature. That was an extremely foolish thing to do, and we're lucky there were no consequences. Yet."

"Yet?"

"I'm not ruling out the possibility that we may still well pay for what we've done here," Finn said gravely.

"And in light of that possibility, let's get the hell out of here, yeah?" Savvy suggested, throwing an anxious glance at the door.

"Savvy's right. They could've detected us the moment we broke that Casting," Hannah said. "They could be on their way right now!"

"I've got what I need," said Finn. "Let's get out of here."

5

THE BLIND SUMMONER

I PRIED ANNABELLE'S TREMBLING HEAD gently away from my shoulder. "Annabelle? We're going to get you out of here. Can you walk?"

It took a moment for all of those words to sink in, but when they did, Annabelle began sobbing even harder. While shaking her head, she managed to answer, "I don't th-th-think so."

"That's okay, don't worry about it," I said softly. "This is Finn. He's the Caomhnóir for our Gateway. He can carry you, if you're comfortable with that."

Annabelle looked at Finn, who had pasted onto his face the most empathetic expression I'd ever seen. Annabelle clutched the afghan more tightly around her body, but nodded.

"You'll have to go back out the way you came," she mumbled. "They put another Casting on the door. They could only leave in pairs, and they had to recite an Incantation before they crossed the threshold."

"That's fine," Finn said. He walked over to the bed, and—keeping his eyes respectfully averted—scooped Annabelle up in his arms as though she weighed nothing at all.

We followed as Finn slid through the window and ascended the fire escape, all without jostling Annabelle in the slightest. She clung to him with her eyes clamped tightly shut—either she was afraid of heights or just too traumatized to take in her surroundings. I heard Finn tell her to duck her head, and they disappeared smoothly into the flat above us.

Savvy was the last through Lyle's window. She slid it shut behind her, snapped the lock into place, and yanked the curtain closed for good measure.

"I don't think anyone was watching us," she announced, as she inched the curtain aside just enough to peer into the alleyway.

"Keep watch while we get her settled," Finn replied. "I'll do a sweep."

Savvy nodded and turned to keep vigil.

"What's going on?" asked Milo, materializing beside Hannah. "What are you—hot damn, what happened to *her*?" he said, staring in unabashed horror at Annabelle.

"This is Annabelle," I explained. "The Necromancers had her trapped downstairs in her flat."

"She looks wrecked! How long has she been down there?"

Annabelle gave no indication that she had heard Milo, which, I realized, was entirely possible; she was sensitive to spirits, but I had no idea whether she could actually see and hear them in the same way as we could.

"Annabelle? How long were you down there?"

I couldn't tell if she'd heard me either. Annabelle's teeth were chattering violently and there was something wrong with her eyes—her pupils were so widely dilated that her irises had been swallowed up almost entirely.

"Come on," I said. "Let's get you cleaned up. Hannah, can you help me?"

Twenty minutes later, Annabelle sat curled up on Lyle's plaid-orange sofa, with a blanket around her feet and her trembling hands gripped tightly around a steaming mug of tea. I had managed to scrub most of the runes from her skin with a hot bath, and Hannah had found her a clean pair of pajamas from the bags of clothes Savvy had purchased at a nearby thrift store.

The hot water seemed to have steamed away much of Annabelle's confusion, and even some of her weakness. Although I'd nearly carried her to the tub, she had climbed out on her own and needed only minor help getting dressed—her fingers had been shaking too badly to fasten her buttons. As she dressed, she had started answering questions more readily, and when I'd brought her back into the living room, she nodded in acknowledgment when Milo pronounced that she was looking better.

While Annabelle clearly couldn't visually see Milo, she could sense—and sometimes hear—his contributions to the conversation. He certainly elicited the first hint of a smile from her by insisting that her hair, freshly washed and still wet, was "runway chic."

As I'd been cleaning her up in the tub, Annabelle hadn't made a sound save for one or two repressed sobs. I hadn't pushed her; I didn't ask her a single question as I scrubbed away the runes. But now, as she sipped slowly on her tea, I eased into the questioning. I was all for letting her recover at her own pace, but unfortunately there were some things that needed to be answered right away, for all of our sakes.

"Annabelle, how did you wind up in that state? Can you remember? I hate to make you talk about it, but we need to know," I said, offering her a plate of scones.

Annabelle started to reach for a scone, but then withdrew her hand, looking nauseated. "I don't think I'm ready for food yet," she said.

I put the plate on the coffee table and waited.

"Nothing happened for weeks," she began in a whisper of a voice. "I started to think I'd been crazy to come here, that no one had been looking for me after all. I don't know if it just took them that long to find me, or if they were waiting for me to let my guard down before they made their move. But either way, they came."

"The Necromancers?" whispered Hannah.

"I never heard them refer to themselves, but, yes, I believe that's who they must be. I have no idea how they got in, or how they knew where I was, but about a week ago, I think, they overpowered me as soon as I walked in the door. They were both huge, and their heads were shaved. They had tattoos all over them. They'd already prepared the Casting that you found me under. Actually, that was the first thing I'd noticed when I walked in; they must've just finished the Casting, because the bed had been placed at a strange angle and I remember thinking 'How did that get moved?' But before I knew what was happening, they jumped out, stripped off my clothes, bound me to the bed, and covered me in those runes. I've never been so scared in my life."

Annabelle was on the verge of crumbling into tears. I squeezed her shoulder gently. "It's okay. You're safe now; they can't hurt you anymore." This was a blatant lie; nothing, as far as I knew, prevented them from bursting in on us at that very moment, but I wasn't about to tell her that. "Go on. What happened next?"

"At first they used ropes, but then they recited an Incantation, and there was a huge influx of spirit energy. It was like... a storm of spirits. I don't know how else to describe it. They were being sucked into the flat from all sides, drawn into a kind of vortex that was centered around my bed. And then…"

Annabelle shuddered as she grasped fruitlessly for the right words. Beside me, Milo drifted closer; his face was transfixed into an expression of terror and he seemed unable to look away. I was glad Annabelle couldn't see him.

"One of the Necromancers lit a black candle and the spirits started screaming, louder and louder, as they were pulled into this spinning energy globe. When they hit the vortex, they were pulled and tugged and torn until they sort of… morphed into a single entity."

"What fresh hell is this?" Savvy muttered.

Annabelle sounded close to tears again. "It was awful… like they'd built a cage out of the pieces of the spirits they'd ripped apart. I never would've believed spirits could be manipulated or destroyed like that if I hadn't seen it with my own eyes."

"I don't understand," I said, looking at Hannah and Finn. "Is this what the Necromancers are known for? I thought they just wanted to bring spirits back from the other side, to reverse death."

"Me too," Hannah said. "But then I guess we have to ask ourselves, once they bring the spirits back, what do they want to do with them?"

"Nothing savory, by the looks of it," Savvy said.

"The Necromancers have always had a reputation for dark and reprehensible magic," Finn said. "Based on what we've seen so far, I'd say that reputation is well-earned." He stood up and turned to Annabelle. "Forgive me. I don't mean to interrupt, but I should check the perimeter and make sure they haven't returned." Without waiting for any kind of response, Finn strode across the room and out the door; he closed it quietly behind him.

I turned back to Annabelle. Gingerly, I asked, "Can you go on?"

"It was like living inside a bubble. Everything was hazy and distorted—the spirit energy created a barrier between me and the rest of the world. I couldn't see clearly, couldn't think clearly. The spirit energy exerted an actual physical force on me; I was too drained to rise from the bed, too drained to think clearly. And the men who'd trapped me there never spoke to me, no matter what I asked them or how many times I screamed."

"Could they hear you?" I asked. "We couldn't until Finn broke the Circle."

"Oh, they could hear me," Annabelle spat bitterly. "I could tell. But other than throwing a few scraps of food and the occasional cup of water at me, they never acknowledged me; I think they'd been trained not to. Once in a while they'd take a call on a cell phone, and sometimes they left for a few hours at a time, but I was never able to make even the feeblest attempt at an escape.

"They kept talking about 'him,' and what 'he' would want them to do. I realized that the two of them were really just henchmen. The real person to blame for my captivity was somewhere else. I had no idea who 'he' was, though, until the fourth or fifth day. That's when 'he' paid us a visit."

I had a feeling I knew exactly who "he" was, but I let her go on. It seemed easier for Annabelle to keep going now that she had started, and I didn't want to interrupt; by telling the story, Annabelle was releasing herself from its grip and weakening its ability to terrorize her.

"You only met Neil Caddigan once or twice," Annabelle said. "I'd only met him perhaps a half dozen times, until two days ago. That's when he walked through the door and sat down on a chair beside my bed. My first instinct was pity: Poor Neil, another luckless bastard caught up in this mess. I figured he'd been captured too, that the other men were going to torture him in front of me. But then he looked at me lying there, trussed up by spirit energy, and... smiled."

For just a moment, a tiny spark of Annabelle's usual fire flared on her face. Although the spark was minuscule and fighting for its life, I was intensely relieved to see it. I knew in that moment that they hadn't broken her, not completely, and that despite how fragile she looked right now, Annabelle would be okay.

She went on, "I knew then. Something clicked. He didn't even have to speak, although of course he did."

Annabelle didn't continue right away. I let her fall quiet for a moment, then prompted her. "What did he say?"

She swallowed something back before she could answer. "He said, 'Pierce sends his regards.'"

I could've exploded. My rage was all-consuming: If Neil had been in front of me right then, I would've killed him without hesitation. I fought not to leap off the sofa and punch the wall. I looked into Annabelle's eyes and we experienced a moment of perfect synchronicity: She would have cheerfully shared in the violence.

"A small part of me still thinks I should have known, somehow. I couldn't have told you exactly why, but I never liked him—not from the very first moment he shook my hand. I always found something about him to be unsettling... I just couldn't put my finger on it."

"I felt the same way," I agreed, thinking back to my own first meeting with Neil; when he looked at me, there had been an eagerness in his expression that bordered on greed. "It was the eyes. There was something really disturbing about his eyes."

"Yes," Annabelle said. "That pale, almost silvery, color. You know, it's not just him. I don't know what causes it, but the two henchmen had eyes just like his."

"Huh," I said, frowning. "I wonder what the connection is?"

"Maybe we should ask Lucida about that too, Jess." Hannah offered. I'd almost forgotten that anyone else was in the room with us, but I winced when I looked at my sister: Hearing all this was as painful for her as it was for me.

I nodded at Hannah, trying not to let my face betray my emotions. Then I turned back to Annabelle. "Go on. What happened next?" I asked, perhaps a little too eagerly.

"Neil never explained why he was there or who he was working for. He just started asking me questions, first about my own abilities, then about yours. Whenever I asked him a question in return, he just smiled and wagged a finger at me, like I was a naughty child who'd spoken out of turn. He'd say, 'Now, now, now, Annabelle, I'm asking the questions here.' He didn't spend much time asking about me, though. It was you he really wanted to know about."

Stewing in my own guilt, I imagined an accusatory edge to her voice. Annabelle wouldn't even look at me now; she had fixed her eyes on the glassy surface of the tea in her mug.

"The questions were casual at first, almost friendly. If I refused to answer, he obligingly moved on to another. But then, as he edged closer to the heart of what he wanted, he dropped the guise of civility. Whenever I didn't cooperate, he'd pull out an old book and start adding to the Castings. With each unsatisfactory answer, he drew another symbol in the room—or on me. Each added a new dimension to my horror."

60

"Like what?" Savvy asked, breathless. She'd abandoned her vigil at the window; she was now utterly captive to Annabelle's story.

"When they first captured me, the spirit energy wasn't unbearable; but then the spirit voices grew louder and their energy began to press upon me physically—it almost felt like an attack of claustrophobia. I've had enough experience with the spirits to be able to tolerate much more of their energy than the average person—I could bear all that. Neil realized this quickly, and decided, apparently, that more drastic measures would make me talk. When I said I didn't know where you were," and here Annabelle shook back her sleeve and traced a crescent shape on her forearm, "he put a symbol here, and suddenly the spirits could touch me."

"Oh, God," Hannah whispered.

"It was like tiny frigid shocks, over and over and over again. The spirits were in agony themselves—disorientated, desperate for help. I think when they realized they could make contact with me, they couldn't stop reaching out. It was torture. I couldn't fill my lungs properly, couldn't move away from them. I held out as long as I could, but if it had gone on much longer, I would've broken. I would've told him everything I knew about you."

"Of course you would've," I said as gently as I could. "That's how torture works, Annabelle. I never would've expected you to hold out like some kind of war hero when they were hurting you like that." I shot Annabelle a gentle, if guilt-ridden, smile. "But why did he stop?"

"One of his henchmen handed him a cell phone. I've got no idea who was on the other end, but a few moments later, Neil left the flat without another glance at me. The other two followed."

"How long ago was that?" I asked.

"Three days, I think."

"Figures," Milo said. "Just before we started staking the place out. Well, at least we can safely say they haven't been around since then. We would've noticed a hulking pair of tattooed guys traipsing in and out. And obviously Jess would have recognized Neil, too."

"And you didn't hear anything that might've explained where he was going?" I asked.

"He had his back to me, and I could barely hear anything over the Spirit Cage," she said. "Of the entire conversation, I'm only sure of one word."

"Which was?"

"Fairhaven." Annabelle took a deep breath, which shuddered and caught in her lungs; the choking noise she made almost sounded as if her lungs had forgotten how to expand.

She took a moment, gasping, before beginning again. "I didn't need to hear any more than that. Whoever was on the other end of that phone probably saved my life. They gave Neil the information he wanted... he didn't have use for me anymore."

Milo, Savvy, Hannah, and I all looked at each other. One word went through all our minds: Fairhaven.

"I wanted to send a messenger like Lyle to warn you. I tried everything I knew about spirit communication, but it was useless. The spirits that surrounded me were mere fragments by then, incapable of real communication... and the Necromancers had Warded the flat against outside ghosts. I tried to tell myself that even if Neil were on his way to Fairhaven, he'd be unlikely to harm you there—that place is supposed to be like a fortress, and I knew the Durupinen would protect you," Annabelle said, with her face growing the slightest bit fiery again. "But is that why you're here? Did the Necromancers attack? Did you have to escape?"

"Yeah, about that," I said, sighing deeply. "Do you want me to warm up that tea for you? This is kind of a long story."

§

A few minutes later, when Annabelle's cup was steaming hot again, I told her the entire story—from the discovery of Hannah's Calling abilities, to the Silent Child, to the revelation of the Prophecy, to our subsequent escape from Fairhaven and inadvertent destruction of the East Tower. Hannah and Savvy chimed in with support now and again, and Milo added sound effects here and there for some much-needed comic relief.

Annabelle's eyes grew wider and wider as she listened; by the time I'd finished, she might have been staring at a nightmarish creature incarnate in front of her instead of my own flushed face.

"Well," she said, when she found her voice at last, "I've said it before and I'll say it again. I knew you were trouble from the moment you walked into my tent."

"Yup," I agreed. "Beware of a college girl with a fishbowl; a sure harbinger of the apocalypse."

"So now you have the Durupinen *and* the Necromancers searching for you?" she asked.

"Yes. Pretty impressive, huh?"

"Well, congratulations," she said, raising one eyebrow in her first recognizable attempt at sarcasm. "You've brought me to the only apartment in the city of London that's more dangerous than the one I just escaped."

"Yeah, sorry about that," I replied.

"And that Tracker you mentioned, Lucida? She's the one who's helping you stay hidden?"

"Yes, and now that you mention her," I said, climbing to my feet and massaging the feeling back into my now-numb right leg, "we really do need to try to get a message to her. She needs to know the Necromancers have been here."

A sharp sound made us all jump. Finn suddenly appeared on the fire escape; the sharp sound was the lock giving as he picked it. He climbed in through the window. Annabelle actually leapt from the sofa at the sight of him, pressing a hand to her heart as she fought to calm her breath. Savvy caught Annabelle's arm as she swayed and helped her back onto the cushions.

"Where the hell have you been?" I asked him.

"I used the *Book of Téigh Anonn* to seal the flat downstairs. If they try to get back in, we'll know," Finn announced, with a grimly satisfied expression on his face.

I turned back to Annabelle. "Go on," I told her.

"Finn, where did you find that?" Annabelle asked suddenly, her voice rather sharp.

Finn looked up. "Where did I find what?"

"That book. Did they leave it in my flat?"

Finn scowled. "No. I brought this downstairs with me. Why?"

"It's just... I recognize it," said Annabelle hesitantly.

"What do you mean? Did they use one to perform their Castings?" I asked.

Annabelle pointed to Finn. "Yes! They had one of those books."

Finn and I looked at each other; his face reflected my own alarm.

"When you say, 'one of those books,'" Finn began, "what do you mean? You mean another old, thick book?"

Annabelle shook her head, her still-damp hair whipping her

face. "No, I mean a book identical to that one. I recognize the design on the cover."

"But that's a Durupinen book," I said. "It has every fundamental Casting that we learn. Your family probably had one just like it, at one point. It's not something the Necromancers should've been able to get their hands on—wait, is it?" I directed this last question toward Finn.

"No," he said, scowling down at his own book. "I don't know how they would've gotten a copy. Of course, it's entirely possible that they've had it for centuries."

"Possible, sure," I said. "But probable?"

"No," said Finn. "No, not probable."

Neither of us elaborated, but I could tell from his expression that we were thinking the same thing: The Necromancers could only have gotten the *Book of Téigh Anonn* from one of the Durupinen.

This meant one of three things. The Necromancers could have had a copy for years, decades—it could've been a recently-resurfaced relic of the power struggle they had lost centuries ago. This seemed, as Finn said, highly unlikely; the *Book of Téigh Anonn* was hardly a grocery store paperback romance; there were very few copies of it in the world. Copies were carefully guarded by the clan to which they belonged—there was no way the Durupinen would allow one to go missing without doing everything in their power to recover it.

The second possibility was that it had been stolen very recently. It might've been easy for the Necromancers to penetrate Fairhaven's defenses now that we'd half-burned the castle to the ground. And of course, there were hundreds of Gateways all over the world—what if one of them had been attacked? If that were the case, the Council may not yet have realized that a copy had gone missing—and that was dangerous in itself.

The last possibility was the most disturbing of all: What if a member of the Durupinen had actually just... handed the *Book of Téigh Anonn* over to the Necromancers?

I couldn't imagine who would commit such betrayal. Except for Savvy and Phoebe—the newest clan to enter the Durupinen ranks—all Durupinen were, to varying degrees, obsessed with being Durupinen. Every single woman revered being part of the Durupinen culture and saw herself as a proud continuation of

Durupinen history. Even Lucida, who clearly didn't follow some of the rules, took her role very seriously—even if she only loved it for the glamour and power it gave her.

No, if one of them were working with the Necromancers, it was someone on the outskirts of the Durupinen structure, someone who felt she owed absolutely nothing to this system, or was herself betrayed and seeking vengeance. But who could that be?

Before I could stop the idea from forming, I suddenly thought of Mary, whose life the Durupinen had sacrificed for their own protection from the Prophecy. With a sudden heaviness in my stomach, I realized there was a caveat to this third possibility: Whoever offered the Necromancers the *Book of Téigh Anonn* didn't have to be *living*. How many of their own had the Durupinen betrayed throughout history?

Breaking into my thoughts, Finn said, "But this doesn't make proper sense. Even if you're right, Annabelle—"

"Which I am," she interjected, with just a slight toss of her hair.

"—there's no way that Neil would be able to read it. It's just not possible."

"And why's that, mate?" Savvy asked.

"Because the *Book of Téigh Anonn* itself exists under a Casting. It appears empty to anyone who's not Durupinen or Caomhnóir—and even then the book remains blank until they begin their training," Finn said in answer to Savvy's question. Then he turned to me and added, "Surely you knew that," in what I thought was an unnecessarily belligerent tone.

"Sort of," I said, crossing my arms defensively. Now that Finn had pointed it out, I remembered that the *Book of Téigh Anonn* had appeared blank to me the first time I saw it. My mother's copy had been given to me as an "anonymous" gift—I had unwrapped it under the Christmas tree in Karen's living room. At the time I'd thought it was a journal, and even attempted to use it as a diary. But ever since we performed our first Crossing, the book had revealed its contents to me: Every page became crammed with runes, Incantations, and Castings. Amid all the recent, incredibly bizarre developments in my life, I hadn't even questioned the sudden appearance of the book's contents. Of course I had a magical book with disappearing and reappearing text. Didn't everyone?

"We were just saying that we should send a message to Lucida," said Hannah, getting to her feet. "We should tell her the Necromancers have a copy of the book, shouldn't we?"

"Yes," Finn said. He looked moodily down at the copy he was holding, as though he blamed it personally for one of its brethren copies having fallen into the wrong hands. "Tell her we need a plan to get out of here safely, as soon as possible. There's no way to know when Neil and the others will be back—and I'm sure they'll be careful to tidy up after themselves. It would be careless to leave loose ends lying about, even if those loose ends are supposed to be trapped in a Spirit Cage."

"I'll come with you," I said, as Hannah turned to leave. "I want to see how this Blind Summoner thing works."

"Okay, sure," Hannah said, smiling.

"Will you be okay until we get back?" I asked Annabelle, who was staring into her tea again; as before, her eyes were fixed and glazed over.

"Yes," she said. "I think... would it be alright if I tried to get some sleep?"

"Of course. I'm just sorry we had to keep you up at all. Get some rest. We'll wake you up if there are any new developments."

Annabelle had already put her mug down and was curling herself into a comfortable position on the sofa before I'd even finished talking. As I started to close the door behind me, Finn stuck his battered black boot into the doorjamb.

"I'm coming with you," he said in answer to my quizzical look.

"Why?"

"Do you need to ask me that? Because you're leaving the flat and the Necromancers could be waiting for you. Don't argue, just go."

It was only with difficulty that I resisted the infantile urge to stick my tongue out at him. Instead, I just tried to ignore his clunking footsteps behind me as we climbed the stairs to the roof of the building.

Out in the late morning air, the London skyline rose and fell in a series of buildings and patches of sky. The Thames was visible only by the break it created as it snaked through the urban landscape, driving the city forcefully to one side or the other with all the entitlement of royalty. I was still taking in the view as Hannah folded herself cross-legged into a Circle she'd chalked onto the tarpaper of the roof. I plunked myself down beside her.

"I've been curious about this ever since you mentioned it," I said.

"It's really useful," replied Hannah, fishing the stub of a white candle out of her sweatshirt pocket. Above us, the sun played peek-a-boo through the spotty cloud cover. "I wasn't sure I'd be able to do it, since Lucida only just taught me how, but it's actually very easy."

Hannah lit the candle and rolled it back and forth between her thumb and forefinger until exactly three drops of wax had splattered onto the ground in front of her. Then she closed her eyes.

Without really knowing what she was doing, I closed my eyes too, since I was sure a little additional concentration couldn't hurt. But before I'd even adjusted to the darkness behind my eyelids, a rustling, breezy presence entered the Circle; I opened my eyes again to see who had joined us.

A middle-aged woman, stout and frumpy, stood before Hannah, blinking bemusedly around as though unsure of how she'd gotten there. Her hands were twisting and untwisting a small tea towel.

"...mustn't leave the flat, he'll be so angry if I go without telling him," she said in a nervous, fluttery voice. "Where am I? I really do need to get back. He'll be expecting me there when he—"

Hannah held up a hand and the woman was struck dumb at once. The woman's eyes stopped darting around and instead gazed fixedly, without seeing, straight ahead of her; her hand, and the tea towel it contained, dropped to her side. At the same time, the candle in Hannah's hand began to spark. The little flame danced wildly, as though something more than air was animating it.

My heart thudded anxiously as I watched its flickering: The flame, I realized, wasn't just a flame anymore, it was something else, something... *living*.

"Hannah, what are you...?"

Hannah shushed me as she lowered the candle carefully into a teacup at her feet. Then she looked up at the spirit and spoke to it. "Lucida, we need to get out of this flat. The Necromancers have been here. They found Annabelle and imprisoned her in a Spirit Cage, but we rescued her. The Necromancers have a copy of the *Book of Téigh Anonn*, and there's a good possibility they are headed to Fairhaven. Finn is sending you pictures of the Casting marks they used, because we don't know what most of them are. Send word or come as soon as you can, please."

The woman's ghost turned and shot away without any sign of acknowledgment.

"How does she know where to go?" I asked.

"Once a ghost has been Severed, they don't need to be told where to go. The sender's message and intentions will automatically bring them to the right place. Cool, huh? I still can't believe I can do it!" Hannah said. She passed her fingers absently back and forth over the flame, which was still jumping wildly despite the lack of wind.

"What do you mean, 'Severed?'" I asked.

"We want her to bring the message, but we don't want her to be aware of what she's doing. That way, if someone intercepts her or questions her, she can't tell them anything," Hannah explained. "We're using her as a vessel to hold the message, and we need the vessel to be empty. So I performed a Severing and channeled her essence into this flame." She pointed matter-of-factly at the candle.

"When you say *essence*, what are you—"

"The part of the soul that makes you human. The part that makes you an individual, with memories and experiences and self-awareness," she said. She caught my eye for the first time since she started explaining and wrinkled her brow in concern. "Jess, what's wrong? You look upset."

Nearby, I heard Finn cease his relentless pacing.

I shook my head, trying to voice my concerns without offending her. "So you basically just turned that ghost into a... coma-ghost?"

Yup, that was me, the queen of tact, at it again.

"No, that's not it at all," Hannah cried. "It's just like she's... hypnotized, or something. When she comes back, I'll release her from the flame and she'll be as good as new. Lucida told me it doesn't hurt them."

"Hannah, I'm sorry, but I don't like it. You're telling me that you're sapping spirits of their humanity just so they can play messenger for us? Doesn't that sound completely wrong?"

"It does when you put it like that!" Hannah cried, tears springing into her eyes. "You make it sound awful, but it's not like that. We need to get word to Lucida and this is the only way to do it safely. In case you haven't noticed, this is a very serious situation we're in."

"I had noticed, actually," I shot back. "Somewhere between burning down Fairhaven and finding Annabelle naked and tortured downstairs, I did indeed figure that out."

"Be serious, Jess."

"I am being serious!" I cried. "We shouldn't be using spirits like this!"

"Why not? Why shouldn't we use them to help us? Why are we the only ones who should be used all the time?" She stood up; her hands, clenched into white-knuckled fists at her sides, were shaking. "My whole life they've been finding me, asking for things, demanding things. They've ruined every home I've ever had. They scared off every friend I've ever made. They've never left me alone."

I had no idea what to say. I'd opened the floodgates. Every bitter feeling Hannah ever had now seemed to be welling to the surface at once.

"Now we're in the most dangerous situation we've ever been in," Hannah continued. "People are hunting us down. They already killed your friend Pierce, and they nearly killed Annabelle. I don't doubt for a second that they'll kill more of us if it will get them what they want. And it's all because of these ghosts! So if I need to use them to protect us, or help us, or get us out of this alive, then I'm going to do it! Don't you think they owe us that?"

"I'm not saying they shouldn't help us," I countered. "We need all the help we can get! But there's a line, Hannah, and it's not always very clear where exactly it is, but I'm afraid we're crossing it. First that quasi-Leeching, and now this? It feels like a pretty damn short walk between what you're doing and what the Necromancers did to the spirits down in Annabelle's flat."

"How can you say that? It's completely different! Those spirits were in pain! I'm not hurting her!" Hannah said, gesturing down to the candle again; the flame was still dancing and swaying with spirit energy. "I'm protecting her! If she was caught trying to deliver that message and I hadn't Severed her, the other Durupinen could use her to get information about us!"

"But we're using her too, don't you see that? We can't lose sight of the fact that these ghosts were human beings! You can't remove someone's humanity just because they're dead!"

"I can, actually," Hannah said firmly, but quietly. "You just watched me do it."

We glared at each other. Finn had stood so still during our argument it seemed possible that he'd been turned to stone.

"Have you ever stopped to think," I said slowly, "what would happen to that spirit if that candle went out?"

Hannah continued to glare as angry tears gathered in the corners of her eyes. "I wouldn't let that happen. I'm protecting her!"

"Good," I said. "I just... let's not lose sight of why we're putting ourselves through all this in the first place. We have a job to do. It's not fair, and I know it completely sucks, but we have to do it."

"I know that. If you think I don't know that, Jess, then you don't know me at all."

What could I say? Wasn't she right? Hannah was my own sister; we'd shared a womb together, yet I barely knew her at all—not in the way I should have. I should've been able to predict the ends of her sentences; I should've known the sounds she made when she slept; I should've known all her favorite comfort foods; and I should've known a thousand other minutely intimate details about my twin. But I didn't. I'd barely been able to scratch the surface of this fragile, damaged, enigmatic person. I was almost too afraid to get below her surface—too afraid she might shatter if I dug too deep. And now we had no choice but to cling to each other, two virtual strangers cast from the same mold.

I was spared the humiliation of agreeing with her. Just then, the candle's flame began to spark and leap unnaturally as the ghost of the woman returned. Her tea towel dangled loosely from her slackened grip as she began speaking in a voice that was half her own and half Lucida's.

"Don't leave the building, whatever you do. They might be lying in wait for you. The Necromancers haven't shown up here, but that doesn't mean they aren't watching and waiting. Tell Finn I got his photos, but I'll need to do a bit more research before I can sort all the different Casting marks. I'll make arrangements to have you moved. Wait for me if you can, but send a message if you need to vacate before I get there. Keep each other safe."

The voice echoed briefly before dying away, leaving the woman's spirit floating, still vacant and unseeing, in the air before us. I looked at her for a moment, as if waiting for something to happen, although of course nothing did.

Hannah caught my eye for a brief moment. Her face was defiant as she turned to the candle and, with the murmured words of her Casting, released the essence back into the waiting spirit's body.

"I... Where am... I really ought to get back. He'll be so angry. Please let me go back?" she pleaded.

My sister looked at the ghost woman for a moment. Hannah's mouth hung open as though she had something to say to her, but instead she blew out the candle. The woman vanished, with her tea towel still clutched between her fretting hands.

6

DISAPPEARING ACT

*T*AP, TAP, TAP.

    I looked over at the window and saw her floating beyond the glass, her tiny fist poised to knock again.

"Mary? Is that you?"

She nodded vigorously and smiled. Despite my confusion at seeing her, I smiled back. I untangled myself from the nest of blankets on the sofa and ran to the window. I yanked and pulled on the battered old lock until it reluctantly squeaked open.

"Come on in. Oh, wait." I pointed to the runes we'd drawn below the sill. "I forgot. We Warded everything."

"Come out here with me," Mary said with a laugh as she floated in a playful little circle, like an ivy leaf in the wind. The breeze caught at her long white nightgown, buffeting her back and forth.

"Sorry, I'm fresh out of pixie dust," I said.

She stared at me curiously, so I clarified. "I can't fly, Mary. I've got this body that gets in the way of things like that."

She laughed again. "You can shed it. Shed it and soar!"

I shook my head. "It's not quite that easy."

"Oh, but for you it is. Go on, try."

I wasn't smiling anymore. "No, Mary. I can't come with you. I have to stay here."

Suddenly she was nose-to-nose with me at the open window, her hair floating around us like mist on the water. "Cut your strings, Jess," she whispered. "Cut your strings and fly!" Then she looked down at my feet and giggled.

I followed her gaze and screamed. There at my feet was my own body crumpled on the floor, and my eyes were glassy and empty. And then I was falling. Falling into the empty pools of those eyes, which widened into chasms that were ready to swallow me whole. A door slammed shut behind me.

73

I woke up with a yelp as I felt my body hit the couch with that peculiar thump that startles you awake from a dream in which you were sure you were plummeting to your death. I looked around wildly. The room was dim with the pale, colorless light that precedes the dawn. Savvy, looking sheepish, was standing by the bathroom with one hand on the doorknob.

"Sorry, mate. Closed that a bit rough. Didn't mean to wake you."

"I… that's okay," I said, a bit out of breath. I frantically patted my hands over my body. It was reassuringly solid, although clammy with cold sweat.

"You okay there?" Savvy asked as she crossed back to the couch.

"Yeah. Just had a nightmare. A weird one. I'll be fine."

Savvy shook her head. "It's one nightmare after another around here, ain't it?"

"Truer words were never spoken, Sav," I replied. I laid back down, but sleep—a fickle friend in the best of times—did not revisit me.

§

Two more days dragged by in agonizing slowness. There was no further discussion about sending Lucida another message. In the first place, there was really nothing new to tell her; in the second place, I think my argument with Hannah about Blind Summoners had shaken her confidence in using them. Although my twin speculated aloud what might be delaying Lucida, Hannah never once suggested that we send another message.

The knot of uneasiness in my own stomach grew by the hour, especially as the sense of health and energy I'd gained from the Leeching began to fade away. Milo had taken to his own ghostly version of pacing, which entailed disappearing and reappearing over and over again in the same pattern of locations across the flat; this continued until Savvy, jumpy from her own highly-strung nerves, shouted at him and threatened to let him be sucked through the Gateway during her next Crossing. After that, Milo contented himself with flickering feebly in and out of focus to channel his anxiety. Annabelle slept for a solid fourteen hours after she filled us in on her captivity, but her slumber was plagued by nightmares that caused her to cry out repeatedly. When she finally awoke, she still looked drained—even after she'd had her first real meal in days. I sent her back to bed as soon as she was finished eating.

We were all teetering on the edge of freaking out, but in no one was the stress more palpable than in Finn. He was wound so tightly I thought he might start pinging off the walls at any moment, like a little silver ball in a pinball machine. Every sound made him jump. Every movement, even from one of us, sent him springing up from his position and poising himself for an attack. He subsisted on adrenaline, a few halfhearted swallows of food, and the strongest coffee we could coax from Lyle's battered old coffee pot. Finn couldn't even focus on writing whatever it was that he usually wrote in his shabby little black books; he would merely huddle over a notebook for a few moments at a time before sighing loudly and shoving it back into his pocket. The only thing he *could* do was be even more snappish and bad-tempered than usual.

It was at the very zenith of our tension, just after Finn had shouted at me for drumming my fingers on the table, when the door to the flat burst open. Everyone screamed, and Finn leapt into action impossibly quickly—which would've been impressive except for the fact that "leaping to action" meant tackling me to the ground and shielding me with his body, which caused a small tower of Lyle's things to topple down on us.

"What the—Finn get OFF me! It's just Lucida!" I cried, wriggling fruitlessly while he processed this information for himself. Then, with one fluid motion, he was on his feet; I was left to mutter mutinously and massage the pain from my upper arms, which he had clamped onto with a vice-like hold in his haste to "save" me.

"Sorry it took me so long to get away, my lovelies," Lucida said. She closed the door behind her, although not before scanning the corridor carefully to make sure she hadn't been followed. "Fairhaven is in a right state, and I had quite a few arses to kiss and tasks to complete before I could get away," she told us while proceeding straight to the window that led to the fire escape. She jerked the curtain back and glared intently into the street below for a solid minute. Then she took out a cell phone, pressed a few buttons, flipped it over, pulled out both the battery and the SIM card, and flung the phone out the window. We heard it shatter in the dumpster below with a hollow clang.

"Have you seen anyone about?" she asked Finn, her eyes still trained on the street.

"No," Finn reported. "No loiterers, and no repeat walk-bys except for the typical commuters. I assume you received my description of the tattooed men? I sent it along with the photos."

"Yes. That pair would be hard to miss, but, then again, I wouldn't expect them to come back. They'd have to be thick to send the same men they'd used before, and I know the Necromancers aren't thick. Marion, on the other hand..." She rolled her eyes.

"What about her?" I asked.

"Well, she's just part of it, really. Fairhaven is a proper mess, and I'm not just talking about the fire damage. The whole central infrastructure has gone tits up. The Council is fighting like mad over whether to reinstate Finvarra, and they can't agree on what to do about you lot. Some of them think it's best to let you disappear—out of sight, out of mind. Others want you found so they can keep you locked up tight in the dungeons under watch. And then there's a small but rather vocal minority who want to..." She drew a theatrical finger across her throat with a horrible squelching noise. "They think the only way to avoid the Prophecy is to make sure you aren't alive to fulfill it. Logical, sure, but just a bit controversial. Whatever else we may get up to, murder is not one of our usual pursuits."

She paused in her explanation, apparently to enjoy the horrified looks on our faces.

"That last bit's not a shock, is it?" Lucida asked. "Surely you all realize that things are deadly serious at this point," she added, smirking.

I swallowed. "Yeah, I guess so. It's just... hearing it out loud like that..."

"Well, no use dancing around the facts, love," Lucida quipped. She took one last peek through the curtains, then walked over to the kitchen; she perched herself on the counter and helped herself to a box of chocolate digestive biscuits. "Of course, Marion is one of that minority, but that's not the real problem. She always had it in for you two. No, the real problem is her attitude toward the Necromancers."

"You mean the fact that she refuses to believe they're back or that they pose any real threat to the Durupinen?" I asked.

"Right in one!" Lucida said, a little too cheerily. "Fairhaven has never been so vulnerable, inside and out, and there's a good chance the Necromancers are going to look for you there. If they come across the place in its current state, they may try to attack—regardless of whether or not you're there—just to take advantage of the opportunity. Everyone needs to be on their proper highest guard. As for me, I needed to find a way to warn the other Council members without their realizing that I'm helping you hide. It wasn't easy, but I laid a false trail in one of the locations where we Trackers have been searching for you."

"How did you do that?" Hannah asked.

"An hour before the other Trackers showed up, I managed to get into one of the flats we were assigned to search. I used the photos Finn sent me and made it look like the Necromancers had gotten there first—Casting marks on the floor, runes on the walls, then I smashed up the furniture just for good measure. Then I circled back around and entered the flat with the rest of the team. It worked like a charm, but when we brought our evidence before the Council, that was another matter entirely."

"They wouldn't believe you? Even with the photos of the Casting marks and all that?" Savvy asked, evidently floored that anyone could be so intentionally stupid.

"Marion wouldn't hear a word of it. She kept insisting that the Necromancers were gone. She said that there must be some other explanation."

"Like what?" I asked.

"Like you lot had staged the flat to throw us off your scent." Lucida shook the last of the biscuit crumbs into her mouth and tossed the empty package aside.

"Ludicrous, considering the complexity of the Castings. No offense, but none of you have the skill or the knowledge to pull off even half of what we showed them. And some of the Necromancers' markings aren't found in Durupinen teachings—where they think you found those, I've got no bloody idea. But I told Marion straight off that I thought the Necromancers were back, and that they were likely looking for you just like we are. I told her to secure the castle and put the Caomhnóir on high alert."

"And let me guess—she's not doing any of it," I said flatly.

"Correct again," Lucida said. "She also forbade anyone on the

Tracker team to alert the rest of the castle. So now everyone in that castle is a sitting duck, and if the Necromancers do show up, infiltrating Fairhaven will be a lark."

"But there has to be something you can do!" Hannah exclaimed.

"Yeah, since when have you listened to Marion?" I added.

"And I'm not about to start now," Lucida said, winking. "I told Catriona all the very same things before I left. She'll spread the word as best she can, but if the warning isn't coming directly from the Council, I doubt many people will listen."

Hannah dropped her face into her hands. "But then how can they—"

"Look, love, I appreciate that you're concerned about them. I am too, but we haven't got time to worry about anyone but ourselves at the moment. We've warned them, and that's the best we can do for now," Lucida said, and her voice, though brisk, was not without emotion. "And speaking of ourselves, we've got to get moving. We're scheduled to be out of this flat and on our way in the next hour, so it's time to pack your bits and bobs."

"We're leaving? Where are we going?" I asked.

"To a safe house I've organized for you. It's a miracle they haven't found you yet, and we don't want to lose any more time... so chop-chop. Pack only what you need. I won't delay for anything once I get the all clear."

Everyone leapt into the preparations. Savvy ran into the bedroom to start gathering our things. A moment later, Annabelle emerged, wide-eyed.

"Savvy woke me up. She says we're leaving?" she asked the room at large. Her eyes fell on Lucida and she froze.

"This is Lucida," Hannah told Annabelle quickly. "She's my mentor from Fairhaven, the one we told you was helping us."

Lucida waved languidly at Annabelle. "The Sensitive, right?"

Annabelle nodded.

"We've never met, but I broke into your shop once," Lucida said casually—as if she were mentioning they had an acquaintance in common instead of admitting to breaking and entering. The shock on Annabelle's face prompted her to further explanation. "I was in charge of making sure no one outside the Durupinen had evidence of Jess' identity. We investigated all her acquaintances from her ghost hunt in the library, including you."

Annabelle's body seemed to relax, although her mouth remained pressed into a tense line.

"How are you feeling?" Lucida asked, in an uncharacteristic show of concern.

"Drained," Annabelle said dazedly as she watched everyone scrambling to pack. "Like I could sleep for a month and still be tired."

"That'll likely be an effect of the Spirit Cage. The spirits would've tried everything to put themselves back together, including feeding on all energy sources around them. You may find your sensitivity to the spirit world is a bit weakened for a time, until your aura replenishes."

"Yes, I've noticed that with Milo," Annabelle said. "I can't always hear him very clearly. Do you think that will improve?"

"It should," answered Lucida, moving back to the window and checking her watch. "I've never seen a Spirit Cage used. That's a dark bloody Casting—even for life and death situations. I doubt there's a Durupinen alive who's ever encountered one. But I've read about them, and the aftereffects ought to wear off. Just try not to exert yourself psychically if you can avoid it."

"I'll try not to," said Annabelle, nodding in understanding.

"Sit down and rest, Annabelle," Hannah said, as she passed her a stack of folded shirts. "We'll get everything together for you."

Gathering Annabelle's belongings wouldn't be hard, since everything Annabelle owned was trapped downstairs in a flat we were all too scared to enter again. Annabelle had been using the same communal clothing pile as the rest of us since we'd rescued her. Fortunately, Finn had had the foresight to grab her passport and purse from the side table before sealing the apartment for good.

It only took about fifteen minutes to gather everything we wanted to bring with us from the odd assortment of belongings we had amassed from convenience and thrift stores. Milo surveyed our pathetic worldly possessions with a critical eye.

"You don't know how lucky you are that I can no longer obsess over my wardrobe options," he said, addressing all of us at once. "You'd all be long gone, but I'd still be here when the Necromancers busted in, weighing the pros and cons of cashmere versus a cotton blend."

"Yeah, we dodged a bullet on that one," Savvy said with a grin. Hannah giggled.

"Right, then," Lucida said, surveying our ragtag group. "You've got everything?"

"I think so," Savvy replied. "We didn't have much to begin with, did we?"

Lucida's newest burner phone buzzed dully against her palm, and she answered it. "Give me the good news," she said, which apparently was her way of greeting whoever was on the other end. She listened a moment, then said, "On our way." She pocketed the phone and turned back to us. "This is it. Keep with me. I'll tell you a bit more about where we're off to once we're safely in the car."

"Who's meeting us?" I asked.

"Never-you-mind. A friend," Lucida snapped. "And he's here, so let's scarper." She looked out the window to the end of the alleyway and sighed. "A gray four-door Volvo. Blimey, can't he ever pick anything with a little style? I'll look like a mum at school pickup driving that thing." She twitched the curtain shut again and crossed the room in a single, fluid bound. "Keep your eyes open for anything dodgy."

I said goodbye to all of Lyle's wacky, teetering piles of royal memorabilia as we filed out the door. I wondered, with a vaguely guilty squirm, what would happen to it all—his life's sad obsession, now most likely headed for the nearest available dumpster. I'd never really found out what had happened to Lyle, who had been so very desperate to return to his den of carefully stacked delusions, but I felt sure that his absence meant he had Crossed when Hannah had opened the Gateway to save me. As I pulled the flat's door shut, I thought that it was all depressing as hell.

And hell, in apparent reply, broke loose.

§

Every light in the stairwell went out at once, plunging us into a thick, gray darkness.

"Go back!" Lucida shouted. "Get back in the flat, now! Before—"

The end of her warning was lost in the sudden echoing cacophony of footsteps that seemed to come from every direction at once; it was impossible to tell how many sets of feet there were, but it sounded like an army's worth. Deep, harsh voices began shouting unfamiliar words and phrases that I couldn't understand but nonetheless recognized as a form of Gaelic. Then the darkness became filled with horrible shouts and moans that rent the air and assaulted my eardrums; a hundred spirits or more flooded the stairwell. Their energy and emotions pressed in on all sides, creating a wild, bewildering chaos. I couldn't see. I couldn't think. I could barely breathe.

In my blind panic, I spun on the spot and tried sprinting the half-flight back up to the door to Lyle's flat, but immediately strong, grasping arms tore at my jacket. I swung out violently with my right arm and heard a gasp of pain as my knuckles collided with someone's skull. I threw another attacker off by swinging the large, heavy bag of shoes I was carrying at him. I heard more grunts as a body tumbled from the landing just above; the body crashed into my leg and nearly pulled me down with it, but I found the railing as I was pushed forward.

I had barely managed to steady myself when another hand closed around my wrist. But as I struggled against it, Finn's voice called over the tumult, "It's me! Hold on to me! We need to move. Now!"

We began to descend the stairs, feeling our way blindly, thrashing and kicking against humans and ghosts alike, without a clue as to who—or what—we were striking.

Another hand grabbed my hair. I clawed at it and heard, "Oi! Jess, it's me, mate!"

"Hold on to me, Sav! We're getting out of here!"

We continued fighting our way, flight-by-flight, down the stairs. Finn stopped abruptly, and we fell back as the sounds of another fight broke out a level or two below us. A foot connected with my shoulder and I stumbled back into Savvy, sending us both crashing into the wall. I cracked the back of my head on the corner of the railing and saw stars for an instant before scrambling to my feet again.

As I got myself upright, I heard Finn shouting into the grayness, "Annabelle, it's alright, it's me, it's Finn!"

I heard Annabelle sobbing hysterically, "I think I... killed him. He fell over the railing!"

More scuffling had broken out on the stairs just below us, and I heard Lucida swearing and grunting as she fought off more of the attackers; then there was a terrible thumping and cracking as one or all of them tumbled to the floor below.

Somewhere below us amidst the din, Milo was yelling something incoherent and Hannah was screaming.

"Hannah!" I called.

"Jess! Where are you? Help me!"

Hannah's voice seemed far away, like every other voice in the discord; how could I ever find her?

"Hannah!" I cried again into the chaos. "Finn, we have to get to her!"

"I know! Her voice is coming from down there! Keep moving!" he shouted back at me.

I couldn't hear myself think; the spirits in the stairwell were bombarding us with an absolute tempest of sound and sensation. It was all I could do to clutch tightly to Finn and Savvy as we struggled forward and fought the collective urge to pass out from the intensity of it all.

Finally, with Annabelle just behind us, our feet found the bottom of the stairs. Finn began sliding his hand along the wall until he reached what he was looking for—the light switch. The sudden return of the light was blinding; we all squinted against it.

Three forms were crumpled at the base of the stairwell. One of the men was stirring feebly, clutching his ribs. Another was trying to stem the flow of blood gushing from a gash on his heavily tattooed head. The third was Lucida.

We all froze in a moment of disbelief. I looked down at Lucida—her eyes were glassy and vacant, and one of her legs was bent up at the strangest angle. Her signature stiletto heel dangled from her foot.

Her lifeless foot.

"JESS!" Hannah's urgent cry broke the hideous spell. Ahead of us, Hannah—while screaming bloody murder and flailing like a captured animal—was being dragged through a door at the end of the hallway by two large, tattooed men.

As the spirits continued to swirl and rush around us, Hannah disappeared through the doorway. But the moment that the men crossed the threshold with her, the deafening spirit attack ceased, leaving the air hollow and empty around us. We raced through the door and burst into the alleyway, where the Necromancers were attempting to force Hannah into the back of a large black van. Milo was flying at them—through them—using every bit of strength he could muster to stop them. That's when I realized that I, too, was screaming, calling out for my sister.

"Let go of her! Get the hell away from her right NOW!" Milo screamed. Milo's energy was so intense that it caused the van's door to slide nearly shut before Hannah was inside; one of the men caught the door with his elbow and forced it open again. As Hannah struggled, she tore the other man's sleeve, which revealed a tattoo of the Necromancers' symbol.

Milo continued his assault as Hannah vanished, still kicking and screaming for all she was worth, into the yawning mouth of the van. But as soon as the door slammed shut, Milo suddenly reeled away from the van as though it had been instantly Warded. He gently floated to a stop and hung in the air, motionless and silent.

"There she is! There's the other one!" a voice yelled.

Two more Necromancers rounded the corner of the building. Finn skidded to a stop so quickly that Savvy, Annabelle, and I slammed into him. Finn stood there for an instant with his eyes darting back and forth between the van and me. I watched the decision form on his face, saw him nod to himself. Then he turned his back on Hannah and looked at us, with his eyes blazing in determination.

"No," he pronounced.

I knew what Finn meant, and I couldn't let him do it. I wouldn't let him do it.

"Run. Now. This way," he ordered, as he yanked us towards the gray Volvo at the opposite end of the alley.

"No, Finn, wait! Hannah! We have to get Hannah!" I screamed as he pulled me further away from her. "Hannah!"

But it was too late. The van peeled away.

From the gap in the alley, three more Necromancers emerged. We ran for all we were worth toward the Volvo. The car was empty, and the driver's side door was standing open, waiting for us. The Necromancers—all five of them—were gaining on us, quickly closing the gap between us as they sprinted in our direction.

Finn reached the car first. He wrenched the passenger side door open and shoved me unceremoniously through it. Savvy piled in practically on top of me, ultimately landing in the middle seat, and Annabelle vaulted into the backseat. Finn ran around to the driver's side and jumped in; his foot hit the gas pedal before the door had even fully closed behind him. The tires screeched as he peeled out into the street; horns blared and pedestrians ran for cover.

"Finn, what are you... you're going the wrong way!" I cried, craning around in my seat. "They took her that way!"

"We're not following them," Finn replied, as he veered the car dangerously into oncoming traffic in his haste.

"We have to follow them! They have Hannah! Turn around Finn!"

"No!"

"We have to go back! We have to go back right now!" I shouted, choking on a rising sob.

"We can't! We can't go back there Jess, I'm sorry!"

"Let me out! Let me out of this fucking car right now!" I cried, pulling in vain on the door handle; Finn had locked me in using the driver's side controls.

"You can pull on it all you want, but it's not going to open," he said, sounding almost relieved.

I ignored him. I yanked on the handle even harder and tried pressing against the door with my foot, but the lock held. "Stop the car, Finn!"

"No."

"We have to go back!"

"If we go back, we're dead! Do you understand me? You saw what they did to Lucida. That'll be us if we go back there! Now stop acting like a lunatic and let me drive!"

I lunged at him. I wanted to hurt him. I wanted to rip that goddamned curtain of hair back from his face so he would look at me. My fingernails scrabbled for his face, but Savvy and Annabelle grabbed and pulled me back.

Annabelle shouted, "Jess, he's right, we can't—"

"Don't you tell me that! Don't tell me we can't go back! That's my sister! They have Hannah, do you understand that?"

"Yes, I do," Annabelle replied, a tinge of sympathy in her voice.

I wrenched my arms away from Savvy and Annabelle and flew at Finn again—this time succeeding in clutching a fistful of his jacket and tugging so hard that he twisted in his seat and almost lost control of the car. He regained control of the wheel, then wrested himself out of my grip by slinking out of his coat, swearing loudly at me as he did so.

84

"We just barely got out of there alive and now you're trying to kill us?" he shouted. "Let go of me and sit down properly!"

Savvy muscled me back into my seat and sat on top of me, pinning me into place. I struggled against her, but I couldn't throw her off. I continued to shout and sob in frustration.

"They have my sister! Why, Finn? Why the hell did you let them take her?"

"Jess, stop it!" Savvy yelled.

"Don't say that to him, it's not fair!" Annabelle cried.

"I didn't let them take her!" Finn began. "No one LET them take her! I couldn't get to her, but I could get to you, so I got you out."

"You should've let them take me instead!"

"They didn't want you!" exclaimed Finn, as if this should've been obvious. "Don't you understand? If they'd gotten their hands on you, you'd be dead right now."

"But Hannah—"

"They're not going to kill Hannah! They want her alive, Jess! Don't you see? She's the valuable one... only she can reverse the Gateway. That's been their goal for centuries! They're not going to let anything happen to her—she's too important to their endgame. But you? Don't you remember what the Prophecy says? You're the dangerous one, from their point of view. You're the one who'll stand in their way, who can ruin everything. If they'd gotten their hands on you, you'd sure as hell be dead now. But they need Hannah. They won't let anything happen to her—not for now, at least. If I could only get one of you out of there, it had to be you."

The argument I longed to scream at Finn got lost on the way to my lips and came out instead as an incoherent sob. My body slackened and fell back against the seat; Savvy, looking intensely relieved, slid off of me and back into her own seat, and yanked her seatbelt across her lap.

"What will they do to her?" I choked out. "She's so fragile, Finn. What the hell are they going to do to her? She won't be able to handle it."

"Jessica, listen to me," Annabelle began. Her tone was so commanding that I had no choice but to comply. "They aren't going to hurt her, at least not too much. You heard what Finn said: They need her. They need her to cooperate, and they need her powers to be at their strongest—neither of those things can happen if they hurt her."

"She's tougher than she looks, that little spitfire," Savvy said. "She's been through a hard lot, but that makes her stronger, mate, not weaker—you told me as much yourself. She'll hold her own till we get her back, you can bet on that. But did anyone see what they did to Milo?"

Savvy's question pulled me out of my panic long enough to look around the car. "Where is he? Did he go with them?" As I spoke, a tiny burgeoning hope popped into being in my heart; if Milo was with her, Hannah might just be okay.

"No," Savvy said. "He was still floating in the alley all vacant-like after the van pulled away."

"I remember now," I said, wiping my eyes with my sleeve and fighting to control the shuddering of my own breath. "I think they performed a Casting on him to keep him at bay. It was like he was in a trance, just hanging there."

"What can we do? Is there any way we can bring him into the car?" Annabelle asked.

"I told you, I'm not going back to—" Finn growled.

"No, I'm not talking about going back," Annabelle said impatiently. "I mean, using your connection to him, Jess. You're Bound to Milo through your Gateway, right? Is there anything you can do to get him here?"

"I'm not sure," I said. "Hannah's the Caller, not me."

"Yes, but you're connected, and that might be enough. I think we need to try. If the Necromancers take him, Milo becomes a liability—a possible source of information. Plus, who knows what they could do to him with their dark Castings. We need to get him back if we can."

"I... I should be able to hear him," I said as I closed my eyes; I searched desperately for a quiet space of calm inside myself where I'd be able to concentrate, despite being so full of noise and terror and grief.

"Milo, can you hear me?"

There was no answer—only a blank, empty buzzing. It felt very, very wrong somehow.

"Milo? Are you there?"

"Anything?" Annabelle asked.

"I can't... It's so strange. He's there—the form of him is there, but it's just... empty." My heart began to race. "What does that mean? What did they do to him?"

86

"I have no idea," said Annabelle. "I'm not a Durupinen, remember."

Savvy shoved her hand into her backpack and extracted her Casting bag. "Summon him."

"But how—"

"Do it right here! We can't just leave him out there!" she said, pulling out her chalk and drawing a sweeping Circle on the fabric of the roof's interior. Then she shoved her candle stubs into the cup holders and lit them with her cigarette lighter.

I hesitated. Savvy tossed her copy of the *Book of Téigh Anonn* into my lap. "You've got to give it a go, Jess. What if they find a way to take him with them?"

She was right. I pulled myself together and started the Summoning. I closed my eyes again, and within the cobbled-together—but nonetheless effective—Circle, I felt out into space, focusing with all my might on the alley we'd just left behind. I found Milo there, although I could barely tell it was him.

"Milo?" I asked tentatively.

A trembling suggestion of something responded, but it was much too weak to be a real answer. Milo was there, and yet he wasn't.

"Come into the Circle, Milo. We're in the car," I said, pulling and tugging at our connection with every ounce of energy I could muster.

Again, there was just the merest trace of a reply, but it was so faint that I almost wondered if I'd imagined it. I continued to focus with everything I had, with a cold and clammy sweat breaking out on my forehead, until I felt Milo break through the boundary of the Circle.

I opened my eyes. Milo was in the car, hanging in the air between the front passenger seat and the dashboard, his eyes as blank and empty as the Blind Summoner's had been. It was a strange paradox, to see a ghost lifeless, but that's what he was. The edges of his form were inchoate—blurry and smoky as if someone had taken an eraser to him—and he looked paler than usual.

"Do you have any idea what they did to him?" I asked Finn.

Finn attempted to drive and examine Milo at the same time. "No," he said finally. "I've not seen anything quite like it."

"How will we figure this out?" I asked, feeling my emotions

starting to close up the back of my throat again. "We don't have anyone else we can ask!"

"The important thing is that we've got him, which means the Necromancers don't," Finn replied. "Let's figure out our next move, then worry about Milo. There might possibly be something in the *Book of Téigh Anonn* that can explain it. The real question is where the hell we're going to go now. Lucida was our only ally, but..."

Fresh tears burned in my eyes as I thought of Lucida sprawled on the floor in that echoing stairwell. However much I may have disliked her, I never would've wished such a fate on her—and the thought that she had died trying to help us twisted my insides into a hard, painful knot. She was gone, and we were on our own. We had nowhere to turn and a seemingly endless army of enemies about to close in on all sides. In that moment, if I'd had a white flag, I would have waved it in surrender.

"There'll be coppers swarming all over that building before long," Savvy said. "I know you lot don't like dealing with them Finn, but couldn't they help us?"

"No," Finn replied sharply. "Both the Durupinen and the Necromancers avoid involving law enforcement at all costs, but that doesn't mean they don't keep tabs on police activity. The Northern Clans will be monitoring the scanners for any sign of us."

"But then, what about the cops coming after us? I know you fancy yourselves all stealthy, but I think just a few people might've noticed that massive punch-up—and the bodies in the stairwell," replied Savvy.

"There won't be any bodies in the stairwell. There won't be anything for the police to find. The Necromancers are very neat, just like the Durupinen," Finn said. "We can't worry about what's behind us right now. We need to focus on finding cover."

"There might be somewhere we can go," Annabelle offered, chewing nervously on a fingernail. "I'd need to make a phone call, and I can't guarantee that we'd be welcomed, but at this point, it might be our best option."

"Where?" Finn asked, with his eyes glinting in the rearview mirror as he locked them on Annabelle.

Annabelle hesitated. "You may not like it very much."

"Is it preferable to a violent death on the side of the road?" Finn asked grimly.

"I will venture to say yes," Annabelle said.

"Then I'm keen on it already. Sounds a good bit better than our current plan," Finn replied. "Go on, what is it?"

"You know my family used to be a Gateway. We haven't been an active family for several generations, so my direct ties to the Durupinen are sketchy at best. But our clan had many branches, and I'm still in touch with one of my distant cousins. She's a member of the Traveler Clans. They've been in England for a generation or two now."

The reflection of Finn's eyes widened in the mirror. "The Traveler Clans? What do you think they could do for us?"

"They might be willing to take us in, protect us, if we ask them."

Finn began frowning thoughtfully. "They've never had much of a hand in the greater power structure. What makes you think they won't turn us away? Or worse, hand us over?"

"I can't say for sure that they won't, but blood still counts for something, especially among the Travelers—and there's a chance it counts for just enough to save our lives." Annabelle paused thoughtfully for a moment before adding, "They might even be able to do something for Milo."

We all looked at Milo again; he remained a floating shell in the space before us. I found myself thinking that never before had the words *ghost* and *haunted* ever been so frighteningly paired before.

Finn, silent, looked back at the road.

"So what do you think we—" Annabelle began.

"I don't know!" Finn growled. "Everyone shut up for a minute so I can properly think!"

As I watched Finn's hands opening and closing on the steering wheel, something clicked in my brain: This was not on him. Just because I was falling apart over Hannah did not mean that Finn was responsible for making all of our decisions. He was just a Novitiate, not yet finished with his training. I doubted that even experienced Caomhnóir like Carrick or Seamus had ever dealt with situations this dangerous.

I took a breath of air that barely found my lungs, but nevertheless allowed me to say, fairly steadily, "We all need to make this decision together; it's not Finn's job. As for me, I don't think we have a choice. If we don't try something, they'll find us before we can take cover. And there's nothing we can do for Milo on our own, but if we found other Durupinen..."

Finn's eyes met mine in the mirror; his gaze was asking questions that I couldn't answer. We would just have to roll the dice and hope we got lucky. Very lucky.

"We're out of options," he said, nodding. "Annabelle, my burner phone is in the cup holder there. See what you can do. Is there a general direction I should be driving toward?"

"Travelers go where the wind blows them," said Annabelle, reaching for the phone and starting to dial. "Just keep driving as far from London as you can get."

§

We drove for nearly four hours, and not once did anyone ask how long it would be before we arrived. No one seemed to care where exactly we were going; what really weighed on us was what we had left behind in our wake—and when it all might finally catch up with us.

Driving on the main highways had been nearly unbearable. Every vehicle that approached made us hold our collective breath until it passed harmlessly by. We were all relieved when we pulled off the main road and began winding through an increasingly narrower network of twisting country roads.

Finally, Finn pulled up onto the grassy shoulder of a rutted dirt road that barely qualified as more than a path. The sky was nearly pitch black by this time, and although we would surely have seen the flashlights of anyone approaching us from a mile away, a sense of unease pressed in as we sat in the blackness, waiting.

"This is the spot, according to the GPS coordinates," Finn said as he killed the engine, which had felt unnaturally loud in the night. "So now I suppose we... wait?"

"Yes," Annabelle answered. "She said they would come for us here."

I shivered and looked again at Milo, who was still an eerie shell beside me—made eerier still in the dull glow of the car's dome light. I decided to fill the awful silence with questions. The more I talked, the less I would have to think, to feel.

"Who exactly are the Traveler Clans?" I asked.

"A nomadic branch of the Durupinen, of Romanian descent," replied Annabelle. "In America, we know them better as Gypsies."

"Gypsies actually still exist?"

"Of course they exist! They aren't fairies or trolls, Jessica, they're just a group of people."

"I know that," I said, bristling indignantly. "But it's not like you hear about them much, or see them in everyday society."

"That's sort of the point," Annabelle said. "They keep to themselves... a floating, independent culture."

"We've got plenty of them here in England," Savvy said. "Not in the city so much, but out in the country. Folks aren't too keen on them settling in their area, usually."

"So all Gypsies are Durupinen?" I asked.

"No, not nearly," Annabelle said. "The Traveler Durupinen are just a tiny fraction of the Gypsy population as a whole. Many hundreds of years ago, when the Durupinen lived fairly openly, the Travelers would use their talents wherever they went, communing with the dead and aiding villages with troublesome spirits. Of course, now they've gone underground like the rest of the Durupinen; but the association between Gypsies and spirit communication still exists."

"And I suppose," I said, as I thought back to my very first impression of Annabelle, with her tarot cards, long skirts, and jingling jewelry, "it would be pretty easy for someone to capitalize on that association and make a nice little career for herself with fortune telling and séances?"

Annabelle very nearly smiled. Nearly. "Yes, I suppose it would. The Traveler lifestyle makes a lot of sense for a Clan Family, if you stop to think about it. They keep to themselves and stay on the move, so they're never in much danger of being discovered for what they are. And because of the... let's say... somewhat negative cultural reaction to Gypsies, people leave them alone for the most part." Annabelle paused. "But most Gypsies don't call themselves *Gypsies* anymore; it's almost a slur. They prefer simply to be called *travelers*. Remember that if you ever meet one—outside of Durupinen Travelers, of course."

As the hours passed, we speculated about who would come, and what their reactions to us might be. When we had talked ourselves out, we waited. We waited and we waited. It became so dark that I couldn't see my hand in front of my face; it was utterly disorienting. With nothing to focus on, and with nothing to distract me, I began to struggle to keep my eyes open at all. Beside me, Savvy's breathing settled into a deep and heavy rhythm.

Annabelle, too, fell silent, and I heard the moment when she slumped over in the backseat. I fought the heaviness fogging my brain. I knew I shouldn't drop my guard, but I was just so tired, so empty of any will to think, to feel, to stay in the present. My present, so full of pain and uncertainty and fear...

Rough hands seized me by the shoulders and dragged me, half-asleep, from my seat. I was too startled to even yell out, but I couldn't have made a sound even if I'd tried; a wad of fabric was stuffed roughly in my mouth. Muffled shouts told me that Savvy, Annabelle, and Finn were also being pulled from the car. Sudden flares of light burst in front of my eyes as I was thrown to my knees into the tall grass; it was by these lights that my eyes adjusted and I could finally see who had attacked us.

The newcomers had created a Circle all the way around our car by pressing into the tall grass and creating something very much like an alien-induced crop circle. Light glinted from four large, but amorphous, torch-like candles, which were little more than misshapen hunks of dripping wax placed atop rough wooden pillars that had been pressed into the earth. The torch-candles offered just enough light to my unadjusted eyes for shapes to begin emerging from the darkness.

There were about a dozen of them, each straight-backed and tall. At first, the men and women were not easily distinguishable from one another—their angular faces were framed in tangles of long, dark hair, and their bodies were obscured by loose, flowing garments. As my eyes adjusted, details emerged. Four of them were women; they wore long skirts, all of which were patched and tattered. Their bare feet and ankles, which were glittering with golden bangles and chains, looked like reflections of their hands and wrists, which also twinkled and shone in the torchlight. Three of the women were older, perhaps in their fifties; from beneath a ragged assortment of head wraps and scarves, their hair, streaked with glimmering strands of gray, peeked out. The fourth woman was much younger, perhaps around thirty. Nestled in the hollows of the throats of all four women were magnificent golden medallions depicting the familiar curves of the Triskele.

The other eight figures were men. Four pairs of them stood at silent attention like stone-faced sentinels; each pair was positioned just outside of the Circle, at either side of the four candles. Their high cheekbones and prominent noses reminded me of old tintype photographs of Native Americans. So, too, did the hard, humorless gazes they now fixed on us.

"Hello, Anca," said Annabelle, addressing the youngest of the women.

"Annabelle," the woman replied, inclining her head. "It has been a long time, cousin."

Annabelle turned to the rest of us with a wry expression. "Jess, Savvy, Finn, meet my dear cousin Anca and her delegation from the Traveler Clans. Famed for their hospitality, as always."

"These are not the circumstances under which we'd like to see you come home," said Anca, gesturing to the rest of us as though we were badly behaved house pets.

"Home is a relative term, isn't it? I must say, this is one hell of a welcome committee," continued Annabelle, tossing her hair with more than a touch of her usual fire. "Does everyone get this kind of red carpet treatment, or do you reserve it just for family?"

Anca didn't acknowledge the joke with even the faintest of smiles. "These are dangerous times, and you bring the greatest of threats here with you. We must take precautions."

"I hardly think all this is necessary," Annabelle said. "I told you we were coming. Surely there could've been a gentler way to receive us?"

Anca shrugged. "I'm adhering to my orders. Were you followed?"

"I don't believe so," Annabelle said, turning to Finn for confirmation.

"No," he said. "Not by any means I could detect, spirit or otherwise."

Anca turned to the nearest man and spoke in a harsh tongue I didn't understand. The man immediately turned and vanished into the shadows.

"And the spirit in the car?" asked Anca, gesturing to where Milo still hung, unresponsive, inside of the Volvo.

"What about him?" Annabelle asked.

"Who is he? What's happened to him?"

"His name is Milo. He's Bound to Jess' sister, and he's pledged as the Spirit Guide to their Gateway. He was attacked by the Necromancers and left in this state," Annabelle explained. "We don't really know what's happened to him. It's part of why we sought you out."

Two of the older women looked at each other; their expressions were skeptical.

"I don't think this bodes well for the rest of the visit," Savvy hissed in my ear. "If this is how they say hello, what do you think they'll do when they hear what's brought us here, eh?"

"Which of you is the Ballard girl?" Anca asked—although she was staring directly at me when she said it.

"I am."

All of the dark eyes in the Circle were now fixed on me. I could feel each pair of them, burning into me from all sides, turning my face flush and my heartbeat into a nervous flutter.

"We've met you here to give you a choice," Anca pronounced. "This is your opportunity to walk away."

"Walk away from what?" I asked.

"We've been instructed to bring you to our own High Priestess. We can't guarantee what she will decide to do once she meets you and hears your story," Anca explained.

I chanced a glance at Finn. He narrowed his eyes as he scanned the Circle.

"We decided as a Council," Anca went on, gesturing to the other women around her, "to give you the option of leaving before you see her. If our High Priestess determines you're too great of a risk to our clan, she may decide to turn you over to the Northern Clans, or to otherwise detain you. We thought it only fair to warn you of this possibility before we took you to see her."

I swallowed and endeavored to keep my voice from shaking, which I failed at miserably. "What would happen if we decided to leave?"

Anca shrugged, almost coldly. "We have cast a Circle here that you won't be able to break until we're miles away. If you choose not to enter our camp, your fate is your own. You won't be able to find us… and we don't trouble ourselves with what happens beyond our own borders."

"And if we go with you and your High Priestess doesn't decide to turn us in? What then?" I asked.

"You'll be offered the protection of the Travelers, which, if I may be so bold, is rather formidable. But, as I said, I can't guarantee that she will choose to extend this protection. Our High Priestess will always put the safety of the clan ahead of all else. That may well mean you're not welcomed here. If you come with us into our camp, you agree to leave your fate in her hands."

I glared at Annabelle. "Blood doesn't count for quite as much as you'd hoped, I guess."

Annabelle smiled grimly. "Not mine, at any rate. Dormants aren't exactly prized in our culture. Still, I must admit I'd hoped for better."

I hesitated, playing for time. If we walked away, where could we go? The Necromancers hadn't just found us: They'd ambushed us. They'd had time to carefully plan and stage an attack. They were probably already on our trail—and were maybe even ten steps ahead of us, waiting for us to play into their hands. What choice did we have? If this new High Priestess was going to turn us over to the Northern Clans, would we really be any worse off than we were on our own? But if—by some miracle—she did decide to protect us, we might have time to regroup, get help for Milo, and come up with a plan in safety.

I turned to the others, prepared to discuss all of this, but they were all staring expectantly at me. I sought out Finn's gaze and he nodded at me as though to say, "The choice is yours. It's up to you."

I took a deep breath. "We'll go with you," I announced. "No chance we take with your High Priestess can compare with the chance we'll take by walking away."

"Very well," Anca said. "Dragos, unlock the Circle and untie them." Then she turned back to us. "For the continued safety of the clan and our camp, we're going to blindfold you."

"Is that necessary?" Finn asked sternly. "Jess is my Gateway; I cannot protect her properly if I'm deprived of my vision."

The man called Dragos, who had stepped forward at Anca's command, looked Finn over with definite disdain. "You are in no position to question our decisions," he said in a quiet, yet somehow cutting, voice. "You have come here seeking our help. We have decided to extend it, for the moment. You will accept it under our terms, or not at all."

"We accept it," I broke in, before Finn could leap into full Caomhnóir mode.

Anca inclined her head toward me. "Very well."

As one unit, the eight Traveler Caomhnóir broke into the Circle, and, as they did so, the surrounding darkness actually seemed to lessen; the light from the torches penetrated further into the night. The four women gathered together, conversing in low voices as they approached us. They began obliterating the Circle's boundary by sweeping their bare feet across it.

It struck me that none of the other women had spoken to us, which surprised me given that Anca was clearly the youngest: I would've thought that age was equated with status. I realized, though, from the little snatches of conversation that drifted over to us, that none of the other women were speaking English. It was possible, I realized, that Anca was not so much the leader of this group, but rather the interpreter.

One of the older women opened the car door and looked at Milo. She called one of the other women over, and they began examining him by the light of one of the candle-torches. I hated to see Milo so helpless and vulnerable; it was the antithesis of the feisty spirit I'd grown to know. He'd made not a sound as the women took control of him with an unknown Casting; as they walked away from the car, he drifted behind them like a grisly, senseless balloon tethered by invisible strings.

Savvy made a sound halfway between a growl and a resigned sigh; I turned to see her steeling herself in preparation for the blindfold that was now being lowered over her eyes. Her hands were balled into fists, and I knew—being the hard-boiled Londoner that she was—that she was fighting against every self-preservation instinct she possessed and restraining herself from punching the nearest Caomhnóir as hard as she could.

The last thing I saw before another blindfold descended over my own eyes was Finn's face, now shadowed by more than the flickering light of the torches. He held his mouth open in a protest that he swallowed—along with, I could see, his pride—as his eyes were covered.

We stumbled and lurched through the forest, over an ever-deepening carpet of leaves and a network of roots so tangled that they threatened to snap our ankles with nearly every step. I didn't get the feeling that the Caomhnóir were trying to be gentle with any of us, which compounded the fear that we were much more prisoner than guest. Ahead of us, the women continued to talk among themselves; it felt like the strange cadence of their conversation was pulling us forward through the woods like the Pied Piper's song.

After what felt like an hour, the ground beneath our feet began to harden and the roots became fewer and far between. Finally, the Caomhnóir guiding me came to a sudden stop. I slammed into his back and had to grab him awkwardly at his waist to stop myself from falling.

"Thanks for the warning," I muttered, righting myself.

By way of reply, he yanked the blindfold from my face, and I clenched my eyes against what, after an hour of pitch blackness, seemed to be a very bright light.

We stood on the outskirts of a large, round clearing that was lit by a blazing, leaping bonfire at the center and a number of smaller campfires scattered around it. Bathed in the orange glow stood about two dozen ramshackle dwellings, including elaborate tents and retro RV campers. There were also a number of wooden wagons, the type of things you'd imagine as part of a circus caravan from a hundred years ago.

"We're taking you directly to our High Priestess. Her name is Ileana. It will be her decision what happens to you next," Anca told us. "Her tent is just over there."

We followed Anca to the mouth of a billowing velvet structure. Two more Caomhnóir waited by the entryway; they drew the doorway's flaps back for us as we approached.

"We're off to see the Wizard..." I sang under my breath.

"What?" Finn whispered.

"Nothing."

7

SACRIFICE

THE TENT'S INTERIOR was lit with fluttering torches and candles—Ileana basically lived in a mobile fire hazard. Her tent was set up like an elaborate office, with carved furniture, steamer trunks full of books, and shelf upon shelf of very old, very mysterious-looking objects—small statues; bottles and mason jars full of herbs; tattered books; candles; quartz crystals; and, horrifyingly, an expansive collection of small taxidermied animals. I couldn't imagine having to move it all every time she changed locations, but then again, Ileana had an army of burly, barrel-chested Caomhnóir at her disposal; I suppose packing didn't trouble her much. Enthroned amid this shrine of oddities, in a high-backed wooden chair, lounged Ileana herself, the High Priestess of the Traveler Clans.

Savvy caught my eye and I knew her thought was the same as mine: We were trapped in some bizarre carnival nightmare, and we both would've been laughing ourselves silly if the situation wasn't so deadly serious.

Ileana looked about seventy years old, and—unlike the leaders of the Northern Clans—she wore every wrinkle and age spot like a badge of honor. This realization heartened me; Ileana obviously didn't believe in Leeching, at least not for beautification purposes. Her long hair, although threaded with white, was thick and shiny. Her wrists, ankles, and long neck were adorned with dozens of chains, jewels, and strings of beads, and her bare feet rested on a pile of embroidered cushions. A wooden pipe dangled from the corner of her smiling mouth. There was nothing friendly or welcoming about her smile: Clearly, she found our wretched state amusing. Behind her right shoulder, a golden cage on a pedestal housed a glossy black raven that glared malevolently from one dark eye; its head, when cocked insolently to the side, revealed that the other eye had been plucked out.

To my right, I could see Finn silently sizing the tent up, counting the exits, searching for concealed weapons, and looking for whatever the hell else his training had taught him to look for.

Anca approached the High Priestess and pressed first her forehead and then her lips to a Triskele medallion, which was strung onto the back of Ileana's hand and held in place by various chains connected to her bulky, jewel-encrusted rings.

"The fugitives have arrived, High Priestess," Anca reported.

"I can see that," Ileana replied, with a slight cackle. I counted four gold teeth. "Leave us, now. Gather the Council and wait for me in the meeting Circle," she added. Anca translated the instructions for the three other women who had accompanied us through the woods, then all four of them bowed and exited the tent. Milo, still tethered, was towed along behind them.

Ileana turned back to us and eyed us beadily before snorting derisively. "So here are the troublemakers—two Apprentices, a Novitiate, and a Dormant. It's a miracle you've survived for as long as you have with the Necromancers in full force on your trail. How did you manage it?"

She seemed to be addressing me, so I answered. "We had a Tracker from Fairhaven who was helping to hide us," I said, endeavoring to keep the tremor of emotion out of my voice, "but she was killed in our escape."

Ileana gave a hacking cough and turned to Annabelle. "Annabelle, is it? Granddaughter of my second cousin Madalina, I believe? The one whose husband dragged her to America?"

"Yes, High Priestess," Annabelle said, rather breathlessly. She bowed her head as a sign of respect.

"How did you get wrapped up in this?" Ileana barked at her.

Annabelle cleared her throat. "One of my colleagues and I were trying to help Jess, well before we knew the nature of her gift. The Necromancers tracked us both down. They tortured us both. They killed our friend David."

"The Necromancers show no mercy. They're quite infamous for it," Ileana said, puffing on her pipe until she resembled a crag-faced steam engine. There was no trace of sympathy in her voice.

"So you do believe us then, that the Necromancers have

returned?" I asked hastily. "The Council at Fairhaven wouldn't even entertain the notion."

"The first thing you should know about the Traveler Clans is that we're not like the Ensconced Clans," Ileana said. "We embrace change—our existence depends on it. We don't allow ourselves to get too comfortable, and that keeps us from becoming complacent. We're always on the move, and, more importantly, on the watch. We see and hear things that don't penetrate into the hallowed halls of our sisters. The Necromancers' rising hasn't been sudden; they have crept, like noisome weeds, spreading and growing over many years. Now they are an infestation which threatens us all."

"So why haven't you done anything about them?" I asked, with my nerves making me sound a bit more combative than I had intended. Annabelle shifted uncomfortably.

"We have neither the resources nor the inclination to battle the Necromancers," Ileana replied, as she poked a gnarled finger through the bars of the birdcage and stroked her raven's chest. "We are too small to invite confrontation without aid. We've reported our findings to the Ensconced Clans, including the Northern Clans. We have been ignored."

"You're not the only ones," I said.

"Before we go on, tell me how you came to be here. Anca has relayed what she could, but I would like to hear the story for myself with these old ears of mine. And do speak up," Ileana added, as she pulled her ankles up and tucked them under her like a small child. She stared at me expectantly, as did everyone else in the room.

I took a deep breath and told her everything—from the discovery of my abilities at St. Matt's, to my reunion with Hannah, to my time at Fairhaven, to the events that led up to our fleeing the castle. Then with Annabelle's help, I explained everything that had happened to us in London, including Hannah's kidnapping, right up until our less-than-hospitable welcome on the outskirts of the woods. Ileana listened intently, taking her eyes off of me only when she needed to stuff more sweet-smelling tobacco into her pipe.

As I sat in the silence that followed the end of my story, I felt much as I did less than two weeks before, when I was standing in front of the Council at Fairhaven waiting to be handed my fate. I had to admit I was growing weary of constantly teetering on the edge of disaster. If I were going to fall, I just wanted to fall already and get it over with; at this point, the impact itself would be sweet relief from this dreadful state of panicky anticipation.

Just when I thought I couldn't take another second of silence, Anca and two of the older Council members bowed their way back into the tent, followed by—

"Milo!" I was so relieved to see him—fully him, fully restored—that I couldn't hide the joy in my voice.

He smiled faintly. "Someday Jess, I'm going to remind you of this golden moment, when you were actually happy to see me."

"Good to see you up and about, mate!" Savvy burst out.

"Are you okay now?" I asked.

"Yeah, thanks to the Witches of Eastwick over there," he said, thumbing back over his shoulder at the Council members who had entered with him. "They worked their magic on me. I don't know what those Necro-assholes did to me, but it was like being paralyzed. I could see you and hear you, but I couldn't move or speak or communicate."

"They put you into Corporeal Shock," Anca said. "It is a way of immobilizing a spirit so it can't harm you. The Shock usually only lasts for a few seconds. I don't know how the Necromancers altered the Casting to make it so powerful, but it was simple enough to reverse. You shouldn't feel any lasting effects, other than a bit of weakness for a few hours."

"Yeah, well never mind about me," Milo said. "What about Hannah? I've been reaching out through our connection since the moment they freed me, but she's not there. Something's blocking her. I'm really freaked out; we've never been disconnected before, not since I died."

I looked at Anca. "Is that an effect of the Corporeal Shock, too?"

Anca frowned. "No. At least, it shouldn't be. They must be using something else to interfere with the connection. I don't know how they could do that, though—I've never heard of a Casting that could separate a spirit from the Durupinen he was Bound to."

Milo turned to me. "Okay well, what else can we do? What have you found out? Do we know where she is? What are we doing to get her back?" he asked, firing off questions with his usual feisty energy.

"We don't know anything else," I said. "I just finished filling the Travelers in on everything that's happened."

Milo turned a defiant glare on Ileana. "Well? You've got the whole story. What are you going to do to find Hannah?"

Ileana looked Milo over with a combination of amusement and condescension. It was a surprisingly threatening expression, and I felt Milo shrink a little beside me.

"Mate, she's like the Queen Mother of the clans around here," Savvy whispered. "I'm sure she could roll you up in that pipe and smoke you if she wanted to."

"Right, okay," said Milo, making an obvious effort to master his emotions before he became the victim of another unpleasant Casting. He turned back to Ileana. "What I meant was, could you, uh, please be so kind as to tell us if you're going to help us?"

Ileana shifted back in her chair so that her face was shrouded in shadows as she answered. "I have not yet decided."

"Stellar," Milo said through gritted teeth, and I realized just how enraged he actually was. "Well, I guess we'll just be going, then, since we have a kidnapping to foil and we're basically wasting our time here. Nice meeting you all."

Milo turned back toward the entrance, but his path was blocked by two of the Caomhnóir. I thought he was angry enough to float right through them, but instead Milo halted in midair, with his nostrils flaring and his hands balled into fists at his sides.

"I'm afraid you must stay and hear my thoughts on the matter, Spirit Guide," Ileana announced. "You are here by my permission; you will leave, or remain, by the same. That was the arrangement."

Milo turned back and hovered to rest beside Finn.

"We're wasting time," Milo hissed to no one in particular. "Every minute we stay here is another minute they could be doing something awful to her. We need a plan." His energy was almost manic—I could feel its intensity rolling off of him in waves; my skin exploded in goose bumps.

"I know," I whispered back. "Let's just behave long enough to find out if they're going to help us. Then we can go from there."

Ileana didn't seem to notice our hushed exchange, or if she did, she didn't acknowledge it. Instead she said, "When Anca first told me about your phone call, I must admit I had no intention of allowing you to come here. You must realize how very real the danger is that follows in your wake."

I snorted with bitter, angry laughter. Danger, really? Right, I had absolutely no idea of our peril—given the multiple attempts on our

103

lives, the kidnapping of my twin, and the violent death of our only ally. So much for staying calm.

Thankfully, Annabelle swooped in and answered before I could open my mouth and put my foot in it. "We do, High Priestess," she said quickly. "And we are sorry. But we had nowhere else to turn."

"Too right," replied Ileana, with a graveness in her tone that hadn't been there before. "That is now true of us all; there's nowhere left for the Durupinen to turn, except into the arms of the waiting enemy. The time of the Prophecy is at hand."

Two or three of the Caomhnóir shifted nervously. Anca closed her eyes and seemed to be praying.

"The strange thing about prophecies," Ileana continued, as she blew a smoke ring into the air and watched it dissipate around her head, "is that they never come to pass on their own. They are always brought about by the actions of those about whom they are made. The Northern Clans have always feared the Prophecy: It's long been suspected that, since the Prophecy was made by one of their own, those it spoke about would also be of Northern descent. The Isherwood Prophecy is—"

"I'm sorry, did you say *Isherwood*?" The question fell out of my mouth before I could stop it. The name *Isherwood* sparked a memory of wandering down Fairhaven's portrait-lined corridor and staring into an ancient, beautiful, and somehow familiar face. "Does that have anything to do with Agnes Isherwood?"

"Of course," Ileana said, eyeing me sideways as if she were trying to decide whether or not I was being impertinent. "Agnes Isherwood of Clan Sassanaigh was the Seer the Prophecy was revealed to so many hundreds of years ago. Surely Finvarra told you that?"

I reeled. My own ancestor, the only member of my clan ever to be High Priestess, had made the Prophecy about me and Hannah, yet every single Council member had kept us ignorant of this. Even Celeste, who I thought had been protecting us at Fairhaven, hadn't deemed this information worth sharing.

"Finvarra hasn't been very interested in keeping me informed," I said when I found my voice at last. "That's pretty much how we got into this mess."

"Finvarra and those before her have shunned the Prophecy and all it could mean for the Durupinen, because they didn't want to face the idea that the Northern Clans could themselves be the cause of our downfall. They've contented themselves with watching for and squelching all possible circumstances that could lead to the Prophecy's fulfillment. It was they who—in direct response to the Prophecy—saw to it that the taboo against Durupinen-Caomhnóir relationships was elevated to a criminal offense... and that the ban was enforced across all clans everywhere on the globe. They have destroyed many of their own in the intervening years, whenever they suspected such a relationship or—worse still—that a child had been born from such a pairing. The Northern Clans focused all their energies on blocking the Prophecy's fulfillment, rather than trying to understand it, but we are not so foolish. The Travelers seek to know everything we can of the Isherwood Prophecy—knowledge may be the only way to alter the outcome."

My anger vanished as a tiny bubble of hope rose in my chest, and I looked Ileana directly in the eye for the first time since entering the tent.

"You think there's still a chance that we could change things?"

"There is always a chance," said Ileana, nodding gravely. "But only if we meet the Prophecy head-on. If the Northern Clans had any sense, they would've studied the Prophecy and learned from it, rather than trying to destroy its fulfillment. History teaches us that this is futile—like cutting the head from a creature that can simply grow a new one. The weakness of the Northern Clans had always been a willful, stubborn arrogance—they've been known for it throughout the ages. This willfulness has, time and again, nearly destroyed them. And now it may destroy us all."

I opened my mouth automatically to defend my own clan, but reason stopped me. I thought of Peyton and the other Leechers stealing energy from the very spirits they were trusted to shepherd, just to appease their own vanity. I thought about Finvarra and her stubborn insistence that the Necromancers had been wiped out. I thought of Marion's cruelly manic obsession with locking us up in the dungeons, as if this were the Middle Ages. I couldn't defend any of them—and, what's more, I didn't want to. They deserved every grim epithet that Ileana had piled upon them.

Ileana nodded again at me as though she understood the conclusion I had just come to, and approved of my ability to put logic before blind loyalty. Perhaps this separated me from the rest of the Northern Clans in her mind, for when she spoke again her voice had lost much of its hostile edge. Then she repeated the words that had been echoing in my head and haunting my thoughts since I'd first heard them.

"When Keeper and Protector shall unite
And forth from this forbidden union shall be spawned,
Two as one from single womb, and Keepers both,
Then shall the greatest of battles commence.
For One shall be Caller with powers unmatched
To reverse the Gates, and call forth the Hordes
To bend to her will and that of our foes.
And One will have to make The Choice
'Twixt blood and vocation, 'twixt kindred and kin,
For she will have the power of sacrifice to end all,
And leave the world until the end of days
To the Darkness or the Light."

I felt Savvy and Annabelle shudder at the ominous words. I'd forgotten that they never heard the Prophecy before.

Ileana drew a deep, longing breath before continuing. "As I said, we have studied the Prophecy with great care. What do you know of your father, child?"

"Nothing. My mother would never talk about him, and the Durupinen have never been able to discover his identity. They've asked both Hannah and me about him, but we know nothing, not even his name."

"Your mother would've wanted to keep him a secret, if he were a Guardian," Ileana said, scratching thoughtfully at a mole on her chin. "The Caller, you say, is your twin sister?"

"Yes. She is... very powerful."

"I don't doubt that, if the Necromancers have this much interest in her," Ileana replied with another cackle. "And you can bet they'll be testing just how powerful she is, now that they've got their claws on her."

Milo released an angry, low, tiger-like growl; I could feel an outburst coming, but Ileana continued before he lost all control.

"The Northern Clans have only ever focused on the destruction foretold in the Prophecy, but the Prophecy could very well mean the salvation of all we hold dear. The key to our survival seems to be in your hands, child. You alone have the 'power of sacrifice to end all.'"

I swallowed hard. "Yes. I'm sorry, but I still don't know what that part is supposed to mean. It's not that I'm not willing to sacrifice something to help us get out of this, but I don't know what that sacrifice is supposed to be. I don't know how I'm supposed to help."

"We believe that we do," Ileana said baldly.

My stomach lurched, as though I'd missed a step while going down a flight of stairs. "You do?"

"Yes."

"Well, what is it?" I blurted out. I feared for a moment that Ileana might mistake my terror for disrespect, but she didn't flinch in the slightest.

"Before I tell you," she went on, "there's something you need to understand about how the Gateways work. I'm sure part of this has been explained to you, but you need to understand all of it. A Gateway's energy is only meant to flow in one direction. The natural flow of the universe dictates that our life energy should travel through a Gateway and beyond the Aether when we die. If your sister manages to reverse even one Gateway, the effects will be devastating. But worse still is that these effects will be irreversible from this side of the Aether. None here on our side will be able to stop it."

Her words dropped into me like a stone. "So what can I possibly do?"

"The Gateway could be closed again, but only from the other side of the Aether."

"But then, how could I be the one to close it? How can I get to the other side, unless... Oh, my G—"

§

The thought collided with the speech center of my brain before my mouth could continue, while—simultaneously—the rational part of my mind denied the realization that had short-circuited my mouth. I gagged, or something very nearly like it, while Ileana gazed at me. She was waiting for the terrible truth to close completely over me, like the dark, dark sea of a watery grave.

The power of sacrifice. The other side of the Aether.

"I... are you telling me... would I need to be... *dead*?"

Milo gasped. Finn stiffened beside me. Savvy and Annabelle both started forward with cries of protest, but quieted at a single look from Ileana. Then the High Priestess surveyed the room imperiously, ensuring there would be no further interruptions.

"A logical question, but a complicated one as well. The answer is both yes and no."

"How can that be?" I asked, my voice rising in my panic. "How can a person be alive and dead at the same time? There's no in-between."

"For most people, this is true. But for the Durupinen, there *is* a way. It's dangerous—and taboo—but in this circumstance, it's the only way you could possibly do what you must and survive."

Here Ileana paused, and a hush fell over the tent. I was at once eager to hear her next words, yet terrified of them. Finn drew himself up into a full defensive stance; I could practically feel the hairs on the back of his neck rise in high alert. Milo, in a rare showing of support, floated over to me and held his hand to the small of my back. The chill of his spirit form was cooling and soothing, a balm for the white-hot trepidation rising within me.

"You must become a Walker," Ileana pronounced.

A gasp came from the Travelers in the tent, but none of us reacted—we didn't know what the hell Ileana was talking about. I glanced over at Annabelle, but she looked as clueless as I felt. I waited for Ileana to elucidate, but it seemed that she wouldn't go on without a direct request; I could barely get breath enough in my lungs to form the required question.

"What does 'become a Walker' mean?"

"A Walker is one who can leave her body and travel the Earth in spirit form," Ileana explained. "While separated from the spirit, the body remains in a state of suspended animation—neither living nor dead, but simply waiting for the return of its soul. A Durupinen who can take Walker form is capable of reentering her body and rejoining the spirit to the physical form."

My heart was thudding so wildly in my chest that I felt sure Ileana could see it twitching beneath my shirt. My heart was the only sound in the tent, apart from the quiet whisper of Savannah behind me.

"Bloody hell," gasped Savvy. I was grateful she had found the exact sentiment that my own mouth couldn't express at the moment.

Ileana seemed not to hear her, and went on, "I should tell you that very few Durupinen are capable of Walking successfully. The danger is acute: It takes a particularly strong will to resist the urge to remain in spirit form. Our souls, you must remember, are protected by our gift. The Durupinen spend so much time in close proximity to the Gateways that our bodies—our very bloodlines—must protect our souls from answering the powerful pull of the other side. So when a Walker leaves her body, her will to return must be stronger than her spirit's desire to Cross. But there's no way to know which pull will win until the body and soul have parted company. And then, of course, it is too late."

I licked my lips, which had suddenly gone dry. "And how do you know I can become a Walker?"

"I don't."

"So I'm supposed to just... try it and see what happens?"

"Yes."

Finn stepped forward and spoke for the first time since we entered the tent. "I cannot allow that."

Ileana raised one black eyebrow. "It is not for you, Guardian, to allow or disallow anything. This is a decision for the Durupinen to make."

"It is my duty to protect her," began Finn, "and I will not stand aside and let her—"

"Your duty is to the Gateway, not to this girl," Ileana snapped.

I bristled as the fear within me turned to anger. "I have a name. And if you expect me to risk my life to save your precious order, you'd better start using it!"

I heard Annabelle's sharp intake of breath behind me. She thought I'd gone too far, but I held my ground. I was not a nameless pawn in this power struggle, and I would not be used like one.

It was clear from her sour expression that Ileana was biting back a scathing response; she swallowed it like something bitter then replied, more calmly than expected, "You are correct, Jessica. Forgive me. Your existence has been theoretical for so long that I haven't fully considered the very human elements involved. This decision will be your own. It will be a difficult one, but I must tell you the Prophecy gives every indication that you will be able to Walk successfully. Remember, it states that you have the power of sacrifice."

"Sure, but it doesn't say how big of a sacrifice I'd be making. Throwing myself off the nearest cliff would be a pretty big sacrifice, but not one I'm willing to make." My voice still reflected more anger than I intended.

"Is any sacrifice too great if it saves the spirits of the world, or saves the Durupinen from destruction?" Ileana asked. "The Necromancers' desires are perverse and destructive."

"What kind of rubbish question is that?" Savvy shouted.

"Savvy, don't—"

"No, it's not right, Jess!" she cried, pushing forward and coming to stand next to me. The Caomhnóir on either side of Ileana stepped swiftly forward, but Ileana waved them back with a grunt, as though she were disgusted that they thought Savvy a threat. Savvy looked as though she would have swung at the Caomhnóir if they'd gotten any closer—and I didn't doubt she could've done some damage.

"You've got some nerve, asking my mate to sacrifice herself for your bloody order."

"Tread carefully, Savannah, or you will be asked to leave," Anca warned.

"No, she's right," I said, as my own ire was reignited from Savvy's spark. My next words practically exploded out of me. "The Durupinen have done almost nothing for me but ruin my life. This so-called gift has been much more curse than blessing. I've lost my mother. My grandfather's been completely destroyed. I didn't know my own sister for almost my entire life—and *her* entire life was spent utterly alone while being poked and prodded by doctors who thought she'd lost her mind. And ever since we were finally clued in to all this Durupinen stuff, we've been ostracized, demonized, and made to feel like freaks because of decisions we had no part in. We only narrowly escaped being thrown into Fairhaven's dungeons, and maybe even worse. And now my twin sister has been captured, and the Necromancers are doing God-knows-what to her at this very moment—while we stand around here trying to figure out what the hell I have to do with the Prophecy. So you'll have to excuse me if I don't exactly have all kinds of fuzzy feelings toward the Durupinen. I'm nowhere near ready to sacrifice my life just to preserve the sanctity of your little club."

"It is your 'little club,' too, lest you forget," Ileana said calmly. Clearly, she was above letting my temper faze her. In fact, judging by the smirk on her face, my outburst amused her.

"Yeah well, I withdrew my membership when they threatened to imprison me," I snapped.

"We both know you can't withdraw your membership—it's your heritage, your bloodline is Durupinen," Ileana said. "And because of this, the rise of the Necromancers will impact you all the more greatly, as you well know."

"I'm pretty sure dying would affect me just a bit more, don't you?" I snarled, clenching my fists at my sides.

"Perhaps, and perhaps not. The reversal of the Gateways will not only affect the Durupinen, but the entire world. The influx of spirit activity will hardly go unnoticed; but that, in comparison, would be a minor issue. What do you know of the Wraiths?"

I was pulled up short. I glanced at Annabelle, but she looked puzzled as well.

"The what?"

"Then you were indeed telling the truth when you said they have not kept you well informed," Ileana said, sounding almost satisfied. "The reversal of any Gateway will unleash a horror we understand only from myth and legend. We don't know of any spirit in living memory that's been pulled back from deep beyond the Gateway, but we do have legends and historical accounts of beings who've come back from the Aether—the space beyond the Gateway but before the next world. This is where the spirits say goodbye to this world; we call the Aether the Fifth Element because it's the plane where a spirit is transformed into the highest expression of spirit energy, and this presence must be present in the Circle. The memories we experience during a Crossing are the spirits letting go of whatever it was—pain, beauty, longing—that tethered them to their humanity, to this world.

"But when a spirit in the Aether is pulled back after unsuccessfully Crossing, it's no longer a spirit as we know them. The humanity, the part of the spirit that remembers who it was in life, has been stripped away; its humanity remains in the Aether, unable to return. When a spirit returns to this side of the Gateway, it's a hollow shell. It retains the appearance of its human self, but the soul is gone."

So, it was basically a ghost zombie. I shuddered at the thought.

Ileana continued, "These shell spirits are Wraiths. Even on their own they can wreak terrible havoc, but even more threatening is that a Wraith can be controlled, manipulated, and twisted to the will of those who've brought it back to this side of the Gateway. If even one Wraith were to return, it would be terrible for anyone it may encounter. But for hordes and hordes of them to return, wielded as a spirit army?"

Ileana let the question hang tantalizingly in the air, begging for an answer. But she didn't need to answer it. I'd seen what would happen if Wraiths were unleashed in the world: I'd scrawled it, with raw and bleeding hands, over the walls at Fairhaven. Destruction. Chaos. Doomsday incarnate.

"And so we do not ask you to Walk only for the fate of the Durupinen. We hope that you'll consider it for the good of all humanity. With Wraiths under Necromancer control, there's no limit to the damage they could inflict on this world."

"Right. So actually, you're asking me to save the world. No pressure there," I said weakly.

Ileana said nothing in response, which only gave her earlier words more time and space to sink in.

I chanced a glance at Finn. He was staring at Ileana with the same dumbfounded expression that I must surely have been wearing. Ileana was staring at me as though expecting an answer imminently. To stall for time, I asked another question.

"Let's say, for the sake of argument, that I decided to do this—to become a Walker. Is there someone who can show me how to do it? Are there instructions at least? Incantations? Or do you expect me to figure this all out on my own?"

"We can offer you training, should you choose to move forward," Ileana answered. For all her lofty indifference, her voice betrayed a definite tone of relief that I was at least discussing the possibility.

"You mean there are Walkers here in camp?" I asked, surprised.

I could've been mistaken, but I thought Ileana hesitated. Her eyes flicked in Anca's direction before she said firmly, "No. But there are those who have studied the practice extensively and can tell you all we know about it."

I took a deep breath. This was not the answer I'd been hoping for. "Okay, here's another hypothetical. If I do actually manage to Walk, and to make it to the other side of the Gateway and re-close the door, how do I get back to this side? Or are you sending me on a suicide mission?" I wouldn't have put "voluntary" martyrdom past any member of the Durupinen at this point in the game.

"You wouldn't be able to return on your own," Ileana admitted readily enough. "But your sister, as the most powerful Caller we have ever seen, should be able to Call you back. She remains here, in the world of the living; the connection between you will tether you to her and to this world. Her gift will be your salvation. That is why it must be you, and no one else, who Walks."

After a good five seconds of loaded silence, Milo interjected, "Aren't we forgetting something important here?"

"What is that, Spirit Guide?" Ileana asked as she pulled a sunflower seed from the folds of her skirt. She poked the seed through the cage and into her raven's eager mouth.

"Hannah!" Milo cried, throwing his hands up in the air. "All of this can be avoided if we can save her from the Necromancers before they force her to open the Gateway!"

"And how do you propose we do that?" asked Ileana, as she searched herself for more stray seeds. The raven cawed impatiently.

"How am I supposed to know?" Milo shouted. "That's not my job! You're the one with the private army of bodyguards and all this info on the Necromancers. Can't you track them down? Find out where they're keeping her?"

Savvy, in her very best respectful voice, echoed Milo. Finn, probably hoping for the chance to go after Hannah and fulfill his duty, watched expectantly.

But Ileana simply replied, "No. It's too late for that now."

"Of course it's not!" Milo cried. "It's only been a few hours! If we hurry we can still—"

"No, we can't," Ileana said firmly, a bite of impatience in her voice. "The wheels are in motion. Even if we were able to rescue Hannah this time, the pursuit would continue. The Necromancers will *not* give up; they've waited too long. Jessica has been lucky enough to escape them for now, but I assure you they are already on the hunt again—perhaps even on the borders of this wood, formulating their attack. Don't you see? I cannot allow our only hope to be sacrificed on a temporary measure. Our resources are best spent helping Jessica to meet what will come, to arm her with the best possible chance of ending this once and for all."

Milo looked around at all of us for support, but no one said anything. Even Finn, whose mouth was working furiously, could find no argument to contradict Ileana's pronouncement. Milo's presence shrank and dimmed as he dropped his head despondently into his hands.

I watched Milo and felt his despair. It would've been wonderfully easy to convince myself that the signs had been misinterpreted, that the Prophecy was really talking about someone—anyone—else. But every time I turned around, another finger was pointing at me, another voice was calling for me. This Prophecy, once so enigmatic, was coming into sharp focus and taking on the form of a great and looming fate—a fate, it seemed, that was intent on backing me into a corner. There was nowhere left to go.

Sighing deeply, I looked up. Ileana stared down at me, expectant, with her eyes boring into mine.

"I can't just decide this right now," I said. "It's all too much to take in. I need some time to think."

"Respectfully, High Priestess," Annabelle broke in, "this is a heavy decision, especially for one as young as Jess. Allow her the night to consider what you've asked."

Ileana frowned. "Very well. We will provide you with lodgings for the night. Dragos will show you to a wagon. Jessica, I will expect your answer in the morning. If you decide not to accept our help, you must leave at once. We cannot have your presence here drawing the eye and the wrath of the Necromancers."

I didn't know whether to scream, shout, or to collapse altogether and dissolve in tears; instead, I decided to hold myself together and nodded.

Dragos stepped toward us as two other Caomhnóir approached Ileana. With a single swish of the tent's velvet drapes, she was whisked out of sight.

8

TORN

A S DRAGOS LED US THROUGH THE ENCAMPMENT, his feet made not a whisper on the grass. He stopped in front of a wagon with a curved top, small leaded windows, and a swinging door at the rear. The wagon was so quaint it almost seemed as if a carnival performer—with hectic calliope music playing in the background— might leap into the driver's seat and drive it away, except that the wagon's wheels had been jammed in place by large wooden blocks.

"You sleep here," Dragos said, gesturing needlessly to the door. It was a Dutch door; the bottom half was held in place by an old-fashioned wrought iron latch, while the top half remained wide open, revealing a lantern-lit, fabric-draped interior.

Apparently, there were no further instructions; Dragos turned on his heel and walked away, darting deftly between the shadows before disappearing beyond the nearest cluster of tents.

"After you," Finn said stiffly.

Savvy, Annabelle, and I clambered awkwardly up the stairs and ducked into the wagon. Inside were four bunk beds, two on either side, built like wooden shelves into the walls. I shuddered thinking how claustrophobic sleeping in the tiny bunks would be. Between the two bunks, there was barely enough room for us to stand single file. On the far wall was a tiny kitchen area, containing the smallest sink I'd ever seen, two cabinets, and a single-burner cooktop.

"Blimey. And I thought Lyle's flat was grotty, eh? Do people actually live like this?" Savvy mumbled, as she squeezed into the back of the wagon and pulled open the cupboards. "I can barely stand up in here."

"The Travelers were forced into a nomadic lifestyle over the centuries," Annabelle said, wedging herself into one of the lower bunks. "They made the mistake early on of peddling their knowledge of the spirits by giving readings and séances. Unfortunately, this bred fear and superstition among the people they sought to help. To escape persecution, the Travelers took to the roads, never settling in one place for too long. They've grown used to surviving with only the barest essentials and in the most economical of spaces," Annabelle gestured at the barely twelve inches of space between the tip of her nose and the bunk above her. "See? Look at that! Plenty of room!"

"If you say so," I said. I crawled into the upper bunk, confident that sleeping in this tiny space would feel like being shut in a coffin; sure enough, the dark ceiling of the wagon was much too close to my face for comfort. I rolled onto my side and closed my eyes at once, not because I was sleepy, but because I couldn't stand feeling so confined.

"Jess, are you... you're not going to sleep now, are you?" Savvy asked from the other side of my eyelids.

"That's the plan."

"Don't you... I mean, shouldn't we... talk this through a bit?"

I opened one eye. Savvy, Milo and Finn were all staring at me. Each face was drawn and anxious.

"In the morning," I half-growled.

"Yeah, but they kind of just dropped a bomb on you," said Milo.

"Yes," Annabelle agreed from the bunk below. "This is a lot to take in, Jess."

"Exactly. Boom. Brain officially exploded. And I am way too exhausted to process any of it. Can we at least try to get some rest before I actually have to deal with it? The sun will be up in a couple of hours."

Savvy shrugged as though this sounded reasonable enough to her, and turned to wedge herself into her own bunk. Annabelle sighed an exasperated "Very well," and I heard her roll over in her bed. Only Milo and Finn remained unconvinced. They shared a doubtful look, with Finn's eyebrows contracting so tightly that they turned into a single "V." Milo looked as though he were about to argue with me, but I closed my one open eye; although I waited for his argument, it never came. A few moments later, when I chanced another peek, Milo had vanished.

I lay there, listening to the soft sounds of everyone else settling down to sleep. What I had told them was partially true. I didn't want to talk right now, but that didn't mean I wanted to sleep. I needed time alone to sort through my own feelings and thoughts about Walking. If we all started talking about it now, I'd get lost in Savvy's blunt observations, Milo's indignation, and Finn's overprotective ferocity. I'd never know if the decision was truly my own, or if they had pressured me into it. Right now, there was only one thing I knew for sure: Whatever I chose, the choice had to be mine and mine alone.

As I lay in the dark thinking, I realized some small part of me had known it all might come to something like this since the first moment I'd heard the Prophecy. I mean, not *this, exactly*. I couldn't have dreamed up the whole Walker scenario, not in a million years. But I had always known the "power of sacrifice" was no poetic turn of phrase—it was always going to mean something very serious on my part. Well, now I knew exactly how serious: There was a very good chance that the "thing" I would be sacrificing was myself.

It would've been easy to dismiss this idea completely, to listen to the very logical instinct of self-preservation. I wasn't going to do it. Of course not. I owed nothing to the Durupinen; in fact, they owed a lot more to me than I ever would to them. So what if the Necromancers wanted to take their power? From what I'd seen, I wasn't even sure that the Durupinen deserved the power they had. Between the Leeching, the corruption rampant in their politics, and Mary's murder, I was half tempted to let the Durupinen fall and allow the Necromancers to take over. I *could* just walk away.

But of course I couldn't just walk away. In the first place, whatever issues the Durupinen might have, I knew in my heart that most of them were devoted to their calling, and that the Gateways were much safer in their hands than in the hands of the Necromancers. Secondly, the Necromancers wouldn't just allow me to exist—they knew I was the one potential threat to their rise to power. They wouldn't rest until they were sure I'd been eliminated; they'd proven that much already. And then, there was the most important factor in my entire decision: Hannah. We had to find her and get her back, despite what Ileana had said. If the Traveler Clans wouldn't help us, then we would have to do it ourselves. Maybe becoming a Walker would be the best way to arm myself for that. Or—I shuddered—maybe Walking would mean that I'd be giving the Necromancers the perfect opportunity to trap me on the other side forever. Ugh.

My tangle of thoughts began to whirl confusedly as sleep crept upon them, but before I could drift off completely, a tiny tapping sound caught my attention. I resisted the reflex that urged me to bolt upright—and crack my head on the ceiling—and instead rolled over and peered through the dusty windowpane. Anca stood in the clearing outside with a lantern smoldering at her feet. She held a small mound of pebbles cupped in one hand; her other hand, which was poised to throw another stone, dropped to her side when she saw me looking out at her. She gestured frantically for me to join her.

I didn't even stop to consider if I would answer her summons. I dropped to the floor from my bunk, grabbed my shoes, then paused for a quick moment to make sure none of the others had awoken. Savvy grunted and rolled over in her sleep. Finn's snores rumbled from the bunk above her. Annabelle's deep, even breathing remained uninterrupted. I crept to the doorway and jumped directly onto the grass, afraid the creaking of the rickety old steps would betray me.

"What do you want?" I asked immediately.

Anca hesitated. "I'm sorry to wake you."

I waved her away. "I wasn't really asleep, so don't worry about it. What is it?"

"I want you to come with me." Anca's voice was weighted with something heavy and dark, and the lantern threw wavering shadows across her face. "There's something you need to see."

"What is it?"

"I can't explain it. You need to see it for yourself. Will you come with me?"

I had no real reason to trust Anca; I'd just met her. How did I know she wasn't leading me into a trap? Then again, there was something about the expression on her face as the amber-hued light rippled across it…

"Okay. Lead the way," I whispered.

Anca nodded, and without another word turned and stalked off into the trees—I nearly had to jog to catch up. In the darkness, I stumbled badly on a root and came very near to breaking my neck. But as I tried to keep from killing myself, I kept thinking that self-preservation was futile—Finn would surely kill me when he realized I'd taken off without telling him. But I didn't care. I didn't want him hovering over me like a disapproving shadow while I did whatever it was I was about to do.

We walked in silence for several minutes, until the trees enveloped us like embracing arms and the stars disappeared above the forest's canopy. If not for the swinging glow of Anca's lantern, it would've been far too dark to find our way. After about ten minutes, just as I was about to ask how much further we had to go, we broke into a small clearing and my destination was revealed.

Under the now-visible light of a nearly full moon, a single dilapidated wagon stood lonely and silent. I would have thought it abandoned, except that a flickering oil lamp hung from a stake near its door. I looked more closely; an elderly man, crumpled in on himself like a ragdoll, dozed in a chair beside the old wagon with his feet propped up against the wheel.

"Andrei," murmured Anca, nudging the man on the shoulder with her lantern.

He sputtered to life, jumping surprisingly quickly to his feet. He looked around with startled eyes until his mind could absorb that it was merely Anca who had awoken him. He heaved a shuddering sigh.

"You scared me nearly to death!" he exclaimed.

"You haven't got that far to go, old man," Anca said harshly, but with the slightest spark of affection. "What do you mean, sleeping on your shift? Dragos will have your head."

"Bah! Dragos can jump off a cliff," Andrei scoffed. "He forgets I knew him when he was pissing in his shorts." He chuckled at his own joke, but he stopped when he finally noticed me standing by Anca's shoulder. "But who is this?"

"Nothing gets by you," said Anca, rolling her eyes. "Haven't you paid even the slightest attention to what the entire camp is talking about?"

"I've no ear for gossip," Andrei said loftily.

"You've no brain for it, more like," Anca said. "This is Jessica. She's from the Northern Clans. I'm taking her in to see Irina."

"Oh, I see. And I'm supposed to let you in without the slightest explanation? What does some Northerner want with Irina?" asked Andrei, narrowing his eyes at me in suspicion.

"You sit out here half-drunk pretending to keep an eye on her, yet I'm supposed to tell you our business?" asked Anca, as she reached around and pulled a flask from behind the wagon wheel.

She shook the flask at him before tossing it to the ground. "She's with me. That's all you need to know."

"Does Ileana know about this?"

Anca didn't answer quickly enough. Andrei chuckled, and waggled a crooked, bony finger in her face.

"Your silence is answer enough, little poppet. I may be half-drunk, but I know I'll get a what for if she's disturbed on my watch!" Andrei leaned down, groped for the flask, shook it slightly, then pocketed it. "I'll lose my position!"

"You won't if you keep your mouth shut and let us by," Anca said. "And I can tell you that you'll lose your position a lot quicker if I show Dragos where your liquor stash is."

Andrei looked genuinely betrayed. Then he shrugged his shoulders and stepped aside with an ironic little bow. "Such an ungrateful granddaughter I was cursed with!" he muttered.

"And such a troublesome grandfather I was cursed with!" Anca shot back. "Go back to your nap. I'll make sure the wagon locks behind us when we go."

Andrei picked up his chair and meandered off, stumbling a bit in the darkness and still muttering mutinously. Anca watched him until he staggered around to the far side of the clearing, then she turned to me as she placed one hand on the wagon's door handle.

"Remember when you asked Ileana if there were any Walkers here?"

"Yes. She said there weren't."

"That was a lie."

My heartbeat broke into a gallop. "There's a Walker in there?"

"Ileana doesn't want me to show you what you're about to see. She doesn't want to scare you away from making the choice that could save us. But she's wrong to keep this from you. You can't truly make your decision until you've seen Irina."

I swallowed hard. "Can you just clue me in a little? What am I about to see? Because I have to admit, I'm freaked out here."

Anca ran a hand over her face. "Ileana, to her credit, warned you that Walking can be deadly. She told you that you could die in the attempt, which, I must admit, I doubted she would do. But death is not the only outcome to fear if you try to become a Walker."

"Are you saying there's something that's worse than death?" I asked, with a tremor in my voice.

"I couldn't say if it's worse or not. But at least death would release you."

"What do you—"

"You must see for yourself. No explanation can convey the reality of what has happened to her," Anca said. "If you know the right Casting to reveal the pages, the *Book of Téigh Anonn* can instruct you how to Walk, just like a textbook can explain the body's physical responses to falling in love—it can tell you how the pulse quickens, how hormones flood your system. But if you've never been in love yourself, you won't ever truly understand what it's like unless you speak to someone who has experienced it. Irina is the only one among us who has Walked."

Anca's hand still rested on the latch of the door. I mastered a powerful desire to knock her hand away before she showed me something I couldn't unsee.

"Don't speak to Irina or approach her until I tell you it's okay. Be ready to leave quickly, if I tell you to. And just... try to stay calm."

Yup, seriously considering the old turn-tail-and-run trick now.

§

The interior of Irina's wagon was bathed in semi-darkness. All was utterly still, and at first I thought Anca had made a mistake. But as she slid her lantern onto a tiny shelf, the wavering light reached the wagon's furthest corner, where a woman lay curled on a mattress under a heap of old blankets.

The lantern light had given form and life to what only moments before could have been a bundle of rags, or even merely a shadow. Irina's long, dark hair was matted and tangled in a wild mess that obscured her face. A thick iron chain trailed out from beneath the blankets and snaked across the floorboards to the wall, where it was fastened to a metal ring. Strewn about the wagon was the wreckage of what had once probably been a table and chair, as well as piles of torn fabric and heaps of feathers that must once have been pillows. The place looked like it had been ransacked by a pack of marauders; but I knew, somehow, that the solitary source of the destruction was breathing gently beneath the blankets.

Runes were scrawled over nearly every inch of the wagon's walls with paint and charcoal, making the space seem eerily similar to Annabelle's flat. In my panicky state, I could only remember the meaning of a few of the runes, but the ones I could recognize did nothing to ease my nerves: Protection, silence, Binding, submission.

"What's wrong with her?" I blurted out before I could form a more polite question.

"You'll see," Anca replied. There was an unmistakable note of fear in her voice as she gazed down at Irina, who stirred and muttered softly in her sleep. Hesitantly, Anca bent down and shook Irina's shoulder. With a grunt and a moan, Irina rolled over onto her back and pushed her mess of hair back from her face.

"What... what do you want?" she croaked.

"Irina, it's me, Anca. I've brought someone to talk to you."

"Who's Irina?" the woman asked, blinking in the light of the lantern.

Anca threw me a quick glance before continuing. "You are. You're Irina."

The woman stared with a childlike fascination at the lantern's dancing flame. "Yes, that's right. I'm Irina. Irina, Irina, Irina," she added, in a little snatch of a tune. "It's a pretty name. But I shall cast it away, away... yes, I shall cast it away."

"I've brought someone to see you," Anca said again. She grabbed my sleeve and tugged me so hard that I stumbled into her. "This is Jessica."

Irina looked at me for a brief moment with just a trace of curiosity. Then she looked back at Anca. "She's a stranger to me. But you—Why do I know you?"

Anca grimaced. "I'm Anca. I'm your niece."

Irina looked for a moment as if the word "niece" was mildly disturbing to her; I was feeling pretty disturbed myself. Anca had never mentioned that she was related to this woman, and, what's more, Irina couldn't have been more than thirty-five years old. Anca herself was that old. How could this woman be her aunt?

In preparing to ask Anca this question, I cleared my throat nervously. When Irina heard me, her head whipped around and she locked onto me with a penetrating stare.

"Why have you brought this one?"

"I told you, Irina," Anca began, "her name is Jessica, and she—"

"Do not tell me her name!" Irina spat. Every trace of sleepiness and vagueness was now gone from her face. "Do not speak to me of names, earthly names! What do I care for names? I cast them away, as you should cast her away. Far, far away. She brings danger with her!"

"We know. That's why we've come," Anca answered, bravely attempting a soothing tone.

Irina's pitch grew shrill as she plunged a groping hand into her blankets and pulled out the chain. "You bring danger to me here? When I cannot defend myself?" She shook the chain in Anca's face. "When I am chained like an animal, trapped like a rodent?"

"Irina, please!"

"No! I will not stay here. I will not be the sacrifice in your games!"

"No one is playing games, and we don't want to sacrifice anyone," said Anca, with her calm facade starting to crack as her voice rose slightly. "We need your help."

Irina dropped the chain and looped her finger under a knotted bracelet, which seemed to be made of hair—her own hair, I realized, as I noticed small clumps of it missing from the back of her head. Having found her bracelet, Irina lifted her wrist to her chin; she opened her mouth as though she were about to bite herself, but then caught my eye and stopped. She looked back and forth between Anca and me, searching for something in our faces.

"Help?" she asked, as if she barely recognized the word and was merely trying it out to see how it felt in her mouth.

"Yes, help," Anca replied, and she knelt at this first sign of cooperation. "Jessica must learn to Walk."

Irina's face broke into a strange, euphoric grin when Anca said the word *Walk*. Irina took a deep, satisfied breath and let her head loll back as she blew it out again. I'd seen my mother do the same thing with the first sip of alcohol after a failed stretch at sobriety.

"Ah yes, to Walk. To Walk," she cooed contentedly.

"Yes," Anca went on quickly. "She must learn to Walk, but no one here can tell her how to do it, not from experience. There's no one among us except you who's ever Walked."

Irina snorted a reproachful little laugh. "Those fools lack the strength of mind. They lack the power. Only I ever found the will to do it." She drew herself up and swept the hair from her face with a dignified stroke of her hand. I could see more runes inked crudely on the skin beneath her jawline.

"Yes, I know that. And now Jessica needs to know everything you can tell her about Walking. It's very important."

123

Irina pouted. "Mustn't speak of it. Mustn't do it. They told me I mustn't do it anymore." She gestured limply at the runes, and I realized they must have been placed there to stop her from Walking.

"I'm not asking you to do it," Anca said. "I'm not trying to get you into trouble, Irina. I just want you to answer her questions. Can you do that?"

Irina didn't say anything, but instead turned to me and sat up straight and expectantly, as if I were about to read her a bedtime story.

I threw a look at Anca, who nodded encouragingly at me. I hated being put on the spot in even the most innocuous of circumstances, but this? I could barely repress the tremor in my voice as I addressed Irina.

"What is it like... to Walk?"

Irina grinned lazily again. "It is like sleeping and flying, like floating and falling. It's discovering the truth of things. It's losing and finding yourself in the haze that's hidden from the rest of the living, breathing world."

A shudder ran down my spine. "Is it... difficult to do?"

"Oh, no. To let go is the most wonderful thing in the world. Snip, snip, snip the strings that hold you down. Leave all your pain behind, all the bonds of the flesh." Irina looked down at her own hands and arms with a sudden, fierce anger, as though she couldn't stand the sight of herself. "This cage, this wretched, wretched cage of bone and blood!" At this, she began clawing at her forearms as a feral, animalistic sound bubbled up from her chest.

I looked at Anca, almost sure she would tell me to ease off, but she nodded grimly for me to continue. I knew I needed to. There was one really important question I still needed to ask.

"Is it difficult to return to your body, once you've left?"

Irina's face fell suddenly into a dark, angry snarl. She bared her teeth at me. "Difficult? Would you find it difficult to return to a cage after flying like a bird through the sky? Would you find it difficult to become a slave again, after a beautiful moment of freedom? Would you?" She raised her hand to her mouth again and whispered a rapid, incomprehensible stream of words into her own palm. Then she placed the knotted bracelet of hair between her teeth and tore it apart.

I opened my mouth, unsure of what would come out, but before

I could form words properly, a familiar feeling crept over me—one that I'd come to regard with less dread and more resignation. It was the very same feeling that I got whenever Fiona was about to experience a Psychic Trance. Irina's eyes rolled back into her head and she keeled over onto her filthy nest, where she began to twitch and shake.

"Back away! *Now!*" hissed Anca, scrambling to her feet.

I leapt back as I watched Irina writhe. Then her spirit shot with disorienting speed from her body, coming to a halt mere inches from my face. Only my shock kept me from bolting out of the wagon in terror.

I stared into the wide, livid eyes of Irina's spirit. "LET ME OUT!" her eyes screamed. "LET ME GO!"

Irina's spirit continued to struggle toward me, but something was holding it back. After several terrifying moments, I was able to see past my own fear, and I realized that Irina's spirit couldn't make contact with me; when I had jumped back at Anca's command, I had landed just outside of the Circle that had been carved into the floor of the wagon.

Being careful not to move any closer, I shifted myself so that I could make out Irina's vacated body. Irina's spirit was still tethered to her corporeal form, connected to it by a number of shining webs. As her spirit thrashed and wailed, Irina's body continued to convulse on the heap of blankets.

"What the hell is happening?" I finally managed to choke out.

"They've placed a Casting on her. Many Castings," Anca shouted, trying to raise her voice over the continued shrieks of Irina's spirit. "The webs holding her together are Bonds. They're meant to prevent her from Walking."

"Yeah, I got that much, but I don't think it's working the way it's supposed to!" I cried, gesturing wildly to Irina's still-seizing body.

"It isn't supposed to work at all," Anca replied. No specific Casting exists in our arsenal to keep a Durupinen from Walking. We don't know if it was lost over the ages, or if it never existed at all. This is a combination of different Castings, a sort of spirit-control experiment."

"How can you experiment on her? She's not a lab rat! She's obviously in pain!" I could barely stand to watch Irina's two selves struggling—the body unaware, the spirit hyperaware, both clearly in anguish.

"I know, but they truly had no choice. When Irina discovered how to Walk, she was the first of our clan in centuries to do it. The Council was enthralled by the possibilities—a Durupinen who could approach spirits on their own plane. Walking meant that Irina could understand everything the spirits were trying to communicate without the need for interpretation. The Council thought they could use her Walking to encourage particularly challenging or violent spirits to Cross, without risking harm to the Durupinen themselves."

Irina's spirit was tiring now; its shrieks dulled to low, guttural moans. It continued to pull at its Bonds, but feebly. It was dreadful to watch.

Anca went on, watching Irina's spirit with a resigned sadness. "At first, Irina Walked only when the Council demanded it. She was proud to be able to serve the clan in such a useful way, and Walking gave her a certain status—a glamour, even. But the sensation was addicting."

"Addicting? You mean she couldn't stop herself from Walking?"

"Yes. When we die, our spirits feel the pull of the other side and give in to it, which is why most spirits Cross immediately after death and don't need our help. Durupinen spirits are the same, although, like Ileana told you, our bloodlines protect our souls from feeling that pull too strongly as we help the spirits Cross.

"But by Walking, Irina was allowing her spirit to leave the protection of her body and its bloodlines. Her spirit began to crave freedom. Soon she was Walking constantly, abandoning her body for months—years—at a time. Over time, her spirit grew stronger and her body grew weaker. Essentially, her spirit began to forget who she was and why she was here. She stopped following orders from the Council. She could no longer be trusted to wander the world, full of the knowledge of the Durupinen. And so, they trapped her there. She's been this way ever since."

"How long?" I asked.

"That's the other thing." Anca sighed heavily. "The body doesn't age while the spirit is Walking. You heard me call Irina my aunt, but actually, she's my great-aunt."

I blinked. "You're kidding me."

"No. I wish I was. Irina is nearly eighty years old."

I looked back at the two Irinas, who were now becoming one being again as her spirit sank, still moaning, back into her body.

Her face, shining with tears, betrayed barely a wrinkle; her mass of black matted hair had only a thread or two of silver in it.

"She looks so frail," I said.

"Her spirit has grown too powerful for her body. She's little more than a shell to house it now," Anca said, nodding sadly.

Irina began to stir. She pulled herself back up into a sitting position, with both hands clasped over her temples as though her head were about to burst. She looked up and cried out, startled to see us standing there.

"Who are you?" she asked us sharply. "What are you doing here?"

"I'm Anca, and this is Jessica. It's okay, Irina, we aren't here to hurt you," Anca explained. Her usually brisk voice was now weary and deflated.

"Who's Irina?" Irina asked, as she again narrowed her eyes in suspicion.

"Don't trouble yourself," replied Anca, as she took me by the arm and pulled me toward the door of the wagon. "We're going now. We're sorry for disturbing you."

"Go, then!" Irina sobbed. "Go and leave me in peace!"

"We're very sorry," Anca said again, then tugged me through the door.

The frost-kissed darkness of the clearing was silent but for the sounds of crickets and snatches of drunken humming from Andrei, who, somewhere out of sight, was deep in communion with his flask.

"Why couldn't she remember us? When her spirit went back inside her body, she didn't even remember we were there," I said between deep gasping breaths. I was fighting to keep something down—although I couldn't tell if it was hysteria or whatever little food was left in my stomach.

"Irina's Bonds are created from psychic energy and emotion. The Castings use Irina's own thoughts and emotions to keep her soul and body connected. It works, as you saw, but at a painful cost to both. Because those thoughts and emotions are being stretched beyond the body to hold her two halves together, Irina loses access to her own feelings and memories. It has driven her into madness—she's almost like someone suffering from dementia. Her mind is battered unpredictably between clarity and confusion."

I had no words to respond, but Anca seemed to have expected

this. She picked up Andrei's lantern, having left her own in the wagon, and turned to head back to the main encampment. With my legs and my heart now much heavier, I trudged after her.

9

CHOICES

WE DIDN'T SPEAK ON OUR TREK back to the encampment: There was nothing left to say. The silence was comfortable enough for me, but it might've been awkward for Anca; she kept looking over at me with her mouth half open as if poised to speak, but she never did. This suited me just fine—my own thoughts were so loud that I honestly don't think I would have heard Anca over them.

As far as I could see, I'd never been faced with a more frightening set of choices. I laid them out as a list in my head: Each option was worse than the last.

Choice number one was obvious: I could run from the Prophecy. I could refuse to get involved, go into hiding, and hope the Necromancers left me alone. Of course that meant never seeing Hannah again, as well as potentially allowing her to destroy the entire Gateway system. It also meant going into a life of hiding and spending every waking moment on the run, just as my mother had. As long as I was breathing, the Necromancers would never stop hunting me; eventually they would catch up with me, and when they did...

I shuddered. No, choice number one wasn't really a choice at all.

Choice number two was to become a Walker. It was the only way to fulfill my role in the Prophecy, the only prayer the Gateways had of surviving. If it were as simple as just stepping in and out of my body, my decision would already have been made—but of course it wasn't that simple. The risks were piling up so fast that I could barely see beyond them. Firstly, I may not have the strength to become a Walker at all, and if I did manage to Walk there seemed a pretty good chance I'd wind up as irretrievably mad as Irina. Then there was Ileana's warning: If I couldn't resist the pull of the other side while Walking, there was no way I could reseal the

Gateway—it all would be for nothing. And finally, if I did manage to Walk, keep my sanity, *and* resist the call of the other side, it would *still* be a suicide mission unless Hannah were able to Call me back. And, despite what Ileana said, the Prophecy was very sketchy about the chances of any sacrifice on my part being temporary. It would've been nice if the damn Prophecy had ended with, "*And then the Caller did save her sister, and the Necromancers did explode into tiny bits.*" Or something like that.

"Well, here we are. I'll bid you goodnight," came Anca's voice.

I looked up, having half-forgotten Anca was even there. The wagon stood before us, silent and dark, as the others slept inside.

"I'd wish you a good night's sleep," she continued, "but I don't want to insult you."

I laughed humorlessly. "Yeah, you've effectively killed all hope of sleep, I think."

"I'm sorry," Anca said. She reached out a hand as though to squeeze my arm, but dropped it again quickly. "I wish I could've shown you something that would make your choice easier. But you needed to know."

"Yes, I did. Thank you for being honest with me. And I'm sorry about Irina."

Anca nodded gravely. "So am I. The price of our gift is steeper for some than for others. Irina has paid dearly for it. I pray the same won't be true for you."

She turned to go. I wanted to call after her and add that I'd already paid dearly for our gift—a gift which I was sure I'd now never be able to look at as anything more than a curse. But, in the instant it took me to consider this, Anca had rounded the end of the nearest wagon and was gone from sight.

I climbed the few steps leading to the wagon's entrance. I had one hand on the door handle when a voice behind me said, "Well now, wasn't that an interesting little field trip?"

I cringed and swore under my breath before turning around. Milo, with his arms crossed, had flared into sight behind me; his spectral foot tapped impatiently.

"Did you follow me?" I asked, attempting indignation.

He scowled. "You're damn right I did... and don't give me that attitude, honey. I'm your Spirit Guide. It's the whole point of my afterlife, following you around."

I sighed, defeated far more easily than usual. "How much did you see?"

"You mean the crazy lady secretly locked away in the woods like something out of a Brontë novel? Every messed up moment of it." At this, Milo began his now-familiar version of spectral pacing, flickering into and out of sight at set intervals. "They can't really expect you to try this Walking thing after seeing something like that, can they?"

"Ileana obviously didn't think so, or she would've shown me Irina herself, right?"

"Oh, and I'll have a few choice words for her when I see her next," Milo said with a growl.

"Don't," I replied firmly. I sank onto a rock beside the wagon. "It's not her fault. She's just trying to save us all. It's natural, I guess, to omit a few details when certain destruction is at stake. I can't say that I blame her."

"Well, you might not, but I'm pretty pissed."

I put my head down between my knees and took a deep breath. My brain was beginning to pound.

I was still staring down at my own shoes when Milo burst out, "There's got to be another way! Some other option to fix this." His voice, while angry, carried a note of sympathy.

"I wish that were true, but—"

"We'll go back to Ileana in the morning. They're just going to have to come up with something else."

I laughed. "Milo, they've been obsessing about this Prophecy for hundreds of years. You really think they haven't exhausted all other options?"

"I don't care! It's their own damn fault the Necromancers are on the rise again, so they'll just have to figure it out for themselves."

"Solid plan," I grumbled. "I'll just tell them that in the morning. I'm sure they'll understand."

"But why does it have to be you?" Milo cried.

I looked up at him, and I was surprised to see the anguish on his face. "Sheer dumb luck, it seems."

Gravely Milo asked, "Why can't I do it instead?"

"Do what?"

"Go through the Gateway and close it from the other side!" he explained emphatically, as if this should've been obvious.

I wrenched my head up and glared at him fixedly. "Excuse me? Why in the world would I let you do that?"

"Because this whole thing is fucked! It doesn't make any sense!" Milo cried, throwing his hands up in the air. "Someone needs to go to the other side of the Gateway to reseal it, and that person should be me!"

I shook my head. "It doesn't work that way."

"Well, it should!"

"Milo, you heard what Ileana said. I have to be the one to go. If the Necromancers reverse the Gateway, the only way to reseal it is to have Hannah on one side and me on the other. One more spirit over there isn't going to make a difference."

"But if I go *knowing* that I have to close it—"

"You wouldn't be able to! I appreciate the offer, but it has to be me."

"But it shouldn't be you! Don't you get it? I'm the one who should be over there!"

Milo's voice was nearing hysterics. I stared at him, utterly unsure of what to say next. It didn't matter, though; Milo took a deep breath—a habit held over from his human days, since breathing wasn't a real action for him anymore—and kept talking.

"It's just—and if you ever tell Hannah this, I will haunt your every waking moment from here on out—I'm not supposed to be here. I know I made the choice to stay, and I'm dealing with it. But the truth is... the biggest mistake I ever made in my life was ending it."

Milo dimmed the moment he made his confession, as if his usual spark were fizzling out. I said nothing. I didn't reply, didn't even move: I was sure if I broke the moment's spell, Milo would never reveal the rest of his story. A story he obviously needed desperately to tell.

"Back then, I'd given up. I had convinced myself that I could never be happy, could never have the things in life that I wanted so badly. I was sure I'd never fall in love—I'd been told time and time again that my way of loving was wrong. And I was sure no one would ever love me—I thought I was fundamentally unlovable because I'm gay. Hell, my own father couldn't love me, and that was his goddamn biological duty. I was an anomaly, a mistake—and what do you do with mistakes? You erase them. You crumple them up and throw them away and start again."

132

"Oh, Milo," I whispered as my heart sank for him. For the first time since I'd met him, I wished I could reach out and touch him, soothe him.

"So I did it. I erased myself. And because of Hannah, I knew that there was a chance I could start over again in a different form. I didn't know what being a spirit would be like, and that's the reason I chose it. It was a gamble, but I honestly thought nothing could be worse than being me and being alive. I told myself that even if being a ghost turned out to be terrible, it had to be an improvement over being me, alive."

Even with everything I'd been through in my own life, I couldn't imagine making that kind of decision. I wanted to say something comforting, but I didn't dare. Milo needed his own space to tell me this—this part of his story that he couldn't share with Hannah. Instead, I sat quietly and waited for what would come next.

"You can't understand what it's like, being like this," he said. "I can't experience things the way you do. I'll never get to do the things I always wanted to do, but I have to sit by and watch everyone else doing them. There's a reason we're not meant to exist this way, and I'm finally figuring that out. We all figure it out, eventually. All ghosts reach the point where we finally admit Crossing over is the best choice. Well, actually, living would have been the best choice for me, but it's too late for that now. The difference is that I can't make the choice to Cross now."

"I'm... really sorry, Milo."

"Me too. So I'm asking you, Jess, please. Just let me do it. It would fix this... awful in-between I'm stuck in. I can help you all—including Hannah—and I can help myself, too. Please. Let it be me."

I wished I could give him another answer, just to extinguish the agony burning in his eyes, but it was out of my control.

"I can't, Milo. It can't be you... As much as I'd like to get rid of you." I added the last part quickly, as a lame attempt at a joke. He ignored it.

I went on, serious once more, "It's not enough to send a spirit across, even one who's connected to us like you are. It has to be me. The Gateway, once reversed, has to have one Durupinen on either side for it to be resealed. But it isn't only that. You can't Cross until Hannah Crosses—and I know neither of us wants that to happen anytime soon. It sucks and I'm so sorry, but as long as

Hannah's alive, I don't think you could do this, even if I wanted to let you try."

Milo shook his head and flickered in and out of view. I wasn't telling him anything he didn't already know, but it still wasn't easy for him to hear.

"I can't understand what you're going through, but I know what your choice meant for Hannah. She never would've made it this far without you, and I could never live with myself if I was the reason for separating the two of you. She needs you, Milo, much more than she needs me."

Milo shook his head. "You're her sister."

"But she really doesn't know me yet," I pointed out. "You're her best friend. You have already been through much more together. As much as I hate to admit it, you're the one she really needs. You chose to stay with her once, and even though it's difficult, I need you to make that same choice again. Because if this goes wrong and I can't get back, she's going to need you more than ever."

"It's not going to go wrong," Milo said, apparently resigned to my argument. "She'll Call you back, I know she will."

I didn't answer. I thought I might burst into tears if I tried to voice my fear of being abandoned on the other side of the Gateway—and this moment was already much too real. I bit it all back, forced it down, and sighed.

"So I guess that's it, then," Milo said quietly.

I realized in that moment my decision had already been made. Had I ever really had a choice at all? I exhaled sharply and nodded.

"They don't deserve it," Milo said. "They don't deserve to be saved."

"Maybe not," I replied. "But I'm going to try anyway."

"Are you going to tell Finn or the others about Irina?"

"No. Because I'm not going to change my mind—their knowing will just make it harder for everyone. But they'll know soon enough, anyhow, because Irina's the one who's going to show me how to Walk."

"Huh?"

"We've got to try to use her. She's the only one living who's done it. I don't care how many books Ileana and her Council have studied about Walking. This isn't something you can learn from a book. Anca practically said so herself."

"You think Irina can remain lucid long enough to teach you anything?"

"No idea. Maybe not. We've got to try, though."

"Finn isn't going to take this very well."

"You never know," I said with greater conviction than I actually felt. "He might be more supportive than we think."

ABANDONED

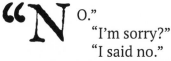**O."**

"I'm sorry?"

"I said no."

Finn's arms were crossed over his chest like a knot that not even the briniest of sailors could untie. His expression was mulish—it had been that way from the moment he'd woken up and seen me sitting there waiting to tell everyone my decision. From the way he had been looking at me, I knew immediately that Finn had already figured out my decision, but somehow this knowledge didn't better prepare him for accepting what I had to say. He had exploded before either Savvy or Annabelle had been able to get a single word in; even Milo had stayed silent and popped out of view.

"I'm not sure you understand the nature of this conversation," I said, crossing my own arms. "You seem to be under the delusion that I'm asking your permission—something I've never done before and will never do. So wipe that disapproving look off your face and do your job!"

Finn blinked at me, incredulous. "Do my job? What the bloody hell do you think I'm getting at? It's been enough of a challenge protecting you from the hordes of people who've tried to kill you. I didn't anticipate having to protect you from yourself, too!"

"Well, good, because I'm not asking you to. Anca and the Traveler Council will help me figure out how to Walk. You just need to stay out of my way."

"This is my duty! I'm not in your way!" he shouted.

"Really? You're trying to forbid me from doing something. I'd call that getting in my goddamn way!" I shouted right back.

"When will you realize I'm not trying to undermine you? I'm trying to help you!"

"And when will you realize I make my own decisions? Mackie

warned me when I got to Fairhaven that the Caomhnóir have a pretty draconian view of women, but you're unbelievable. Seriously, if you don't want me to do this, why don't you just hit me with your club and drag me back to your cave?"

"You didn't have a problem with me or my club when I stood up with you in the Council Room, or when I was driving like a maniac through London to save you from the Necromancers!" Finn's voice rose to a frustrated, angry pitch that I'd never heard before, and his livid face was now so red it looked about to burst. "Either you want my protection or you don't, Jess, but you can't have it both ways!"

"Yes, let's talk about wanting it both ways! You keep claiming that your only job is to protect and preserve the Gateway. Every single time you've helped me, you've made it painfully clear that your help has nothing to do with my own personal well-being. Well, here I am, getting ready to risk my well-being for the sake of the entire Gateway system, but suddenly you won't allow it? So which is it, Finn? Are you safeguarding me or the Gateway? Because it looks like you'll have to choose between the two. We both know how you've chosen in the past, so I don't know why you're fighting me on this. We all know you care a hell of a lot more about the Gateway than you do about me!"

Finn's face twisted with something painful; he leapt off the far edge of the bunk and toward me in one sudden movement. For one wild, incoherent instant, I thought he was going to attack me, but he charged straight past me and out of the wagon; he slammed the door so hard that one of the drapes separating the bunks fell into a dusty heap on the floor, and several candles tumbled from their wooden holders. Savvy jumped up quickly and stomped on the curtain as it started to smolder.

I didn't even consider following Finn. I sat in the wagon and watched the dust settle, attempting to let my own anger settle among the motes. Annabelle and Savvy sat in the stillness with me, waiting for me to break the silence.

"What about you guys? Do you forbid me from going through with this?" I asked.

Annabelle smiled weakly. "I'm impressed with you, frankly. And don't worry about Finn; he'll come around."

"I don't know about that, but thanks anyway," I said.

"You're welcome," she said as she stood up and pulled her

sweater over her head. "I'm going to find Anca and see if she can rustle us up some breakfast. I'll be back soon." Annabelle slipped out the door and into the dim morning, where the light filtering through the trees was still as much shadow as brightness.

As I watched her go, Savvy blew a long breath out through her teeth. "Blimey, Jess, do you always have to be so hard on him?"

My anger instantly redirected itself; I whipped around to face Savvy and hissed, "Excuse me? What do you mean, I'm hard on him?"

"Oi, Jess, think: You never let him do his job without going at odds! It's ridiculous having the men as protectors, yeah, but it ain't his fault... it's how the system works. He was born into it just like you were and he's gotta make the best of it, doesn't he? He's been told his whole life that his duty is to protect you, but here you go getting yourself into all these situations where you come this close to snuffing it—"

"I'm not getting into these situations on purpose!" I shouted. "Do you honestly think I want any of this?"

"Don't you go yelling at me! The point is, if all this goes tits up, he's going to blame himself, and I know you don't want that. So... try to understand his point of view, yeah? That's all I'm saying."

I was caught completely off guard. When Savvy sounded more rational than I did, I knew I needed to reevaluate. I took a deep breath.

"Fine," I said grudgingly. "There's a possibility you might be right, but it doesn't matter. I can't change my mind on this."

"I know you can't. So does he. That's likely why he's so cross about it," Savvy answered. She walked over and sank into the bunk next to me, then flung a chummy arm around my shoulder. "I'm not all that keen on it myself, to be honest."

"Neither am I."

"I'd be scared shitless if it were me, mate."

"I am," I said. "Believe me, I've tried to talk myself out of this at least a dozen times since last night. But no matter how I look at it, I keep coming back to the same decision."

"Yeah, I know. We really didn't know what we were getting into, did we?"

"Not a clue."

"To think I used to complain about a bit of bookwork back at Fairhaven. Now look at us—on the run with a bleeding Traveler caravan," Savvy said, chuckling. "I should've slammed the door in Celeste's face when she turned up to recruit me."

"If only you'd barged into someone else's shower, you could've avoided this whole mess," I said, putting my head down on her shoulder.

"Yeah, fate works in mysterious ways, doesn't it? But then I'd have missed out on your magnificent tits," Savvy chided. "So really, a fair trade in all."

I laughed before I could stop myself. I punched Savvy in the arm and we started cackling madly. It was the first decent laugh we'd had in weeks.

A sharp rap on the wagon door silenced us both. The door opened before either of us could cross the wagon to answer it. It was Anca.

"Ileana sent me for you. She wants to know if you've come to a decision," Anca said.

I reached into my bunk for my bag and shouldered it. "Wow, before breakfast, huh? And I'm assuming we'll be escorted out of the camp if she doesn't like my answer?"

Anca frowned down at her feet. "Caomhnóir will be standing by, yes. I've already sent Annabelle to Ileana's tent."

"Right hospitable that is," said Savvy.

"Well, let's get this over with," I said.

"Where was your Caomhnóir going?" Anca asked as we stepped down onto the grass.

"Probably somewhere to go cool off," I answered. "I'm sure we'll find him sulking behind one of these wagons."

"No, I don't think so," Anca said as she led the way. "He asked Dragos the way to the nearest road. You really don't know where he was going? I assumed you'd sent him somewhere."

"I'm not in the habit of sending him places," I said. "He's not a messenger boy. You saw him leave the camp? Did your people actually allow him to do that?"

"They allowed him to go, but not before swearing an oath as a Guardian not to reveal the camp. He had his things with him."

I stopped walking and looked back at the wagon; Finn's rucksack was indeed missing from beside the door. I traded a nervous glance with Savvy. Anca, realizing she'd outpaced us, turned around.

"Is everything okay?" she asked.

"Yes, I think so. Finn and I had an argument about Walking. He stormed out."

"I see," Anca mumbled, looking unconcerned. "Should we send someone after him?"

"No," I said quickly. "I'm sure he'll be back. He was just upset."

"Very well. Follow me, please. We shouldn't keep Ileana waiting."

As we walked, the absence of Finn beside me began to feel like the presence of something painful and gnawing.

§

"Well then, Muse. You have reached your decision?"

Ileana was perched again in her carved wooden chair; she drummed her fingers on its arms.

"Yes, I have."

"And?"

"Yes. I will try to learn to become a Walker."

In a low whoosh, Ileana let out a breath that I didn't even realize she was holding. Anca closed her eyes and bowed her head. Even the stone-faced Caomhnóir betrayed expressions of surprise and relief.

"You've made a wise and brave choice," Ileana pronounced.

"It might be brave, but I'm not so sure about wise," I said. "But I'm making it anyway, on two conditions."

The raven cawed as though raising its own objections to the idea of conditions.

Ileana frowned. "Conditions?"

"Yes," I said, being careful to keep my voice as respectful as I could. "I realize that you're not planning to engage in battle with the Necromancers, but if I'm going to risk my life to become a Walker, you'll need to take a few risks yourselves. We need to know where my sister is, and we need you to help find her."

Ileana's dark, heavy brows rose so high that they nearly disappeared into her hairline. "We are taking plenty of risks as it is. We've agreed to shelter you and teach you all we know about Walking. You will have our full protection while you're here. Isn't this enough for you?"

"No," I said flatly. "Walking will be pointless if my sister remains missing. I can't Cross through our Gateway if I don't know where she is. I also refuse to treat the Prophecy as if it were set in stone. There may be no need to reverse the Gateway at all if we can find and rescue my sister first."

"I already told you, I will not—"

"I'm not asking you to help us rescue her," I said. "Even though we could obviously use all the help we can get. But we have no resources to look for her, and no idea of where to start. I think you have both of those things."

Milo materialized beside Savvy suddenly, scaring the living daylights out of her. With what I could tell was a great effort, Savvy managed not to scream in the presence of the High Priestess.

"Yes, and I'll help," Milo said firmly. "That's what I'm here for; we need to find her."

Ignoring Milo, Ileana ran a finger over her mouth. With a shrewd expression on her face, she asked me, "What is your other condition?"

"Irina has to be the one to teach me how to Walk."

Ileana could no longer feign composure: Her mouth fell open and her ruddy complexion went pale.

"How do you know about Irina?" she asked. She then answered her own question by shooting a baleful look at Anca, who dropped her eyes to the canvas floor of the tent.

"Does it really matter?" I asked. "It's enough that I know. I get why you wanted to hide her from me; I've seen the state she's in. But honestly, Irina's the best resource I have. I want her there as a guide when I try to do this."

Ileana shrugged. "Very well. I can't imagine that there's much help to be had from the likes of Irina—you've seen what she is. But I leave that up to you. If you want her there, we'll find a way to bring her to you. But I can't guarantee that she'll be as useful as you hope, and if she grows impossible to control, she will need to go back—for her own safety as much as ours."

"Fair enough," I said. "What about the first condition?"

Ileana hesitated, then spit into her hand and held it out to me. "We shake on it, and then I release my own Trackers to begin the search. Again, I can promise nothing."

"Neither can I," I said grimly, taking her hand and shaking it.

"We begin then!" Ileana cried, jumping up from her chair with such great verve that her raven squawked in surprise. "Anca, convene the Council in the meeting Circle. We must devise the best plan for removing Irina safely from her Bonds. Then alert the Scribes. They'll need to prepare all our scrolls and books about Walking so we can decide how best to proceed with Jessica's training."

Anca shuffled out of the tent at once. Ileana approached me and clapped a bony old hand on my shoulder. Every movement she made created a tinkling, jingling sound, almost as if she were a human wind chime.

"By the bonfire at the center of camp, you will find food. Help yourselves and eat up. You will need your strength, I don't doubt, for what lies ahead of you."

"Thank you. And those Trackers?"

"I will send them at once."

"Thank you, High Priestess," Annabelle said.

Savvy and Milo echoed Annabelle's thanks, and we all turned and exited the tent. The morning air still had a damp cold to it as we approached the bonfire, where a long trestle table stood loaded with bowls of fruit, roasted vegetables, loaves of rough bread, tureens of soup, and a number of ambiguous cured meats that could've been made from any number of animals. It was like stumbling onto an ancient bacchanalian feast in the middle of the 21st century. It was one of the strangest and most anachronistic moments I'd ever experienced. Just yesterday, my breakfast had consisted of a packaged pastry and cereal in a Prince William mug, yet today I was sitting on a log like a forest nymph, eating from a rough wooden bowl.

Savvy looked down at her food and sighed. "Who do you think I'd have to screw to get a ciggy around here?"

"Aren't you starving?" I asked her, dunking my bread into a bowl of hearty brown stew before wolfing it down almost without chewing. It might have just been how hungry I was, but at that moment the Travelers' simple bread and warm stew were the best things I'd ever tasted.

"Mate, I haven't had a fag since yesterday 'round midday. I nearly tackled that old gypsy bird for the tobacco in her pipe," Savvy said, with more than a note of desperation in her voice. Her knee was jiggling up and down rapidly.

"Plenty of the Travelers smoke," Annabelle offered. "It's part of the culture. They roll their own, of course, but I'm sure if you ask around..."

"Brilliant! It was either that or a shag, and I don't much fancy a romp in the wagon with any of these blokes. Back in a mo," Savvy said. She jumped up and disappeared around the corner of the nearest wagon, where several Caomhnóir were talking and laughing raucously.

I looked over at Milo, who was hovering extremely close to the bonfire and staring into it; his thoughts were far from the encampment.

"She'll be okay," I said.

"That's what I keep telling myself, but I can't stand not knowing," Milo replied. Any living person would've been uncomfortably warm being so close to the flames, which were sparking in the misty, early morning air.

"I know."

"I just… I haven't been truly disconnected from her since I met her. I feel sort of…"

"Lost?"

"Yeah."

"It's like Finn said, they aren't going to hurt her, not really. They need her at her strongest."

"Speaking of our burly bouncer," said Milo, tearing his eyes from the fire and changing the subject. "Where's Finn run off to?"

"I don't know. He was really angry about my decision to try Walking. Anca said she saw him leave the camp with his backpack."

Milo frowned. "He's just blowing off steam. I'm sure he wouldn't actually leave us here. He takes his job too seriously for that."

"That's why we fought," I said. "I think I make protecting our Gateway too hard of a job to stick with."

§

It was two long days before Ileana and the Council deemed everything ready for my first attempt at Walking. Having to wait those two days was just about the worst thing for my resolve. It gave me way too much time to consider all of the various and terrifying ways that Walking could go wrong; self-doubt seeped in as well, and I began having a hard time remembering all of the reasons I had agreed to Walk in the first place. When I wasn't consumed by my own concerns about Walking, I was obsessing over what awful things Hannah might be subjected to at the hands of the Necromancers. And, if I managed to put either of these two issues out of my mind, I found myself preoccupied about Finn, wondering where he had gone and if he was safe.

In those two days, Ileana's Trackers hadn't managed to locate Hannah, although Anca assured me they were following several promising leads; she was confident that we would have information about Hannah soon.

"I promise you, we'll let you know when we have news," Anca told me when I stopped by her wagon for the third time in those two days. "Don't you trust us?"

I laughed before I could stop myself. "I'm not sure who I trust anymore, including myself."

"Trying times draw colors to the surface that we never knew we had inside. Then we must create with them as best we can," Anca said solemnly.

"Is that a Traveler proverb?" I asked.

"No, just an observation," she said, a trace of a smile on her face.

"That's great. You should write fortune cookies," I replied. But when I saw the utterly bewildered look on her face, I quickly added, "Never mind." Of course Anca had no idea what a fortune cookie was—she lived in a caravan in the middle of an English forest.

"Finding your sister is our task," Anca said. "Let that be our focus. Your focus is needed elsewhere."

"By elsewhere, I assume you mean Walking."

Anca nodded. "Of course. That's the one task which no one else can take on for you."

I didn't reply. I felt like heavy weights were being dropped, one by one, onto my shoulders. Hannah's gone. *Clunk.* Finn's gone. *Clunk.* Learn to Walk, but don't die in the attempt. *Clunk.* Reseal the Gateway and save the world. *Clunk. CLUNK, CLUNK, CLUNK, CLUNK.*

"You seem troubled," Anca said, as though she were merely observing the weather.

I laughed again, loudly this time—a harsh peal of laughter that resounded through the trees and echoed in the clearing. Several large black birds took flight over our heads, squawking loudly.

"Do I? I can't imagine why." I was getting eerily good at deadpan.

Anca looked at me thoughtfully for a moment. "I don't sense that you believe in things like proverbs or superstitions, but I'm going to tell you one of ours."

"Super," I said dully. "Lay it on me."

Anca pointed up to the small unkindness of ravens now perched in a distant, bare treetop. "Travelers have always believed that ravens bring bad luck. We curse at them and shoo them away when we see them. We blame them when something goes wrong. I suppose that sounds silly to you."

I shrugged. It did sound dumb, but I wasn't about to say it.

"It sounded silly to Ileana, too, but not because she doesn't believe in luck and omens—she *does* believe in them, just like the rest of us. But unlike so many of us, she doesn't believe she is powerless against them."

I looked up, shaking myself out from under my distractions; I gave Anca my full attention for the first time.

"I'm sure you've noticed Ileana's caged raven?" Anca asked.

"I did, yeah. It's sort of hard to miss."

"The night Ileana became High Priestess, she went out into the forest alone and came back with that raven. She returned covered in peck marks and scratches, because she caught it with her bare hands; the struggle cost the bird its eye. She brought the raven into her new tent and locked it in that cage. At first, the Council members were horrified. 'Why would you bring such bad luck into your home?' they asked her."

I suddenly found myself breathlessly waiting for the answer. "Why did she?"

"She told them, 'I will have my share of bad fortune as High Priestess, but I will not lie down and wait for it to befall me. I will embrace it. I will tame it. I will bend it to my will. Misfortune and I will look each other in the eye, and we will know each holds power in her own way.'"

Anca let the words sink in for a moment before she took me by the shoulders and shook me. "And so I say to you, Muse: This Prophecy is approaching, whether you like it or not. But you don't have to lie down and let it befall you. Embrace it. Tame it. Bend it to your will. You are not powerless—It is but a raven."

I took a deep breath. And the breath went deeper into my lungs than any breath I'd been able to breathe in weeks.

"Thanks. I... I'll do my best."

146

"And we'll do our best to locate your sister."

As much as Anca did to try to ease my worries about Hannah, Dragos did nothing of the sort when it came to Finn. None of the Travelers had seemed concerned about Finn's disappearance at first, but when they saw he hadn't returned the next morning, they reluctantly agreed to send someone to look for him. It had finally occurred to Dragos that Finn's oath may not have been enough: If Finn were caught by the Necromancers, they could potentially torture enough information out of him to find the encampment. By noon on the second day, the borders of the camp had been reinforced with every protection and Casting the Travelers could muster.

By the second night, Savvy's reassurances that Finn would be back any moment grew less and less confident, and Milo had started shushing her whenever she mentioned his name. As my anger at Finn cooled, it was replaced by a miserable guilt, even though I kept telling myself—over and over again, in a smaller and smaller voice—that I'd done nothing wrong.

II

PREPARATIONS

BY THE TIME THE SUN ROSE on the morning that I would Walk for the first—and possibly last—time, my nerves had caused all my organs to contract into hard, pulsing lumps. I started my day by forcing down a few bites of breakfast—which immediately came up again.

"You look like death warmed over, mate," Savvy said when she caught sight of me stumbling out of the bushes, where I had just deposited my breakfast.

"I'm swell," I said. "Just anticipating the possibility of my imminent death."

Savvy slapped me on the shoulder with a resounding smack. "Buck up, you'll be alright. Anca told me they've got everything set up to keep you safe. If it looks like this isn't going to work, they'll get you back into that beautiful bod." Savvy winked one of her trademark winks, and I knew she was doing her damnedest to cheer me up. She'd been sating her own nerves by chain-smoking hand-rolled Traveler cigarettes all morning; she was patting her pockets for another when Dragos appeared behind her.

"I've come to take you to Irina's clearing. We're ready for you," he said solemnly.

With a Herculean effort, I swallowed back another urge to vomit and stood up on shaky legs.

"We'll be right there with you," said Annabelle, standing up as well.

"No, you will not," Dragos snapped. "No one else is permitted, for their own safety. You will stay here in the camp."

"Like hell we will!" Savvy nearly shouted, jumping to her feet as the glowing butt of her latest cigarette fell from her lips. "We're not letting her do this on her own!"

"We'll get as close as we safely can, and that's where we'll wait," said Annabelle, stepping swiftly between Savvy and Dragos before Savvy could start throwing punches. "But we *are* coming with you as far as we are allowed," she added firmly.

Dragos looked for a moment like he might argue, but decided—after a long look at Savvy's expression—that it wasn't worth the effort. "Suit yourself," he grumbled, then turned toward the woods.

Milo, Savvy, and Annabelle walked with me through the woods. I could feel their anxious stares boring into me so intensely that I half-wished they had stayed behind. They were somehow making me more nervous than I already was, and yet without the swishing of their steady footsteps beside me I seriously doubted that I would've been able to keep my own legs moving forward. I felt like I was being led to the gallows while holding out for an eleventh-hour pardon.

It seemed to take far less time to reach Irina's clearing than it had a few nights before—probably because I was fighting the impulse to run in the other direction. Sooner than I thought possible, the light shafts filtering in through the forest's canopy widened, and the spaces between the trees grew larger until they gave way altogether. In the daylight, I realized that Irina's clearing was a fairly small and circular space—a space that, by its very nature, was ideal for a Circle since it had ready-made boundaries. And a Circle was exactly what the Travelers had turned the clearing into.

If I hadn't already been familiar with the runes, candles, and other basic trappings of Durupinen ceremony, I would have thought that we'd stumbled into a horror movie. The entire perimeter of the Circle was on fire. Twelve women in flowing and ragged gypsy attire were spaced at intervals just inside of the Circle's flames, rocking and muttering under their breath. Dozens of ropes hung in the tree branches, and from them dangled huge runes. Some of the runes were woven from a sort of rough, plant-based cloth; others were painted onto fabric swaths; and still others had been cobbled together from large, gnarled vines and branches.

In the middle of the Circle, a bizarre webbed dome had been created from ropes and netting. The dome enclosed an area about twenty or thirty feet wide and some twenty feet in height. More runes had been scrawled onto its outer surfaces with broad strokes of black paint. Within its confines, I could just discern a dark, still shape in the grass.

"What the fuck?" Savvy whispered.

"Welcome, Muse," came Ileana's voice.

I spotted Ileana on the far side of the clearing. Having no idea what would come out of my mouth if I dared open it, I just nodded at her. She beckoned me forward and I followed the crook of her finger as though hypnotized. Annabelle, Savvy, and Milo remained behind, unsure if they were allowed any further. I didn't want them to follow me; nothing that was about to happen would be made any better by having them close enough to be endangered.

I shuffled over to Ileana as my eyes darted repeatedly to the cage-like structure that I was skirting. I knew who the dark shape inside was, although I was almost afraid to look carefully enough into the dome to confirm this knowledge. Ileana was puffing on her pipe, but not in the same imperious manner as when we'd first met; now she sucked on it like she needed it to keep herself composed, and I realized she was nearly as nervous as I was. She understood as well as I did just how much rested on the experiment we were about to conduct.

"Thank you for coming," she said quietly—and with a good bit less authority than I anticipated. It was almost as though she had expected me to change my mind and not turn up at all.

"I'd say you're welcome, but..." I shrugged; my voice was dry and hoarse.

"We've done all we can to ensure your safety," said Ileana, waving with a grand gesture to the structure behind us.

"What is it?" I asked.

"There is no real name for it," Ileana said. She frowned, as though she were hoping a name for the structure would present itself from somewhere amid the tangles of rope. "We've been experimenting with a combination of Castings, and this is the result. But I can't guarantee that it will protect you, and I can't guarantee that it will hold Irina. We must hope for the best."

"Okay," I said slowly. "Tell me how it's supposed to work... in theory."

"If Irina is to instruct you on how to Walk, she must be able to do it herself, but Walking is very dangerous for her. Irina's spirit is very strong; much stronger than her body's ability to contain it. After so much time outside of its proper confines, her spirit longs for freedom—when she releases it, it will attempt escape permanently."

"Yeah, I saw a bit of that the other night."

"This structure is meant to prevent that. Her soul, when freed from her body, should be trapped inside this dome. It will be free to roam within the structure, but trapped just the same."

I looked again at the enclosure. As I focused on it, I could feel an energy rolling off of it in dizzying waves. Whatever the Travelers had built, however experimental, was powerful.

"Great," I said, almost as a question. "And how is it supposed to protect me?"

"Much in the same way. Once your spirit leaves your body—if you do manage to separate the two—there's a very good chance it will want to escape. Again, this structure should prevent that. The other Durupinen will be standing by with Castings designed to, uh... *encourage* your spirit to return to your body. Even if things go badly, we should be able to get your two halves back together again."

"Great," I said again, although this time my voice was so faint that I almost couldn't hear myself. I refocused myself and asked, "What can I expect if it does go well? How will I know if I can really Walk without endangering myself?"

"You will continue to feel the pull from your physical body; it will act as a sort of root for you—although you will roam, you will also know where you belong. In theory, you will feel the pull of your living form more powerfully than the pull of the Gateway. At least that's what the scrolls tell us. We have several firsthand accounts of what the experience is meant to be like, in addition to all we've gleaned from Irina's gibberish."

"She talked to me a bit about it," I said, thinking back with mild horror to my introduction to Irina. "I think, with a little encouragement, she might be able to tell me more."

"There is one thing you should know," said Ileana, refusing to meet my eye. She ran a soot-blackened finger along the inside rim of her pipe.

"Oh, I think there's more than one thing I need to know," I said. "But which one are you talking about?"

"The Casting for the moment of parting," Ileana said. "We don't have the full instructions in our possession."

My heart shuddered. "Isn't that pretty much the most important part?"

"It's crucial, yes," Ileana said with a grim smile. "We know all of the materials the Casting requires, but it will be up to Irina to show you the rest. We possess none of the words to be recited—if indeed there are any—and we don't know the steps required to achieve the parted state. You must find a way to coax it all from Irina, if you can."

I couldn't help it: I turned right around and heaved the very last of my breakfast into the nearest bush. Ileana didn't seem to care in the slightest. She watched me with detachment until I had wretched myself into silence, and went on. "We've prepared the necessary materials for you. This way."

I followed Ileana across the Circle to a table where the other Durupinen were poring over heaps of scrolls and books. Many of their texts looked as old as the ones at the library in Fairhaven; even in my current situation, my inner bookworm sent up a quiet, yet fervent prayer, hoping that the fire hadn't decimated Fairhaven's irreplaceable collection. I shook my head to refocus myself.

"This is Flavia," said Ileana, gesturing to the woman with three nose piercings who sat nearest me. Flavia looked to be about twenty-five; her long black hair, shaved close to her scalp on one side, hung down her shoulder in a heavy braid. Her eyes swam at me from behind a pair of magnifying goggles, which she pushed up onto her forehead to better focus on me.

"Flavia is our newest but most prolific Scribe. Her special field of study is obscure and antiquated Castings. We planned the set-up of the Circle based largely on her research," Ileana said.

"I'll only take credit if it actually works," Flavia said to Ileana in an unusually soft-spoken voice. She smiled very gently at me. "I've done my best. This is fairly uncharted territory."

"Thank you," I said.

"Certainly. Let me show you what we have for you," said Flavia, sliding out from behind the table. The other two Scribes, both much older, didn't even look up.

"The earliest writings about these Castings describe in great detail the preparation of materials, so we have a really good handle on how to start. The Casting utilizes a double Circle, which we've already taken care of. It has to be cleansed by burning sage and lavender, and all other residual spirit energy needs to be expelled. It seems that this cleansing, and the double Circle itself, will not be necessary as your Walking abilities progress, but for the first attempt you do need the spiritual space to be as empty as possible."

"Is it okay for Irina to be in there?" I asked, looking at her properly for the first time. Irina was still in chains. She appeared to be asleep.

"We think so. There is mention in the early writings about the helpfulness of a guide who can instruct in the Walking process. That guide would need to be within the sacred space in order to interact with you once you have parted company with your body."

"Okay then," I said, as my eyes fell on a row of bracelets on the tabletop. "Are those for me, too?"

"Yes," said Flavia, picking up a bracelet and laying it into my upturned palm. "These are the most important element of the Walking process. No matter how skilled of a Walker you become, you will always need one of these to perform the act. It's called a Soul Catcher."

"These are what Irina has been making for herself," I said, turning the bracelet over and examining the knots; there were seven in all, each of which looked both unique and complex. "She was weaving them out of hair that she'd been pulling out of her head."

"Yes," Flavia said sadly. "Soul Catchers are not generally made from hair, of course, but that was all Irina could get her hands on. We've woven these from hemp. They're exact replicas of the only known illustration of a Soul Catcher we have, which we found in a scroll from pre-medieval times." Flavia's voice flared just for a moment with a touch of academic excitement, and I could tell that she was restraining herself—for my benefit—from completely geeking out over all of this.

"Why do I need so many?" I asked.

"You don't... at least not today. Today you only need one. Each time you Walk, you will need to use one as a part of the Casting that separates soul from body. We've simply made a stock for you, so you don't have to make them yourself—you can just focus on practicing. But eventually you'll need to make your own, when you've exhausted this supply."

I looked at the eleven Soul Catchers remaining on the table; I desperately, desperately hoped that I'd get the chance to use them all.

"So how do I use them?"

Flavia's gentle smile faded away. "That's the biggest gap in our knowledge," she said. "We don't have the exact steps for the Casting itself. We know that Irina knows them, because she has successfully Walked many times and still continues to make attempts. You'll need to coax the right words out of her to complete the Casting. More generally, though, I can tell you that you tie the Soul Catcher to your left wrist and cut it away here," and she pointed to the space between the third and fourth knot, where a red thread had been woven in, "while saying the appropriate words at the moment you wish to separate body and spirit. The cutting of the Soul Catcher enables the separation and allows the spirit to wander free." She picked up a small pocketknife from the table and handed it to me.

I remembered how Milo had once described dying as cutting the ties that held him to this world, and how Irina had talked about cutting her strings and floating away. It sounded almost too easy, too pleasant, too... literal. Nothing so gentle and natural could end with a state like Irina's, could it? I shuddered as I clutched the Soul Catcher more tightly in my hand.

"So that's it? I just put it on, say the magic words, and snip, snip?"

"According to everything we have on the subject, yes," Flavia replied. "If you're meant to Walk, the ties that bind you to your body will be loosened, but should still root to your spirit—you should be able to return whenever you choose. Your body and soul should reconnect without trouble."

"That *should* is pretty demoralizing to hear right now," I said flatly.

Flavia's face crumpled. "I'm sorry, I..."

"No, no," I said, waving a hand at her. "Sadly, it's the only appropriate word at the moment. Is there anything else I need to know?"

Flavia shook her head. "I can't think of anything else that wouldn't overly complicate things for you." She gestured to the Soul Catcher. "Just put that on and get Irina to give you the right Incantation. The rest will sort itself out."

"What about getting back into my body?" I asked. "To be honest, that's the part I'm most worried about."

"There's nothing ceremonial about it, as far as we know—no Castings need to be performed. If you're meant to Walk, you will be able to reenter your body at any time, and the two elements will rejoin without a problem."

"And if I'm not meant to Walk?" I asked.

Flavia grimaced. "We will do what we can, through Castings, to help you. I can't say for sure if anything will work. There is no Casting I know of that can force the rejoining of body and soul, but we can bring the two together—in proximity, I mean—and hope your will to live is strong enough to bridge the remaining gap."

I laughed mirthlessly. It was a slightly hysterical sound. "I've been seriously questioning my will to live just by agreeing to do this."

Flavia reached out and gave my upper arm a friendly squeeze. "I would stake my role as Scribe on this going well today. You are doing a wonderful thing. Every source and every sign I've studied points toward the same conclusion: You are meant to be a Walker, and that ability is the key to salvation for our entire order."

I wouldn't have thought words from a virtual stranger could comfort me so much in this moment, but I found myself fighting the urge to fling myself at this woman and hug her. Instead, I smiled and said, "Thank you for all you've done to help."

As she smiled back at me, I had a strange, fleeting, déjà vu-like moment; I found myself imagining an alternate universe where both of our lives were normal, where Flavia was just the local young-adult librarian who read manga at the circulation desk and made great recommendations when I returned my books.

Maybe she sensed it too, for her smile turned a little sad as she said, "You're welcome. I'm only sorry you needed me to do it at all. Best of luck to you."

I turned back to Ileana, who had lit her pipe during my conversation with Flavia; Ileana's face floated toward me out of a sweet haze, as if it were materializing from a fog.

"Are you ready?" she asked me.

I gulped. There were no more runes to examine, no more questions to ask, no more scrolls to read: There was nothing left to keep this moment from coming.

"Yes," I replied, with a decisiveness I didn't feel. "It's now or never."

Ileana pointed to a space just wide enough to crawl through on the far side of the enclosure. "You enter there."

I thought about taking one last look at Savvy, Annabelle, and Milo, but I knew that whatever I saw in their faces would only weaken my resolve, not strengthen it; I kept my eyes trained on the dome's opening, and focused all my energy on forcing my feet to keep moving forward. There was an upsurge of excited whispering from the surrounding Travelers; it sounded like a strong breeze was rising up around me.

This was it, I told myself. "*For she will have the power of sacrifice to end all...*"

§

Silence and stillness met me on the inside of the dome; it was as though everyone and everything outside had ceased to exist. I didn't know why I found this thought comforting, but for some reason it calmed me. I didn't have to think or worry about anything beyond the immediate; in here, it was just Irina, me, and the challenge at hand.

I stood up straight and looked above me, where the runes hung like constellations. I felt comforted by their presence, even though I couldn't recognize half of them. The runes seemed to give order to the chaos of the crisscrossing vines of the dome's ceiling.

I tore my eyes from the runes and found Irina, still huddled in the fetal position, on the grass. From where I stood, only the back of her head and the curve of her back were visible, along with the dirty soles of her feet. I walked forward and knelt down beside her. I thought about reaching out and touching her, but I didn't dare. Not yet.

With the silence pressing in all around, Irina's breath, even and yet harsh, sounded abnormally loud in my ears. Her hand twitched in her sleep; I very nearly jumped backward like a skittish animal. Then my eyes fell on a row of at least a dozen bracelets woven from glossy black hair—the grisliest of jewelry—that adorned her wrist. I realized with a jolt that I still had my Soul Catcher clutched in my sweaty palm; I fumbled as I tied it securely around my arm. As soon as the Soul Catcher was fully fastened and resting on my wrist, I felt my pulse quicken beneath it, as if my very blood knew what was coming.

It was not easy to convince my hand, which was now shaking violently, to extend toward Irina's shoulder. I meant to shake her gently, but I never had the chance. Before I could so much as lay a finger on her, she jerked awake, her eyes wide and hyperaware the very moment they snapped open. Her lips lifted back from her teeth in a snarl.

"What do you want? Who are you?" Irina hissed.

"I'm Jess Ballard," I choked out from behind the knot of terror threatening to obstruct my windpipe. "I'm the—"

"The Northern Clans," Irina said, as recognition flickered to life in her eyes. "The girl who brings the danger."

Well, there was a badass nickname I had absolutely no desire for.

I nodded. "Yes. We met a few nights ago. Anca brought me to see you."

"They said you'd be coming here," said Irina, and she seemed to take in her surroundings for the first time. "They told me, but I didn't believe them. They never tell the truth, not to me."

"Well, they were truthful this time. I'm here, and I still need your help."

She simply stared, childlike, into my face, eager and expectant. She tucked her legs beneath her and clasped her hands together in her lap, waiting.

At least she wasn't leaping out of her own skin to attack me yet. I took that as an encouraging sign and went on.

"You say I bring danger. I want you to know I didn't bring it on purpose. It has followed me here, and I am trying to protect us all from it, including you—and especially my sister."

"What have they done to her?" Irina asked very seriously. I couldn't tell if she knew that 'they' referred to the Necromancers. Perhaps she thought I meant the Travelers, since they were the ones who had kept her locked up for so long.

"The Necromancers want my sister, my twin, to do something very, very bad," I explained. "She is extremely powerful, and they want her to reverse the Gateway and bring the spirits back to our human realm."

Irina frowned. "Bring them back? That cannot be."

"I know," I said. "No one should be able to bring spirits back. But my sister can—she's a powerful Caller, and I'm afraid that they'll torture her until she does their bidding. I need you to help stop them... and her."

Irina nodded solemnly. "We must not let her. The spirits are happy where they are. They're at peace. We must be sure they stay there."

"Yes," I said, relieved that Irina had understood so much of what I had told her; I had half expected her to burst into angry gibberish the moment she'd laid eyes on me. "But," I continued on, while Irina was still lucid, "I'm the one who can help the spirits stay on the other side. I'm the one who can make sure they stay happy."

Irina smiled at me, but it was a mechanical movement, devoid of actual happiness; I wondered if she, in her wretched state, could remember what it was to be truly happy herself.

"Well done, you."

A short bark of laughter escaped me, and Irina flinched. "Thanks," I said. "But don't congratulate me yet. I'm still not sure how to do what I have to, and that's why I need your help. You have to teach me to Walk."

As she had done when I met her in her wagon-prison, Irina became anxious the moment I mentioned Walking. Her fingers found the row of bracelets on her wrist and began to twist them in agitation. "I haven't done it. I've stayed here. I've stayed in the cage."

"I know," I said as soothingly as I could, despite my voice's trembling in fear. "And the other Travelers know it too. You aren't in trouble. In fact, they want you to help me; that's why they've brought you here." I gestured around to our surroundings. "They've made this place for us. They're standing by, just in case we need them. I need to learn to Walk—just like Anca told you—and I need you to show me how to do it."

Irina narrowed her eyes at me. "Are you trying to trick me?"

"No," I said. "No Irina, I don't want to trick you. See?" I held up my own wrist so she could see my Soul Catcher. "They made this for me, but I don't know how to use it. I know I need to cut it, but I don't know what to say. I need you to tell me what to say."

"Why would I do that? Why would I enable another to do what is denied to me?" she asked. She pouted, making her look momentarily like a small child about to throw a tantrum.

"Because," I began, as I smiled in what I hoped was a conspiratorial way, "they've left us alone in here. They've taken the Bonds off of you, Irina. You can Walk in here. See?" I gestured around us once again.

Irina took in her surroundings properly for the first time, noticing the specific runes in the space above us. Then she looked down at her arms and chest, from which the runes had been scrubbed away. As comprehension slowly dawned, her face lit up like the sun peeking over the horizon. She bowed her head a moment, taking a deep, satisfied breath. When she looked at me again, she was transfigured by her joy, almost unrecognizable.

"I'm... free?" she whispered tenuously, almost as if she didn't dare wish it to be true.

"In this dome, you are," I said, crouching closer and pasting on a grin. "You can leave the cage of your body, Irina, as long as you agree to show me how to do it as well. But first," I tried to keep my smile in place, but my fear was threatening to overwhelm me, "is there any way to... can you tell if... if I'll be able to Walk safely?"

She cocked her head to one side, considering me. Then Irina leaned forward and reached both of her hands out for mine. I extended my palms, and she grasped them with surprising force. Her fingers were cold and dry as she pulled me even closer. She stared into my eyes for one long moment. I tried not to blink as her fathomless eyes bore into me.

At last she said, "You can if you choose."

I nearly cried with relief. "I can?"

"If you choose," Irina repeated, nodding. "You are strong in soul. I can see it in the spaces behind your eyes. But you must choose. The choice is the hardest part."

"But if I choose to return, will I be able to?"

"Yes." Her expression turned momentarily skeptical. "If you really want to. But the other... it's wonderful." Her lower lip trembled as she spoke.

"I know. You keep telling me that." I pulled myself back together with a cleansing breath. This was it. "I want to feel it too. Will you Walk with me?"

It seemed Irina couldn't resist such an invitation. She looked around, but no one was visible beyond the barriers of the enclosure. "You must cut your Soul Catcher here," she whispered, indicating the place between the third and fourth knots that Flavia had shown me.

"Yes. That part I know," I said, with my heart beating so

160

frantically now that the rhythm felt more like a hum. "But the words! What are the words, Irina? What do I say?"

She beckoned me forward with the crook of her finger. "In the old tongue, and so that the spirits of old will hear you, you must speak it here," she placed a fingertip on my mouth, "and here," she moved it over my heart.

"Sínim uaim thar dhoras mo choirp
Ach an eochair coinním fós,
Bheith ag Siúl tráth i measc na marbh
Agus filleadh ansin athuair."[1]

As I fought to remember the words without knowing what they meant, a gust swept through the structure, whipping around us and tossing Irina's hair into a frenzy. Her face was now aglow with anticipation. Then, without another word, she bit through her Soul Catcher and her spirit burst forth; in the same moment, her body fell in a lifeless heap at my feet. As I watched it crumple, I was struck by the truth of it: Although her body looked the same as it had a moment before, there was nothing left of Irina there. Everything that made her who she was now soaring above my head. I looked up.

The joy. She was flying through the air like a bird, arms outstretched, her face alight with a happiness I could not comprehend. It was this, perhaps, that gave me the courage to take the Soul Catcher and the blade between my trembling fingers.

"I will choose to come back," I told those same trembling fingers. Almost like a prayer, I told it to my breath, my racing heart.

"Sínim uaim thar dhoras mo choirp
Ach an eochair coinním fós,
Bheith ag Siúl tráth i measc na marbh
Agus filleadh ansin athuair."

I cut through the Soul Catcher with a single decisive swipe.

---

1. I reach beyond my body's door and yet retain the key, to Walk awhile amongst the dead and then return again.

12

GLIMPSES

AND I WAS GONE.
   Or, I was really here for the first time; it was hard to tell which.

Gone was every physical sensation. There was no pain, no frightened fluttering of my heart, no connection to anything physical at all. It was an unfathomable relief that I never even knew I needed—as though I'd been in pain all my life without knowing it. Freed from my body, the "pain" suddenly stopped, and I felt what it was to be really, truly at peace. I was nothing but weightless, floating consciousness; I was completely at my ease in this small, quiet bubble of solitary contemplation. I did not see. I did not hear. I just... was.

Being completely stripped of my senses didn't disturb me at all; I found it natural in this state. I didn't need them to experience my surroundings fully. But as I thought of my senses, I thought of my body; as soon as I thought of my body, I found myself wishing I could see.

The moment I wished for it, I gained a sort of vision. It wasn't exactly like seeing things with my eyes, but I could see nonetheless. I took everything in, gauging my relationship to objects nearby. I was hovering very close to the top of the dome the Travelers had built to contain us. I knew I couldn't touch the dome in the way I had when I was in my body, but something about the energy radiating from the dome stopped me from trying to touch it while in spirit form. Even as I floated nearer to the dome's top, part of me wanted to cringe away from it. I focused instead on the space below me, where I saw a figure lying supine on the ground. It took a moment to associate that figure with myself: I knew it was my body, but even mere moments after vacating my human form, it felt entirely foreign to me. Was that really what I looked like?

Was my hair really so dark, my skin so pale and drawn? Was my face, so young in comparison to others, really that careworn and dejected?

I looked for a long time at my right hand, which was sprawled open in the overgrown grass. That hand seemed to be telling me that living was a sad and empty thing sometimes. I felt a twinge of longing: I wanted to rejoin with that hand, to re-fill that body so that it wouldn't be so empty, so alone.

"Isn't it exhilarating?" a voice said from nearby.

I tore my attention from my body below and focused instead on the spirit who was now hovering level with me. Irina was alight with happiness—her form had expanded with energy like an inflated balloon. As I watched, she soared around the enclosure, looping and diving and weaving like a stunt plane in an air show.

"Yes," I admitted. "It certainly is."

Irina looked as I remembered her, and yet she seemed entirely new, like a shining, rainbow-colored version of her human self. In this form, she was glowing and pulsing with unrestrained energy.

"You don't look like a ghost," I told her.

"I'm not a ghost," she said. "A ghost is an imprint, an echo. I am so, so much more than that. Imagine a spirit with the energy and vibrancy of the living, but unfettered by a human body. That's what I am. That's what you are."

"What do I look like?" I asked, more to myself than to her. I held up a hand before my eyes. It shone and gleamed in a spectrum of colors, pulsing and flowing, and an aura trail of light followed my fingertips as I wiggled them back and forth. I looked down at myself—or rather, at this new representation of myself. How strange it was to have a form and yet feel nothing physical.

But if I was up here, then who was down there? I looked down at my body again. It drew my eye with a powerful attraction, and I felt the urge to approach it, to study it more closely.

"Why are you looking at that cage? Forget it. Let yourself go!" Irina laughed, flitting about so fast that she seemed to be in three places at once.

I didn't think of my body as a cage, but when I was away from it, I understood how it would've been so easy, in that moment, to forget about its existence entirely, to abandon it down there in the dark blanket of grass.

"*I will go back,*" I told myself. But first I would feel what it was like to really Walk, since I'd gotten this far.

"Irina, how do I... move?" I asked. I had no real control over myself in this purest of forms. I couldn't understand how to propel myself through a physical space now that I no longer had a physical existence.

"You must stop thinking that you have a form which must be moved with muscles and bones. You control your movement with your being," she said, soaring past me.

"Do you think you could be a little more specific? I don't seem to be able to control anything with my being—probably because I have no idea what the hell that means!"

Irina actually laughed, and I saw in her spirit face the girl she really was, the girl she could never be again in her body. It was beautiful and sad at the same time. "You must will yourself to occupy each new space. Visualize yourself in it, and you will begin to move."

"That sounds like a lot of work," I said. "Couldn't I just float or something?"

"It's not work. It couldn't be easier. Just try it, Northern Girl," Irina sang.

I focused on an empty patch of air across from me in the enclosure. No sooner had I pictured myself occupying that space than I was there—with no clear perception of how I had moved. I tried again, this time focusing on a thick patch of grass below. Again, I found myself instantly upon it, and disoriented at the speed of my own travel. I reeled from a sort of mental dizziness.

"No, no," Irina giggled. "You must envision the journey itself, not just your final destination. You must imagine yourself existing in every step along the way, or you will never know what it is to fly!" With this, she soared past me in an arc, her arms spread like wings.

I gathered myself for another attempt, although I could already feel myself tiring. Or at least, I think I was tiring. If I were a light, I would've been dimming. My colors seemed to fade as I watched them. My eyes were drawn to my body; it no longer looked foreign, but inviting. It looked like my bed might have looked after a very long day.

"Should I be tired already?" I asked Irina.

She stopped rocketing around for a moment, although she

looked annoyed. "Yes. It is very hard, at first. Returning will perhaps seem easy this time, but do not be lulled into a false security. When you truly Walk, when you embrace it with all that you are, your spirit will thrive on it. That earthly body will reveal itself to be the prison it really is."

I did my best to ignore her admonishment. I couldn't worry about that now. I had work to do. If I couldn't control my path while I Walked, the ability was useless. I needed to be able to propel myself into the Gateway without getting tired or disoriented, or else what good would I be in the struggle ahead? I focused instead on the practical part of Irina's advice: I imagined myself occupying each step along the path to my next destination.

I started to move and then, quite suddenly, lost all momentum. It was too much. I'd already tried to do too much; I could feel myself starting to drift, without control over where I was. My form came to a slow stop in the air. As I hung, suspended, a terrible thought occurred to me, flooding me with panic: What if I couldn't get back to my body?

It wasn't physical panic, of course. I had no "physical" in this form—a thought that only deepened my nonphysical panic. Nonphysical panic was sort of a buzzing of the mind, a scattering and shaking of my thoughts. In my fear, I concentrated on the one thing that was anchoring me to the living world—my body—which lay immobile in the grass below. I envisioned myself not flitting around the dome, but back below, tucked safely inside the body I'd left behind. I allowed the vision to fill me, to spread through every shining, multi-colored particle of myself. As I concentrated, I wished—more fervently than I'd ever wished before—to somehow find my way back into myself. Then my body, as if answering my call, began to do the work for me; it seemed to cast out an invisible net and ensnare me in it. Whatever it was that tied me to my body was starting to tug and tighten, reeling me back in.

As I watched Irina in her glory, I both envied and pitied her; I knew that rejoining the two halves of myself would be a relief for me, but for her, it would be utter torment.

"I will go back," I said aloud as I imagined the ties that connected me to my physical self winding around me. "It is home," I told myself. "Home is where you return to."

My body moved closer—or rather, I moved closer to it. I could see tiny beads of sweat glistening on my brow, could see the light glimmering on the tips of my eyelashes.

We... I... connected. Reconnected.

I drew a breath that filled every inch of my being; I sucked the air in as if I'd been forced underwater until the very moment I could hold my breath no longer. I was awash with an onslaught of disorienting sensations as my five senses returned. Smells attacked my nose. Lights popped and exploded in front of my eyes. Every pore was afire with feeling. I was overwhelmed to the point of terror until I remembered that this was what it felt like to be alive.

"She's back! I can see her! She's moving!"

"Jess! Jessica! Are you alright? Someone get her out of there!"

Rough hands seized me and dragged me backward by my arms through the opening of the enclosure and into the soft, dewy grass of the clearing.

"Jessica! Are you okay? Say something!"

"I... I think I'm okay," I gasped with difficulty. I tried to remember how to focus my eyes, and Dragos wavered into view above me. Anca was beside him; her hair was hanging down around my head, blocking out the light. A poking and prodding at my arms and legs revealed a number of other Travelers marking me with runes in dark, dusty charcoal.

"What are they doing?" I asked, still panting as if I'd run a marathon.

"Protective runes, to make sure your spirit doesn't attempt flight," Anca answered. Her expression was already transforming from concern to wonder. "Aren't... don't you want to Walk again?"

"Not particularly," I said, watching as nearly every visible patch of my skin was marked by the women. "Hey! Watch it!" I cried, slapping away one woman who was attempting to lift my shirt so she could mark my midriff.

"Stop!" Anca demanded. "Stop marking her! She's... fine. She has reconnected."

I swatted another hand away and tried to sit up. My body was reluctant to obey my thoughts, and Dragos, seeing what I was trying to do, helped me into a seated position.

"We weren't sure how long to let you go, so we began the Casting to pull you back, but you returned before we completed it. Did you return by yourself?" Anca asked. She was still looking into my eyes as if she couldn't believe she was seeing me look back out at her from behind them.

"Yes," I said. The dizziness and disorientation were fading. I began to gently move individual fingers and toes, testing my control. It seemed to be returning. "It was exhausting. That was as much as I could do, for a first try."

Anca's face split into a grin. "It was miraculous."

A scuffling nearby drew our attention. Milo, Savvy, and Annabelle were struggling to get through to where I was sitting.

"Oh, I *know* you did *not* just try to expel me," Milo shouted, in full-on fierce mode. "I am this girl's Spirit Guide, do you hear me? And you will let me do some guiding or I will haunt your ass until doomsday!"

I grinned even more widely than Anca. "Let them through, please," I called.

The protective circle of Travelers that had formed around me broke apart as Milo blasted through them, with Annabelle and Savvy right on his heels. Annabelle looked pale and shaken, and Savvy's mascara was smudged suspiciously under her red-rimmed eyes, but Milo was smiling from ear to ear.

"Atta girl!" he said when he reached me. "I knew you'd be a natural. Never doubted it for a second."

I smiled back. "I couldn't let you have all the spirit-form fun. Now I can annoy you even without a body to dress in clothes you hate."

He chuckled gleefully. "No worries, sweetness, I'll just find something else to rag on you about."

It was the first time he'd ever used his signature pet name on me, and I didn't take it lightly. He winked, as though to say he'd meant it.

"Blimey, Jess, that was... well, I'm glad you're back—you gave us all a bloody heart attack," Savvy said tremulously.

Annabelle managed a smile. "Well done. Truly."

"I must agree. Well done, indeed." Ileana appeared as the Travelers parted for her—and her trail of pipe smoke—like the Red Sea. "What brought you back? We didn't need to force you, I see."

"No, I wanted to come back."

"Wanted to? You mean you could feel the connection to your body?"

"Yes. I was free of it, but I could always sense it there. It was still connected to me."

Ileana flashed a wide, gold-toothed smile with an approving nod. "The Prophecy did not lie. You are truly meant to do this. Perhaps one Durupinen in a century could exist in spirit form and actually want to return. It was always a struggle, even in the earliest days, for Irina to return. That was a shorter Walk than I expected, though. Why did you return so quickly?"

"Walking is... well, I couldn't do it for very long, at least not this time. It takes a lot of energy. Irina said it would get easier; she certainly had no trouble with it. But it's going to take some practice before I'm good enough to do anything useful."

"Well then, practice you shall have," Ileana pronounced. "This structure and all the assistance we can give to you are yours, until you feel ready to Walk on your own. Our Scribes will continue to search for anything that might assist you."

"Great," I said, as a wave of exhaustion worked its way from my soul into my body, making both feel as though they were suddenly made of lead. "I'm going to need all the help I can get. And speaking of help," I glanced back at the enclosure, inside which Irina was probably still rocketing around like an escaped firework, "what are you going to do about her?"

"Do you still require her assistance?" Ileana asked.

"Yes, definitely."

"Then we will keep her there, inside the enclosure, until you no longer need her."

I continued to watch the cage; I was almost sure I could sense Irina gleefully flitting about.

"And then?"

"Then she will need to return to her body," Ileana replied.

"She won't go voluntarily, I can tell you that right now," I said.

"We are prepared to assist her."

"To force her, you mean."

Ileana eyed me beadily. Her silence was answer enough.

"It seems so cruel," I said. "Can't you just... let her go?"

"No," Ileana shot back. "It wouldn't be right or safe. She is much more of a danger to all of us if she's allowed to roam free. I assure you, after Walking for all these years, she is a formidable force. She has long since forgotten her allegiance to the Durupinen. She fears and hates us now; I cringe to think what she would do if she were free of us forever."

"I know," I said. "I just hate to think of her like that again."

Ileana looked into the enclosure at Irina's abandoned body; her expression, though resigned, was not unkind. "As do I. I knew Irina before she became what she is now. She was a great and powerful woman once. It gives me no pleasure to keep her caged like an animal, but there is no other way—especially if the Necromancers are looking for you."

"So when my practice is over..."

"She will return to the existence she led before you came. She cannot ultimately be free until death, but she will never truly die if her body lies abandoned and un-aging. It's regrettable, but not all that we regret can be changed."

I nodded; as I did so, I thought about Evan, and Pierce, and my mother, and even Lucida. Some regrets linger; we simply had to learn to live with them.

13

CONNECTION

OR THE NEXT FOUR DAYS, I WALKED.
Each morning I entered the enclosure and braced myself for the weightlessness, the disorientation, and the deep discomfort that came as I started to feel a little too wonderful being freed from my body. As far as my ability to move around was concerned, the second day was no better than the first. Within minutes I was utterly drained and had to return to my body out of sheer necessity.

Each time after I Walked, I staggered back to our wagon and slept for hours. Each time I awoke with a pounding headache and an odd tingling sensation all over, like pins and needles throughout my whole body. This sensation lasted until the next morning, when I would achieve total relief when I started Walking again.

"I think I know why Irina hates reconnecting so much," I grumbled after several days of this. "Being back inside my body is definitely uncomfortable. Not that I'm complaining, really. It's better than the alternative of not being able to return at all."

Flavia, who was taking volumes of notes on my experiences, nodded thoughtfully. "The ties that connect you to your body are being stretched to their limits. The more you stretch them, the easier it will get, just like with any type of exercise." A ballpoint pen bounced against her lips as she spoke.

"I hate exercise," I said, rubbing my throbbing temple.

She bent over her notebook again, as though my hatred of exercise was worthy of note. "And how was moving around this time? Any better?"

"Not really. Irina keeps telling me that I'm not letting go, but she won't elaborate on what that means, so I can't fix it." I picked up the glass of water someone had brought for me and drained

171

most of it in one gulp. "To be honest, Irina's not very interested in helping me now that she's free. The problem is that she's going to get bored inside the dome really soon. I can already see her testing its edges, looking for places she might be able to sneak through undetected."

"There are none," Flavia said flatly. "I've been over every inch of that space, and there's no way for her to get out, as far as I can tell."

"Well, that won't stop her from trying." I glanced back at the structure; I could sense Irina's blithely soaring form within. "I just hope I can squeeze a little more information out of her before she starts ignoring me completely."

Speaking of ignoring me completely, it had been nearly a week and there was still no sign of Finn. Ileana's Trackers were supposedly on the watch for him, but he had vanished as completely as Hannah, who they still had no leads on. I asked Ileana about both of them every day, and every day her answer was the same, "We continue to search with every resource at our disposal."

Each day, I bit back the observation that, perhaps, the Travelers just didn't have enough resources. Milo was absolutely beside himself with worry; I wasn't sure how long I'd be able to keep him from doing something desperate.

I was feeling pretty desperate myself. I lay awake at night, torturing myself with images of what the Necromancers might be doing to Hannah. And whenever I could tear my brain away from that, I replayed my last argument with Finn over and over in my mind until I was positively writhing with hot, bubbling guilt, while cringing in fear over what might've happened to him.

I knew that wherever Finn was now and whatever he was doing, my actions had driven him there. What if he'd gone looking for Hannah on his own and the Necromancers had captured him as well? What if they were torturing him for information about where I was hiding, like they'd done to Pierce? Given Finn's Caomhnóir training and his general stubborn streak—a stubborn streak that rivaled my own—I trembled to think what he would endure before he would divulge even the smallest clue.

Now that I'd managed to Walk without serious consequence, my stubbornness wanted to find Finn just so I could shout, "I told you so!" at him. If he'd only listened to me. If he'd just had a little bit of faith that I could make the right decision on my own, without his hovering over me like a dark cloud of primitive patriarchy. But no, he had to storm off in a fit of rage, and now who knew if we'd ever see him again.

As frightened as I was for Finn, it angered me even more when I realized that he might be choosing—of his own accord—not to return. It might've actually been his own choice to stay away, without so much as a word about his safety, leaving us to stew in worry and fear. In some ways, that thought was even worse than the thought of his being captured by the Necromancers.

As it turned out, I wasn't the only one worried about Finn's absence. Ileana and the other Travelers helping me to Walk were concerned as well, although not exactly for the same reasons.

"We need to discuss your protection," Ileana said after my fourth attempt at Walking. It had gone better than the previous one; I had managed to cross from one end of the enclosure to the other in one fluid, controlled movement. I had also managed to return to my body without feeling so completely and utterly drained.

Ileana now stood over me as I sat on the border of the clearing with Flavia; Flavia was scribbling down a transcript of my experiences, and I was sipping water and attempting to regain my bearings in my body—it was a bit like acquiring sea legs.

"What about my protection?" I asked.

"It's traditional for the Gateway's Caomhnóir to stand guard over the Durupinen's body while she is Walking. I say *traditional* for lack of a better word, since of course we know there's nothing traditional about this situation. Nonetheless, the scrolls tell us that a Durupinen's body is left vulnerable to attack while Walking. Having your Caomhnóir present limits the chances of the body being harmed or tampered with while it's incapable of defending itself."

"But my body isn't in any danger while we're here practicing like this," I replied.

"Perhaps not," Ileana conceded. "But as you say, we are practicing. It's important for us to consider and prepare for all possibilities. When the time comes for you to Walk in fulfillment of the Prophecy, your body is likely to be at risk. If your Caomhnóir is truly lost, we must make other arrangements for safeguarding your body. Not doing so would be foolish in the extreme."

"That makes sense, I guess," I said, fixating a bit on the word *lost* and all the unknowns those four little letters contained. "What do you suggest, since Finn is... not back yet?"

"It's time for your Spirit Guide to take a greater role in your protection," Ileana declared.

"Is that why I'm waiting over here?" came Milo's impatient voice as he instantly appeared beside us. "Anca said you wanted me for something."

"Yes," Ileana said. "Flavia will explain."

With an excited flurry that reeked of academic fervor, Flavia looked up from her notes and spoke.

"The Walker's body is protected by the Soul Catcher's Casting from outside spirit invasion. Other spirits cannot leap into the body and take it over while it is abandoned. Think of the Soul Catcher as a key to two doors; it opens the front door so that the soul can Walk, but it also locks the back door so that no other soul can enter. The Spirit Guide is the single exception to that rule."

"You mean I could still get in?" asked Milo, perking up with interest.

Flavia nodded and held up an ancient book, where a curling, yellowed page bore a diagram of a spirit entering a body. "Yes. As her Spirit Guide, your connection enables you to occupy the space inside Jess's empty body, and even control it in her absence. So if the body were in jeopardy, for instance, you could move it."

"And if it were the victim of ill-advised fashion choices, I could give it a makeover?" Milo asked brightly.

Flavia just stared at him for a moment, then turned to her book almost as if she were concerned about having missed a paragraph on fashion and Walking.

"Ignore him," I said. "He's joking."

"You wish," said Milo, flashing a huge smile and waggling his eyebrows at me.

Flavia looked back and forth between us, unsure of how to proceed.

"That's enough foolishness," Ileana said sharply from behind her pipe's smoke. The fumes wafted straight through Milo, causing him to float back in disgust. "Go on please, Flavia."

"Right," said Flavia, trying to pick up her lost thread of thought. "Well... the Spirit Guide can act as a protector in this way. So in the absence of your Caomhnóir, we thought we ought to teach your Spirit Guide how to practice Corporeal Habitation."

A faint bell went off in my brain. This was something I already knew about.

"We've done it," I said, looking at Milo.

"We have?" he asked, raising his eyebrows.

"You have?" Flavia gasped in similar surprise.

"Yes," I replied. "I realize we're navigating in uncharted territory here, but I did manage to pay attention to the little bit of training we received at Fairhaven, and we already covered Corporeal Habitation. Milo and I have done it."

"Remind me?" said Milo.

"When we snuck off campus with Savvy to go to London, remember?" I paused, then clarified for the others. "Annabelle sent a message to me asking me to meet her in London. We used Corporeal Habitation to sneak off Fairhaven's grounds because Habitation masked our human energy as we crossed the Wards."

"Oh right!" Milo cried brightly. "Why didn't you just say, 'Hey, remember that time we shared a body?'"

I ignored him.

Flavia looked impressed. "Did that actually work?"

"Yup. Savvy figured it out. She wasn't Walking, obviously, so she didn't vacate her own body, but we learned that a spirit can share our physical space, at least temporarily. As long as a spirit came along for the ride, the Wards could only detect the spirit, not the living person. Savvy made tons of excursions without permission, so she had lots of opportunities to refine her technique."

"Interesting!" exclaimed Flavia, beginning to scribble. Ileana, however, placed a wrinkled old claw on top of her pen.

"Let's keep that information to ourselves," she said. "I'd rather we didn't have the young ones trying to sneak away from the camp when we're within walking distance of a city. They get restless enough as it is."

Flavia seemed to shrink a little. She stuck her pen into her elaborate braid.

Ileana turned back to Milo. "So then, what say you, Spirit Guide? Are you willing to attempt this? It would strengthen our defenses if you could protect Jessica's body in this way."

Milo stopped grinning and became unusually solemn. "I should've realized this Spirit Guide thing would get serious eventually," he said with a sigh. "So... yeah, I'll do it. I want to help, if I can."

175

I very nearly opened my mouth to protest, but thought better of it. It was true that I didn't relish the idea of Milo being in sole possession of my physical person; in fact, the thought of anyone walking around inside my body—or of my body actually living without me—was repugnant. But Milo was already beside himself with his eagerness to help, and I hadn't forgotten his heartbreaking offer to close the Gateway in my stead. If Corporeal Habitation was something he could do to help me while also making him feel as though he were doing something to help Hannah, I had to let him try.

I just smiled at Milo. "Just don't cut my hair, okay? And no pink."

He grinned back. "No pink. Cross my heart."

"Do you think you're up for it now, or would you rather wait until tomorrow's Walk?" Flavia asked me.

I chugged the rest of my water and handed the cup to her. "Let's do it now. If this part is also going to take practice, we should get started." Milo nodded in agreement.

As I tied on a new Soul Catcher, Flavia walked us through the process. Once I was inside the enclosure and had vacated my body, Dragos would perform a Casting that would allow Milo to enter the dome as well. Getting Milo into the enclosure needed to be done quickly, and without Irina's noticing, since the Casting that would enable Milo's entrance might—for a few seconds—breech the integrity of other Castings on the dome. If this happened, it could be possible for Irina to escape before Dragos sealed up the dome again. My job was to distract her while Milo entered. Then, Milo would enter my body and attempt to control it. I would allow him as much time as I could. When I was too drained to Walk anymore, I would reenter my body, with Milo still Habiting inside, and we would exit the enclosure together.

"Have you got all that?" Flavia asked.

"Of course," I said, throwing a look at Milo and grimacing as I did so. "What could possibly go wrong?" I wanted to add that Finn would kill us for this, but I bit my tongue—this wasn't the time.

"A walk in the park," Milo agreed. "Ready when you are."

I crawled back into the structure, and noticed, once again, the energy the Castings created within. The very air weighed on me; it was a constant reminder of the many forces that limited my existence when inside.

176

"You're back so soon?" Irina asked. Her smile was so knowing, nearly smug. "I knew you'd soon enjoy it too much to stay away."

"It's not that, although I think Walking is starting to get easier. Ileana is angry with me," I lied, hoping my theatrical pout was convincing. "She says I'm not making progress quickly enough. She ordered me back in here to try again."

Irina laughed. It was a rainbow-colored sound that shattered and bounced around the space and fell like oversized raindrops onto the grass. "How nice to have someone else in trouble with me for a change!"

"Thanks for your sympathy," I said baldly. "Maybe if you tried a little harder to help me, I wouldn't be in trouble."

"Perhaps if you enjoyed yourself a bit more, I would be of more help. But I can't help someone who won't embrace Walking," she countered.

"Well, here I go. Let's see if I can have a little bit more fun." I recited the Casting and cut the Soul Catcher; I felt the fetters of my body fall away, and I heard the now-familiar dull thump of my body sliding softly to the ground behind me. As I floated away from my body, I fretted that—with Milo Habiting inside—my body might feel different when I returned to it… sort of in the same way your bed would feel different if you returned after a stranger had spent a week sleeping in it. The thought made my skin crawl, but I shook it off and focused instead on the task at hand: Distracting Irina.

I wanted to draw her eye away from the dome's opening to ensure that she didn't see Milo entering; I chose a spot as far from my body as I could and willed myself there. My movement across the enclosure was still patchy, and I felt as if I were riding a bumper car over an unpaved road as I propelled myself.

"What am I doing wrong?" I asked, looking around me. "This is the spot I envisioned, and I think I'm imagining myself along the path, too, like you said. Any pointers?"

Irina sighed and came to rest beside me, with the air of a teenager forced to babysit a younger, obnoxious sibling. "Do you really wish to spend your energy on such trifles?"

"What do you mean?" I asked.

"This," Irina said, as she waved a dismissive hand around the enclosure, "is not worth your time. You're destined to Walk the wider world, are you not?"

I hesitated. "I'm not sure. I think so. I'm still hoping I won't have to Walk at all, at least as far as the Prophecy is concerned."

"You cannot hope to truly appreciate the joys and freedoms of Walking until you are free. I mean entirely free, without the boundaries of this larger cage to confine you."

We both stiffened at a small but obvious atmospheric disturbance within our little bubble. Irina's chin perked up, and she raised her nose into the air like a predator scenting blood.

"What was that? Did you feel it?"

"Oh that," I said, keeping my tone casual. "Yes, they're adding more protections to the enclosure today."

Irina stared at me, nostrils flaring. "Adding protection? What else could they possibly come up with to keep us trapped? Every inch of this dome is crawling with runes to keep us here."

"Oh, no, not protection to keep us in," I invented wildly. "Protection from an outside attack. The Caomhnóir have intelligence that the Necromancers may be closing in on me, and they want to make sure we're protected if they find us."

Irina cocked her head to one side. "They want you that badly?"

"Yes, actually, they do," I answered, confident that this part, at least, wasn't a lie.

"What is it about you, Northern Girl? What is it that makes you so fierce and formidable?"

I shuddered. "Nothing. My sister is the fierce and formidable one."

"But they fear you."

"I'm nothing. It's Hannah they should fear. They might look at her and think she's just a helpless little thing, but they have no idea who they're dealing with."

A strange sensation came over me. It was as though a fog settled over my new form, fading the rainbow colors and dulling my razor-sharp perceptions to a sluggish, intoxicated haze.

"What's happening?" I managed to slur, but my question was lost to Irina's shriek.

"Who are you? What are you doing here?" she cried in indignation, while pointing a shaking finger at something far below us.

I turned with great effort and struggled to focus on what she was seeing. On the far side of the enclosure, Milo was crouching next to my body, with one hand extended into my chest as though he were caressing my heart; I knew that this was Milo's way of silently cooing to my body, trying to enter it gently.

Irina shrieked again, and Milo pulled his hand back; instantly my vision and thoughts became sharp again. Even as I frantically tried to find an excuse to explain Milo's appearance, I realized that we had discovered a potential problem: If Milo's presence in my body was going to cause my spirit form to become disoriented, that could spell trouble later on.

But that was a problem for another moment. Right now, Irina looked ready to attack Milo; her claws were already outstretched. I placed myself clumsily between her and Milo.

"It's alright, Irina," I said, as calmly and reassuringly as I could. "That's just Milo. He's my Spirit Guide, and he's part of the protection I was talking about."

"Spirit Guide?" She glared at Milo like she didn't believe a word I was saying.

"Yup, that's me," Milo said. "Just your friendly neighborhood Spirit Guide. Nice to meet you."

Irina totally ignored him and turned back to me. "But he's a spirit! What's he doing in here? How did he get in? I've been over every inch of this place. They've completely Warded it!"

"I'm not sure. The others must have let him in somehow," I lied, shrugging in an offhanded way.

"But then," continued Irina, lighting up like a firework, "if he's gotten in... there must be a way out!" She began to rocket around so fast that she was merely a blur, pausing only to probe at various points on the dome.

"I don't think so," I said, dizzy from watching her manic, desperate attempt. "They're pretty determined to keep us in here. I don't think they'd allow any loopholes."

"But then, how will he get out again?" she moaned, as she crept along the bottom edge of the dome, as if she'd dropped something irreplaceable in the grass. She turned a mad-eyed, feral look on Milo, who jumped back in alarm. "Do you intend to stay here forever, Spirit Guide?"

"No, not forever," Milo said quietly as he looked to me for help.

"Well then," Irina began—and in the space of half a second she was almost offensively close to Milo's face— "you're the one I ought to cozy up to, aren't you? Because when you go, I'm going, too."

"I... well, that's not exactly how it works," Milo stuttered.

Even as I rushed to help him, a part of me was amused to see him so clearly intimidated by Irina. His usual level of sass meant he was typically very hard to intimidate.

"Irina, he's not going out as a spirit. You won't be able to leave with him."

Irina turned to me and barked, "What do you mean? What other form could he take?"

But I couldn't answer. Milo had finally snapped out of his panic long enough to do what he was supposed to do, and was now vanishing into my body. I was overcome with the same dizzying sensation as before, but this time it was so powerful that I hardly knew where I was or how to regain my bearings.

I tried to focus and saw my own eyes staring back at me.

It was probably good that my vision was hazy, or I might have panicked completely. There was my face, but not as I was used to seeing in a reflection. Although the features were familiar, something alien was staring out at me from my own eyes, and some other person's expression twisted my mouth. That person chuckled, and I heard his voice wrapped in the cloak of my own.

"Wow. So this is what it's like to be you, huh?" said Milo from behind the timbre of my own voice. "No offense, but it feels really weird."

I tried to respond, but I could hardly force my spirit form to create the words. I also couldn't hear myself think; Irina was absolutely beside herself, screaming at the top of her lungs in confusion.

"Impossible!" she was shrieking. "The Walker's body is protected from possession. What is this witchcraft? What are you? How are you doing that?"

Milo, who seemed a little braver now that my skin stood between us and him, addressed Irina. "Calm down, would you? I'm her Spirit Guide, remember? It's one of the perks of the job." Then, lifting an arm clumsily in front of his—my—face, he said, "It's hard to move you. It's like I forgot how to drive one of these things."

"It'll come back to you," I stammered. "Just hurry up and get it—me—uh, my body—across to the entrance so we can get out of here."

"Are you okay?" Milo asked, clearly alarmed at the disorientation I was exhibiting.

"I can't think or see straight when you're in there. So just hurry up," I said again.

Irina was trilling something in her terrified confusion. I made out the words "impossible," and "demon-spirit."

"Can't you shut her up?" Milo asked from somewhere nearby. "I'm kind of busy here." I watched as Milo attempted to move my body into a seated position.

"Irina, it's okay! I told you, he's my Spirit Guide! I know him! I trust him! Stop shouting!"

"What's her problem?" Milo said through my mouth, in my voice.

"She was taught that her body is safe from other spirits while she's Walking. What you're doing shouldn't be possible, as far as she's ever known," I explained, trying not to look at him. Watching my body move without my consent seemed to make the dizziness worse. Summoning all my strength, I moved away from Milo—me—and closer to Irina, who was now skittering around the far side of the enclosure like a bird trapped behind glass.

"Irina, he's just practicing, do you understand? Listen to me! We're connected, and that's why he's able to enter my body. No other spirit could do it. He needs to practice, so he can protect my body if I ever need it," I said, speaking much more slowly than usual so I could concentrate on keeping the words clear. The slow pace of my speech had the fortunate side effect of slowing Irina down as she listened. By the time I had finished, she was sort of spirit-pacing side to side, with her eyes darting from my spirit form to my Milo-inhabited body. Milo was now clumsily attempting to stand my body up.

"I've never heard of this. You're connected?" she asked, her tone still skeptical.

"Yes," I said. "He's Bound to my sister and pledged as the Spirit Guide to our Gateway. Spirit Guides are the only exception to the Soul Catcher's protecting the body from Habitation. They probably never told you this because you don't have a Spirit Guide... it didn't matter for you."

Irina had slowed to a stop now. "What of your Caomhnóir? Why can't he protect you?"

The guilt and worry rolled through me in this new form, rocking me more deeply than I'd ever felt it before. "He's gone. We argued, and I now don't know if he's ever coming back. I can't count on his protection."

"Hey!" I heard my own voice shout. "Hey, Jess! Take a look! I think I've got the hang of it. Shit, this feels freaky!"

I chanced a look back at Milo and my body and instantly regretted it. I had only the briefest glance at my own figure, tottering and weaving like a drunkard, before my vision became clouded and blurred; If I'd had a digestive system, I surely would've emptied it heartily.

"Hurry up!" I said, though my words were barely distinguishable. "I'm really not feeling right. I seriously can't even watch you, it's draining my energy."

"Okay, okay. I'm walking back now. I'll tell you when I'm done."

Even through my blurred and fuzzy vision, I could tell Irina was laser-focused on me. "How is he leaving?" she asked.

"In my body."

"Then how are you going to get out?"

"I'm going in my body, too."

Irina laughed, although I couldn't see what was funny. "You cannot occupy the same body together."

"We can," I said. "We've done it before."

"Two spirits within one body? Can this be?" Irina whispered. She was now staring down at my body as Milo steered it across the grass.

"Yes," I replied, still disoriented. "Now please stop talking so I can concentrate."

Finally, I heard myself call, "Okay Jess, I'm ready for you. Are you okay?"

"I think so. You're at the entrance?"

"Yeah, I think I've figured it out. Let's get out of here."

"Thank God. I'm coming."

It happened before I could stop it: Irina looked from me in spirit form to my body with an intense, but unreadable, expression; then she streaked, with terrifying purpose, toward my body below.

"No! Stop!" I fought desperately to gain my bearings, to force my spirit form into motion, but I could barely bring my destination into focus. I watched in helpless horror as Irina tried to force her way into my body, which jerked and writhed as my mouth opened and screamed with a pain I could neither feel nor comprehend.

I gathered every particle of strength I had and launched toward myself.

I hit my body with a force that felt almost physical—though of course I had no physical form at the moment—and seemed to bounce off of it. My body was screaming, but it was not actually my pain, I realized; Irina's pain was manifesting in the screams coming from my body's mouth. And I could see her, faintly, as she pressed herself, again and again, against my body, as if battering herself against a door that was fortified against her.

"You can't get in, Irina!" I shouted. "You're only torturing yourself. Get away from here, now!"

"No!" I heard her moan, even though it was my mouth that spoke. "I must escape. I cannot stay here! Take me with you in this cage!"

"We can't!" I shouted as Irina attempted to fully break into my body.

Milo, muffled and struggling, shouted, "Get out of here you crazy bitch! You know how it works! You can't get in here, and you'll only hurt yourself—or Jess—trying!"

I shuddered and gathered my strength again—although what I was going to do with that strength, I had no idea. I just knew I needed to enter my body again. But how could I, when Irina was attacking it like this?"

"Milo, brace yourself. I'm coming back," I said.

"Just get us out of here!" he cried.

Irina's strength was fading. She knew it, and fought even harder trying to incorporate herself fully into my body.

I had absolutely no idea of what to do next, when a sort of soul-to-body self-preservation instinct kicked in. I concentrated on the space inside my body that Irina was inhabiting, and propelled myself towards it with every bit of power I had left. I felt our spirit forms collide, felt Irina being expelled from my body; in that same moment, I felt my spirit and body reconnect.

§

The screams ripping from my throat transformed from outside noise to internal sensation as my senses came flooding back. I stifled the screams at once, biting back my sobs as I readjusted to having physical sensations once again—readjusted to pain, to exhaustion, and to all the darker aspects of having a physical form.

I opened my eyes. Even though I was now back in my body, for some reason I was still able to see Irina's spirit form; she was a huddled, faded, flickering, heaving mass on the ground. She was paler than I'd ever seen her, and she seemed utterly unable to do anything but keep still and cry quietly. Her form was barely distinguishable from the ground on which it twitched and shuddered.

"Milo?" I asked—not aloud, but inside my own head. My head, which I now realized, felt huge and unwieldy, like someone had strapped a ten-pound weight to it.

"I'm here," he mumbled. "What the hell happened?"

"Irina's gone," I replied, with the response transferring from my thoughts to his thoughts almost seamlessly. "I forced her out when I entered."

"I... she... that was bad," he stuttered.

"Did she hurt you?"

"She hurt *you*, I think," Milo replied. "At least, I was feeling real pain, like when I was alive, so I think it must've been physical."

"Yeah, I still hurt," I answered, tentatively moving my fingers and toes, arms and legs, "but I think I'm okay. Wow, that was really... messed up. I can't believe Irina..."

"Jess, are you sure she's gone?"

I pulled my attention away from my physical inventory. "Huh?"

"Are you sure she's gone? I think I can still hear her in here."

I looked again at Irina's nearly translucent form on the ground nearby.

"Yeah, she's definitely gone. I can see her over there."

"So then who am I hearing right now? That's not you, is it?"

"Is what me?"

"The humming."

I stopped everything I was doing and listened hard.

"Can you hear it now? What is it?" he asked. Milo's voice echoed inside my head, blotting out any other sound.

"All I can hear is you! Shut up a second and let me listen!"

The moment we stopped communicating, I heard it—a tiny melody in the recesses of my head. It was slow and a little sad, like a nursery rhyme, and it repeated as I listened.

"Yeah, I can hear it, but... that's not Irina's voice."

"No, it's not," agreed Milo. "Wait... It... didn't this happen before?"

Milo was right. Without my realizing it, the tune was already stirring my memory: The last time we'd Habitated, Milo and I had heard the same thing—a faint, constant presence of another voice. This same voice. Singing this same little tune, in this same, oddly familiar way. Without knowing why, it made a lump rise in my throat and made tears spring unbidden into my eyes.

Our realization was simultaneous. I couldn't have said whose thought it was that first zipped across our consciousnesses, but it was Milo who spoke first.

"Oh, my God! Oh, my God, Jess, it's Hannah!"

I cringed as his excited voice bounced around the inside of my skull. "Milo, seriously, calm down! It hurts when you yell."

"Sorry, sorry," he whispered impatiently. "But listen! That's her, isn't it?"

With my heart now pounding, I focused in on the humming again while trying my best to block out all of the uncomfortable sensations I was still readjusting to. Sure enough, the more I listened, the more I was sure Milo was right: It was Hannah's voice.

"You're right."

"Of course I'm right!" Milo said. "Don't you think I know her voice? I can't believe I didn't recognize it the last time it happened. I guess I couldn't concentrate that night—I was too distracted by sharing your body. But that's her, I'm sure of it!"

"What do you think it means? Why can we hear her?" I asked.

"I have no idea. This Spirit Guide thing just keeps getting weirder and weirder," Milo hissed. "I haven't been able to communicate with her at all since they took her. I've been trying and trying, but they've blocked our connection somehow. It must take the two of us together, for some reason. And if we can hear her..."

He didn't need to finish the thought; the same light bulb flared to life in my own consciousness. "Try to talk to her Milo! Say her name, see what happens!"

"Hannah? Hannah, it's Milo. Can you hear me, sweetness?" Milo said in a quiet and tentative voice. The humming went on unbroken, except for an occasional sniffle. She was crying.

"I'm going to try louder. Brace yourself," Milo warned.

I cringed as he shouted inside my head, with every decibel

resonating against the inside of my skull like a clanging church bell. We waited a moment: Nothing happened.

After Milo's failed attempt, I tried. I shouted for Hannah mentally, then out loud. Finally, after a half-dozen attempts, we had to conclude she couldn't hear us.

"Now what?" Milo asked.

I glanced over at Irina, who was starting to raise herself from the ground.

"Let's get the hell out of here, before Irina unleashes herself on us again and someone has to perform an exorcism to get her back out."

"Good thinking."

With every muscle in searing pain, I crawled laboriously toward the opening. It was hard to move; my head felt as if it were full to the brim with sloshing, rolling water.

"Do you feel as shitty as I do right now?' I asked.

"I think this is probably the worst I've felt since I've been dead. So yeah, I'd say so."

I collapsed onto the grass just outside the enclosure. As usual, Flavia, Anca, and half a dozen Caomhnóir descended on me.

"Back up!" I shouted, raising my hands in front of me as Flavia reached toward me with a candle. "Everyone just back off for a minute!"

"But Irina! Isn't she…"

"No! She's still inside, and you'd better check on her, because I have no idea if she's okay. In fact, she's probably not okay, because I can still see her—and she doesn't look strong. Now back off, please, I'm trying to concentrate here!"

My voice rang with an authority I didn't know I could muster, and everyone backed away obediently. I pushed them all out of my mind so I could concentrate. The voice—Hannah's voice—was still singing softly.

"Okay, let's think here," I said—thought—to Milo. "Do you think we're hearing inside her head right now, the way we can hear inside each other's?"

Milo concentrated a moment. "No. I don't hear any thoughts, do you?"

"No. Just the humming. Let's see if we can hear anything else."

I felt our energy sync up as we both focused on Hannah's voice. Other sounds became audible around her. A high-pitched buzzing—perhaps a fan or an air conditioner? The steady ticking of a clock. A tapping noise, like a pebble being repeatedly dropped on the ground, or maybe dripping water. A scratching, like fingernails in the dirt.

"I can hear where she is!" I said, with hope bubbling up in me for the first time in days.

"Me too!" Milo said. "It sounds kind of echo-y, doesn't it? Like she might be in a basement or something?"

I focused again, and I immediately heard what he meant. There was a hollow quality to the sounds, and even her humming itself had a faint echo to it. "Yeah. She's definitely inside. It's sort of like one of the bigger rooms at Fairhaven, with the way the little sounds bounce off the stone walls."

My imagination, inspired by my fear for my sister, began to conjure images of dank prison cells and desolate castle dungeons. I felt Milo shudder, and I knew the images disturbed him just as much as they did me. As much as I would've liked to keep these thoughts to myself, I couldn't—my thoughts filtered from my mind across to his, like foreign waves lapping up onto his shore.

"Okay, she can't hear us, but we can hear her," said Milo. "What's going on?"

"It must be part of being Bound. Maybe you're like a bridge between the two of us."

"No one ever said anything about being able to hear each other in our heads!" Milo snapped. "What the hell? No one thought we might need that information?"

"Yeah, well they also failed to mention a prophecy that all but ensured our mutual destruction—so their track record on giving us important information is pretty shitty."

Suddenly, I realized the pressure in my head was starting to build; it was getting harder and harder to concentrate. "Milo, can you come out for a minute? I think I'm reaching my limit for how long you can stay in there."

Then there was a strange pulling sensation, and all the pressure lifted as Milo appeared beside me. He was barely visible, and he was panting as if he'd just run a fifty-meter sprint.

"Me, too," he said. "Wow, being inside you is no picnic."

I stared at him in shock; the absurdity of his innuendo, however unintended, was hilarious.

Milo caught my eye mischievously and started cackling. "Okay, wow... things I never thought I'd say to a girl."

I joined in his laughter, but it died out quickly as the gravity of what we'd just discovered hit us both.

"So this is it. This is our best chance to find out where she is," I said.

"Yeah, I guess so. All we need to do is tolerate the Habitation long enough to hear something that will give us a clue," Milo replied, nodding. "It's not going to be easy, though. I could feel it draining my energy."

"You don't look good," I said.

He smirked at me. "Please. I always look good. Don't hate."

I rolled my eyes. "You know what I mean. You look... depleted. We have to take it easy. We don't know what we're doing. We might even be hurting you."

"I know, you're right," Milo conceded. "Just give me a few minutes to recover."

We sat in charged silence, exhausted yet abuzz from the excitement of our discovery. I was vaguely aware that Flavia, hovering uncertainly a few yards away, was waiting for a signal giving her permission to approach me again.

"Did you notice," I said as my head finally started to clear, "that it sort of got brighter when we concentrated together?"

"Now that you mention it, yeah, I did. What do you think that was about?"

"I'm not sure, but I have a theory. We can already hear everything that's going on wherever she is. Maybe if we concentrate hard enough, we might be able to see something, too?"

Milo frowned, deep in thought. His form was beginning to brighten, as though he were catching his spirit breath.

"Sometimes, when Hannah calls to me, I can almost see her surroundings. It's like... I'm not really sure how to explain it; I can still see where I am, but it's almost like someone puts a filter over my eyes and there's a pale impression of her surroundings printed on it. I've never really thought too much about it—it's a natural part of our connection. So maybe you're right. Maybe if we can focus ourselves in the right way we might be able to see something."

188

"Do you feel up to trying now, or do you think we should wait a little longer?" I asked.

Milo looked down at the specter of his own hand, considering. "Let's give it a few hours. I'm still feeling sort of... weaker than usual. And besides, you've just been through a lot, too. Your body probably needs some time to recover, don't you think?"

"Yes, let's wait, then," I agreed. "But not tonight, though, or she might be asleep. We don't want to waste your energy if there's no real chance we'll get anything. We need to make sure we're taking our best shot at seeing some real information. As much as I hate to say it, let's wait until the morning."

Milo looked as torn as I felt, but he nodded. "You're right. Let's not screw this up by rushing it."

I motioned to Flavia, who scurried over. "We need to talk to Ileana," I said.

"What's happened?" she asked, handing me a glass of water.

"I think we might've found a connection to Hannah."

Flavia's jaw dropped. She looked in confusion from us to the enclosure. "But how..."

"I have no idea. But we need to tell Ileana, and anyone else who's been involved in the search for my sister." I chugged the water, flopped back onto the grass, and closed my eyes. "And then I need to sleep for about a year if we're going to try that again."

A breeze swept through the clearing, bringing with it the faint echoes of Irina's tortured sobs. It was, without a doubt, the most heartbreaking sound I'd ever heard.

14

MANIPULATIONS

T HE SAME STEADY DRIPPING. The same echo-y sound quality.

No humming. No sniffing. Only steady, slow breathing.

A dank room came mostly into focus, as if we were watching the scene through a rain-washed windowpane. The walls and floor were made of stone. High above, a narrow, slanted opening allowed in the room's only natural light, casting a long strip of relative brightness across the floor. In one corner stood a brass bed made up with a pale blue blanket. Two slender legs lay bent upon the blanket, and two dirty knees were cupped by slender, grubby-nailed fingers; the figure, although facing us, was balled defensively into a fetal position, which obscured her face. To the left, a small wooden side table held a tray of food and a glass of water. A single yellow flower, a daisy, stood propped up but drooping slightly in an old milk bottle.

I wasn't sure what I had expected from this Corporeal Habitation mission, but I was surprised when I realized that the perspective coming into focus wasn't from Hannah's eyes, but from Milo's—as if he were in the room floating off in a corner, rather than sharing my mind and body here with me in the encampment.

A door opened, revealing the bright light of the hallway. A man stood in silhouette, with his arms crossed over his chest.

"You've not eaten your food. Again." His voice was deep and gravelly.

"I'm not hungry. Again." Hannah's voice, although tiny and cracked, was defiant as she uncurled herself.

"Very well," said the figure as he strode across the room. He bent to pick up the tray, but froze at the sound of a second voice.

"Leave it, Simon. Our guest may change her mind."

191

"I won't," said Hannah as Simon turned and exited the room. Then I realized the owner of the second voice had been in the room all along, sitting on a stool in the shadows. It was Neil Caddigan.

His strangely pale eyes shone brightly beneath bushy white brows. His white hair was much longer than it had been when he first appeared in the Culver Library in the guise of an earnest scholar. He wore a long black coat over his dark clothes, and a silver pin gleamed at his throat. His hands were folded leisurely in his lap as he sat, apparently at his ease, on the wooden stool.

"Now now, Miss Ballard. You'll need your strength in the days ahead," he said. "I assure you the food is quite good. Simon is an exemplary cook. I apologize for the interruption, however. Shall we have that talk I mentioned?"

I was almost sure Hannah would curl up and shut Neil out again, but she turned and met his eyes.

"You're Neil, aren't you?" she asked. "I recognize you from the drawing Jess did, after you tried to run her off the road."

"How rude of me," Neil began. "I ought to have introduced myself straight away, although I see it wasn't entirely necessary. Yes, I am Neil Caddigan. I do apologize for my delay in coming to see you. I didn't intend to leave you without explanation for so many days, but I had other pressing business to attend to, and I'm afraid the Castings we used to subdue you took some time to wear off. How are you feeling today?"

Hannah glanced at the tray, where her food had congealed together into an unappetizing lump. With a swift, decisive motion, she kicked the tray, sending it flying off the side table; it crashed into the opposite wall. The little flower went with it; its petals scattered on impact.

Neil didn't even flinch. He chuckled. "And here I thought your sister was the feisty one."

"Where's my sister? What've you done with her?"

Neil raised his eyebrows, as if the question surprised him. "Nothing whatsoever. We don't know where she is—although we're searching, of course."

"And what about Milo? I can't connect with him. What have you done to him?" Hannah was clearly attempting to keep her voice calm, but panic was creeping in and driving her pitch upward.

"Your Spirit Guide is fine, as far as I know. We merely interrupted your connection temporarily, so that we could speak to you without his interference. I assure you... when we've concluded our business, your connection will be restored, and it will be as clear as ever."

Hannah hesitated, as if Neil's polite answers were throwing her off. "What about—"

Neil actually laughed. "Hannah, you needn't worry. We're doing everything we can to locate your friends and bring them here safely."

Hannah paused again, still seemingly confused by Neil's lack of outward animosity. Finally, she asked, "You're a Necromancer, aren't you?"

"Right again. Clever girl. You're better informed than I might've imagined, although I think I may still have one or two things yet that will surprise you," said Neil, as his smile broadened.

"I'm not listening to anything you've got to say. I know what you want, and I'll never agree to it. You're wasting your time," Hannah replied, a tremor shivering through her voice.

"Those are hasty words from someone who, forgive me, is very ill-informed about what I have to say," Neil said, wagging his finger at Hannah as if she was a disobedient puppy. "I've not asked you to do anything, Hannah, nor will I force you into doing anything that you do not readily agree to. I hope we can be clear about that, right from the off."

Hannah sat up a little straighter. "But... you've me locked in here! You kidnapped me!"

"Now now, *kidnap* is a harsh word. We did abduct you, true, but it was for your own protection, Hannah," Neil explained, as though this should have been abundantly obvious. "We have no desire to hurt you... or else, I assure you, we would've done so already. All we've done is ensure that the Durupinen now hunting for you won't be able to capture you.

"We've brought you here, and we've done all we could to ensure your safety. I realize these old castles are drafty and a bit antiquated in style, but we've endeavored to make your quarters as comfortable as possible." Neil gestured sweepingly around the room. "We've not tied you up, nor starved you—although you are making quite the valiant attempt at starving yourself." Neil paused and looked ruefully at the food spattered across the floor. "I do wish you would see this as a rescue, for that's undoubtedly what it is."

"A rescue? I'm supposed to believe you were rescuing me?" cried Hannah, her voice breaking. "You killed my mentor! Lucida is dead because of you, but I'm supposed to trust you? You're out of your mind!"

Neil, oddly enough, was still smiling. "I'm going to show you something. I hope, after you've seen it, that perhaps you'll be a bit more receptive to what I have to say." He stood up and walked almost casually toward the door; there was so much bounce in his step that he might have been whistling. He opened the door and crooked a finger at someone who was obviously waiting on the other side.

Lucida, flashing a dazzling smile, walked into the room. "Surprise, love."

"Lucida!" Three voices—Hannah's, Milo's and mine—shouted her name all at once. In our shock, Milo and I came dangerously close to breaking our focus and losing the connection to Hannah. But our desperate desire to know what the hell was going on kept us clinging to our focus, even as we fought to keep the vision clear and steady.

Hannah gasped. The gasp twisted into a sob, and then into a strangled, "Lucida! But you were... I saw you... oh, my God!" Then Hannah staggered to her feet and into Lucida's waiting arms, which closed around my sister and hugged her tightly.

"I know. I know, and I'm sorry, love. But I had to make everything neat and tidy for the Durupinen who came to investigate."

"But I don't understand. You were dead, I saw you."

"Not dead, love. You remember I told you I'd done a bit of Leeching before I came to fetch you? Well, actually, I'd done a whole bloody lot of Leeching. I stored the energy up, so I could heal myself when we staged the accident."

"Spirit energy can do that?" Hannah asked in awe.

"Yes, if it's done properly. Oh, Hannah, there are so many things that our power as Callers can bring to us. The Necromancers are the only ones with the vision to realize it!"

"I still don't understand. Are you working with them?" asked Hannah, pulling back from Lucida slightly.

"Now now," Lucida replied. "Sit down and listen. You trust me, don't you?"

"I... yes. I mean, I did trust you, but—"

"If you trusted me then, you can trust me now," cooed Lucida, stroking Hannah's hair. "Have I ever led you astray?"

"No. No, you haven't."

"Then listen to me, love. Listen to both of us," she said, as she stretched an arm out toward Neil, who had resumed his seat on the stool. He took Lucida's hand, gave it a quick squeeze, and released it.

Lucida began, "Many years ago, when I was just a few years younger than you, I discovered I was different. I don't mean that I was a Durupinen—I'd grown up surrounded by ghosts. I knew who we were and what my future would hold. I accepted it... I was *eager* for it... proud that I'd soon get my turn to protect our family secret. But when I was fifteen, my gift began to change. I had real power over the spirits I communicated with—I could draw them to me, and I could just as easily push them away. I could even exercise a certain measure of control over their actions. My mother was scared, and she brought me to the Council. And that's when my gift became a curse.

"The Council didn't see me as a prodigy; they saw me as a threat. Callers have always been linked to the Prophecy, and so I scared the living shite out of them. Before I could say 'Bob's your uncle,' I was ripped from my home, separated from my family, and all but imprisoned. They did tests on me, bloody *experimented* on me. My entire family was interrogated, and I was poked and prodded and made to dance like a circus monkey for weeks before they finally determined I wasn't the Caller from the Prophecy. As in, 'Oops. Our mistake. Move along.'"

"And then I was supposed to give the rest of my life to them. I was supposed to serve without question, to subjugate myself to their rules and traditions... and I was expected to do it with a bloody smile on my face. You ought to be able to imagine how I felt about that—I know your sister struggled with the same thing."

Hannah nodded her head. "I do. I do understand."

"I know you do, because they've done the same to you," Lucida said. "When my training at Fairhaven was nearly over, I began wondering how I could stand to live my life this way. That's when Neil found me."

Neil smiled in an almost paternal way at Lucida, although he did not interrupt her.

"The Necromancers had been keeping an eye on me, too,"

Lucida went on. "They knew what I was, but—unlike the Durupinen—they saw me as a blessing rather than a threat. One day when I'd snuck out to the city, Neil found me and told me the truth—a truth that changed the course of my life." And she turned to Neil, like a child awaiting a treat for good behavior.

Neil obliged by picking up the thread, and Hannah, now transfixed, turned to him. "You've heard of us through Durupinen history," he said, "but history, as you know, is written by the victors. We have been vilified through the ages, well beyond what we deserve. We've made our mistakes, yes. We've had leaders who got carried away, it's true. We've stood up for our own power and our own beliefs—and we've fought, and killed, and died in the name of our society. But the very same can be said for the Durupinen. This does not make us evil, although the Durupinen would have you believe otherwise."

"That depends on what your beliefs are," Hannah said, a hint of the defiance in her voice. "Fighting for what you believe in isn't okay unless you're fighting for good. You want to destroy the Gateways and control the spirits. You want to drag them back and enslave them. There's nothing right or good in that!"

"And here, my pet, you are wrong again. I cannot blame you," Neil countered. "I expected you'd be spewing this sort of rubbish. What else would they teach you but their own propaganda?"

"It's not propaganda!" Hannah cried. "I've heard the Prophecy. I've seen what you do to the people who get in your way."

"And what of the people who get in the Durupinen's way? What would have happened to you if you hadn't managed to escape before the Council had its way with you?" Here Neil paused, letting the question hang unanswered in the air for a moment. "But I'm getting ahead of myself. Let's return to when we found Lucida." He turned to Lucida and added, "Perhaps you'd better tell Hannah about it after all. I fear she and I are not yet good enough friends to carry on with this conversation."

"I'll never be friends with you," Hannah spat.

"Never say never, my dear," Neil charmed.

Lucida jumped in before Hannah could retort. "That night, Neil sat me down and told me the truth about the history between the Durupinen and the Necromancers. The Durupinen have always maintained that we exist to regulate and maintain the

Gateways—that we alone can open and close them, and only we can control the flow of spirits through them. This is a lie."

Hannah blinked. "A lie?"

Lucida nodded solemnly. "A lie, love. The truth is that the Gateways should be open all the time, so spirits can pass freely through them. The Gateways should be monitored, certainly, but it's not for us to decide when, or if, a spirit should seek rest. The Durupinen took this power and perverted it. They might've started out with good intentions in the beginning, but the purity of those intentions eroded over time. Surely you've seen it for yourself—the corruption, the blatant abuse of power. I've seen it... hell, I've been a part of it. But in truth, the Durupinen aren't entitled to the power they wield. They seized it, knowing full well that one day someone would take it back and set things right."

Hannah looked back and forth between Neil and Lucida, as if waiting for one of them to explain further. When they didn't, she asked, "I don't understand—who is supposed to take that power from them?"

"You are," answered Lucida.

"Me?" Hannah jumped back in shock.

"Yes, you," Neil said. "Why do you think they fear you so much, Hannah? They don't deserve their power. They've known this for centuries. They've known that one from amongst them would rise to claim that power for her own—and that the Necromancers would be the ones to teach her how to wield it. Their fear is not for the Gateways, or the spirits, or any other noble cause: They fear their own downfall, nothing more. Over the centuries, they've done everything they could fathom to thwart it—and destroyed many lives in the process. But they have failed. In spite of all their carefully laid plans, in spite of everything they did to prevent it, here you are."

"I... but I'm not... it can't be me," said Hannah; her voice was a terrified squeak.

"But it is," Lucida insisted. "It *is* you. Your sister's Prophecy mural—that's not you reversing the Gateway and allowing sinister spirits through. That's you *reopening* the Gateway, restoring it to its rightful state. And if the spirits in the drawing seem just a touch irked at the Durupinen after being cut off from this world for centuries, I think you can understand why, love. And just think, Hannah, just think what you could—"

"That's enough, Lucida," interjected Neil, placing a gentle but restraining hand on Lucida's shoulder; his touch extinguished the smolder of excitement in her eyes. "Poor Hannah has enough new information to digest... and we must let her digest it, if we are to move forward."

Lucida smiled and ran an affectionate finger down the side of Hannah's face. Hannah didn't smile back, but she didn't brush Lucida's hand away, either.

"You're right Neil," said Lucida. "We'll have time for all that. Nothing but time."

"Now Hannah," Neil said, "I understand you like books."

Hannah nodded warily, as though she thought Neil might produce a book and throw it at her head.

Neil did in fact produce a volume, but he didn't throw it; he laid it with great care on the bedside table. "I like books myself. In fact, as an academic, I quite revere them. I hope you will consider reading this one. It will tell you everything the Necromancers have learned about the Prophecy. It will also tell you a bit about what we stand for, and why you might consider working with us." Neil paused momentarily, then raised both hands as though in surrender and backed away. "As I said before, I will not force you. But knowledge is power, and I think you ought to well inform yourself before you make a decision, don't you?"

Hannah seemed to be trying to find something to argue with in this suggestion, but it was too logical. She nodded instead.

"Marvelous," Neil cried, clapping his hands together and then extending one to Lucida, who took it and rose from the edge of Hannah's bed. "We'll leave you to get some rest. And in the meantime, I don't want you to worry. We're doing all we can to find your sister and the others before the Durupinen do. We shan't let anything unfortunate happen to them if it's in our power to prevent it."

Again, Hannah nodded.

Lucida and Neil were on the threshold of the door when Hannah, suddenly and loudly, spoke up. "Lucida, would you... could you... stay with me a little while?"

Lucida, beaming, practically purred. "But of course, love. You need only ask, and you know I'm here for you." She slunk back across the room and flopped back onto the bed.

"And... do you think... sorry, but is there any more food?" Hannah muttered.

"Yes, of course," Neil laughed. His laugh was a silvery, slippery thing, and it sent a shiver up my spine. "I'll get Simon to bring you something as soon as he cleans this up."

Lucida turned and looked Hannah in the eye, and as she did, Hannah's eyes looked at once paler and brighter than I'd ever seen them. They were huge, like harvest moons.

"Now pet, why don't you tell me about—"

§

Suddenly, the vision transformed into a whirl of blurred colors and warped sounds. A loud *pop* ricocheted inside my skull as the last vestiges of the vision vanished.

I reeled dizzily for a moment, then realized that Milo, too weak to hold on anymore, had dislodged himself from my body.

"I'm sorry," he gasped. "I just... couldn't... do it... anymore."

"Where are you? Are you okay?" I asked.

"I don't know... I feel like I'm going to fade to nothing. Can you see me?"

I squinted in the direction of his voice, but I could make out only the faintest outline.

"Barely. Rest for a minute. Don't try to talk."

We both lay still for a long time, with only the sound of our exhausted breathing between us. Occasionally our panting was punctuated by one of my groans—my head was pounding from the prolonged presence of too many thoughts. For a moment, I was almost glad Finn wasn't around—if I told him what we'd seen, he would've been just as disturbed as we were.

We rested in the overgrown grass just outside of our wagon. It was dusk, and here and there around us, the Travelers began to light their lamps. It was like watching giant fireflies flare to life one by one. I watched the lights until they transformed from amorphous glowing blobs to clear orbs bobbing in the gathering darkness. Finally, Milo spoke.

"I think I'm recovering a little. That worked better than I thought."

"Me too. And we know Hannah's okay. For now, anyway."

"So Lucida's alive."

"Yup," I replied, shaking my head—a movement which I instantly regretted as the pounding increased. "I *knew* I never liked her. I knew it. She always had that attitude, like she was above everything Durupinen, like our troubles amused her, you know? And now we know why. She was working for the enemy the entire time."

"And to think I was actually starting to like her. Bitch is going down," Milo murmured.

"Do you know what the most disturbing part of that was?" I asked.

"That Neil managed to make himself sound like a benevolent savior, even after what he did to Annabelle and Pierce?"

"Yeah," I said, shivering even in the absence of any cold. "Not to mention that even I was half-convinced by the time he stopped talking. Like, I actually found myself thinking that maybe the Necromancers aren't so bad, like maybe they're just misunderstood."

"The guy's smooth, I'll give him that," Milo agreed. "He's done his homework on Hannah, too. He knows what a nightmare her life has been, and he knows he can spin it to make the Durupinen look like the ones at fault."

"He doesn't even have to spin it that hard," I said with a rueful smile. "I spend half my time thinking about how this whole mess is the Durupinen's doing. But then I remind myself of everything we've seen of the Necromancers for ourselves, and I can safely say the Durupinen are definitely the lesser of two evils."

"This... this is bad though, isn't it?" Milo asked. I looked at him, and his face—as pale as it was from the exertion of the Habitation—was clearly awash with worry. "I know Hannah's a good person. We both know it. But good people can only be abused and manipulated so much before they start to lose faith in things. If she has to listen to much more of that—"

"No," I said. "After what she saw them do to Annabelle? After Pierce?"

"She never knew Pierce," Milo pointed out. "I'm not trying to be harsh, but that man didn't mean anything to her. She only cared about him because of what he meant to you... and I'm sure Neil will be able to explain Pierce's death away. He's making the Necromancers smell like roses!"

"What about Annabelle? Hannah saw her there, stripped down and tortured. How could she ever just—"

"She barely knows Annabelle either, and I don't think Hannah's ever really forgiven her for luring you into London that night—it *did* almost get you killed. Plus, since Annabelle's connected to the Durupinen, Neil will paint her as the enemy, too. The more opportunity he has to demonize the Durupinen, the more reasonable his abuse of Annabelle will seem."

I opened my mouth to argue but closed it again. There was no point. He was right. I always hated it when Milo was right, but I especially hated it now.

"If he turns her, it's all over. This Prophecy is going to come down with a vengeance on everyone."

"I know," I sighed. "I just don't know what to do about it right now—in some ways that's scarier than anything else."

We looked at each other, with our fear bouncing back and forth between our eyes.

"We've got to tell Ileana what we saw," I said. "And I need to draw a sketch of the place where they're keeping her, in case it helps the Trackers find it. Neil definitely called it an old castle, but that's the only clue I remember. Did you hear anything else?"

"No. And I think I need to blink out for a while and get some beauty rest, afterlife-style, especially if we're going to try that again anytime soon."

"Okay. You rest. I can go see Ileana myself," I said, swaying a bit as I struggled to sit up. "I'll tell you one thing, though. I still think the Necromancers are the bad guys in all of this, but it sure as hell isn't as black and white as I'd like it to be. Between Lucida and the Necromancers, and now maybe even Hannah... the Durupinen are damn good at creating their own worst enemies. Hell, they might even deserve them."

15

SCRIBBLINGS

"**A**ND YOU ARE SURE THAT'S EVERYTHING?" Ileana asked. She was staring through a swirl of pipe smoke at the drawing and the stack of notes I had given her.

"Yes. I went over it all with Milo. That's every detail we could come up with between the two of us."

"And where's your Spirit Guide now?"

"He's resting. He's very weak. He couldn't even rematerialize over here, or he would've come too. Habitation takes a real toll on him, or else we would've maintained the connection longer, tried to find out more."

Ileana nodded but her expression was full of disappointment. I could feel my defenses shooting up around me—a sort of invisible shield, like the Wards.

"Look, we did the best we could."

Ileana looked up, saw the expression on my face, and pulled her pipe from between her teeth. "I'm not criticizing you, child. I know you did your very best, and that you want to find your sister just as much as we do. But I'm troubled by what you saw. Deeply troubled."

I bit my tongue, hoping she would explain further.

Ileana did not oblige right away. She handed the stack of papers to Dragos, who turned at once and exited the tent at a jog.

"How well do you know your sister?" she asked bluntly.

"I..." I didn't know how to answer the question. In some ways, I felt like I knew Hannah better than I'd ever known anyone else—discovering I had a sister meant connecting with someone in a way I'd never known was possible. In other ways, I didn't know her at all. "I think that question is more complicated than you might expect."

Ileana tried again. "Can she be broken?"

"She's already broken," I said, my heart swelling with a familiar, protective anger. I knew Ileana meant a different kind of "broken," but the word had triggered something in me that bordered on being irrational; I swallowed it back, but it didn't go easily.

I expected Ileana to demand further explanation, but it seemed she needed none. Apparently, even the reclusive Traveler Durupinen had enough ears to the ground to know a bit about Hannah.

Ileana amended her choice of words, and when she did, her tone was less harsh. "Do you think your twin can be swayed by rhetoric like theirs?"

"Yes, I do—but not because she's weak," I said, with the words tumbling over each other in my haste to defend my sister. "If anyone else had been through what Hannah's been through—if anything she's stronger than anyone. But she's damaged. They've damaged her. All those years of being tormented by spirits without knowing why. All those years of foster homes and psychiatrists. And the worst part is that none of it needed to happen. If only she'd known what she was, if she'd had someone to explain it all to her. She could've been alright."

"I expect that's exactly what Neil will say, if she still remains unconvinced," Ileana said. "What about you? How much of it did you believe?"

"I know what the Necromancers are. They killed Pierce. They nearly killed Annabelle. And if it hadn't been for Finn, they would've killed me and Savvy, too. You should've seen the sick, sadistic Casting they placed on the spirits they were using to imprison Annabelle. The spirits were—I don't know how to describe it—dismembered, or something. And I never trusted Lucida, not from the moment I met her. If I were the one they had imprisoned right now, they'd be wasting their breath."

"But you're not."

"No, I'm not. So I'd tell your Trackers to get searching, and fast."

Ileana scowled. "You're sure your drawing is accurate?"

I snorted. "I suck at a being a 'good' Durupinen, but I was drawing long before the spirit world hijacked that skill set. It's accurate. I promise."

Ileana actually smiled. "Very well. If that's all the information you have for now, you should head over to the enclosure. Flavia and the others have been waiting for you to Walk again."

"I don't think I can right now."

Ileana's thick black brows contracted. "What do you mean? Clarify yourself."

"I mean, I don't think I can Walk and spy on Hannah in the same day. Habitation is almost as draining for me as it is for Milo. It takes everything I've got to share my body with him and reach out to Hannah like that. I wouldn't last five seconds Walking right now."

"Hmm," said Ileana, as she reached almost absently between the bars of her raven's cage. She stroked the bird's glossy feathers; he nipped at her fingers, but she ignored him. "This is a daunting problem. I think you must stop contacting your sister, for a time."

"What? No!" I said, much more loudly than I intended. "How are we going to rescue her if we stop trying to find out where she is?"

"You have given us a solid lead. My Trackers can make much of the information you've provided, I'm sure. You should be pleased with yourself for discovering it. But your focus now must be on Walking."

"But if we can keep connecting with her, we might overhear something that gives away where she is. If we could just find her and get her out of there, we could foil this whole damn Prophecy before it has a chance to—"

"No, Jessica. It will not work like that."

"It's just Jess, actually," I snapped as my frustration rose, "and why won't it work like that?"

"Because the Prophecy is imminent, can't you see that?" Ileana retorted. "There's no question anymore about stopping it. It's coming upon us as surely as the sun will rise in the east. Now all we can do is prepare for it as best we can."

"So that's it?" I asked. "We're just going to lie down and let this Prophecy devour us? What the hell is the point of looking for Hannah if..." My voice died in my throat as a terrible thought occurred to me—a thought made all the more terrible because of how sure I was of its truth. It was like a dawn of understanding peeking over the horizon and revealing what once was hidden by the dark.

"Oh, my God. There are no Trackers out searching for her!"

"Of course there are," Ileana said with a dismissive wave of her hand.

"But none with any intention of rescuing her!" I had to take a long breath to control myself. "Oh, sure, you're looking, but you said it yourself—you aren't a large or powerful clan. You aren't going to engage with the Necromancers in any kind of battle, even if fighting means foiling this whole Prophecy and crushing it into a myth. No, that's too risky for you. So even if you do find her, you'll just watch and wait."

Ileana didn't respond, but instead sized me up with her shrewd gaze. I took her lack of outright denial as confirmation of my theory.

"That's why you're investing all this time and energy in my Walking," I continued. "You don't have a contingency plan. You aren't allowing for any other ending to all of this."

"It's not a question of what we will or won't allow. It is coming," Ileana said firmly.

"Yeah, it is—because you're holding the fucking door open for it," I shouted. "And you won't even risk a small confrontation to prevent it, but I'm supposed to lay down my goddamn life and hope that somehow—by some miracle—my sister might be able to do something to bring me back!" I laughed, although nothing in my life had ever been less funny. "It's no wonder the Necromancers persuaded Lucida to join them. It's no wonder they can make themselves sound like saints! At the slightest provocation, look at how quickly the Durupinen throw their own 'sisters' to the wolves!"

"Jessica, I hardly—"

"It's Jess. At least learn a girl's preferred name before asking her to die for you!" I spat. "I will not be Walking today. I'm not sure if I'll be Walking ever again, to be honest. Do us all a favor and don't come looking for me unless you have something worth sharing about Hannah's whereabouts."

I turned my back on the High Priestess of the Traveler Clans and stalked out of the tent, not giving a single damn about a word I'd just said—except, perhaps, to consider a few more choice phrases I would've liked to have hurled at her withered old face.

I stomped back to our wagon, wondering how long it would be before we had a pair of Caomhnóir show up to escort us out of the camp. How long would Ileana let us stay if I wasn't going to follow her rules? With enemies at every turn and nowhere left to hide, this ought to have been a major point to consider, but—upon further reflection—I realized that I didn't actually care: Let them chuck us out.

Savvy was sitting in the grass just to the left of the wagon's steps, which she had folded up so she could lean back against them.

"Oi, there, Jess," she called nonchalantly as she saw me coming. She had been bent over something in her lap, but when she caught sight of my expression, she hastily stowed whatever it was away. "What's happened to you? You look like you could breathe fire."

"What gave it away?"

"The smoke properly curling from your nostrils, that's what. What happened?" she repeated as her smirk collapsed into lines of concern. "Did you have any luck connecting with Hannah? What did you find out?"

I explained, as quickly as I could, what Milo and I had seen during the Corporeal Habitation, and then about my conversation with Ileana.

"So that's why I'm so pissed. The Travelers are laying themselves down like doormats and letting the Prophecy steamroll right over us all."

"Huh? You're not making sense, mate."

"Hannah. They aren't the least bit concerned about rescuing her. They're just counting on me to save the universe with my weird new out-of-body trick."

"Hey, at least you can do that trick. Can't hurt to have it as a backup, now can it?" Savvy said, trying to add a touch of reason into the madness. She reached an arm out to slap me on the back, but as she did so a small, flat something slipped from under her arm and into the grass at my feet.

"What's this?" I asked, looking more closely.

"It's nothing." Savvy attempted to hide the item by snatching it up and sitting on it, but I grabbed the corner of it and yanked it out from under her. "It's nothing. Don't—"

But I'd already recognized it. "Where did you get this?" I asked, as I looked wildly around the clearing with my heart now pounding. "Did he come back? Is he here?"

"No," Savvy said quietly. "No, mate, Finn's still gone."

"But where—"

"I found it right here," Savvy said, patting the ground at the base of the wheel, where the overgrown crabgrass was nearly knee-high. "He hung his bag right on that hook up there, so it must've fallen out when he grabbed his stuff and stormed off."

I looked down at the little black notebook; it was one of the many Finn habitually carried with him. Its leather cover had been handled and thumbed so often that the sheen had dulled away in places. Within its covers, the edges of the pages were frayed and curling together in wavy clumps.

"Just now?"

"This morning. I was putting out a ciggy and stepped right on it. The dew from the grass has seeped in a good bit, but it's still legible."

"You read it?"

"Well, not the whole thing," Savvy admitted, looking uncomfortable. "I didn't realize what it was at first, did I? And by the time I did, I'd already read too much, so... so I just kinda kept on going."

I looked down at the book again. How many times had I seen Finn writing in it, and how many times had I wondered what was so important that he couldn't wait to record it? A kind of manic recklessness overtook me: Maybe it was the anger at Ileana still coursing through my veins, or maybe it was a residual anger at Finn for abandoning us, or maybe it was even anger at myself for pushing him away, but something smoldering turned into a true flame within me. I suddenly didn't care that the book wasn't mine, or that I had no right to read Finn's writings. Somehow I felt every word in the book—whatever was in there—was owed to me. I pulled open the front cover.

Savvy reached out and flipped the notebook shut again before I could read even a single word. "Mate, I'm not sure you want to do that. I already feel like a knob for reading just that little bit, and I can guarantee you're not—"

But I slapped Savvy's hand away. She pulled back, looking shocked at whatever ugly thing was splashing itself across my features. She said nothing else, but she shook her head ruefully. Her warning only stoked my curiosity: What was in this book, this stupid book that Finn had pulled out in front of me a hundred times and scrawled in so intently? What was he so desperate to hide?

I opened the cover again and stared down at the first page, which contained twelve lines in tiny but incredibly neat handwriting. If

I hadn't seen Finn writing in it, I never for a moment would've guessed that his hand could produce anything so neat and oddly elegant.

If

If the wind could carry her to me—
Effortless, a leaf upon a breath of breeze,
Then I could catch her between my outstretched fingers.
If music could play the song of her,
Then she could float in through my ears
And root there deeply in the rhythm of my pulse.
If the early light of morning,
Could tip her over my horizon,
Then she could spill into the shadows of me.
But instead we stand, the breadth of a world between us,
And I cannot so much as endeavor
To extend toward her a single, trembling hand.

"It's poetry," I said blankly. My voice sounded as though I'd never heard of such a thing before.

"Yeah. Stop reading it."

I ignored Savvy and flipped open another page. I scanned the page, and then another. They were poems. All poems.

"So all this time I thought he was writing a handbook on how to be antisocial or scribbling hateful entries about how much he loathed me, but he was actually writing... this?"

"Yeah, mate."

"These... are poems. Love poems," I went on blankly.

"Yeah."

I didn't know what else to say. I was so thrown, utterly confused. Finn a poet? Finn, who could barely construct a sentence in a woman's presence that wasn't a veritable manifesto of misogynistic bullshit?

After a minute of my dumbstruck silence, Savvy mumbled, "People are complicated, Jess. And sometimes the ones that seem the easiest to read are the most complicated of all. It sure would shed an interesting light on why he left, if those poems are what they seem to be."

I looked Savvy in the face; she was smiling at me in the saddest way, but for some reason, this only made me angrier. Angrier because things were complicated enough. Angrier because I didn't have a shred of anything inside me left to give. Angrier because there wasn't a single free corner in my head to process anything else.

"I don't have time for complicated," I said, flinging the book back at her. "You can wipe that smirk off your face, because those poems have nothing to do with me. In case you've forgotten, Finn hates me. He practically had to be dragged kicking and screaming to his Initiation, and he's barely tolerated me since. And I hate poetry."

Yet even as I said it, the vision Finn's poem had painted danced through my overwrought thoughts and forced its way into my head. The poem burrowed in beside the anxiety and fear, making itself at home and entwining itself around the gaping, wretched question mark that was Finn Carey.

16

ONE LITTLE WORD

D ESPITE MY HAVING SCREAMED IN THE FACE of the High Priestess of the Traveler Clans, no Caomhnóir brigade arrived to kick us out of the encampment. No pitchforks, no torches. In fact, the Travelers completely left me alone the entire next day and well into the evening.

I was starting to wonder if we were being strategically ignored when Annabelle returned to the wagon after having an after-dinner walk; our dinner had been left on a tray outside by a young girl who had all but fled when we came out to get it.

"Ileana sent Anca for me," Annabelle answered, after I'd asked where she'd been. "Seems the High Priestess wanted the advice of a Dormant," she added, a little flare of pride in her eyes.

"About what?"

"About how to get back in your good graces," Annabelle replied with a grim, but knowing, smile. "Ileana knows she's alienated you, and the Traveler Council is in a panic. They're afraid you're no longer willing to Walk, and worried that Ileana has destroyed any chance at foiling the Necromancers. Ileana's afraid she's going to be voted out of her position."

Savvy snorted. "She deserves the sack, the old cow."

"So what did you tell her?" I asked.

"I told her I had absolutely no sway whatsoever over what you decide to do," Annabelle said firmly. "After all, I'm just an old gypsy fraud who once threw you and your pet fish out of my tent—then swindled your roommate out of five dollars."

I grinned slyly at her. It felt strange to smile, like my face had forgotten how to do it. "Well, that's almost true," I chided.

"Ileana's getting desperate. I told her that her best bet was to put her effort into finding Hannah. I know she's been meeting with groups of Trackers all day, so I think she's probably stepping up her efforts."

"Thank you."

"Of course. She wanted you to know that Flavia is in the Scribes' wagon and at your disposal should you need her. I also agreed to ask if you would consent to go see Ileana tomorrow morning. I told her I could make no promises, but that I would pass along the message."

"I honestly thought she would kick us out," I said.

"She's too scared you'd never come back," Annabelle replied. "They're not stupid, Jess, they know it's your decision. And don't be afraid to leave them hanging a little. They might be inclined to offer more help if they think you really might not Walk again."

"Have they still got the dome set up?"

"Oh, yes. Everyone is in position, ready and waiting in case you decide to show up."

"Hmm," I said. "Well, maybe I'll let them wait, at least until tomorrow. Milo should be here any minute. We're going to try to connect with Hannah again. We're not giving up on finding her, even if Ileana thinks it's pointless."

"Good for you," Annabelle said. "Let them squirm. But do be sure to update them in the morning, alright? No need to interrupt the entire clan political structure to prove a point."

"No need," Savvy interjected, "but making 'em sweat a bit feels damn satisfying, doesn't it?"

Annabelle nodded. "Very well. Oh, I almost forgot. Ileana is offering you a Caomhnóir for protection, if you want one."

The smile slipped off my face. "What? Why?"

"Because you don't have one here at the moment. And they know how precious a commodity you are," Annabelle explained. "So I suppose you can think about that, too, and let Ileana know tomorrow. Honestly, though, it might not be a bad idea. I know we're all hoping Finn comes back, but in the meantime, it's better to be safe than sorry, don't you think?"

I could feel Savvy's eyes boring into me. I ignored her and nodded at Annabelle again.

"Well then, I'm heading in. Goodnight, Jess, Savvy."

As Annabelle swept past us and into the wagon, Milo materialized with a tiny popping sound. He looked awful; he was pale and drawn, even for a ghost, and there was something lacking about his usual pearly luster.

"Hey, are you ready?" Milo asked flatly.

"I'm off, then," Savvy said. She stowed Finn's little black book in the back pocket of her jeans. "I'll let you two get on with it. Good luck. I'm off to hit up my cigarette connection."

As Savvy stalked off toward the main clearing, I turned my attention back to Milo. I bit my lip as I looked him over again. "Are you sure you've rested enough? We just did this yesterday. Maybe that's not enough time for you to recover."

"I'm peachy keen, jelly bean," Milo said with a wan smile.

"I can't believe you just said that. What are you, a bridge-playing grandma?"

"Don't sass your elders," Milo quipped. "I told you I'm fine, so I'm fine. Now move over in there."

I rolled my eyes and barely had a moment to brace myself before Milo expanded inside my skull like a mental balloon; I felt as claustrophobic in my own body as a commuter on a packed rush hour subway.

"You okay? It feels cloudy in here," Milo said. Once again, his thoughts transferred seamlessly to my thoughts; I was never going to get used to this.

"Yeah," I said. "I'm just tired. I'm not sleeping."

"Neither am I," Milo said snidely.

"Yeah, but the difference is that you don't sleep. Ever."

"True," Milo chuckled. "But I can't let you feel all tormented and misunderstood. It's not good for you."

"Just shut up and focus please," I thought-spoke. "With both of us compromised, who knows how long we'll have."

We both quieted down and found the place in our shared mind where Hannah could be reached. Now that we knew how to focus on her, it was almost as though she were waiting for us.

At first, the only sounds were a gentle sniffing and the occasional turning of a page; Hannah was reading, apparently, and seemed to be alone for the moment. We listened to the quiet of her solitude for a few minutes.

"Do you think we should pull apart and try again later?" I asked as Hannah's silence stretched on. "There's no point in wasting all this energy if she's just by herself reading."

"Yeah, maybe we should jus—" Milo began, but his thought cut out abruptly as a voice joined Hannah in her room.

"Hey there, love. Care for some company?"

It was Lucida. I didn't need the loud, echoing *shh* from Milo as we both focused in on Hannah again and concentrated for all we were worth. Hannah's room, with its stone walls and dim, slanting sunlight, shimmered into view.

"Sure," Hannah said, closing her old leather book. "Any word yet? About Jess or the others?"

"No, not yet, love. We'll let you know right away when we find them, I promise. I just hope we can get to them before Marion does," Lucida said as she stepped out of her signature four-inch stilettos. How she managed to maneuver over the castle's uneven floors in such things was a total mystery.

"I hope so, too. At least, I think I do," Hannah said. "Do you really promise me that the Necromancers won't hurt them?"

"Yes, I promise, pet," Lucida answered with her overweening Cheshire-cat-smile that seemed to put Hannah at ease. "All we want is to find them and bring them here."

"And are you sure I can't just talk to Milo?"

Lucida shook her head sadly. "No. We've already lifted the Casting on your connection, but it's being blocked from the other side, somehow. We're working on it, but the easiest way to open things back up will be to get him here."

"I can't even Call him. I've tried it," Hannah said, as her voice broke in a dry sob; I felt Milo's answering whimper reverberate through my head.

"I know, love. But you'll be together again soon enough. I just know it... Now, tell me, are you making heads or tails of that?" she asked, as she curled like a cat on the bed and tapped a perfectly manicured fingertip on the cover of Hannah's book. The cover was printed in runes instead of letters, with the symbols stamped onto the cover in flaking gold leaf.

"I don't know," Hannah said, sighing. "There's just so much of it, and it's hard to tell fact from theory. It's like trying to navigate through an entirely new culture." She paused and laughed a little. "Actually that's exactly what it is."

"I don't know that you can get a proper feel for it from a pile of old books," replied Lucida, shaking her head. "Experience is always best when you want to understand something for yourself."

"Yes, and the only experiences I've had with the Necromancers have been pretty awful," Hannah said. "Running Jess and Finn and Savvy off the road? Kidnapping? Torturing Annabelle?"

"No one's perfect," Lucida quipped. Hannah's expression turned momentarily incredulous; Lucida hurried to amend her meaning. "I'm not saying all their methods are laudable, pet, but just think what might've happened at the Durupinen's hands if we hadn't gotten you out of Fairhaven when we did. The Necromancers have made some mistakes in their efforts to find you, but ends can justify means sometimes, Hannah. This is so much bigger than any of us."

"You mean the Prophecy?"

"Yes, the Prophecy, but you need to understand something else, too. The Durupinen make the Prophecy sound like the end of everything, but it's not. All it means is the end of their control of the Gateways. For us, that would just be the beginning."

"But the beginning of what?" Hannah asked. "I still don't really understand what I'm being asked to do, because no one seems to know what will happen after we do it. I mean, I understand the Necromancers' eventual goals—that part's pretty clear from the books. They want to explore beyond the Gateways. They want to know what death is, and where we go when we Cross, and maybe even find the way to reverse death. I understand that. I think everyone wants to know those things. But it almost sounds like they're chasing... well..."

"Immortality," Lucida whispered, and even as she said it, her face lit up with an excitement that seemed slightly manic. "Free passage back and forth between the worlds of the living and the dead. Just imagine it."

"I'm not sure if I want to," Hannah said. "I don't know if we're meant to."

"But what if we are? What if we're just wasting the chance because we're too scared to see what moving between worlds could be? The Durupinen are stuck in the past, afraid to seize opportunity. But the Necromancers are visionaries, love. Together we could discover extraordinary things."

"You make it sound so exciting." To my dismay, there was a trace of longing in my sister's voice.

"It is exciting! Haven't you spent enough time being scared?"

Hannah didn't answer. She didn't need to. Of course she'd spent enough time being scared. She'd spent most of her life being scared.

After a moment, Hannah asked, "What made you decide to join them? You grew up with the Durupinen. You were always taught the Necromancers were your enemy. What was the thing that changed your mind?"

Lucida hesitated; she seemed to really be considering this question, and she bit her bottom lip as she thought. "You know me, pet, I've never been one to sit still. I make my own way. But... at the end of it, I think it came down to the idea of power."

"How?"

"I've seen what spirits can do. Many are just lost and harmless, sure, but I've seen some destroy lives, torment people, and wreak havoc. You should know what I mean."

Hannah nodded. "Yes, I do."

"And here I was with this power not only to communicate with them, but to control them. Why would you or I be born with that power if we weren't meant to use it for some purpose?"

A little "Oh," popped out of Hannah's mouth as if she were surprised. It seemed as though a light had gone on in her head—a light she'd never known was there before. "I never really thought of it like that before."

"Of course not. You were too busy being terrified, fretting over when the next ghost would show up to torment you."

"You make the spirits sound awful. They weren't all like that. A lot of them were just scared. They're people, Lucida."

"No pet, they *were* people. People are alive, Hannah, and this side of the Gateway is our world. Why should the dead have any control here in the world of the living? Why should we be at their mercy when they aren't even meant to be here?"

Again, Hannah didn't respond. Her hands, which had been fidgeting a few moments before, had gone very still in her lap.

"I'm not saying we shouldn't help the spirits when they need it," Lucida went on, tucking her legs up under her and wrapping her arms around her knees, "but surely we aren't meant to be enslaved, forced to do their bidding night and day. Especially not you. The Durupinen talk of nothing but duty. They would have you believe that you've no choice but to serve the spirits. But look what you can do!"

"It scares me," Hannah whispered.

"It shouldn't! Now you can finally stop being afraid! Think, Hannah. All those years with those damn spirits controlling your life... they made living an absolute bloody hell for you, yet all the while you could've been controlling them! All that pain and doubt, all those doctors and institutions—you suffered for no good reason! All those years you could've turned those spirits on anyone you wanted, freed yourself at any time. But no, you suffered alone. The Durupinen did that, don't you understand? Our so-called sisterhood left you to rot, defenseless and alone, purely because they feared your power."

"They didn't know about me, though," Hannah pointed out, with the air of someone trying to inject a note of diplomacy into the conversation. "How could they have told me all this if they couldn't even find me?"

"But it comes to the same thing, don't you see, Hannah? If it weren't for them, your mother would never have had to hide you in the first place!"

"My mother," said Hannah wistfully, sounding as though she were using the word without knowing its meaning, as if "mother" were an entirely foreign concept to her. "I wish I knew why she left me there alone. I mean, I know what she was trying to do by separating us, but... well..." As I watched, I could tell Hannah was struggling with a thought she was ashamed of—or else a thought that was too large, too complicated, too heavy, for her to voice easily. "Why was it me? I know our mother couldn't have predicted which of us would be the Key. I know she couldn't tell which of us would experience Visitations first, but... she must've had a *reason* for choosing one of us over the other, right?"

Lucida merely shrugged. My blood boiled; Lucida wasn't going to help Hannah work through all of her complicated feelings surrounding this very legitimate question—a question which I, as the "lucky" twin, had to admit I hadn't given a lot of thought to. But already I could see Lucida turning all this over in her mind, considering how to best manipulate Hannah's pain and doubt.

"Easy... Stay calm, Jess," said Milo, interrupting my thoughts. "I can feel you slipping. Don't lose your concentration." The vision went fuzzy for a moment as I refocused.

"But how could she do that!" Hannah cried. "How could my mother leave me when she knew what I might be, when she'd spent her own childhood talking to people no one else could see?"

"Would you like to ask her?" asked Lucida, jumping up from the bed.

Hannah looked up into Lucida's face, where the faintest suggestion of a smile was playing about her lips and a wry sort of knowledge gleamed in her eye. "Lucida, what do you mean? I can't ask her. No one can. She's gone."

Lucida's smile bloomed, wide and satisfied. "Oh, my dear little poppet, that's what I've been trying to tell you. Of course you can."

Hannah said nothing, although her hands began to tremble violently in her lap.

"You alone have that power. Do you want your mother to answer your questions? Do you want to hear her reasons, her apologies, for yourself? Open the Gateway. Call her back. Bring her before you. Demand your answers and your portion of truth. Your mother owes you that, surely."

"I... I could see my mother? I could talk to her?"

"Yes. You alone hold the key to that door. Anything you ever wanted to tell her, you can. You could demand any explanation you need from her."

"No," Hannah squeaked, withdrawing momentarily into that too-familiar shell of hers. Then she shook her head violently as though trying to dislodge the very words she had just heard. "Even if it's true—even if I could do that—it wouldn't be right. Spirits, including my mother, want to be on the other side. They're meant to be there. Bringing them back would be terrible for them, wouldn't it?"

"Have you ever asked the Durupinen what's on the other side of the Gateway?" Lucida asked.

"Yes, of course I did."

"And what did they tell you, pet?"

"That we aren't meant to know what's on the other side. That it isn't our job to know. We're just supposed to send the spirits across and trust that they're supposed to be there."

"And were you satisfied with that answer?" asked Lucida, twirling her finger around a tendril of her own hair.

"No... I accepted it, but I wasn't exactly satisfied."

"I should hope not," Lucida scoffed, "because I remember asking the same question and getting the same answer. And I remember having a knot in my stomach every time I closed that Gateway after a Crossing. I remember wondering if I could keep sending those spirits into the bloody unknown. What if the other side isn't the right place for them?"

"But then why would they want to go so badly, if that's not where they're supposed to be?" Hannah asked; a flutter in her voice betrayed her fear.

"When do we ever want the things that are best for us?" Lucida asked. "Think of all the things we lust for—none of them are good for us. Why would our spirits—especially new spirits who are lost and confused—be any different?"

Hannah, pensive, didn't answer. I was beginning to wonder how much more new "information" my twin could take in before she stopped questioning Lucida's methods entirely.

"The Necromancers aren't willing to take anything for granted. They believe that the more we know, the better prepared we are. They want to know everything they can about the other side. Knowledge is power, Hannah, and you are the ultimate source of power, love."

Again, Hannah remained silent—she seemed to have lost the ability to argue. Lucida pressed this to her advantage. "I know you want to do right by the spirits, love, and that's admirable. But what about doing right by yourself? What of taking back what's rightfully yours? You've only now begun to understand what your powers can do. The Durupinen don't want you to explore that. But you owe nothing to them, Hannah. Nothing to them, and nothing to the spirits. You've already given enough. Aren't you tired of being a victim? Aren't you exhausted living a life for others, when you could finally be living *your* life for yourself?"

Hannah stammered but formed no real words. I could tell that her head was awhirl with too much misinformation and too many questions, that too many old wounds had been opened in both her heart and mind.

Hannah hugged herself tightly and began rocking back and forth, soothing herself. She began humming quietly; Milo and I—with a simultaneous start—recognized her tune immediately—and the fearful desperation behind her melody. Lucida had finally worn my sister down.

Lucida let Hannah rock—terrified and confused—for a few long moments, before sitting back down on the bed and taking Hannah's face in her hands. "Love, you want control of your own life, don't you?" she asked.

Slowly, Hannah whispered, "Yes." It was a tiny word. One little word, but so very, very important.

"Good girl. Of course you do. So when Neil comes to ask for your decision?"

Hannah didn't answer right away. She shook her face free of Lucida's grasp. She looked down at her own hands, turning them over in her lap and running her fingers over the crisscrossing little scars that evidenced her years of pain. Scars that were footprints left behind by the spirits that had trod across her childhood and destroyed any hope she'd ever had for a normal life. Yet, as gruesome as her scars were, I knew they were nothing in comparison to the scars she carried deep inside her being.

"Yes," replied Hannah, with a deep, achy sigh. "I'll tell Neil *yes*."

§

Milo lay on the ground doing his ghostly version of gasping for air. We had disconnected with a violent motion that left me reeling.

"That's it!" he cried, as he began struggling to sit up. "They've twisted her mind! They've got her... that 'yes' is what the Necromancers have been waiting for. We need to find Ileana. Now."

"Wait, Milo," I began. "Just wait a second!"

"Are you out of your damn mind?" he shouted. "What the hell are we waiting for?"

"Because Ileana isn't going to do anything about it!" I cried. "I told you what she said the last time. The Travelers don't care about stopping her. They've given up on any hope of thwarting this Prophecy before it can come to pass."

"So what? So we just sit here on our asses? How is that any better than what the Travelers are doing?" Milo was shouting at me with much more force than I would've thought he could muster after a Habitation. "And Hannah needs me, Jess! Lucida preyed on every fear she's ever had, turned every ounce of her self-doubt and hurt into a weapon! The moment Hannah's alone she'll shatter into a thousand pieces. I'm the one that's supposed to keep her from falling apart—I'm supposed to take care of her!"

"I know that. That's not what I mean," I replied. "I just don't think Ileana is the right person to tell. She doesn't care about getting Hannah out of there. If we go to her with this, she's just going to keep us here and force me to Walk every second of the day until Hannah forces the Gateway open—and then that old crone will probably push me through the goddamn thing."

"Plus..." Milo began, as he made a concerted effort to calm himself and think more logically, "we'll deserve every doomsday-inspired second of that Prophecy if we just hang around here and do nothing. So what do we do?"

I remembered Anca's advice. "Milo, the Travelers believe the Prophecy is already in motion, and maybe it is. But what we need to do right now is take control of ourselves. Nothing else will change until we do."

"Those sound like pretty words, Jess—pretty but empty. We're under that hag's thumb."

"Which is why we need to get ourselves out of here, and soon," I replied. "We'll need to get past the Wards and out of the camp before Ileana suspects anything."

"Don't you think she already has extra protection up, in case we decided to make a break for it?" Milo asked.

"Probably," I said. "Honestly, I'm surprised she hasn't trapped me inside that dome and forced me to Walk twenty-four hours a day in preparation for the apocalypse. But we can't worry about that now. We already know how to get across Wards; we've been doing it for the last fifteen minutes."

"Okay," Milo began, clearly still fighting his own battle to keep it together, "and what do we do next, assuming we can escape this place... which I doubt?"

"We keep connecting, as often as we can, with Hannah. At some point, someone is going to say something that will give away their location, especially now that Hannah is cooperating."

I fell quiet for a moment. Saying it out loud punched a gaping hole in my stomach: Hannah was going through with this. Despite everything the Necromancers had done to us and to the people we loved, despite the bond between us, Hannah was choosing them over me. I would've been sick then and there if I hadn't been trying to stay focused on Milo.

"Right," he said, calm enough now to think things through. "And all we need to do is hide from Marion's Trackers, Ileana's Trackers, and the Necromancers. Cool. No problem."

"No problem," I repeated; we each savored the sarcasm in our own bitter way.

"Jess..."

"Yeah?"

Milo's voice shook. "What Lucida said... about how spirits *used to be* human..."

"Don't, Milo. Don't even think about that bullshit."

"But she believed it. Hannah believed it."

"Hannah wasn't thinking of you when she accepted that."

"I know. That's the point. She wasn't thinking of me. How could she be talking about spirits and not remember me? We've lost her, haven't we?"

I swallowed back the fear that was threatening to choke me. "No, Milo. Not yet. She's not lost yet."

17

COUNSEL

THREE HOURS LATER, I stood outside the scribes' wagon. I shivered in the moonlight; a chill had crept into the air, or perhaps my own exhaustion was sapping the warmth from my body. It had taken me the whole three hours to gather enough resolve to make the walk across the camp.

I knocked softly on the knotty wooden door, but the sound still managed to reverberate through my head like a battering ram. Flavia poked her nose out of the door like a mole scenting the air, then started violently at the sight of me.

"Jess! I wasn't expecting you to come! Ileana told me to wait, but I never thought... What can I do for you?"

"I need your help."

"Of course! What is it?"

"I'd rather not say out here. Can I come in?"

Flavia nodded, stepped back, and opened the door fully.

My first thought was that if I had to move into the Travelers' camp permanently, I could've happily resided in the Scribes' wagon. Except for Ileana's tent, the Scribes' wagon was much larger than any other dwelling I'd seen. It was fashioned from an old train car, and the walls were lined with shelves and cabinets full of old books. The floor was covered in a thick red carpet; the train's original plush seats remained; they were tucked under the wooden tables at which the Scribes worked. A fire crackled invitingly in a small pot-bellied stove. Flavia had clearly just extricated herself from a little nest at one of the tables; a cup of tea was steaming beside a candlelit chair, and the quilt she'd been wrapped in looked cozy and welcoming. I fought the overwhelming urge to steal her spot while it was still warm.

Flavia motioned for me to sit in the chair across from hers and, reading my mind, pulled open a large chest, then handed me a patchwork quilt.

"Tea?"

"Yes please," I said, dropping into the chair. It was velvety and smelled like old books.

Flavia handed me a cup of tea and then pulled the blinds on the windows. She sat down and fixed her eyes on me with an analytic gaze, as if my reason for visiting might be written on my face.

"What is it, Jess? How can I help?"

"Are we alone?"

"Yes. Yasha's already gone to bed."

I could only assume that Yasha was one of the other Scribes, but I didn't bother to confirm this. "I need to ask for your help, but before I do, I need you to promise me something."

Flavia looked nervous. "I will if I can."

"If you can't help me with what I'm about to ask, that's okay. I don't want to get you in trouble—and I don't want you to do anything you're not comfortable with. You've been really nice to me, and I'm sure I never would've learned to Walk without your help. But if you can't or don't want to help, will you promise—swear to me—that you won't tell anyone what I've asked?"

Flavia considered this with a thoughtfully furrowed brow. After a moment, her expression cleared. "Yes. I think I can promise that. Okay, yes, I give you my word."

I relaxed just enough to take a sip of tea. I felt it warm me all the way down into my stomach. "Do you remember the other day, when Milo came into the enclosure for the Corporeal Habitation?"

"Yes, of course."

"And I told you that we had Habitated before, that it had gotten us across Fairhaven's Wards without detection?"

Flavia nodded again. "Yes."

"Well, do you think you could help me figure out if that would work here?"

"You mean you want to leave the encampment undetected?" Flavia asked.

"Yes. But it's not a want, Flavia, it's a need."

We looked at each other for a long moment; Flavia chewed her lip in apparent agitation. Finally, she said, "Is that all you're asking me for? Merely my opinion on whether it will work?"

"Yes," I replied quickly. "Just some information on how the camp is protected would be helpful."

"Can you tell me why you are trying to leave? If I promise not to tell anyone?" Flavia asked.

"If you help me determine whether I can actually leave," I began thoughtfully, "then, yes, I'll tell you why I'm doing it."

The worry in Flavia's expression passed from her face. Perhaps it was because I was confiding in her, but she smiled at me. "Alright, then."

I smiled back. "Great, thank you."

"Don't thank me yet. I might not have the information you need. But," she slid out of her chair and walked to the nearest bookshelf, "I must admit that after you told me about Corporeal Habitation, I looked into it myself."

My smile widened. "Of course you did."

Flavia giggled. "Hey, I'm a sucker for obscure Castings. Plus, I live in the most oppressively boring subculture in the universe, so having a reliable escape route sounded pretty appealing." She ran her finger along the books' spines until she came to a large red volume and pulled it from the shelf. She laid it open on the table.

As I watched Flavia thumb through the book, I suddenly realized she reminded me strongly of Tia, and I thought my heart would burst from both the pain of missing my roommate and the fear that danger would find her—despite Karen's promise to hide her safely. I'd heard nothing since Tia had gone into hiding. Generally, I forced myself to believe that no news was good news, but at the moment nothing could sate the gnawing feeling in my chest: If something happened to Tia—my best friend—it would be all my fault for dragging her into the disaster that was now my life.

"Are you okay? You look... worried." Flavia was staring at me with a frown of concern that pulled at the corners of her mouth.

"Yeah," I said, as I tried to rearrange my features into a more neutral expression. "I just have a little too much on my mind right now."

"With the fate of the living and the dead resting on your shoulders? Yes, I'd say you have quite enough to be distracted by," Flavia replied, as she fumbled with a pair of dark-framed reading glasses that she had tucked into her hair for safekeeping. Perching them on her nose, she muttered, "Ah, here we are," before sitting back down at the table and beginning to read aloud.

The grounds of Fairhaven Hall and many other Durupinen strongholds employ non-binding Ward boundaries, which allow non-hostile spirits to wander in and out freely. Patrolling these boundaries falls to the Caomhnóir, who can expel spirits at their discretion. But, as the Wards only sound their alert when broken by the living, the castle's borders must be policed with regularity, and spirits must be further Warded against entering forbidden areas on the grounds.

Flavia looked expectantly up at me. "Uh, yeah, that sounds about right," I said in reply.

"A list of the different types of Wards Fairhaven uses is in here too," Flavia added, turning the page and running her finger down it. "I cross-referenced them with the Wards used to protect our encampment, and they're identical. We may do some things differently around here, but when it comes to Warding our borders, we all seem to follow the same rules."

"So our Habitation trick should work again?"

"Yes, I don't see why not," Flavia replied. "If it worked at Fairhaven, it should work here. You are free to leave the encampment undetected, although," she closed the book and frowned, "I can't imagine you will get far. Once our Trackers and the Caomhnóir know you are gone, they will surely come after you. And I must say that they are very good at their jobs."

"We'll cross that bridge when we get to it. I really just needed to know if we could get out. We're already going to have a veritable army of people after us, so what's a few more?"

"You should escape by the boundary nearest to Irina's wagon," said Flavia, stowing the book back on the shelf. "The only Caomhnóir on duty there is Andrei, and he's a... well, he's not very reliable. He's supposed to have a partner, but none of the other Caomhnóir will work with him."

"Anca's grandfather? Yes, I met him. I think we'll be able to get by him without too much trouble. If nothing else, we would simply sneak something stronger than usual into his flask and wait for him to pass out."

"So, why are you leaving?" asked Flavia, tucking herself back into her chair.

"How much did Ileana tell you about our... disagreement?"

"Nothing, but the story spread like wildfire. There is no such thing as a secret when you live in a Traveler camp," Flavia replied with a wry smile. "If you sneeze in the privacy of your own bunk in the middle of the night, a hundred people say, 'God bless you' and another hundred hand you a handkerchief."

I couldn't help but laugh; I couldn't have come up with a more apt description of Traveler culture. "Right. Well, Ileana's decided that the Prophecy is going to happen no matter what we do, but I haven't given up. Someone needs to find my sister—not just to keep tabs on her, but to actually get her out of... wherever the hell it is they have her," I said. "And since we've run out of people who are willing to help us, that someone has to be me."

Flavia was a scholar. She could've lectured me about the likelihood of the Prophecy coming to fruition, or about the many references throughout history that pointed to its fulfillment. Hell, she probably could've written a book about how my lack of a solid plan would lead to certain disaster. But she didn't.

Instead, she said, "No one can say for certain what may happen. But surely we can't complain about it if we choose to do nothing."

"Exactly."

I took a long sip of my tea, buying myself some time as I tried to frame my next question. "Do you think," I asked, "that there's a possibility she's already done it?"

Flavia's brow furrowed in confusion. "That who's done what?"

"Sorry. I mean, do you think there's any chance that Hannah has already done what the Necromancers want her to do and reversed the Gateway?"

Flavia looked startled. "I don't think so. We would know, surely."

"But how would we know? What will happen?"

"I don't know. No one does. We can't know until it happens. But the consequences have been foretold as dire, so I think it would be obvious somehow. An upsurge in spirit activity. Disturbances across our individual Gateways. And of course, the appearance of the Wraiths."

My hands tightened around my teacup. "Those are the ghost-zombie things Ileana was talking about, right?"

"Was that really the first you'd heard of them? Didn't your own Council tell you about them?"

"Flavia, no one even told me about being a Durupinen until a few months ago," I said baldly. "And even then, no one seemed to think it important to mention the Prophecy until a few weeks ago."

Flavia shook her head. "I'm sorry. It's mind-boggling how little you've been told, especially since it concerns you so closely."

"Tell me about it," I replied with an exasperated sigh.

"It's such a sad thought that sometimes a spirit can get trapped in the Aether, instead of Crossing all the way through. And the worst part is, there's no way to tell if it's happened once the spirit enters the Gateway. We just have to assume everything goes well—that the spirit traverses the Aether successfully and arrives in the world beyond. Of course, there are certain factors that can increase the likelihood of a spirit getting trapped."

"Like when greedy Durupinen decide to Leech away some spirit energy during a Crossing," I said. Even though Hannah had asked for the spirits to donate their energy, I still writhed with guilt as I said it—spirit energy was the reason I was still alive.

"Yes, that's one instance, and an unfortunate one. I understand it's a fairly regular practice in some other clans. Here among the Travelers, unless it was a true emergency—life or death—you'd be severely punished for such an act."

"Really? What would they do to you?"

"Your Gateway would be sealed and you would lose your right to Guardianship. You would lose both your purpose and your protection."

My mouth fell open. "Permanently?"

She nodded seriously. "Yes. The Gateway would not be reopened again until the next generation was ready. As you know, closing a Gateway will cause spirits to plague the Durupinen involved until the Gateway is opened again—and there'd be no Caomhnóir to help deter them. It's a terrible punishment, not least because it disturbs the balance."

I let out a low whistle. "I wish the Northern Clans would take Leeching as seriously as you do."

"So do I. The number of spirits they've gotten trapped in the Aether is probably great. And that will mean more Wraiths if the Gateway is reversed."

"Can you tell me more about them? How will we know a Wraith when we see one?"

"Well, like I said, there are a few reasons the spirits might be stuck in the Aether. Leeching is one. A spirit could also be torn about its decision to Cross and deplete its own energy trying to stay behind or turn back. Or a spirit can be weakened for some other reason. If the Gateway is reversed, those spirits will be brought back to our side, but they will be… different."

"Different how?"

"They will no longer be themselves. That essential part that makes them human, that knows who they are, will be gone. The trip back to the world of the living will sap that essence, and all that will return will be a shell. That shell will retain the appearance of the spirit, but it will be devoid of humanity. Once in this form, they can be controlled completely."

"I've seen it," I said, bolting up straight in my chair. "The Blind Summoner!"

"The what?"

"Blind Summoners." I stared at Flavia, surprised. "Haven't you heard of them?"

"No, never. What are they?"

"It's a spirit whose essence has been trapped in a flame, so you can give it a message to deliver, and—" I closed my eyes as the truth hit me. "Of course. I'm such an idiot!"

"What is it?" asked Flavia with genuine alarm. I hadn't meant to startle her, but the realization had hit me so hard that I'd practically shouted my last few words.

"It's not a Durupinen Casting at all, is it? There's no such thing as a Blind Summoner in Durupinen culture, is there?"

Flavia shook her head. "No. I've never read a single reference to them anywhere."

"Of course you haven't. Because Lucida was already working for the Necromancers. She was already dabbling in their magic, and testing their messed-up theories for herself." I dropped my face into my hands but kept speaking, causing my voice to muffle. "And then she started teaching those Castings to Hannah, to see what she was capable of. I should've known. I knew it was dark, I just knew it. And I told her, I *told* Hannah it wasn't right."

"Jess, what are you talking about?" Flavia asked with even more concern than before. The poor woman must've thought I'd lost it completely.

"The Necromancers are anticipating the arrival of the Wraiths. They're experimenting with ways of controlling spirits who have had their essence stripped, and they're using Hannah to do it! God, this is so messed up."

"They've found a way to create Wraiths without the Gateway?" Flavia gasped, horrified.

"I think so, yes. At least, they found a way to temporarily induce a state similar to a Wraith's."

"The Necromancers may have begun as a scholarly brotherhood, but scholarship is the furthest thing from their true agenda now," Flavia said, and I could see that—as an academic herself—she felt personally affronted. "For centuries now, they've been about power, not knowledge. If they can create Wraiths, with or without reversing the Gateway, they will have total control—the very thing they crave the most!"

"But there must be some way to fight them, right? I mean, the Durupinen must have some kind of measures in place to deal with Wraiths. We seem to have a Casting for just about everything else."

"No, and that's the most devastating part. All of our Castings will be useless, because they're meant to be placed on spirits that still have their humanity. Expulsion, Binding, Caging—none will work on a Wraith. We'll be helpless against them if the Necromancers use them to attack. We'll be decimated."

We stared at each other; the horror expanded between us, filling the space like something noxious and choking.

"Jess, I know you don't want to admit that the Prophecy may be happening, and I agree that you should do everything in your power to keep it from coming to pass, but I hope you're formulating a plan... in case of the worst."

"Yeah, it's becoming clearer and clearer that I'm going to have to do that."

We sat in silence for a while, sipping our tea and watching the flames dance in the belly of the stove. It was a very cheerful sight, and it made me feel strangely alone—despite Flavia's sitting within three feet of me. When I had drained my tea to the dregs, I placed it on the chipped old saucer and willed myself out of my chair.

"I'd better get going before I fall asleep in that chair for the night."

"You're welcome to. I've done it many times," Flavia said with a gentle smile.

"Better not," I said. "Thank you. I won't tell anyone you helped me. You've been a really good friend to me, and I appreciate all you've done. If I do have to Walk to end this whole thing, and if I manage to pull it all off, it will be mostly because of your help."

"If you have to Walk to end this, it will be your strength alone

230

that gets you through it. And you have that in abundance; we've all seen it. We have faith in you."

"Well, thanks again," I said. I turned into the darkness before Flavia could see the tears that had sprung suddenly into my eyes and were now racing each other down my cheeks.

18

THE HEAT OF BATTLE

W E TOOK THE NEXT DAY TO FORMULATE OUR PLAN. Milo felt he was still much too weak to attempt fleeing the camp without a few days of solid rest, so we decided that we would wait until the upcoming Saturday, four days away, before making a break for it. And as much as we hated to, we also agreed that we wouldn't connect with Hannah again until after we'd made it past the Wards. We couldn't risk the journey—and the probable subsequent chase—if Milo couldn't keep up with us. "Us" included Annabelle and Savvy.

"Are you kidding, mate? Get me the bollocks out of here!" was Savvy's refined response upon hearing we were planning our escape. "If this godforsaken wasteland had proper walls, I'd be climbing them by now. And you'll need all the help you can get, won't you? Of course I'm bloody well coming!"

Now that we'd landed among her extended family, I wasn't sure that Annabelle would want to join us, but she agreed readily.

"Are you sure?" I asked her. "You've got roots here. I wouldn't blame you at all for wanting to stay."

"Those roots don't run as deep as I hoped they would," Annabelle said with a bitter little laugh. "I'm more like the weed among the roses around here. No one has much interest in a Dormant who can't even claim a direct living Durupinen relative. It's been... interesting being here, but I'm ready to leave whenever you are."

"It's not just that we're leaving," I explained. "This will be out of the frying pan and into the fire, Annabelle. We're actually going to look for the Necromancers—the people holding Hannah, the people who killed Pierce. I don't know what's going to happen. And you've experienced better than any of us what the Necromancers can do. They didn't just imprison you, they tortured you in that Spirit Cage. Seriously, no one would blame you if you decided not to come."

"But that's just it. They killed David. If I can help finish them, I will. End of discussion," Annabelle declared firmly.

I met her eye, and the fire in hers felt like a direct reflection of the fire in mine. We understood each other.

"I think you should go to Ileana," began Annabelle, looking thoughtful, "and tell her you want to Walk again."

"Why the hell would I do that?"

"I think it would be an excellent way to throw her off track. After your, um... outburst, Ileana's probably expecting you to leave, and she'll be prepared for it. But if you tell her you want to Walk again, and maybe even throw in a well-rehearsed apology, she may let her guard down. We'll have a better chance of sneaking out unnoticed."

"I don't know if I can stomach an apology," I said with a grimace, "but that's a really good idea. Unfortunately, it means I'll have to Walk again."

"Yes, it does, but you really are getting better at it, and it can't hurt to give it one more shot—especially since you might need to Walk for real in the near future," Annabelle said.

There was too much sense in this to reasonably argue against it. We knew our plan was the ultimate long shot. Escaping undetected; evading the Travelers and the Northern Durupinen and the Necromancers; finding the castle where Hannah was being held; rescuing her before she reversed the Gateway while also de-programming her brainwashing—the odds were stacked so heavily against us that accomplishing even one of these feats would be miraculous. But continuing to improve my Walking skills, as unappealing as this prospect was, was a good idea no matter what.

And so I played my part. I went to Ileana and told her I would continue Walking. Even she, with all her lordly airs, couldn't hide her relief. I showed up at the enclosure on Thursday afternoon, hiding my reluctance and knowing that I shouldn't waste this opportunity to practice. I even managed to swipe a handful of Soul Catchers from the stock on the table without anyone noticing, in case I *did* need them in the future. Pocketing them was easier than I had expected; the other Travelers kept their distance from me, as if one false move might spook me and spoil everything—although I thought Flavia might've given my hand an extra squeeze of support as she tied another Soul Catcher to my wrist. Even Anca, who stood guard at the entrance to the enclosure, nodded respectfully and took a wary step back as I approached.

"You may find Irina uncooperative today," Anca reported as I started to crawl through the entrance.

I paused, with both hands on the ground. "You mean more than usual?"

"Yes. Ever since your last Walk, she's hardly risen—in either body or spirit form. She's realized that this dome is really just a bigger cage, and she's just about given up hope of finding a way out of it." Anca, frowning, looked past me and into the enclosure. "I don't think she'll be inclined to help much."

"Thanks for the heads up," I said, then continued into the dome.

As I sliced through the Soul Catcher and rose into the air, I realized that Irina's spirit form wasn't soaring around the dome as usual. She was sitting, right beside her body, in the corner of the enclosure with her arms clasped around her knees.

Concentrating intently, I envisioned myself sitting beside her—and before I could even blink, I was next to her. I couldn't feel the ground beneath me, but the proximity of her spirit gave off a sort of warmth that grounded me in the space.

"Irina? Are you okay?"

She didn't reply. Her chin, resting on her knees, was trembling.

"Talk to me, Irina. Tell me what's wrong."

Again, she didn't answer. She did, however, throw me a scathing look so venomous that I nearly backed away from her.

"Can I help you?"

"You don't care about helping me," she whispered.

"I do care," I said, and I meant it. "We've spent all this time Walking together, tell me what I can do to help."

She glared at me with hollow eyes and pointed a finger at her body, which was crumpled on the grass beside her. "You can reach over to that... *thing* on the ground and snap its neck."

"I'm not going to do that. You know I can't."

Irina dropped her hand. "Fine then," she spat, with her voice hitching as she repressed a sob, "Open this prison and let me out."

"You know I can't do that either."

"I know. You don't care."

"It's not that," I said firmly. "But it's not my decision. Your clan's

Council built this enclosure for us—they're the ones keeping you here. Why don't you speak to one of them?"

"You think I haven't tried? You think I haven't used every word, every argument, every plea? They have long stopped listening to me," replied Irina, staring over at her body with a curiously detached expression. "I cannot make them hear me. I cannot make them understand what it is to live like this—this endless, torturous, longing."

As I looked at Irina in her misery, I was revisited by a sudden and startlingly detailed memory of a senile old man in a nursing home; he was sitting in a plush green chair at a window, but he was far from comfortable. Every muscle in his decrepit body was tensed in anticipation of the freedom he so desperately hoped would come. My grandfather's anguished voice reverberated back to me across the intervening months: *"I've seen it! Send me back! I want to go back!"*

In that moment, my sadness for Irina pressed upon me like a suffocating weight.

"I will talk to them for you," I offered. "I've got some bargaining power."

Irina looked away from her body and stared at me instead. "What do you mean?"

"I mean that they need me to cooperate. So I'm going to make it clear that they need to release you if they want my help. We're the only two Walkers on Earth. That counts for something, in my book."

"Don't lie to me," Irina replied, although it was more of a plea than a threat.

"I'm not lying. I mean it. I can't pretend to understand exactly what you're going through, but I do understand it better than you might think. And you shouldn't have to suffer like this anymore."

Irina's mouth twitched into a semblance of a smile. "I would be forever in your debt, Northern Girl."

"No, you wouldn't," I replied. "You don't owe anything to anyone. Not anymore."

We sat together a moment, and then she asked, "How do you feel?"

"Me? I don't know. Fine, I guess."

"You aren't disoriented? Dizzy?"

I took stock of myself. I'd been focused so intently on Irina that I hadn't been paying attention to myself. But now that she'd mentioned it...

"No! I feel... comfortable!"

"You let go," said Irina, nodding approvingly. "You were so distracted by your spirit state before that you couldn't allow yourself to just be."

It was true. I'd been so focused on the actual act of Walking that I couldn't allow it to happen freely. I'd been preoccupied with all the what-ifs—with all the pressures of what would happen if I failed. But when my focus was on Irina, I'd managed, without realizing it, to cut those last few mental strings. I felt better than fine. I felt wonderful!

I imagined a long and looping flight for myself and took off—flowing like water, floating about like a breeze. It was bliss. Irina watched me and laughed—actually laughed.

"You've got it now, Northern Girl," she cheered.

And she was right: I had it. Now I just had to pray I never ever needed to use it.

§

The wagon was empty. We'd packed up our assortment of temporary belongings. Savvy and Annabelle had gone off to the center of camp to secretly scavenge for as much food and other supplies as they could, while Milo and I made our way, quickly and quietly, to the encampment's western border, near to the clearing of Irina's now-abandoned wagon. By the time we arrived, so had nightfall.

"Right, let's make it quick," I said, as we reached the boundary. A rune carved into a nearby tree marked the place where the Casting for the Wards had been performed. A spindly light glimmered off the rune, like light hitting a spider web.

"Savvy and Annabelle will be here soon. I know it's tempting to connect again so we can check on Hannah, but we need to make sure you've got enough strength to take us all across."

"I know, I know," Milo agreed, a little sulkily.

"I want to see her, too," I said.

"I know you do. So let's get this over with so we can see her for real," he said. "Ready?"

"Ready."

Milo surged forward and stepped into my space, expanding immediately inside of my head. I'd taken only a single step toward the Ward when something I couldn't define made me stop. A powerful something that made me turn and look over my shoulder.

"Uh, Jess? Wrong way, sweetness," Milo's voice said inside my skull.

But I had seen her. Mary stood on the edge of the clearing; her tiny frame, luminous in its spirit state, was aglow from within. She held a candle between her grubby fingers.

"Mary?"

"Jess, is something wrong?" asked Milo. "Everything's gone dark."

"Shh! There's a spirit. A friend. Give me a minute," I replied.

Mary nodded at me and lifted a finger to her lips, begging my silence. I walked toward her, moving—or so it felt—with the strange gliding motion of a dream.

"What are you doing here?" I asked.

She wasn't looking at me. She was looking down at the candle's flame, watching it leap and dance in the semi-darkness. Her expression was stoic, unreadable.

"Mary? Did you come from Fairhaven? Is everything alright?"

She kept looking at the candle, and so I stared at it too while wondering what was so fascinating.

"They are coming," she whispered.

I snapped my gaze back to Mary's face. She was looking at me now; her eyes were wide and anxious.

"What did you say?"

"They are coming!" Her voice answered me, but her mouth didn't move. In fact, her voice seemed to be emanating from the candle.

"Who's coming?"

Mary said nothing, but leaned down and blew out the candle. At that same moment, twin flames lit in her eyes, bathing her face in an orange glow and utterly transfixing me. She opened her mouth wide and revealed a yawning cavern of flames. And then she began to scream.

I came to my senses suddenly; Milo simultaneously leapt from my body as though he had been burned.

I was drenched in cold sweat. As I wiped the icy beads away from my eyes, I thought for a moment that the screaming was just an echo, a remnant of the vision in my consciousness. But as I blinked the last vestiges of Mary away, I realized that the screams were coming from through the trees, from the direction of the camp.

"What the hell? What just happened?" Milo asked.

"I had a sort of... vision? I don't really know. Didn't you see it?"

"No. But I couldn't see or really hear anything else, either. After you turned around, it all went black and sort of quiet. What was it?"

"It was Mary. The Silent Child. She said they're coming."

Milo didn't ask who Mary had meant: There could only be one "they" that could inspire the fear now coursing through us both.

Another scream. A shout echoed in the darkness.

"Stay here," I said, struggling to my feet. "I'm going to see what's happening."

"What? No! You can't go back there! That's got to be the Necromancers! We've got to get you out of here, Jess!"

"Of course it's the Necromancers!" I cried. "But we're not leaving without Savvy and Annabelle. And you need to blink out so the Necromancers don't see you."

"No, I'm coming to help!"

"Don't you remember what happened the last time they put a Casting on you? You could wind up like that again, or worse! Just blink out, Milo. Don't communicate and don't show yourself! I want you to go as far and deep into your spirit realm as you can, and don't come back until I say so. Got it?"

"Okay, okay!" Milo conceded. "But I don't like it! For the record, I'm acting under duress!" And with that, he vanished.

I took off through the forest, following the cries of distress rather than the path. For a few moments, I could feel Milo's presence with me—just a suggestion of a bright spot somewhere in my peripheral vision. But then he faded away, deep into the spirit world, as I rounded one last bend and threw myself behind a massive oak tree.

Hell had broken loose in a much more literal sense than I ever would've thought possible. Pandemonium reigned. Everywhere I looked, spirits were jetting through the air, flinging themselves at people, toppling wagons, and shredding tents. Flaming logs from the central bonfire were soaring through the air, and screams rent through the night as the Travelers scattered in all directions. Grunts and shouts joined the din as the Caomhnóir, wielding both

Castings and brute force, tried to protect the camp. And everywhere, with their black cloaks swirling around them and their faces covered by skull masks—like *calaveras* come frighteningly to life—the Necromancers swarmed.

"Fan out! Search every inch of this camp! Find the Ballard girl!" a deep booming voice called over the tumult.

I stood rooted to the spot with panic buzzing loudly in my brain. I wanted to do something, anything, to help; but I was utterly incapable of acting. I watched, paralyzed, as the ghost of an old man sent a red-hot crumbling log through the air and onto a tent, which collapsed on one side and immediately caught fire. Three dark-haired figures crawled out of it a moment later, coughing and yelling.

"Jess! Come here! Now!"

I looked around for the voice, but before I could find it a small cold hand began tugging me into a nearby clump of bushes. I opened my mouth to shout for help, but the hand leapt from my wrist to my mouth, covering it.

"It's me, it's Flavia!" She watched the recognition flare in my eyes and dropped her hand.

"Flavia, what are you—"

"There's no time," she hissed, reaching for my arm and pushing my sleeve up. She pulled a Soul Catcher from her pocket with shaking fingers and began knotting it around my wrist.

"What's this for?" I asked.

"Saving your life," she replied. Even though she was whispering, I could hear a terrified tremble in her voice. "They will keep destroying and killing until they find you. This is the only way to stop their attack. You can't run and you can't hide from them. They will start torturing people soon. This is the only chance."

"But how will this—

"Shh! Follow me. Quickly now." We took off out of the bushes and sprinted to the edge of the clearing. Bewildered and terrified, I followed her, crouched in an effort to stay out of sight.

We fled across the camp, darting from tree to tree for cover. Twice we skirted around smoldering, ruined tents before we reached the Scribes' wagon. It was aflame, like nearly everything else, but Flavia ran toward it.

"No, get back!" I cried. "It looks like it's going to collapse at any—"

But Flavia, coughing and sputtering, yanked me forward into the shadow of the wagon's wheel. She wrenched back her sleeve and, with a dry, hysterical sob, reached underneath the nearest corner of the wagon. Then she pulled her hand out again and began rubbing something dark and sticky onto my face and neck.

Blankly, I allowed her to keep rubbing, but then realized what she was doing; the smell gave it away. An unmistakable, metallic-like smell: Blood. Flavia's hand, and now my face, were both smeared in thick red blood. Flavia was sobbing uncontrollably and muttering something incoherent as she reached under the wagon again. Then her hands reemerged, red and dripping in the flickering, smoky darkness.

With a horror that rippled through every cell of my body, I bent and peered under the wagon. Anca's body, with eyes wide and glassy, lay in a pool of her own blood—the same blood that Flavia was still smearing on me. I gawked, unable to take in the reality of what I was seeing.

"Anca came to help me save the scrolls," Flavia spoke in gasping whispers so quiet that she didn't even seem to be speaking to me. "Then this spirit... it was screaming. The glass in the windows exploded, and the stove... I couldn't stop it."

She looked me over, then she wiped her shaking hands on her jeans. Flavia cast one last, agonized look at Anca, then pulled me away from the wagon and off into the darkness again. We began stumbling through the underbrush, and had to duck nearly flat as a flaming piece of debris sailed over our heads and crashed into the trees. We continued on, but didn't get far before a fight broke out so close to us that Flavia was knocked off balance and into me; thankfully, I was able to push her back onto her feet, and we somehow barely missed a step.

I didn't ask where we were going. I just ran, with the scent of Anca's blood burning in my nostrils, until Flavia stopped so suddenly that I slammed into her. We crouched behind a monstrous oak tree a few feet away from Ileana's tent. Her tent was one of the few that hadn't yet caught fire, although one side had been torn away from its stakes.

Flavia turned to me, her eyes swimming with tears. "Listen carefully. Every one of those monsters is looking for you. When they see you're dead, I can only hope they will call off the search and retreat. It's the only way."

"When they see I'm dead? Flavia, what the hell are you..." But then logic fought free of my fear and I understood. I understood because she was holding a pocketknife out to me and pointing it at the Soul Catcher she'd tied to my wrist: The Necromancers would find my abandoned body, and would hopefully think the last threat to their plan had been eliminated.

"Won't they know what I've done?" I asked.

"No. I'd bet my life on it," Flavia replied. I knew full well that she was, in fact, betting her life on it.

"But all those spirits. They'll see me, won't they? They'll be able to tell the Necromancers."

Flavia was already shaking her head. "No. They don't see anything. They don't hear anything. They're nothing but empty shells."

"You mean... Oh God! Wraiths? It's happened already?"

"No, I'm almost sure it's what you told me about. Like Blind Summoners. But instead of messages, the spirits have been given instructions to destroy the camp."

"Are you sure? How do you—"

"Didn't you tell me Summoners' essences were trapped in flames?" she asked.

"Yes, but—"

She grabbed my hands, staring into my eyes. "The fire, Jess. Listen to the fire."

I tore my gaze from hers. I focused on a wagon, mere feet from us, which was engulfed in flames. I heard the pops and crackles. And then I heard something else in the very fabric of the sound; at first it was indistinguishable, but once I heard it, the roar became nearly deafening.

The flames themselves were screaming.

I looked back at Flavia; mutual horror passed between us. The fire itself was alive with souls—weaponized souls, torn away from their spirit forms. And when the flames at last died out...

"You need to get out into the open so they'll be sure to discover your body," Flavia said urgently. "Or they'll have no reason to stop the destruction."

"What will you do?" I asked.

"I will keep watch for as long as I can," Flavia promised.

"No. Get out of here," I begged. "Please, you've got to protect yourself!"

242

"Just go, Jess. Do it! Now!"

No words could suffice; I squeezed Flavia's hand gratefully. Then I looked quickly around to be sure all was clear, then bolted into the clearing. Keeping low to the ground, I prayed that the smoke and chaos would conceal me just long enough to position myself.

I flung myself into the grass next to the entrance of Ileana's tent. There was a large rock protruding from the dirt a few feet from the tent's nearest stake. I lay my head against it, hoping to make it appear as though I'd cracked my skull open; this would explain my bloodstained face. Then I pressed my face to the dirt, closed my eyes, and whispered the Casting as I sliced through the Soul Catcher.

The fear and heat and every other awful sensation melted away as I rose, effortlessly, away from my body and high into the air. I embraced the disconnection this time, allowing it to carry me above the stink and grit of the smoky attack below. I actually enjoyed a selfish instant of bliss, knowing I was safe—knowing nothing below could touch me—before rationality caught up with me and my fear returned in full measure.

Sailing like a bird, I observed the scene below; each new detail I saw magnified my dismay. Figures littered the ground below me; some were writhing horribly, but others were terrifyingly inert. Still more figures darted among the flames, fighting and shouting, or dragging others out of harm's way. The flames had spread rapidly—the Travelers' dwellings looked now like torches in the darkness below. In my spirit state, the voices of the flame-trapped spirits were now even clearer. I could hear each individual word; each was at once separate, yet part of a deafening din—a din that would surely echo in my head forever. The agony of it rippled through me.

Concentrating for all I was worth, I floated lower, through the haze of smoke, so I could keep my body in sight. I was acutely aware that my body was in much more danger than I'd ever dared to leave it in before, but I also knew that I had no choice.

"Jess! Jess, where are you?" A familiar voice was just distinguishable from the anarchy below. It was deep and panicked. I knew that voice, but the noise of the attack made it impossible to identify; I couldn't even discern the direction it was coming from.

"Jess? JESS!"

As I continued trying to find the source of the voice, two spirits with vacant eyes drifted through the smoky air over my body. They stopped, then approached my body warily, examining it. With my spirit form abuzz with a fear-like energy, I bit back the urge to fly at the spirits, screaming silently in my head for them to leave my body alone. A third spirit circled above me like a vulture, but—even though it passed within a few feet of where I was hovering—it didn't acknowledge me.

A moment later, all three spirits vanished simultaneously; my body was left alone in the sweltering semi-darkness, looking strangely alive in the light dancing from a nearby blaze. Barely a minute later, two Necromancers hurtled around the side of the tent. They skidded to a halt beside my body.

"That's it! There she is."

"They said she was dead. Go check her."

One of the Necromancers started forward warily, as if my body might leap up and attack him at any moment. He reached out and felt for a pulse in my neck. He lifted my eyelids. He poked and prodded my body for a long, tense moment.

"Well?" the other one shouted, waiting for a pronouncement.

"Dead!" the first cried triumphantly.

"And you're sure it's her?"

"Yes! She has purple streaks in her hair. See for yourself!"

The second Necromancer darted forward and shoved my hair roughly back from my face. After a moment, he raised his head and let out a maniacal crow. He pulled a cell phone from his pocket and took a picture of my "dead" body.

"Signal the others. Abandon the fight. We must tell Brother Caddigan it is done!"

§

"Jessica! Answer me! Jess!" came the angry, panicked voice again.

A lone figure stumbled out from behind Ileana's tent just as the two Necromancers began their dark revelries. The figure, obscured by the smoke, was coughing and retching. He stepped forward from the haze as he pushed the loose hair from his ponytail away from his soot-streaked face.

It was Finn.

Finn's eyes fell first on the Necromancers, then at the body by

244

their feet. I watched as realization spread across his face: The sound that escaped him was guttural, animalistic. He launched himself forward, and, with a ferocity I'd never seen in anyone, he tackled one of the Necromancers. The intensity of his attack obviously shocked the man, too; it was a solid few seconds before the Necromancer beneath him could do anything other than cover his head protectively. The second Necromancer dashed off into the night as he shouted loudly, proclaiming my death. Others took up the call, reveling in my supposed demise. Their cries echoed again and again on all sides.

Finn, meanwhile, with incoherent sounds spewing out of him, was hammering away at the other Necromancer. The Necromancer never had a chance: With a final grunt, Finn slammed a fist into the side of the man's head and knocked him out cold instantly. Then Finn shoved the man's limp form aside and threw himself onto the ground beside my body. Finn passed his violently shaking hands over me, as if he were afraid of damaging me further.

"Jesus Christ. Please, no! No—" he cried, and the emotion in his voice choked off the rest of his words. Feeling for a pulse, he pressed two shaking fingers to my neck, but I knew he would find no signs of life. My body was entirely still—no breath, no heartbeat, no pulse—and would remain lifeless, suspended in time, until I returned to it. But there was no way for Finn to know this, of course.

"Finn! Finn, I'm here! I'm alright!" I called from above, but he didn't acknowledge my cries; he couldn't hear me over the commotion in the camp—and, I suspected, his own grief. Actually, I wasn't even sure Finn could hear me at all in my Walking state.

Finn was wailing uncontrollably now—sobbing, pulling at his hair, and beating his bloodied fist against the ground. I couldn't bear to see him this way, couldn't stomach the utterly forlorn sounds coming from his mouth. Amid all the death and destruction around us, Finn's anguish was singularly the one thing I couldn't bear: I couldn't let him spend another moment thinking he was too late.

Without thinking, without considering my own safety, I—just to end Finn's agony—looked down at my own body and imagined myself back inside it.

As I flew home, it happened as if in slow motion: All I could do was watch. Finn reached down, cradled my head in his arms, and lifted me against his chest. And at the moment I reconnected, he bent his face to mine and kissed me.

The kiss filled every cell of my body so intensely that there was barely room for me to expand back into myself. My lips, my heart—every inch of me seemed to be on fire. And as I pulled a desperate first breath back into my lungs, I was filled with Finn's breath, his tears, and every wild, intense, out-of-control emotion burning upon his lips.

All reason left me: Not one single rational thought stayed behind to guide me. Instead of pulling away, my arms shot up, wrapped around Finn's neck, and I kissed him back—like it was the last thing I would ever do.

I felt his arms tighten around me for an instant, but then a strangled, muffled cry of relief escaped from our locked lips; Finn pulled away in shock. Our eyes met. Our breaths came in sharp, shuddering gasps.

"Why are you kissing me?" I panted.

"Why are you alive?" he said.

"Why are you kissing me?" I repeated.

"Don't you think my question is just a little more important?" Finn cried.

"Not really!" I struggled into a half-sitting position. "What the hell is going on here? I hope you don't think this is a Sleeping Beauty kind of moment, because that is *so* not what is happening here."

"Sleeping what?"

"Oh my God, you really are where all cultural references go to die. What are you doing here? I thought you were gone for good!"

Finn ignored my question and began looking me over with a wildly bewildered expression in his eyes. Then he looked down at himself, now covered in Anca's blood, too. "But all the blood! You were dead, properly dead. You had no pulse!"

"It's not my blood. I was Walking."

Before my eyes, his own eyes went cold. Finn pulled away sharply as his face twisted with anger. "Walking? You mean you figured out how to... I thought you were dead!"

"That was the idea!" I exclaimed. "The Necromancers were coming for me. It was my only chance of getting away from them!"

The mention of the Necromancers seemed to snap us both back into the parlous, gruesome reality surrounding us. We both looked

246

wildly around, as though a hoard of Necromancers were going to leap from the trees and descend upon us, but there was no one.

"Do you think the attack is over?" I looked over at the motionless, unconscious Necromancer Finn had fought.

"I'm not sure," answered Finn cautiously, lifting his chin into the air as though he could scent danger. "It sounds like they've retreated."

"I heard them just before you..." I changed my tack awkwardly, "just before I reconnected. They were proclaiming my death, celebrating it. If that's what they were hoping for, then they probably left the camp, right?"

Finn nodded, although he did not look at me. We both listened hard. The camp wasn't silent, but the sounds of the struggle were gone. Voices still rang out, but they were the cries of an after-attack. The Travelers were calling out for loved ones, crying for help, and working to put out the fires that were still burning everywhere. A few were keening into the night, sobbing—no doubt—over a family member's dead body. The Caomhnóir were shouting instructions to each other as they resecured the encampment. Despite all this activity, a muffling heaviness had fallen over the camp; the heaviness of loss and tragedy pervaded like a gas, creeping over everything.

Finn turned back to me. "If that's not your blood..."

I didn't let him finish. "Anca's. She's dead."

Finn cursed under his breath. "What about Annabelle? Savvy?"

My insides turned to lead and dropped into my feet. "I don't know. Milo and I were near the western border when it happened, looking for a way around the Wards. I haven't seen them."

"We've got to find them and get out of here," Finn said as he pulled his arm unceremoniously from behind my back and jumped up. I collapsed to the ground with a thunk. "Where did you see them last?"

"Our wagon, but they could be anywhere now," I answered, fighting my way to my feet. There wasn't a snowball's chance in hell of my asking Finn to help me up, despite how weak and disoriented I felt.

"We haven't got time to look for them. We've got to get you out of here before the Necromancers realize you're still alive," Finn declared.

"But that's just it, Finn. They already think I'm dead. That was their mission, and as far as they know, they've accomplished it. They've gone. I don't think we need to hurry."

He considered this for a moment. "There's something to that."

"Gee, you think?"

"Stay here then, but get under cover," he said. "Get into the tent and stay there."

"Don't talk to me like—"

"We don't have time for this, Jess! You can get properly offended later, but for now do as I say!" he shouted. Then he bent over the unconscious Necromancer and, with a grunt, hoisted him into a fireman's carry before hurrying off toward the center of the camp.

I watched Finn's retreat as I boiled over with the absolute strangest mixture of emotions I'd ever experienced in my life: relief at seeing him again; anger that he'd left in the first place; fear that something would happen to him before he returned; plus a whole host of other, less-easily-definable concerns and emotions that I didn't have the desire or ability to cope with right now. I pulled back the flap of Ileana's tent and stumbled inside.

A single overturned lantern lit the tent with a flickering golden light, revealing the utter disarray. I scanned the space for anyone who might be hurt—or worse—but it was deserted. Ileana's throne-like chair had been toppled. The raven's gilded cage lay battered on its side, yet the raven—apparently unharmed—stood ominously silent within.

I went to the raven and looked into its one good eye. I expected the bird to squawk in alarm, but it didn't; its silence seemed almost defiant. I remembered the tale Anca told me: Ileana had bent this creature to her will, yes, but that will would now mean the bird's death if I didn't release it. I searched the raven's eye as if what I found there would reflect things yet to come, but instead I found things past—there was Anca, cold and lifeless, beneath the wheel well of the Scribes' wagon.

I jumped back with a start as a cold sweat raced to my brow. I knew I needed to release the raven—and not just to save the bird from a slow, wasting death. I needed to free it because I could do nothing to bring back Anca, could do nothing to save the others in the camp; what I *could* do was give the raven back its rightful freedom, give this omen of misfortune a chance to create its own fate. I brought the cage to the far side of the tent where the fabric had been torn, then released the raven into the night.

I turned back to the room, refocusing on my surroundings. A large table stood in the center of the room, with chairs pushed haphazardly away from it—everyone at that table had clearly left in great haste. A large number of scrolls and papers littered the tabletop; Ileana had been in the middle of a meeting when the attack had begun.

A familiar image caught my eye, and I walked around to the other side of the table for a better look. Right in the table's center was a huge blueprint with its curling edges weighted down by large, smooth stones. There was no mistaking the building—it looked just as I had first seen it just a few months ago: Fairhaven Hall.

"What the hell?" I asked into the emptiness. I half-expected an answer; these days I never knew who—living or dead—might be around to answer.

I was sure I wasn't supposed to be looking at anything on this table, but I was also sure that I didn't give a damn what I was "supposed" to do. Not now. I pulled several more papers toward me. One was a map of Fairhaven's grounds, marked up with notes in Gaelic. Another was a roughly drawn map of what appeared to be the dungeons. A third map was covered in notes about specific Castings that protected various points of the castle.

I looked back down at the table, bewildered. As I pushed aside the Casting map, Hannah's face, staring up at me from a photograph, appeared.

I tossed the papers aside and snatched up her picture. It looked like a surveillance photo—one that had been taken from a great distance and then blown up. Hannah was being led across the central courtyard of Fairhaven.

The photographer had snapped the photo just as Hannah had turned her head toward the camera. Her expression was calm, even happy. Perhaps Lucida, who was out of focus but clearly discernible, had said something amusing the moment before. Lucida's hand rested comfortably on Hannah's shoulder, and, as I noticed this, I felt a desperate urge to reach through the picture and slap Lucida's hand away and remind my sister that this woman was her enemy. But I fought past this desire and focused instead on the disturbing implications of the picture.

Hannah was at Fairhaven—and Ileana knew it. An entire room full of people had known it, discussed it; everyone in that room knew full well that I was desperate for any scrap of information about my sister's safety, that I was wild for any shred of evidence that pointed to Hannah's not yet having sealed the fate of our whole universe with her tiny, bare hands.

But how could Hannah be at Fairhaven? How could Lucida and the Necromancers be at Fairhaven, when we knew that the castle was...of course! I laughed out loud—I'd been such an idiot. The only information we had about Fairhaven had come from Lucida, and she'd been in Neil's pocket all along: We had no reliable information about the true state of Fairhaven. It might've even been possible—and this new thought enraged me even further—that Lucida herself had gone back to Fairhaven and facilitated the Necromancers' takeover of the castle from the inside. Everyone we cared about there—Mackie, Celeste, Fiona—could be imprisoned, or worse.

But what did it all mean? And why would the Necromancers want to bring Hannah to Fairhaven in the first place?

My first thought was to find Ileana and unleash my rage—how could she have kept this from me? My second thought was that the first thought was not worth my energy. I now had the information we needed; we knew where we were going next, even if we had no idea of what we would do when we got there. I made the conscious choice to focus on this fact instead of my anger. We were going to Fairhaven. But what was waiting for us there?

I scanned the tabletop again, hoping it would contain further useful information that we could take with us. Another photograph showed the east side of the castle, where a single, narrow window was circled in red ink. Could this be the window of the room where Hannah was being kept?

"Jess!"

I screamed and flung the nearest large object—the raven's empty cage—in the general direction of the voice.

"Calm down! It's me!" Finn shouted, lowering his arms from in front of his face.

"You sneak in unannounced after what's happened here tonight, and you tell me to calm down?" I nearly shrieked. "What's going on out there? Where are the Necromancers?"

"Gone. Fled after they found your body."

"What about Savvy and Annabelle?"

"They're right here, I've got them. Let's get out of here!" he said, pulling the tent flap back. Savvy and Annabelle were revealed; they were both streaked with soot and looked badly shaken, but seemed otherwise unharmed. Annabelle gasped when she saw me—I'd forgotten for a moment that I was still covered in Anca's blood.

"Thank God!" I sighed. "Are you two okay?"

"We'll live, mate," Savvy answered grimly. "Which is more than some here can say."

I swallowed hard. "Is it really that bad?"

"Yeah, it's bad. The Travelers are gathering near the enclosure. I saw some people being carried there. They were burned and screaming, and..." Savvy's voice failed; she shook her head.

At that moment a violent drumming began, accompanied by an instrument that sounded like a primitive violin. A ghastly wailing followed.

"What the hell is that?" cried Savvy, raising her fists as if she were prepared to swing a right hook at the sound itself.

"They're mourning," Annabelle said softly. "From birth to death, every Traveler life event is celebrated or mourned with music. This is a tribute to the dead."

We all stood transfixed, listening. Their song was horror turned into music. The combination of sounds was so wrenching I could hardly endure it; my very skin felt alive, as if Anca's blood was wailing too.

"Do we know who else is...?"

"No, and we don't have time to find out," said Finn, much more harshly than the moment warranted. He realized this and softened his voice. "We can't risk being caught here. The Necromancers could come back, and we don't want to be here if they do."

"You're right," I agreed, causing Finn to look at me like I'd said something bizarre. I gathered up as many of the papers as I could and shoved them into Savvy's arms. "Here. Stick these in your bag."

"Right, yeah, sure. And... what are these?" Savvy asked.

"This is the intel the Travelers have on Hannah. It'll make finding her easier."

"I know where Hannah is," said Finn, waving a dismissive arm at the scrolls. "She's at Fairhaven."

"I know she's at Fairhaven!" I cried, pointing to the blueprint still spread across the center of the table. "How do you know where she is?"

"I'll explain when we're safely out of here. Now let's make that happen. Immediately."

"Yeah, okay," I answered, handing an armful of papers to Annabelle; she stuffed them into her backpack. "We should get moving. Unless..." I felt my heart speed up. "Has anyone seen Flavia?"

"Who's Flavia?" asked Finn, but I ignored him as I watched Annabelle and Savvy shake their heads.

"Okay," I said, biting back a sob. "She's fine. I'm sure she's fine. Let's go."

"Can we really do that?" Savvy asked. "Leave? I mean, I know we need to be safe, and I know we've got to find Hannah, but it *is* sorta our fault that the camp's been attacked, ain't it? Shouldn't we help clean up the damage, or organize some aid? Or put out some fires?" She gestured behind her, where smoke and flames were still engulfing the camp.

Finn shook his head. "I feel poorly about it too, but we need to go. We're endangering them further by staying here, I promise you that."

"And we can't put out those flames," I said. "Have you listened to the fires?"

"Listened to the fire?" asked Savvy, her tone dubious. "Nope, can't say that I have, what with all the ear-piercing shrieks and such. And why the bloody hell would I listen to a fire when I'm doing my damnedest not to be burnt to a crisp?"

"Because it's not a normal fire; it's alive. Remember the Blind Summoner I told you about? The spirit essence trapped in a candle?" I asked.

Annabelle figured out first; her eyes grew wide with horror. "I wondered why I never sensed them coming," she whispered, turning and looking over her shoulder at the nearest blaze. "So many ghosts used in the attack, and not a single one of us was able to feel their approach. It didn't make any sense."

"That's because they aren't human spirits. Not anymore," I said bitterly.

Savvy caught up. "Blimey! You don't mean... are they still in there, in the flames?"

"Yes, Sav, just listen."

We all froze again, listening. Added to the melancholy dirge of the Traveler's music was another layer of sound; in the crackling of the fires around us, hundreds of spirit voices were calling out incoherently, their words lost in a twisted, agonized chorus.

"We have to tell someone," Savvy whispered; her eyes sparkled with budding tears.

"They know," I replied. "At least Flavia does, and I'm sure she'll tell the others. But I honestly don't know if there's anything they can do. This is a Necromancer Casting; the Durupinen haven't encountered it before."

"Well, just tell them to keep the bloody fires going!" Savvy cried, as her tears spilled onto her cheeks, which were now reddening with anger. "Keep piling on the firewood until someone figures it out!"

"Savvy, they can't..." Annabelle began.

"They bloody well better!" Savvy shouted, dropping the papers I'd handed her. "They're Durupinen! It's their job to help these spirits—they can't just let the lot of them snuff out with the fire! What the hell will happen to those spirits, with no idea who they were or why they're still here?

I jumped forward and caught her by the shoulders, shaking her slightly until she met my eye. "Sav, I don't know," I told her. "I have no idea what's going to happen to them. No one does. But I can tell you what's going to happen to us if we don't get out of here. If the Necromancers come back—and they might—we are all dead."

"But *they'll* be worse than dead!" said Savvy, sobbing in earnest for the trapped spirits now.

"And there's not a thing we can do about it here, Sav. But if we get to Fairhaven, and if we end this thing, we can make sure this doesn't happen to any other ghost ever again. You're right, we are Durupinen. As much as we hate it sometimes, and as much as we wish it was someone else's responsibility, it's ours. So let's get out of here and do the one thing that can finally protect all these spirits from the Necromancers for good. Let's end this."

She stared at me a moment, as though my words were traveling a great distance to reach me; as they sunk in through her hysteria, Savvy relaxed her body beneath my hands and nodded slowly.

More calmly, she asked, "And what about Milo? They didn't get him? They didn't trap him in one of those fires?"

253

"No, Savvy," I soothed. "He's safe. I sent him away when the Necromancers first attacked. I'll Summon him back when it's safer."

"Good," Finn said. "Very good. Okay, let's get out of here. Everyone follow me."

We re-gathered Savvy's papers and took off after Finn, who had skirted around to the back of Ileana's tent. We caught up with him along the border of the clearing.

"Where are we even going?" I asked, struggling to keep pace.

"To the road that runs north of the clearing. It's the same one they met us on when we arrived, as far as I can tell. It's also how I got back here."

"Yeah, and that's all really interesting," I said, as we crouched past a thicket of holly bushes. "But how are we going to get out of here without a car?"

Finn stopped short; we all crashed into him. "Shh! We're going to pass the enclosure. Not a sound now, or they might stop us!"

We skirted through the trees, making as little noise as possible—although I couldn't see how anyone could hear us over the crackling of fires and the Travelers' symphony of sorrow, which was now building to a crescendo. Tears blurred my vision; I blinked them away so I could see where I was stepping. I fought the impulse to break away and run into the clearing; I desperately wanted to ask someone—anyone—how many had been killed, how many besides Anca had given their lives to protect us. I wanted to know their names and see their lifeless faces; I wanted to lift my own voice into the chorus of grief that was pounding like angry fists into my eardrums.

§

"Where are you going, Northern Girl?"

The voice seemed so close to my ear it might have been inside my head. I leapt in alarm as Irina, grinning at me through the trees, shimmered into view.

"Irina! What are you doing?" I hissed.

"I asked you first," she said, grinning wider.

"I'm leaving. We need to get out of here. I don't want the Necromancers coming back here again because of me." It was true, even if it wasn't the whole truth.

"They've caused great damage here. The Council is in shambles. The encampment is nearly destroyed," she said.

"I know. I don't even know what to say. I'm so sorry." I blinked back the tears in my eyes once again.

"I'm not," replied Irina bluntly.

"Come again?"

"The Necromancers destroyed my prison. They scattered my jailers and broke the Castings that held me. I'm free!" she proclaimed, stretching her arms wide and lifting her face to the sky—a sky she could now traverse as far and wide as she chose.

"What about your body? Your life here with your people?" I asked.

She dropped her chin and looked at me again. "I have no life here. Only the torture of enslavement."

"They only want to protect you. You should go back, Irina."

"They don't care about protecting me—and you yourself promised my freedom," Irina said. "They only care about protecting themselves. You ought to know that now, before you sacrifice everything. They care naught for your suffering, as long as it serves to preserve their precious order. Remember that, before you honor them with your sacrifice."

I had no way to argue with her; I knew there was more than a little truth in Irina's words.

"Good luck, Northern Girl." And with the joy of a long-caged bird, she soared into the star-strewn darkness, which swallowed her up.

"Who was that?" Finn asked.

"No one we'll ever see again," I said.

"Do you think she'll tell the others she's seen you?"

"No. She's been planning her escape for a long, long time. I doubt she'll ever show her face here again, let alone speak to any of the Durupinen. Come on, let's keep moving."

We plunged into the woods beyond the edge of the camp and walked until our legs cramped with the effort, pausing only for a moment by a small pool to wash the blood and soot from our faces. We emerged onto a dirt road, lit only by the pale glow of the clear night sky and a round, full moon.

"Now where do we—" Savvy began, but Finn interrupted her by inserting two fingers into his mouth and whistling loudly.

Two headlights flared to life immediately, followed by the roar of an engine. A large black SUV rumbled out of a nearby ditch and stopped beside us. Savvy, Annabelle, and I were too shocked at its sudden appearance to do anything but gape.

The driver's side window retracted. A round, freckled face appeared.

"You got everyone?" Bertie asked Finn, wiping nervous beads of sweat from his upper lip.

"All accounted for. Let's get out of here," Finn said. He opened the back door and motioned with one impatient jerk of his head for all of us to get in. "I'll explain when we're on the road," he replied curtly in answer to my bemused look.

We piled into the car, with Savvy sputtering incoherently at the reappearance of her Caomhnóir.

"Hello, Ms. Todd. I hope you're well," Bertie said with an odd sort of salute.

I turned to her, smirking. "Ms. Todd?"

"Don't get me started. I've told him at least a hundred times to bugger off. No one's ever called me Ms. Todd in my life but my headmistress before a proper telling-off. It gives me the creeps." Savvy shuddered, then looked back at Bertie. "What the devil are you doing here, then?" Her tone was almost accusatory, as if Bertie had done something wrong by remaining unharmed.

Bertie shook his head. "I wasn't in the castle when the fire started," he said. "When I saw you slip out of the meeting in the Grand Council Room, I followed you in case you needed protecting. But I couldn't find you—I was searching the grounds when the fire broke out."

"Bloody hell! So why did Lucida tell me..." Savvy began, but I cut her off.

"Everything Lucida told us about Fairhaven was a lie. I don't think she went back to Fairhaven at all—or at least, she didn't go back to check on everyone. She's with the Necromancers, remember? She must've made up all those details about the aftermath to cover her tracks."

"That cow!" cried Savvy. "She had me thinking this bloke got his lungs well-toasted trying to save me."

"I kept looking for you for days and days after the fire," Bertie continued. "Then I thought you might've crossed the Wards with a ghost, like you'd done before, so I went to investigate. I was on the very outskirts of Fairhaven when the Necromancers attacked.

It was awful. Then I lost track of Phoebe, too. I figured I had a better chance of finding her, at least, if I got some help, so I took one of the cars and made a break for it. I had to run one of the Necromancers down to get away." He pointed to a crack in the windshield and shuddered violently. "I think I killed him, but I didn't stop to find out."

"And what about Phoebe?" Savvy asked. "Is she—"

"She's fine," answered Finn, cutting her off. Then he turned to me and added, "Bertie found me later, when I went back." His tone told me that no further explanation was coming, so I let it drop. Then he cocked his head toward the driver's seat; Bertie unbuckled his seatbelt and slid over to the passenger side obediently, looking relieved to let someone else do the driving.

"Where are we going?" Bertie asked as Finn threw the car into drive and started down the tree-lined road.

"Back to Fairhaven," Finn replied, without so much as taking his eyes from the road.

"And what are we going to do when we get there?"

"I haven't gotten that far yet."

19

TRUTH OF THE HEART

I PRESSED MY FOREHEAD against the back of the driver's seat headrest and closed my eyes; it felt easier to ask the next question without having to chance seeing Finn's face.

"So are we going to talk about it?" I asked.

All was silence but for the hum of the car rocketing along the highway. Savvy, Annabelle, and Bertie had fallen asleep an hour ago, and Milo, true to my order—and probably trying to save his strength so we could Habitate and check in on Hannah when we got to Fairhaven—hadn't materialized or truly communicated since we'd left the camp. Every once in a while, I knew he was nearby, though; I could feel the quiet pulse of his presence.

After we'd put a good few miles between us and the remains of the Traveler camp, we had all settled into a temporary bubble of relaxation—cherishing this brief moment between crises—as the car covered the distance between one terror and another. Now, with the others asleep, Finn and I were more or less alone. I sat directly behind him as he drove—our heads were separated by only a few mere inches of fabric and padding, yet the silence between us covered a much larger, much murkier distance.

"Talk about what?" Finn asked brusquely after a moment.

"Don't. Don't do that. You know what I'm talking about."

He sighed. "I don't know where to begin."

"Why don't you begin with why you left?" I demanded in a quiet, but firm, tone.

"You already know why, don't you?" he asked.

It was a cop-out and he knew it. I didn't dignify his equivocation with a response, but Finn didn't expect me to. He sighed again.

"I couldn't stay. I couldn't stay and watch you risk that much. What if it had gone wrong? How do you think I would've felt if you were lost, knowing that my one function in life is to protect you?"

"It's not your one function in—"

"It is, Jess. It is. I can't understand what it was like growing up not knowing who you were, just like you can't understand what it was like growing up like I did. The Durupinen defined everything. It was the only lens I ever had—it was my whole world. Everything I did was valued by whether or not it would help me be a better Caomhnóir, even by my own mother. We didn't have discussions about what I wanted to do with my life. There was no, 'What are you going to be when you grow up?' And if I showed interest in anything beyond being a Caomhnóir, it was ignored—or actively stamped out. Caomhnóir. Period. Full stop.

"So, Jess, just try to get that, can't you? That was my whole life—from the cradle on through. So if I seem a bit... obsessed with your safety, it's because I am. It's what I've trained and prepared my entire life for. And I'm failing! Every time I turn around, I'm failing again."

"You're not failing. You're doing the best you can," I said, not without sympathy.

He laughed incredulously. "The best I can? I've already lost half my Gateway. Your sister was kidnapped right from under my nose! And *you*... you've nearly gotten yourself killed more times than I can properly count! And now, every Durupinen and Necromancer in Britain is after you, yet here I am, made a fool again—I'm driving you right into the viper's den."

"But you're doing it for the Gateway. That's what you're really protecting."

"It's supposed to be," he said. "But I've failed at that, too."

"What do you—"

"Because somewhere along the way I got lost!" he cried, raising his voice in anguish loudly enough to cause the others to stir. He watched them anxiously in the rearview mirror for a few moments, ensuring no one had awoken. When he continued, his voice was hushed, but urgent. "At first, protecting you and protecting the Gateway were the same thing. I could do both. But then you decided to Walk—and I had to choose, don't you see? Suddenly the Durupinen and the Gateway were endangering you; I had to decide which one I was supposed to be protecting!"

I shut my eyes tightly; this didn't make any sense. "If you were so worried about protecting us, why did you leave? How could you protect us if you were gone?"

"Add it to the list of failures!" Finn cried. "I was furious. Pissing fire. I was working my arse off to keep you alive. Yet you woke up that morning and told me you were going to risk it all—needlessly!"

"It wasn't needless!" I could feel my old anger rising—the frustration that only Finn could inspire in me—and I did my damnedest to keep it out of my voice. I wasn't trying to pick a fight; I needed answers.

"Any risk to your life feels needless to me. So I left. I left and told myself that I didn't care. If you didn't care enough to protect your own life, then neither did I. If you were going to make my job impossible—if you were going to make me choose—then I was done trying to do either."

"So... why did you come back?"

"When I left, I decided to go back to Fairhaven. It took me days to get back. I was able to hitchhike a bit of the way, but I mostly stayed off the main roads for cover. When I finally arrived, I knew I couldn't let anyone see me, but I thought I could at least sneak onto the grounds, assess the damage, and find out what happened to my sister."

I sat up straight. "Oh my God, Olivia! Was she... is she okay?"

"She's fine," Finn answered. "Or at least, she was when I left. I set up a surveillance base in the woods and caught sight of her on my second day. I was lying low, deciding whether to risk contact, when the Necromancers attacked.

"That was three days ago. The Necromancers blitzed—there were far more of them than I could ever have imagined. I don't know how they got to be so powerful without the Durupinen detecting it, but there was a veritable army of them. And they have hundreds of spirits completely under Necromancer control. Well, actually..." he glanced into the rearview mirror, catching my eye, "they're under Hannah's control."

"Hannah's control? How do you know that?"

"I saw her," he said, almost apologetically. "She was walking with the Necromancers, heavily protected, working a Casting. She was carrying a torch, and the torch was... wailing—screaming like the fire at the encampment. The Necromancers were giving the spirits orders and the spirits were obeying without question. They're hypnotized, I think."

I put my hands up over my face. "They're not hypnotized.

They're using Blind Summoners as Wraiths. They're empty, Finn—they don't even know who their human selves were. Every scrap of their humanity is trapped in that Spirit Torch. Or at least it was—God only knows what will happen to them if Hannah ever lets it go out."

"She wouldn't let it go out," Finn replied, and I could almost hear a question in his voice.

"I honestly don't know what she would do anymore."

"But surely she's not doing it voluntarily," Finn reasoned. "They must be forcing her. Why else would she cooperate?"

"It's Lucida," I said. I plunged into the entire story, explaining how Milo and I had discovered the connection between us and Hannah, then I told him about everything we'd seen during our Habitations. When I'd finished, Finn's mouth hung open in disbelief.

"Lucida's alive? But how did she..." he couldn't even finish the question.

"She Leeched. She stored up the spirit energy somehow, then used it to heal herself. She must've learned how from the Necromancers. And Lucida's probably the best method of persuasion the Necromancers could have—Hannah's always trusted her."

"So they've turned her?"

"I think so."

Finn paused; he took a deep breath and blew it out again. "Well, that changes some things."

"Yeah, it does."

A long and loaded silence stretched between us, making the space between the front and back seats seem suddenly enormous. I almost didn't have the courage to break the spell.

"So tonight..."

"Yeah?"

"Why did you come back?"

"When Fairhaven was attacked, I had to get help. I almost stayed to fight, but when I saw that army of ghosts, the Wraiths, I knew there was no chance. At best I'd be captured, and that wasn't going to help anyone. I thought if I could get back to the Travelers, they might offer to help—or at least point me to other clans that would. I was on my way to their camp when Bertie found me. We drove here nonstop—I remembered the GPS coordinates to the north

262

road. From there it was easy to find the camp; I saw the smoke, and I knew the Necromancers must've located you. I told Bertie to wait with the car while I found you."

"And when you did," I said, "you thought I was dead." It wasn't a question.

"Yes."

I waited, but he wasn't going to mention it. It was up to me.

"And you kissed me."

Pressing, pressing silence. Then a weak, but audible, "Yes."

"Why, Finn? Why'd you do that?"

"I don't know. It was a mistake. Forget about it," he replied, with every ounce of his usual brusqueness.

"A mistake? Seriously? No, a mistake is if you tripped and fell and landed with your lips on my face."

"I said forget about it. Can't you just let it go?" he asked.

"No! I can't just pretend it didn't happen. I deserve an explanation, Finn."

"What is there to explain?" he asked.

The question seemed so blatantly dumb that I couldn't help myself: I laughed scathingly. "Gee, let's see; how about telling me why someone who hates me ends up kissing me."

"I don't hate you."

"You hate all of us!" I cried. "That was all part of your upbringing, wasn't it? Durupinen are evil temptresses who steal your soul, wear your testicles as earrings, and all the rest of that bullshit. You've hardly said a single word to me that wasn't insulting at the worst or condescending at the very best. Hell, you even had to be dragged kicking and screaming to our Initiation! That's how badly you wanted to get away!"

"That... wasn't what it looked like," Finn said sharply.

"Oh really? You didn't turn up until halfway through the ceremony... and only after another Caomhnóir found you and forced you to come. What am I supposed to think?"

"I didn't... I... I couldn't face it, okay?"

"And you still can't! You left us, Finn! So why would you turn around and kiss me like that?" It was getting harder and harder to keep my voice hushed.

"I... you don't..."

"And what I *really* can't figure out is why—even after all of your training—you would risk your life to protect me when you can't stand the sight of me. And who can blame you? Women are evil, and Hannah and I—coming from this outcast family who screwed up your whole precious system—are *particularly* evil. But now you're stuck with us, and we keep landing in worse and worse trouble."

Finn growled. He actually growled like a trapped animal before spitting out, "Just... here!" and flung something small and hard over the back of his seat and into my lap.

"What's this?" I picked it up and recognized it in the passing brightness of some oncoming headlights. "What do I want with this? I already know what you write in these!" I said, throwing it back at him. "You dropped one near the wagon when you walked out on us."

Finn balked—I watched his face fall in the rearview mirror. Then, with an intentional calmness, he said, "I was wondering where that one got to. You read it?"

"Some of it. I admit I was surprised. Up until last week I was pretty sure these were full of page after page of 'All work and no play makes Finn a dull boy,'" I said, in a pathetic attempt at a Jack Nicholson impersonation.

"What?"

I knocked my head against the window in frustration—had he really never seen a single movie, ever? "Nothing. Never mind. I don't see what any of this has to do with why you left."

The little book came sailing back over the seat and smacked me in the forehead.

"Ouch!" I exclaimed a little too loudly.

"Shh!"

"How about 'sorry'?" I hissed.

"Sorry, sorry," he grumbled. "But... you need to read it. Page one."

"Reading this is going to help me understand why you left?"

"Yes. And also why I came back. And also why I... Damn it, Jess, just read it."

Sighing deeply, I opened the little book, grabbed a penlight from the cup holder, and began reading.

JESS
She abides with darkness.
It clings to her like ash,

264

From the tips of her eyelashes to the soles of her feet,
Darkness wraps about her, a soft gossamer shroud,
Shielding the world from the shining heat of her eyes.
If I could brush this ash, like stardust,
Away from the constellations of her cheeks,
And see beyond her caliginous veil,
To the blossoming sorrow beneath—
What mightn't I give to be so blinded?
All within me, surely, the pulse of every cell,
For a single brush of lip upon lip.

I read it again. Then again. And a third time. I couldn't turn the page. I couldn't move beyond this single collection of words.

"What's this?" I finally asked.

Finn hesitated, as though he thought I was asking a trick question. "A poem."

"No. Yes, but... what *is* this?" I asked. "The title is 'Jess.'"

"Yes."

"And it's... but you... you don't even like me."

"That's not true," he said quietly, with a shyness I'd never heard before in his tone.

"Yes, it is. You're not even nice to me! You don't like me," I repeated, still staring down at the words on the page, which were causing my stomach to churn in the strangest way.

"You're right. I wasn't nice to you. But it wasn't because I didn't like you." And here Finn paused, causing me to look up. His gaze found mine in the rearview mirror. "It was because I fell in love with you almost the first minute I saw you—and that goes against everything I've ever been taught."

"I... you... what?" I said helplessly, as the strange, spongy feeling overtook my stomach and tangled my tongue.

"I can't explain it. It was... like you read about in books, the sort of thing you never think happens in real life, to real people. But Jess, I walked into that classroom and saw you... Then my beastly cousin started picking on you... and something in me... changed... and that was it!

"And I was terrified and angry. The Senior Caomhnóir told us we'd be tested—that it was the mark of the true Caomhnóir to resist that temptation. I thought I was ready, but there you were on the very first day, tearing my resistance to shreds!"

I tore my gaze away from Finn's and realized I was mouthing wordlessly, agog. This was not happening.

"I tried to poison myself against you. I listened to all the gossip, but it just stoked this fire inside me—it was all I could do not to tear down anyone who spoke against you. But at the same time, I knew I had to get away from you. I knew I couldn't be tied to you for life—the agony would destroy me.

"I went to Seamus and asked to be reassigned. When he refused, I went over his head to Finvarra. I never told either of them the true reason. They assumed I was prejudiced against your clan, just like everyone else. I panicked when the Initiation came, so I ran... ran like a coward! As you know, I didn't get far. Suddenly there we were, bound together. A twisted, cosmic joke—I always had to be near you, but could never be *with* you. And perhaps the worst part of it all was that you so clearly despised me!"

"Finn!" I gasped, "I don't... I didn't... I just thought you hated me, so I put my guard up." I couldn't bring myself to look into the rearview mirror. It was so much easier to keep my eyes glued to the words of the poem, the words that grew more and more beautiful every time I read them.

"Of course you despised me! I made sure you did! You were quite clear on your feelings about having a Caomhnóir—I used that to put as much distance between us as I could. Since physical distance wasn't possible, I kept building that wall. But all the while, these feelings for you kept burrowing under it, so I trapped them between the pages of my notebooks before I could give myself away."

"Mission accomplished," I said weakly, before adding a totally unnecessary, "I had no idea."

"That morning in the wagon, I snapped. Properly snapped. I couldn't stay and watch you risk your life by Walking. I couldn't stop you, but I couldn't save you, either. So I ran. Again. But, Jess, I regretted it instantly. If the Necromancers hadn't attacked, it would've been a matter of a few more days before I came back. Within hours of leaving I knew I wouldn't be able to stay away long. I fought every hour not to tuck my tail between my legs and run back to you, to beg your forgiveness. And then I did come back... and I saw you dead on the ground, and I thought..."

Finn's voice was swallowed by emotion, and I looked up again. His eyes, reflected in the rearview mirror, were glistening with

266

pooled tears. Yet I still couldn't believe any of this. I was in the fucking twilight zone.

"I'm in love with you, Jess. It's impossible and reckless, but I can't fight it. I'm tired of trying."

All I could see was the glint of those tears in Finn's eyes. All I could hear was the pounding of my own heart.

"Jess, say something. Please, say anything."

"I... Finn... I..."

Beside me, Savvy suddenly snored loudly and startled herself awake, saving me from having to answer Finn. She flailed her arms so violently that she smacked Annabelle in the face while simultaneously kicking the back of Bertie's seat. Thankfully, neither of them woke up.

"Oi! What's that? What's happened?" she slurred.

"It was you," I told her, shutting Finn's book and stowing it carefully out of sight. "You snore like a cartoon character, Sav."

"Sorry, mate," she said, giving me a curious look. "You alright?"

"I... I'm..." I glanced into the rearview mirror without meaning to and caught Finn's eye. He was still looking at me: The intensity of his gaze sent blood flooding into my cheeks. I dropped my eyes quickly to my lap. "I just couldn't sleep. I'm too worried about Hannah."

But Savvy wasn't convinced: She smelled a rat, and I knew it. She began looking back and forth between Finn and me with her eyes narrowed in suspicion. Thankfully, whatever her suspicions were, she dropped them, and instead shoved her sleeve back so she could check her watch. "We must be nearly there, then?"

"We are," Finn answered, tearing his eyes from me and refocusing on the road. "And we need to come up with a plan."

20

REVELATIONS

I KNOCKED MY FISTS REPEATEDLY AGAINST MY TEMPLES. I couldn't do it. I couldn't think anymore. I had absolutely no ideas. I would never have another idea as long as I lived—a life which, at the moment, wasn't looking like it would be very long.

We had driven until we were just beyond Fairhaven's borders. Every paper, scroll, and photo we'd stolen from Ileana's tent was spread on the grass between us, lit only by the headlights of the SUV. We'd been over and over them; every time one of us had an idea, another of us shot it down—although we all emphatically vetoed Bertie's brilliant idea of "just winging it."

"Even if we manage to get onto the grounds and into the castle without being detected—which, by the way, sounds basically impossible," I began, "we haven't got a clue where in the castle Hannah is." I pulled out a photo, which had a window circled. "I mean, this room obviously means something, but we have no idea what."

"And if what Flavia said is true, then this book is bloody useless," Savvy said, throwing the *Book of Téigh Anonn* one long, disgusted look before tossing it into the grass. "How are we supposed to get past the Wraiths if the Castings won't work on them?"

"It's true," Bertie said, speaking for the first time in so long that I'd actually forgotten he was there. "We couldn't expel them. Nothing we did had any effect at all." He paused for a moment, then added guiltily, "By 'we,' I guess I mean the other Caomhnóir at the castle. I didn't actually fight the Wraiths myself. I would've, of course, but I was already at the border, so..." Bertie's voice died away. He swallowed hard then dropped his eyes to the map he was holding, as though it had suddenly become fascinating.

Savvy rolled her eyes and turned to Finn. "Finn, you saw a good

269

bit of fighting at the Traveler camp and at the castle. Wasn't there anything that put a dent in 'em?"

Finn shook his head. "The only time I ever saw a spirit stop attacking was when someone doused one of the fires. But even if the Spirit Torch is still lit, I'm sure it's being kept in a safe place."

"And we can't just extinguish it, even if we do find it," I said. "All of those spirits would just... well... die. For good." I knew "die" wasn't exactly the right word, but I couldn't think of another way to describe it. No one challenged the term; they all knew what I meant.

"But surely giving the spirits their essences back would work as well?" Annabelle asked. "They're only obeying the Necromancers because they have no choice. So how do we find out how to release the spirits from the Torch and restore their essences?"

"The only people who can tell us that are Hannah or the Necromancers," said Finn. "Only a Necromancer traitor would give up that intelligence—it's the key to disabling their army. And Hannah..." Finn looked at me inquiringly.

I shrugged. "I want to think she'd help us, but I just don't know anymore."

"Well, this is bullshit!" Milo burst out. "How did the Durupinen defeat the Necromancers all those years ago? I mean, they won, right? They must've had some tricks up their sleeves. You don't win wars without learning to fight dirty."

"Don't look at me, I never read anything for Celeste's class, did I?" Savvy said.

"We never learned about anything like that," I answered. "Our books glossed over the messy stuff—we learned that the hard way, didn't we? If the Durupinen ever played dirty, we aren't likely to know about it. Plus, they didn't have to deal with Wraiths before, did they?"

Finn shook his head. "We've spent a lot of time learning Casting tactics—both defensive and offensive. Every Casting we have needs the spirit essence to work properly. I can't think of anything that would disable the Wraiths."

"Neither can I," added Bertie. "Finn's right."

"They're like floating weapons," I said, knocking over a pile of scrolls in frustration. "There's no way to reason with them, no way to appeal to them; they're literally floating vessels of violence! They feed off mayhem... they're the incarnation of Necromancer hatred! Spirits who know nothing but negativity, who thrive on it, and... and..." I trailed off as a crazy, not-quite-formed thought swooped down on me.

A crazy—and quite possibly brilliant—thought.

"I've got it!" I exclaimed, as the last bit of the thought coalesced in my mind.

"You've got what? What the hell are you on about now?" Finn demanded.

"The Durupinen aren't so pure. They've used a being just as awful as the Wraiths to torture people. But it's not in our books—the Durupinen weren't dumb enough to record it for posterity."

"Are you going to tell us what you're talk—"

"The Elemental," I said.

Bertie, Savvy, and Annabelle looked confused. Finn looked pensive. But Milo's face split into a wicked grin.

"Oh girl, you *are* good," he said, smirking.

I gave a mock bow. "I try."

"There's an Elemental on the grounds?" Annabelle asked, looking alarmed. "A real one? I thought they were just legends."

I nodded. "Hannah and I were trapped in a Circle with it right after we got here. Long story. But I can tell you from personal experience that there's no more effective weapon in the world."

"But could we control it?" Finn asked.

"I have no idea," I replied. "But I do know it's being controlled right now by the Durupinen. They've got it contained in the *príosún*."

"Yes, and for good reason," Finn said. "If given free reign, that thing would wreak absolute havoc."

"Isn't absolute havoc exactly what we need?" Milo asked.

"Not if we can't aim that havoc at the right people," Finn replied. "Who's to say it won't start attacking every single person in its path?"

Poor Bertie, looking more confused—and terrified—than ever, finally burst out, "What is this... this... Elemental? I've had no training! How am I..."

Annabelle, with a touch of sympathy in her voice, cut him off. "I'll explain later, Bertie. Just trust us."

"I know Finn, but that might be a risk we have to take," I said. "But I think the Wraiths would be the perfect lure. Don't you remember how positive thoughts drove the Elemental away? The Wraiths don't have *any* positive energy; the Elemental will feast on them!"

"I suppose," Finn said slowly, before jumping up and starting to pace, "if we had the ability to trap the Elemental again when it had served its purpose, it might be worth the risk."

"So can we?" I asked. "How did you and Carrick banish it last time?"

Finn stopped pacing and looked stricken. "I don't have that Casting, it's too obscure," he said. "It wasn't in the *Book of Téigh Anonn*. Carrick knew it; he told me what to do, what to say. I don't think we can do this without him."

I groaned. "Back to the drawing board, I guess."

"Hold on. Why can't we just ask Carrick?" asked Milo.

I stared at him. "Uh, probably because Carrick isn't here," I said flatly.

Milo rolled his eyes at me. "Don't get sassy with me, we don't have time. I know Carrick's not here now, obviously, but he must be in the castle. He's Bound to Finvarra—he can't leave her—and Finvarra is probably in the dungeons now; I think our best bet is to find him. He'll have the information we need."

"That's all well and good, mate," Savvy said, "but how are we supposed to find him? It's the same problem. We can't very well get into the castle without being discovered, can we?"

"But Jess can. She can Walk," Milo answered, before turning to me. "Didn't you say the Wraiths can't see you when you're Walking?"

I nodded my head in both amazement and as an answer to his question. "It's true. They were flying right past me at the Traveler camp. Not one of them even acknowledged me. Milo, you're a genius!"

"Obvi," Milo sang.

"No, no, this is no good," Finn said in his best Caomhnóir-taking-charge voice. "We can't send Jess in there alone. What if she's caught? What if we can't get her back out? No. We can't afford a mistake like that."

"We don't have time for caution," I insisted. Finn caught my eye; his gaze burned with such intensity that I had to look away. "If we don't try it, we're done for. I'll head straight for the dungeons, find Carrick, and get back here. The Necromancers will never even know I was there."

Savvy nodded. "She's right. We've got one shot at this. You've got to let her do it, mate."

I nearly shouted down Savvy's idea of Finn's "letting me" do anything, but I bit my tongue and kept my eyes on my hands.

After what felt like an interminably long pause, Finn said, "Fine. But Milo is going with you; wrap him inside your spirit form, if you can. And Milo, you stay within Jess' shielding for as long as you can. Don't leave her unless you need to go for help. And no playing hero, either of you!"

"Fine," I said flatly.

"In and out, quick and dirty. Promise," Milo said earnestly.

"Right," began Finn. "We'll cut through the woods, then wait by the *príosún* with your body until you come back."

My heart began beating a violent tattoo against my ribcage. "Let's go."

§

I'd thought Fairhaven's grounds were beautiful from the first moment I saw them. But they were even more beautiful when floating—bathed in chilling moonlight—weightlessly above them. I propelled myself on mere thought over Fairhaven's gentle hills, and around its wending walls and flower beds. Milo, invisible, hovered close by me; as he promised, he hugged tightly to my spirit form, as if we were overlapping just a bit. We came to a stop at the base of the castle and waited in the shadows, taking stock of our surroundings.

Across the grounds, Wraiths wove through the air like moths, or else hung suspended—eerily still—waiting for a trigger that would cause them to unleash their dark instructions.

"What do you think would happen if they could see us?" Milo asked. His thought drifted into my head like a song.

"I don't know. They'd attack, probably. I'm sure they've been programmed to watch for intruders."

"Hey, I know that one!" Milo exclaimed, and even without seeing him point, I could follow the direction of his thought toward the ghost of a strapping man floating about ten yards away.

"Remember him? He was the one Savvy used to cross the Wards the night we went into London."

"That's right," I said, observing him more closely. "What was his name?"

"Martin, I think." I felt Milo shudder. "He just doesn't look right like that. None of them do."

"I know. But focus, Milo—the quicker we get this done, the quicker they'll be themselves again."

"Okay," began Milo. "According to the map, the highest level of the dungeons should be just on the other side of this wall." I turned to the wall itself and examined it closely; the Necromancers hadn't added any runes that I could see, at least not to the outside.

I was about to enter the castle when a new thought struck me. As often as I'd practiced Walking, I'd never actually tried to move through a solid object before, which—now that I stopped to think about it—seemed like a glaring omission in my training. Why the hell hadn't Irina showed me how to do it? What if there was some trick to it I didn't know?

"Hey, Milo, any advice for going through solid objects?" I asked a bit sheepishly.

"If it's anything like the way it is for spirits, it'll feel strange at first," Milo offered. "You'll feel sort of... compressed. Don't think too much about it or you'll get disoriented."

"Right, okay," I said, psyching myself up. "Just do it. Piece of cake." I held my breath—even though I didn't need to breathe in spirit form—and pictured myself on the other side of the wall. Whatever it was that made me up—Cells? Particles? Energy?—was compressed very, very tightly; I felt for an instant as if I might implode and vanish from the world with a tiny *pop*. But then, almost as quickly, I was inside the castle.

The sensation lingered. I shook off the compressed feeling as best I could as I tried to keep my wits about me. I found myself in a long, dark hallway lit by torches that had been jammed into crude, wrought iron brackets. The passage looked like it had been hewn roughly into the stone, unlike the meticulously constructed upper levels of the castle. Every few feet, a thick wooden door with a small barred window was set into the wall.

"I'll start looking inside the cells," I said. "Stand guard here. What will you do if a Wraith shows up?"

"Back through the wall, quick! What am I, an idiot?" Milo hissed.

I began my search of the dungeon. The first three doors revealed nothing but piles of crates, broken furniture, and tattered mounds of burnt fabric. Before the Necromancers had arrived, the Durupinen must have used these rooms to store the things damaged in the fire. Then I rounded the first corner and froze.

At the bottom of a set of stairs, Mary, with her face slack and expressionless, paced the hallway. Even as I watched, she turned and stared right at me—through me—then continued her patrol with measured, soundless paces.

Relief and sadness coursed through my spectral form in equal measure. I still didn't know why the Wraiths couldn't see me while Walking—my best guess was that Walkers were unknown to the Necromancers, and that, by extension, Wraiths weren't told to attack a Walker—but it was a small comfort to know that my invisibility applied to all Wraiths and not just to the ones at the Traveler camp.

I slid carefully past Mary, pausing for a moment to look into her face. If I were still in my body, my eyes would've filled with tears at the sight of her—Mary, freed from centuries of Caging only weeks ago, was enslaved again. With Mary being a Wraith and unable to recognize me, I wondered how she'd managed to visit me at the Traveler camp and warn me about the dangers to come. Maybe she'd only been recently converted; I didn't have time to think too much about it now.

I continued down the hallway, more determined than ever to find the Spirit Torch and restore the essences trapped within it. None of the doors in the hallway had locks, but rather each was barricaded with a heavy wooden bar held in place with metal brackets. The bars would be simple enough to remove from the outside; if we managed to get down here, we could release everyone.

I reeled with emotion as I peered through the wall into the next room. Fiona, with one arm heavily bandaged, lay inside; she was breathing in the slow, even pattern of deep sleep. Heavy iron cuffs bound her hands together behind her, perhaps to stop her from using her abilities as a Muse. The walls, ceiling, and floor were covered in runes, just like Annabelle's flat had been when we'd found her.

I fought a mad desire to save Fiona. I wanted to break the door down, rip the cuffs from her wrists, then use her irons to beat the shit out of every Necromancer who had the gall to stand in my way. But I swallowed my anger back; I forced it down into a place where it smoldered, but couldn't explode. I had a job to do. "We'll be back for you soon," I promised in a whisper, hoping some comfort would seep into Fiona's dreams.

I crossed the hall and peered into the next cell. I nearly shouted in surprise. Lucida was inside, battered and bruised, with a number of runes painted on her bare skin. An alarm bell went off in my mind: If the Necromancers still had control of the castle, what was Lucida—their accomplice—doing here, chained as a prisoner? There was no time to investigate; if I woke her, there was no telling what she might do. I moved on.

Two doors away, Finvarra was leaning stiffly against the wall, upright and regal, even though she sat on a filthy, straw-strewn floor. She was not facing me. Her gaze was fixed on the narrow strip of moonlight visible through the high window, which filtered down through the murky gloom and lit her long, silver hair with an unearthly glow.

"Finvarra!" My voice, although restrained to a whisper, seemed to resound through the cell like a gunshot. I concentrated hard on materializing; I'd only done it once or twice in my training and it was still a bit difficult.

Finvarra's head snapped up and her mouth dropped open when she saw me. "Jessica?" Her voice was hoarse and cracked, like she hadn't used it in a while. "What are you... What's happened to you?"

"I'll explain later. Where's Carrick?"

"But you're... a ghost!" Finvarra whispered.

"I'm not, I promise. I know I look like a ghost, but... I really can't get into it right now. Where's Carrick?" I asked again. "I need his help."

Finvarra was shaking her head. "Carrick? He's trying to find a way out, although I'm held here by many Castings. He's convinced he will find a chink in their armor if he keeps searching. I'll Summon him back." At this, she closed her eyes and moved her lips silently for a moment. "He's on his way." She stared at me again. "What are you doing here? How did you get in?"

"I'm here to stop all of this, if I can," I explained. "Do you have any idea where the Necromancers are keeping my sister?"

Finvarra's eyes widened. "Has it happened? The Gateway, has it...?"

"Not yet. That's what I'm trying to prevent, if I can just—"

But Finvarra interrupted me, speaking in low, anguished tones. "Jessica, while I have the chance, I must say how very, very sorry I am that I doubted you. You tried to warn us all about the Necromancers. We should have listened. We were fools to ignore the signs. We were so convinced *you* were the danger that we couldn't see the true dangers looming up before us."

"Yeah, well, it's a bit late for that now," I retorted, in no mood to be at all charitable. "Is everyone okay? Have they locked all of you down here?"

"The teachers and Council members, yes. I was the first one they brought down here, but I witnessed the others being locked up, too. As far as I know, they've got the Apprentices up on the main floors of the castle, locked in their rooms. I think the Necromancers are hoping they can use them, somehow—or perhaps convert them. I do not know where the Caomhnóir and Novitiates are being held, but they must still be on the grounds somewhere."

"And what about the ghosts? Did they capture every spirit on the grounds? Are there others besides Carrick that are still free?"

"As to that, I do not know. We've been betrayed. Lucida was working with them all along. She must have instructed them on the best ways to take down our defenses."

"Yeah, we learned about Lucida the hard way," I said. "Have you heard anything about Hannah? Have you seen her?"

"She was with the Necromancers when they arrived. She was carrying a torch, and the spirits were under her control. I've never seen anything like it before." Finvarra shook her head. "These... spirits they're using... what are they?"

I sighed, and told Finvarra everything we'd learned about the Spirit Torch and Blind-Summoners-as-Wraiths.

"Blind... but... is this a Necromancer Casting?" Finvarra asked.

"Yes. We think they must've discovered Blind Summoning because of their obsession with Wraiths. If the Gateway reverses, they'll have legions of true, more powerful Wraiths to control—thanks largely to the Durupinen's Leeching."

"My God," she sighed, drawing a weary hand across her forehead. "We reap what we sow. As ever, we reap what we sow." Finvarra hung her head for a long moment, but then recomposed herself. "But you still haven't told me why you're appearing in this form. What have you—" She broke off and looked up expectantly. "Here comes Carrick."

"Jessica's here? But how did she get in?"

Carrick's voice preceded him as he materialized in the far corner. He took one look at me and his face crumpled with such devastation that, had I been connected to my own heart, I surely would've felt it stop.

"Jessica! Oh, God! What've they done? What've they done to you?"

Carrick's reaction seemed so overblown and unusual for a former Caomhnóir that I could barely find my voice. Why did this ghost of a man, who I'd known for only a few weeks, care this much about me? "Carrick, it's okay! I'm not—"

But Carrick wasn't looking at me anymore. He had dropped his face into his shaking hands as his entire form became racked by an onslaught of sobbing.

"I'm sorry, Elizabeth. Oh, God, I'm so sorry. I've failed them. I failed you. I'm so sorry!" he gasped into his hands.

Finvarra stared at him in alarm. "Carrick, what's wrong with you? Calm yourself at once!"

But Carrick just kept wailing into his hands, ignoring Finvarra. "I'm sorry, Elizabeth. I'm so sorry. Jessica, I'm so sorry."

Somewhere deep inside me, something woke up. A primal and ineffable something—triggered by the sight of this man in this wretched, anguished state—stirred in me: Suddenly, I knew what that something was. I knew it as though I had always known it—it was intrinsic to my being, to the blood flowing in my veins.

"Carrick. Look at me."

He shook his head. "I can't. I can't see you like that. Please don't make me."

"Look at me. I'm not dead. Do you hear me? I'm not dead!"

At this, Carrick's head shot up. His tear-stained face went blank with shock. "What?"

"I'm not dead. I'm a Walker."

Carrick looked completely befuddled, but Finvarra understood.

278

"A Walker? But we haven't had a true Walker in centuries! How could you possibly have learned to Walk, Jessica?"

Carrick looked back and forth between us, still not understanding.

"I'll explain that later," I said, still looking at Carrick. "The point is, I'm not dead. I've just left my body. But my body is fine, and I can return to it safely whenever I want to."

Carrick sunk to his knees with a strange half-laugh. "You're alive?"

"I'm alive," I repeated.

He laughed again, and then seemed to regain himself. He looked at Finvarra and dropped his head again into a respectful bow.

"I am sorry, High Priestess. I am sorry for deceiving you."

"What are you talking about, Carrick?" Finvarra demanded.

Carrick ignored her once again and turned to me. "It is time to confess. Long past time, truly, but there's nothing I can do to remedy that now." He took a long, deep breath. "There's something I ought to have told you the first moment we met."

I couldn't speak. I couldn't think. I knew what Carrick was going to say, yet I had no idea if I wanted to hear it.

"I'm your father, Jessica."

21

SPIRIT LEGACY

C ARRICK'S WORDS FELL UPON ME and rolled off without sinking in. Surely, I'd imagined his confession. Surely, I was in a strange waking dream, and this would all become a half-remembered figment of my sleeping brain. Yeah, that was it. Surely.

"What did you say?"

"I said, I'm your father," repeated Carrick. His words were softer but more deliberate. I knew he was delivering his confession slowly and intentionally so I could absorb it.

"I... You didn't... What?" I'd been reduced to babble.

In my bewilderment, I turned to Finvarra—Finvarra, who always seemed to have an answer or explanation for everything. If she confirmed it, it was true. But the confusion on her face rivaled the confusion on my own. She had no more inkling of my parentage than I did, and for some reason Finvarra's ignorance made me even more convinced that I had misunderstood Carrick.

"We never meant for it to happen," Carrick began softly. "There was no intention, no flirtation—harmless or otherwise—between us. I would never have allowed it, and Elizabeth was much too focused on her training to give thought to such a thing. Even if she had, she would never have chosen me as the object of her affection; I was nearly twice her age and treated all Durupinen as I was taught a Caomhnóir should. In a logical world, there was no chance for any relationship to bloom between us. But the strongest love can be insidious, like a creeping vine—before we could recognize it for what it was, it had entangled us completely."

He paused here, perhaps waiting for some reaction or interjection from me, but I was still too shocked to respond. After a cautious look at Finvarra, Carrick continued.

"I was working as an instructor here. My duty was to train the

Caomhnóir in defensive Castings. I was, if I may be permitted to say so, particularly good at my job. I had always had an intuitive ability to sense a spirit's intentions... and therefore to pre-empt altercation. Finvarra can attest to this; I was the Caomhnóir to her and her sister Narissa, in addition to teaching."

Finvarra had recovered herself a bit, and although she didn't have words to respond yet, she permitted herself to nod in confirmation.

"From the moment your mother and aunt came to Fairhaven, there were murmurings about their strength. As you know, we have always kept a close eye on anyone who could be described, even in part, as the Gateway foretold of in the Prophecy. As twins, they were flagged for close observation. It fell to me to watch them carefully. I also had to conduct an investigation into the family, to eliminate any possibility of their father being a Caomhnóir." Carrick paused again before adding, with the faintest suggestion of a smile on his lips, "The irony of all of this is not lost on me."

Distracted from my mission by Carrick's bombshell, I lost focus on why I had come here in the first place. "You thought my mother and Karen might be the ones in the Prophecy?" I managed to croak out.

"Not really, no," he said. "We ruled them out quickly. Apart from being twins, we found no evidence linking them to the Prophecy. But as a result of the investigation, I had to work closely with Liam, your mother's Novitiate. This meant, of course, that I saw much more of Elizabeth and Karen than any of the other Apprentices.

"You remind me so much of your mother, Jessica. Although she grew up with much clearer expectations of what Fairhaven would be like, just like you, she loathed the Durupinen-Caomhnóir dynamic. While I was busy ruling her out of the Prophecy, she was busy trying to sabotage the clan's relationship with Liam."

"What do you mean by sabotage?" I asked.

"She resented him, as I'm sure you can understand. Liam treated her with the customary curtness and mistrust, and Elizabeth—being the spitfire she was—did *not* respond well to it. She was much too proud to allow someone who treated her with such disdain to hold even the slightest control over her."

Yes, that definitely sounded like my mother.

"The other teachers thought her willful and disobedient,"

Carrick continued. "I found her to be spirited. She opened my eyes to the inherent faults in our system and traditions. Elizabeth believed that the Durupinen-Caomhnóir relationship should be mutually respectful—a relationship which would allow both parties to appreciate each other's gifts while still maintaining the Sanctity Boundaries. She asserted, again and again, that there was no point in having a protector who resented and mistrusted the people he was sworn to protect. I could make no reasoned argument against her."

Neither could I, I thought. Little rankled me more than the misogynistic views of the Caomhnóir. Yet, even through my shock, a tiny part of my brain applauded my mother for standing up to it all; she'd always taught me to be fiercely independent, and it was comforting and satisfying to know she practiced what she preached. I said none of this aloud, though; I was much too focused on Carrick's story.

"Jess? Did you find him?" Milo's voice came buzzing through our connection. "What's taking so long?"

"Not right now, Milo. Go keep watch at the entry point." I thought, pushing him away with my mind.

"But I—"

"Not. Right. Now." And with an enormous effort, I actually lifted Milo out of my thoughts. This was about me. Me and Carrick. I had the right to this moment, uninterrupted and whole.

Suddenly a lightning bolt of anger shot through me, quick and hot. If I had had a corporeal form in that moment, I would've beaten someone bloody. It wasn't enough that Finn had declared his unrequited love a mere few hours ago. It wasn't enough that my sister—apparently suffering from history's most dangerous case of Stockholm syndrome—had been held captive for weeks. Hell, it didn't even matter that I was—literally—in the middle of saving the world. Now I had *this* to deal with? Carrick couldn't have told me this one day after class, or while I was out sketching, or—oh, I don't know—pretty much at any other moment than *now*?

I felt my form flicker momentarily, but got control of myself before I disappeared. I calmed myself as well as I could, and said, "Go on, Carrick." Then, just to jab at him, I added, "Quickly. I *am* in the middle of something here."

"It happened one day during a training exercise." Carrick began again. "The Novitiates were being tested on their expulsion skills, and the Apprentices were assisting. Liam's Casting went rather badly wrong, but instead of taking responsibility for it, he faulted your mother and your aunt—shouting at them, blaming them, even accusing them of sabotaging his test. Your mother stormed out of the courtyard; I was forced to go looking for her.

"I found her just beyond the forest. She had drawn a protective Circle around herself and, although she endeavored to hide it, I could tell that she'd been crying. I told her to return to the courtyard. She refused, saying that she would not be spoken to in such a manner. I tried to calm her. I made excuses for Liam—I explained that he was embarrassed, upset with no one but himself. Elizabeth would have none of it. In response, she fixed on me with a gaze that pierced me to my very core; to this day, I remember every single one of her words:

"'Don't you think I know that? Hell, everyone in the courtyard knew that, but that isn't the point, is it? The point is, you did *nothing* to stop him. No one ever does. This culture is toxic. You're undermining the very relationships you're trying to build. If we don't learn to respect each other as human beings before anything else, everything will fall apart. We won't be able to trust each other. Don't you get it?'"

"Yes, that sounds like my mother," I said as a twinge of mourning swept through me. So much had happened since she died—so often I had to push her from my thoughts so I could focus on the dangers in front of me. But the truth remained: I missed her with a deep, terrible emptiness. That emptiness gurgled to the surface now; if I'd been in my body, fresh tears would've welled in my eyes.

Carrick resumed speaking in his own voice and continued. "Your mother's resistance was jarring. It made me stop and notice, for the first time, this gaping flaw in the system: If we were to continue to protect our Gateways and ensure our existence, shouldn't we encourage our young members to question, to test, to improve? Your family was one of the most powerful old Council clans—it was, quite frankly, unheard of to encounter anything but utter submission and acceptance from such an influential family. But your mother, so brazen with her questioning—so very American—ultimately made me realize that traditions turn to shackles when they prevent evolution. Just look where we find ourselves now: We're at the mercy of the Necromancers once again.

"Elizabeth began filling my thoughts before I realized it. Day and night I asked myself who was this girl making me question everything I'd taken for granted about the world I defended? I couldn't stop thinking about her—her defiance, her ideas, had captured my attention. I never thought of love. I didn't realize what truly was happening; my attachment took root before I could defend myself.

"When I watched Elizabeth drive away at the end of her training, I was filled with a strange emptiness inside, although I bit this away. I focused on my relief—I'd most likely never see her again. Never again would I have to wrestle with the strange, powerful feelings she'd ignited.

"I threw myself into my work. At that time, Finvarra was being groomed to become the next High Priestess as Calista's health was fading." He paused and turned to Finvarra. "As the new High Priestess, I knew you'd need my protection more than ever."

Finvarra nodded solemnly, but didn't reply—words weren't needed. She and Carrick held a shared gaze between them for a long moment.

Carrick broke away from Finvarra's eye. "But then, less than a year later, I got a panicked phone call from Liam. The girls' father—your grandfather, Jessica—had stumbled upon them in the middle of a Crossing. Liam, as a new Caomhnóir, didn't know how to handle the devastating fallout. He blamed himself, although he had no reason to. I was handpicked by Finvarra as part of the team that would fly to Boston."

"You didn't want to go," Finvarra said. She looked at Carrick with sad new understanding in her eyes. "You fought me on it, and I couldn't understand why."

"I'm not sure I knew myself, High Priestess," Carrick replied. "Something inside me was raging against seeing Elizabeth again. I put forth every argument I could think of to stay behind."

"And I, convinced this was the first test of my new authority, would not listen to you," Finvarra said, shaking her head. "I ordered you to go, determined to quash any dissension in my ranks."

Carrick nodded. "So of course I went. But what I found in Boston was so much worse than I was prepared for. John Ballard had suffered irreparably, but I could only see Elizabeth's devastation. When I found her, alone and sobbing, I simply could not let her suffer if it were in my power to comfort her. In her grief, we came together."

My rage had subsided: Now I couldn't find a single emotion within me. All I could feel was a blank, buzzing astonishment and a vague frustration that my mind couldn't absorb what Carrick was telling me as quickly as I needed it to. I was scrambling to keep my head above a rising tide that threatened to drown me at any moment.

"That night, I was blissfully happy. The next day, however, I was consumed by horror. You must realize," he said, meeting my eye for the first time, "that all my life I'd been taught nothing was more abhorrent than what I'd just done—I'd been conquered by the very temptation that had threatened the Caomhnóir since the dawn of our brotherhood." Carrick's voice rose with a note of true desperation. "In my shame—and without saying goodbye or offering even the flimsiest explanations for my cowardice—I fled back to Fairhaven, determined to never see Elizabeth again."

"You just abandoned her?" I asked flatly. "When that happened to my grandfather, that was probably the most horrible moment of my mother's life. And you're telling me that you slept with her and then... just left her there, in that hellhole of a situation?"

"Yes." He said it baldly—devoid of any apology and without even the slightest pleading in his voice. It was as though he knew I wouldn't accept any of this, knew that he didn't deserve my forgiveness.

"Did you ever see her again after that?" I asked.

"No—but not for lack of trying," Carrick answered. "I missed her terribly. Each day, my resistance waned. It was all I could do not to cross the ocean to be with her—expectations be damned. But not even two months later, your mother Bound her Gateway and disappeared. When the news reached me at Fairhaven, I was sure I was the cause of her departure. It wasn't until I arrived back in the States to help Liam search for her that I learned the whole truth—I learned of your impending arrival, Jessica. It made me even more determined to find her.

"One night, we set off in Liam's car chasing a lead from our Trackers. When we found Elizabeth, I told myself, I would never let her go again. I would tell her how I felt, even if it broke every rule.

My distraction made me sloppy. Liam and I were flying down an icy road when a car sideswiped us. I never knew it was behind us, never saw the headlights in the rearview mirror."

My heart was in my throat. This was the instant Carrick had died. This was the instant my *father* had died—yet here I was listening to him describe it. This might've been the most singularly bizarre moment in my entire life—and that was saying something.

"As we crashed, I experienced an instant of clarity. I'm sure it only lasted a second or two, but it seemed I had a long time to think about it just the same. I knew I was about to die as surely as I had ever known anything. I also knew that I couldn't leave this realm without making sure Elizabeth and our child were safe—free from the claws of the Prophecy. At first I thought, for a mere fraction of a second, of Binding myself to Elizabeth, but as I was dying—in the instant that it mattered—I Bound myself to Finvarra and my sworn Gateway."

Carrick did not look at Finvarra as he made this confession, but instead kept his eyes averted—not out of shame or embarrassment, but out of respect. Finvarra, on the other hand, was looking directly at Carrick as though she had never really seen him before.

"It was a strategic decision, one that made perfect sense for what I felt I needed to do," he explained, with eyes still downcast. "Despite all else, I had sworn to protect Finvarra's Gateway, and I did not take that duty lightly. But there was more to it, I admit. Finvarra was the High Priestess. Any leads on Elizabeth would surely be brought directly to Finvarra, and she would make any decisions regarding Elizabeth. Finvarra would also be the one trusted to interpret the Prophecy—which, I admit, I was terrified of. Therefore, the most crucial place to be, in order to keep an eye on Elizabeth—and on you, too, Jessica—was with Finvarra."

"You Bound yourself to me because of her?" Finvarra asked slowly. It was barely a question, almost as though she were just testing the words to see what they sounded like out loud.

"I did. I am deeply sorry," Carrick said, still looking at the ground.

"So many times I consulted you about the Prophecy!" Finvarra began, with her ire now rising. So many times I sought your opinion, trusting you implicitly in everything. And now I discover that your true goal was never to protect the Durupinen, but to mask your own shame!"

"I never intended to deceive you, High Priestess, and I would never intentionally cause you any pain. I didn't—"

"How am I ever to trust you ever again, when the entirety of our Bound relationship has been built on lies!" Finvarra spat. "What am I supposed to think?"

Carrick raised both hands in a pleading, supplicating gesture. "I never stopped protecting you," he insisted. In his upset, his form wavered and flickered fitfully, like a candle in a draft. "I may have loved Elizabeth, but that didn't mean that I couldn't also protect you!"

"And if you had had to choose?" Finvarra demanded. "If you could only have protected one of us at any given moment? What then?"

Carrick's silence spoke volumes. Finvarra stood up, turned her back to us, and began staring through the cell's arrow-slit of a window. Twilight had deepened to velvety blackness, and the stars had revealed themselves, glittering one by one, through the window's sliver.

"When you appeared beside me as a spirit, before the news of your death had reached anyone's ears, I was so sure you had stayed for love," Finvarra said, "simply because I'd never known a spirit to Bind itself for any other reason. I was correct in my assumption, but I was quite wrong about who your love was truly for."

Carrick still couldn't answer. Finvarra didn't seem to expect a response, however; she continued staring at the twinkling stars. As the silence spiraled deeper and deeper between them, I increasingly felt that I was intruding on something terribly private—even though what Carrick had just revealed could not have related more closely to me.

Finally, Carrick realized that his confession was not yet over; he took a shallow breath and went on, addressing me once again. "I never allowed myself to grieve for what could have been between your mother and me. It was a luxury I told myself I didn't deserve. Instead, I focused on my new role as a Bound spirit to the High Priestess. Here I was able to keep tabs on what was happening to your mother, for the Council was following the situation most closely. I was one of the first to know when you were born, Jessica, and I was always alerted when the Trackers had any leads on your mother."

"Did you know about Hannah?" I asked before I could stop myself. I didn't know what difference his knowing about my twin would have made, but my curiosity raged nonetheless.

"No, Jessica, not for many years. Your mother was able to conceal Hannah's existence even from the most skilled of our Trackers. We found no trace of your sister until early last year, when Lucida stumbled upon a link. A foster family curious, no doubt, about Hannah's origins, had requested information about you."

"And that was when you started looking for Hannah, too?"

"Yes. But within a few months of that discovery, your mother... she..." He couldn't finish the sentence.

"Died. The word you're looking for is *died*," I said, almost harshly. The irony of a ghost being unable to speak of death was nearly too bizarre to process; I had a brief, wild desire to laugh out loud, despite the moment's gravity.

"Yes," said Carrick, rather shakily. "And of course that set off an entirely more pressing set of events which distracted us from searching for Hannah. But once we had located you both and had begun our investigations, the rumors began."

"About the Prophecy?"

"Yes. The Council still knew nothing of my relationship with your mother, but they knew enough about the two of you to suspect that your father was a Caomhnóir. The Council came—more or less—to the conclusion that your mother and Liam had been together, but with both of them gone, there was no real way to confirm this. I tried to thwart the idea, but it gained momentum as the Council discovered more and more about you. I knew I would need to remain closer than ever to the High Priestess and to the Council if I was to have any chance of protecting you, but of course..." Again Carrick trailed off. There was no need to finish the thought. He had not been able to protect us: No one had.

"Why did you wait so long to tell me?" I asked.

He looked me in the eye again and winced, but did not turn away. "Because of the look on your face right now! I've never been more crippled by fear! I've been afraid to confront this very moment, to see that look on your face right now. It's piercing me as surely as if I had a body! But I assure you, you cannot despise me more than I despise myself for the way I treated your mother." He stared at me harder, as though trying to punish himself with whatever expression I had on my face. "The Caomhnóir pride ourselves on our bravery, but when my bravery was truly tested, I failed—I failed her, I failed you, I failed your sister. I've spent every moment of my afterlife trying to atone for it!"

§

In the long, painful moment that followed, I could do nothing but watch as waves of misery and shame washed over Carrick. I knew I should say something—anything—but I had no idea what to say next. Mercifully, I was saved the trouble of figuring out my next words by the appearance of Milo by my side.

"What the hell is going on here?" he hissed.

I turned to him. "You're supposed to be keeping watch at the entry point!"

"And you're supposed to stay in contact with me at all times, so don't you start sassing me!" he exclaimed. "You went silent, I got worried. I'm your Spirit Guide, that's my job. Now, what's going on? Did you get the Casting from Carrick or not?"

"I... haven't asked him yet."

"Haven't asked him yet? What the hell have you been doing, trading life stories?" Milo cried. I shushed him as I threw an anxious look over my shoulder.

Milo got the message and changed subjects. "There's a Wraith at the other end of the dungeon, I just checked," he said. "It's the Silent Child. Did you see her?"

"Yes, I did."

"I was hoping they hadn't caught her," he said sadly. "She's patrolling on a pattern—it must be part of her instructions. She won't be back down this way for another three minutes."

"Well, we better hurry up then," I said.

Milo looked genuinely hurt, and a little angry. "Why do you think I came to—"

I turned back to Carrick and Finvarra, who were both staring at me now. "We don't have much time, and we've wasted too much already. I can... we can... talk about this again later, if we get the chance. Right now, I need you both to focus: We have one chance at thwarting the Necromancers. I need the Castings to Summon and banish the Elemental. They aren't in the *Book of Téigh Anonn*, but Finn knows you have them.

Both of their faces went blank in surprise. "The Elemental? What does that creature have to do with this?" Finvarra asked.

As quickly as I could, I explained our rough plan. When I had finished, Carrick nodded in agreement. "It's risky, of course, but you're right—it's the only thing that might work. How will you remember the Castings? Have you got a way to write them down?"

"I don't need to, not in this form. It's hard to explain, but I'm hyperaware right now. There's nothing to get in the way of my mental energy. If you tell me, I'll remember."

Carrick rattled off the instructions, including a fairly complicated Summoning in Gaelic. Normal Jess would have heard nothing but gibberish, but not Walker Jess. Even as shocked and drained as I was, I could still appreciate the ease with which I instantly stored the words in my mind—as if my brain was tucking them safely on a shelf, to be plucked later.

"Carrick, can you tell us anything about what's happening in the rest of the castle? Do you know where Hannah's being kept?"

Carrick shook his head. "They've Warded the entire central courtyard area, including all the surrounding rooms; I can't get anywhere near it. Only the ghosts they're controlling can gain access. I think Necromancers are holed up in there."

"If they truly are going to reverse the Gateway, the most powerful place would be the *Geatgrima*," Finvarra said. "That's surely why they've returned here."

"But I thought the Gateways were a part of us," I said. "They aren't physical places, are they?"

"Not in the usual sense, no. But there are places, like Fairhaven, where the Gateways have been opened so many times that the barrier between the worlds has become worn down, like the tiny cracks in the walls that separate the worlds of the living and the dead. Our presence creates those cracks. The energy channeled at the *Geatgrima* is stronger than a hundred individual Gateways. If your sister manages to reverse it..."

The horror of the thought swallowed us all. I remembered the first moment I'd seen the *Geatgrima* towering over the assembly of white-clad Durupinen, its devastating allure tugging at each and every one of us.

I pushed the thought away. There was no time.

"What about that torch Hannah carried with her when they attacked? Have you seen it?"

Again, Carrick shook his head. "Not since they entered the castle. I couldn't risk discovery. But I can tell you the Caomhnóir are being held in their barracks."

"Okay, thanks," I said. "If this works, we'll free you all as soon as we can. If it doesn't... well, we'll come up with something else, I guess. We'll see you soon."

Carrick's face was twisted with a dozen different painful emotions. "Wait! Jessica, let me go with you. I can help!"

"No," I said, shaking my head firmly. "You need to stay. If the Elemental gets out of control, you need to be here. The Necromancers won't know what's coming—they won't be able to protect themselves. But you can make sure that thing doesn't harm any of the Durupinen in here."

"Jessica, I..."

"Not now," I said flatly, cutting him off before he'd even started speaking: I already knew what he was going to say. "I can't... I'll see you later. I promise."

And, without another word to the man who I'd known only for a few minutes to be my father, I turned and left, my heart and mind too full of inexpressible things.

22

A DEAL WITH THE DEVIL

I PUT AS MUCH DISTANCE BETWEEN ME and the castle as I could, as fast as I could.

"What was that all about?" Milo asked as we flew through the night.

"Nothing," I grumbled in my best "mind your own business" grunt.

"Jess, I can tell you're upset. Can't you just—"

"No, Milo. No, I can't."

Something in my tone made him give up. We flew in silence until we reached the cover of the trees. We saw not a soul—living, dead, or in-between—anywhere on the grounds. Their absence struck me as ominous.

We reached the *príosún's* clearing and saw Finn, Savvy, Annabelle, and Bertie crouched around my body, waiting. Finn's eyes were closed and he was muttering something to himself. It seemed difficult for him to look at my lifeless body, even though he knew I wasn't forever gone from it. Seeing Finn's tortured, restrained tenderness added a hollow, painful lump on top of the mounting pile of other things I could not possibly cope with. The pile teetered, threatening to bury me; I shut it away as I reentered my body.

"Jess!" four voices chorused.

"You alright?" Finn asked. "That took longer than I thought. Did you get it?"

"Yes," I gasped. "Give me a pen and paper."

Annabelle thrust them into my hands, and I wrote down all of Carrick's instructions before the barriers of my physical form had a chance to dull and cloak these essential details. I handed my notes to Finn, who started to take them from me but stopped; he looked into my face with concern.

"Are you sure you're okay? What's happened to you?"

"Nothing. I'm fine," I replied, knowing the lie was utterly transparent.

"No, you're not. I can see it in your eyes."

"Of course I'm not! It's just... everything! I mean, are *you* seriously okay right now?" I burst out. I calmed myself a bit before adding, "I'll be okay when this is all over," and climbed awkwardly to my feet. Finn put out a hand to help steady me, but I brushed it away.

"They didn't know anything about where Hannah is, or where the Spirit Torch is, but they do know the Necromancers have blocked off the entire central courtyard and surrounding rooms," I reported, looking at Savvy and Annabelle instead of Finn. "Milo and I will need to Habitate to see if we can find out more."

"What's so important about the central courtyard?" Savvy asked.

"The *Geatgrima*. Finvarra thinks the *Geatgrima* is most likely where they'll try to get Hannah to reverse the Gateway."

Finn's eyes widened. "That would be..."

"Cataclysmic? Devastating? Apocalyptic? Yeah, I think that's the idea," I said impatiently. I turned to Milo. "Are you ready? This means you might not be strong enough to go with us when we enter the castle."

Milo nodded stoically. "I know. But this is important. The more intel we have, the better. If this is the best way for me to help, then let's do it already."

I closed my eyes. "I'm ready."

Milo surged forward and I felt the now-familiar expansion of his consciousness inside my own. Almost at once my head was filled with a stormy, wounded crying.

"That's Hannah!" Milo cried, with his fear infecting me before my own could even form. "What's wrong with her?"

"We won't find out by panicking, Milo! Focus in!" I thought-spoke to him.

"Right. Right. Okay, get a grip, Milo," he said to himself, and I felt the steadying hum of his concentration as it aligned with my own.

A room resolved behind my closed eyes. Hannah was in the Grand Council Room, but it was barely recognizable. The walls were charred and soot-blackened. A huge section of the north wall

294

directly behind the Council benches had crumbled away, framing a jagged snatch of dark, starry sky. The chandeliers, once lit with electricity, were now alight with waxy stumps of candles.

"I cannot express how very sorry I am," said Neil, who knelt beside my sister. One of his long pale hands cupped her shoulder. "We were too late." Just over his shoulder, the Spirit Torch burned in a holder that had been placed upon the High Priestess' throne; the Torch and the throne were enclosed in a Circle and surrounded by candles and runes.

"I don't believe you. I *won't* believe you," Hannah said, her voice cracked and broken.

"They were staying with a band of Travelers, an obscure clan. No doubt their companion Annabelle took your sister to them—I understand she has relatives there."

"But that doesn't make any sense!" Hannah cried. "Why would they go to another Durupinen clan when they knew our clan was looking for them?"

"As to that, I cannot say. Perhaps it was their only option. Perhaps trusting another clan was a gamble—a gamble they lost. Someone amongst the Travelers must have tipped off the Northern Clans; their Caomhnóir attacked the camp. They left no survivors but for a few Traveler children who told us what happened. I've sent Lucida to the camp to look for other survivors. Perhaps we'll know more when she returns."

"No. None of that is true! I won't believe it, I won't!" Hannah shouted, slapping Neil's hand away from her shoulder.

"I thought you might need evidence, although I hesitate to show it to you," Neil said in a tone so affectedly delicate that it made my skin crawl. "It's not my wish to cause you further distress."

Hannah remained silent for a moment before squeaking, "What is it?"

"I do not wish to show you this Hannah, truly," Neil repeated. "But it will help you accept the truth..." Was I the only one who could hear the note of amusement, however faint, in the folds of his velvety voice?

"What is it?" Hannah asked again.

"A picture," Neil replied, "sent to me by one of my men. He sent it as proof of the state of the Traveler camp when he arrived." Neil held the cell phone in his hand, looking down at its screen. Without even seeing the picture, I knew the screen showed me "dead" on the ground. Neil had believed the ruse too well, and he was now twisting my ploy to serve his own ends—and tormenting Hannah in the process. The guilt swelled in me; I almost lost my connection with Milo as my heart broke.

Hannah leaned back but trained her eyes on the glowing screen, as though the phone were a weapon being pointed at her. Then she held out her hand. Neil, trapping her eyes in his gaze, dropped the phone into her outstretched palm.

Hannah let out an indescribable sound—a strange, primal thing that made all the hairs on my arms stand up. Then, as her mouth seemingly remembered how to form words, she sobbed out, "I'll bring her back! I'll Call her and she'll come back! Jess wouldn't leave me without saying goodbye!"

"We tried, Hannah," Neil began. "I asked Lucida to Call Jess here for you, but apparently she's passed through the Gateway already. Crossed over." He paused for a calculated moment. Then, with a particularly cruel snideness, he added his coup de grâce. "Left you behind without a second thought. Like mother, like daughter."

A wave of nausea hit Hannah so hard I could see it reflected in her face. "What about Milo?" she sniffled.

"No sign of him," Neil replied. "Your sister may have forced him through the Gateway with her, perhaps for her own protection, as she Crossed." Neil barely bothered to hide the sadistic satisfaction in his voice; were Hannah not so devastated, she would've been able to see the bald baselessness of his lies.

Hannah—her face tear-streaked and puffy—doubled over, shaking and shuddering, then fell to her knees. She knelt there—a tiny, crumpled heap—for a moment so long it seemed endless. When she spoke next, her voice was smaller, more devastated, than any voice I'd ever heard.

"There's nothing left," Hannah whispered at last. "They've taken absolutely everything I have. Everything." She took one last longing look at my picture before letting the phone clatter to the floor.

Neil reached out and grasped her arm; his gesture was eerily paternal. "Tonight we take it back, Hannah. We take it all back. Tonight you can demand answers from your mother, from Jess, from anyone else who's ever abandoned you."

With an unexpected jolt, Milo pulled himself away from my mind without warning. I staggered; my vision went black before the surrounding faces of Finn, Savvy, Annabelle, and Bertie, all tense and anxious, came into view.

"Those bastards! Those bastards!" shouted Milo, as he began his trademark version of spectral pacing.

"What happened? Could you tell where she was?" Finn asked.

"Hannah's in the Council Room, and the Torch is there, too. She's falling apart, Finn. Neil showed her a picture of my body from the Traveler camp. She thinks we were all killed by the Durupinen."

Annabelle covered her mouth with her hands. Savvy grunted angrily. Bertie looked as though he might be sick.

"Oh sweetness, what are they doing to you!" Milo wailed, addressing Hannah as if she were a spirit hovering above. He blinked in and out of view in agitation before turning to me. "That's torture, Jess! Psychological torture! We've got to get in there and show her we're all okay before she does something stupid. Do you know how bad this is? They told her you're dead! She thinks you've betrayed her, abandoned her! You're the only living person on Earth that she loves, but now she thinks you're dead—and that you've forced me away from her forever. If she hasn't completely cracked up already, she will any minute!"

I blinked. The only living person she loves. No, I didn't quite realize that. Neil's manipulations were even crueler and more twisted than I'd thought. I pushed back the idea—adding it to the towering pile of emotional shit I simply couldn't deal with today.

"Calm down, Milo," I said.

"Do not—do *not*—tell me to calm down!" Milo shrieked. "That's my girl in there, do you understand?"

"I do!" I cried, stepping forward and wishing desperately that I could hug him. "Listen, Milo," I began gently, "you need to save your strength. Hannah needs you, but you won't be able to help her if you can't materialize. Because now there's no way we're going in there without you. So do it for her, okay? Calm down, blink out, and rest."

I watched the wild light fade from his eyes. Then Milo nodded once and, with a strangled little half-sob, flickered out of sight.

"Okay," I said, turning to the others. "It's time to make a deal with the devil."

§

If someone had told me a day would come when I would step into the *príosún* voluntarily, I would've said that I would rather die first.

Well, as a Walker, I would've been half right, anyway.

I floated a few feet above my body, hesitant to put too much distance between these two very crucial parts of myself; I knew Finn was standing by, ready to protect my physical self, but the variables at play with the Elemental were too unpredictable and potentially devastating to take any chances. I entered the Circle, but I kept myself close to its boundary.

I remembered, with dread, the night that Hannah and I had been trapped in a Circle with the Elemental—a cruel hazing joke that had gone horribly wrong. Just a few minutes with the creature left me so weak and disoriented that I barely knew who I was; all I had known in that moment was that I would've gladly welcomed death if dying meant the pain and terror would end. Hannah very nearly *did* die—another few minutes with that creature and we could've lost her. But now, despite my own lingering terror, we had to use the Elemental—the cruelest being in existence and the Durupinen's ultimate torture device—to our advantage. Right. No problem there.

Somewhere to my left, I could hear Finn muttering the words of the Summoning that Carrick had given us. Any moment now...

A panicked sort of moan escaped me, despite my best efforts to suppress it.

"Jess, you okay in there mate? We can't see you." Savvy called.

I'd forgotten to materialize. "Yeah. Yeah, I'm alright. Just freaking out, that's all," I said, as I flickered into view.

To calm myself, I talked through our plan in my head, to remind myself why it was necessary to face this being again. Yes, I decided. Yes, the Elemental would join forces with us. The temptation of feasting on the spectral embodiments of hate would be too delicious for it to resist. To the Elemental, the Wraiths would be—

But before I could complete my pep talk, my thoughts were overridden. A thought leapt into my brain—a thought that I did not put there. The thought felt like an intrusion, strange and foreign and unsettling.

298

"We recall it, do we not? This morsel. We taste it on our tongue, and we know it. We have tasted it before."

"But the form, the form... what is it now?"

"I'm here to speak to the Elemental of Fairhaven Wood," I declared, hoping my voice betrayed something less than my utterly crippling fear. "Will you show yourself and speak with me?"

"It seeks us. That is bold."

"Shall we speak to it? But what is it?"

"More than human, more than spirit. We cannot fathom it. We must know."

Suddenly, from nowhere, the Elemental appeared. In one way, it looked very much the same as when I had last seen it—human-like in form but constructed entirely of rippling, swirling negative energy. But last time, the Elemental had chosen the form of a woman; this time the embodiment it chose was a pair of twins—two young girls joined together in one being, connected to each other by a long, swooping, shared braid. The braid floated above the Elemental's twin heads in an arc, creating a mock-halo. Ever-changing, terror-inspiring images flickered across the entirety of the creature. For half a second, I even thought I saw my own tortured face projecting from the face of one of the twins.

My heart, if I'd been attached to it, would've stopped. My stomach would've disgorged its contents, and my knees would've buckled beneath me. It seemed the damnable creature formed itself from my darkest fears for Hannah and me. How it picked these fears out of my brain when—at the moment—I technically had no brain to pick was terrifying... and a shock I was, quite frankly, woefully unprepared for. I felt my form flickering rapidly; I struggled to master my torment and hold tightly to my materialized form.

"We have tasted it before," the Elemental repeated as it hung in the air before me. *"We will taste it again."*

The Elemental's hiss sparked my memory. The night we were hazed, my love for Hannah—a love so quietly powerful that even I was surprised by its depths—was the very thing that forced the Elemental to loosen its grip long enough for Finn to expel it. The Elemental had tasted then all my confusion and concerns about my new relationship with Hannah. I realized that the twin form the Elemental now chose had nothing to do with anything that had happened since—the beast had simply formed itself from the imprint of those fears. The Elemental was betting that the fears it had fed on before would—given the right prodding—outweigh my love for my sister.

Not today, you soul-sucking bastard, not today.

A confidence surged in me. "Speak!" I commanded. And much to my surprise, the Elemental did exactly that.

"*What are you, my beauty, my love? Not spirit, no. No, not a ghost.*" The twins' mouths moved in unison as the Elemental spoke through them. It was creepy as fuck.

"No, I'm not a spirit. I'm a Durupinen and a Walker," I said. My voice seemed to ring unnaturally loud through the clearing.

"*What brings you here, Walker?*"

"I request your help," I replied emphatically, as if my plea were almost a command.

"*Help? What can any being ask of us? We do not help. We feed. Yes, feed. And you, my sweet, are mouthwatering.*"

At this, the Elemental opened its mouths and lashed its two tongues at me simultaneously—finding my fear, my anger, my guilt, and every other negative emotion I harbored. But unlike at our last meeting, the Elemental couldn't take hold of my negativity. It couldn't use my own emotions to weaken me; either it didn't know how to feed on a Walker in spirit form, or was simply incapable of feeding on Walkers altogether. I could feel myself nearly expanding in triumph—and relief.

The Elemental froze and cocked its heads to one side. I had stumped this embodiment of evil; the creature didn't know what to do with me.

"*What means this?*"

"*How does it thwart us?*"

"*What trickery is this, to Summon us but deny us sustenance?*"

"*To taste but not feed? Ah, agony!*"

"I did not Summon you here to feed you with my own emotions!" I hissed. "But a feast awaits you, if only you will hear me out."

"*A feast? What does it mean?*"

"It will explain itself, or it will leave this place!"

In its anger, the Elemental expanded itself. The twins grew larger; the colors of their many flickering images intensified as their shared braid pulsated even more brightly with waves of poisonous negativity. Again, I was momentarily enthralled by my own immunity to this beast's powers; it was satisfying to see the Elemental so utterly impotent, but I also didn't want to push it. I needed this vilest of creatures to cooperate.

"The Durupinen are under attack," I began. "The Necromancers have invaded Fairhaven Hall and are going to destroy this world if we don't stop them."

"What care have we for the struggles of humans?"

"They win, they lose, it matters not. We feast upon them all and relish their pain."

"The more they battle, the more they suffer. The more they suffer, the more mouthwatering they become."

"I know you don't care who wins, but if you'll help me, I will offer you the chance to glut yourself on morsels formed of the purest suffering," I said loftily, trying to keep the disgust out of my voice. "Isn't that what you want?"

The Elemental said nothing, but continued to size me up with its ever-changing faces.

"The Necromancers have taken over with the help of ghosts without essences, called Wraiths. They've been filled with all of the things you feed upon—hatred, greed, violence. The Wraiths are all over the grounds, unable to defend themselves. Wouldn't you like a taste?"

The Elemental seemed to shrink; the twins' limbs of swirling color slunk limply toward the ground.

"The witches have trapped us here. We cannot leave this place. We cannot hunt the bounty you promise."

"I alone can release you," I said, but even as I spoke the words, I panicked slightly at the recklessness of them. "If you agree to feed only on the Wraiths, and *not* on the humans, I will free you from this place. When the battle is over, I will send you back here. But you will have free reign to feed upon every Wraith that you can find during the battle."

"No humans? No taste of human pain?"

I cringed. But despite my disgust, I continued negotiating this deal with the devil. "I'll sweeten the pot. You will know the Necromancers by the skull masks and black robes they wear. Consider them fair game as well, but only them."

This last enticement piqued the Elemental's greed. The monster launched into an argument with itself—its many voices wrapping and twisting, rising and falling, as they came in unison from the twins' mouths.

"*It cannot free us. What power could it have? We fed upon it once. It was helpless to fight us.*"

"*But now! It defies us now. We lash and it does not crumble. It is a wicked thing, a powerful thing.*"

"*But we have drained it before. It had no such power then.*"

"*But it got away from us then. It has changed since then.*"

"This is your one chance at freedom," I bluffed, "and it's about to be pulled off the table. Take it or leave it."

"*We cannot trust it. It is one of them. It is surely a trap, a trap.*"

"*We are already trapped. Trapped and caged and locked away these long, long years. What have we to lose?*"

"*To lose, to lose, so much to lose. A moment of freedom, yes, but it will return us to this place.*"

"*But so much to be gained, if it speaks the truth. A feast, it says, a feast.*"

"*We shall return here, but we shall be sated for the first time in many years.*"

"*A feast. A feast.*"

I knew the Elemental would agree before it said the words. The hunger reflected now in its ever-changing faces was as clear as the echoes of pain that lingered there.

"*We agree. We shall feast only upon the Wraiths and the Necromancers.*"

"Very good," I said. "But understand this: If you feed even for a moment on someone else, I will know. And I will destroy you."

The Elemental stared at me as I fought to make my own face reflect a power that I did not possess. I had no idea if I succeeded or not. Like so many parts of this plan, all I could do was hope.

"Our attack will begin shortly," I said. "I will release you soon. Remember our agreement. I *will* destroy you if you break it."

And the Elemental merely stood, as a pair of confused children, while I flew out of the Circle, reconnected to my body, then stumbled away.

"That was brilliant," Savvy whispered. "You were brilliant. Totally badass." Bertie and Annabelle remained silent, but they each looked at me with awe.

Finn nodded curtly. "Well done. I don't think we could've wished for better."

"Thanks, Finn," I replied, knowing that even such a brief congratulations from him was tantamount to lavish praise. "I just hope we can control it once it's been unleashed. We're playing with serious fire here."

"You were right, though," Finn said. "It's the only chance we have. The Necromancers don't know about the Elemental, as far as I can tell, so they won't know how to fight it. By the time they sort it, it'll be too late."

"And if it starts attacking the Durupinen?" I asked.

"It won't," Finn insisted.

I glared at him.

"But if it does, we'll be ready. I've used the Casting before; I can do it again. Don't be bothered about it."

I nodded, but the knot in my stomach—ever-present since Hannah had been kidnapped—tightened just that much more.

"I hope you're right," I replied. "When do you think we should—"

A strange rumbling began beneath our feet. Through the woods came a sudden, collective shift in energy so enormous that we were all dizzy from the force of it. My head swam and my ears rang. Beside me, Savvy lost her footing and fell into me as she clamped her hands over her ears. As she struggled to regain her footing, Bertie moved to shield her, but she shoved him away. I righted myself as a wind barreled through the trees. But it was a wind that had nothing to do with weather and everything to do with an almost-seismic shift in spirit energy.

"What in the world is—" cried Annabelle, clutching her head.

A wailing, moaning sound filled the grounds, cutting her off. A thousand voices rose in a single threnody, all singing as one. Their cry was composed, it seemed, of the very essence of longing and sadness and the desperate desire for all that lay out of reach. As the song rose, a thousand spirits appeared above, trapped on a current that was drifting toward the castle.

A smaller moan broke through, and Milo—shivering with restrained emotion—materialized; he braced himself as if he were a child in a windstorm.

In a tone graver than any other I'd ever heard him use, Milo declared, "We have to do it now. It's started."

23

THE FEEDING

"**M**ILO! STAY WITH US!" I cried, reaching my arms out helplessly toward him, as if I could somehow hold his spirit form in place. But Milo was already shaking his head.

"It's fine, I can resist it, but I think it's only because I'm Bound. It wants to suck me in—I can feel it—but it's like I'm tied down in a storm."

We all watched for a few horror-struck moments as the spirits of Fairhaven drifted over us, pulled helplessly toward the central courtyard. Above the *Geatgrima*, they vanished into a great swirl of sentient mist.

"This is it!" Finn cried over the renewed wailing. "Time to release the Elemental. We'll follow it to the castle."

"And the Necromancers will what? Just let us in?" Savvy asked. "I've had my share of pub fights, mate, but I won't be much use against those bastards."

"The Elemental will do all the fighting for us, believe me," Finn answered. "Annabelle and Savvy, you two stay together. Bertie, you go with them. Once the coast is clear, head to the dungeons and release the prisoners. You'll need the *Book of Téigh Anonn* to undo the Castings, but once the Elemental has taken care of any Wraiths or guards, you'll have plenty of time to work."

"Won't we need keys? Savvy asked. "What good will Castings do if we can't open the bloody doors?"

I shook my head. "There aren't any locks on the cells. They don't really need them; the prisoners are helpless. There are wooden bars across the cell doors, but you should be able to move them easily enough."

"I can attest to the power of the Castings keeping the prisoners helpless," said Annabelle with a grim smile.

"Find one of the teachers first," I said, seeing the nervous look on Savvy's face. "Give the *Book of Téigh Anonn* and the Casting materials to one of them, and let her figure it out."

Savvy's face relaxed. "Right. Yeah, Castings aren't my cup of tea. I should've stayed awake in a few more classes."

"Live and learn," I replied with a quick smile.

"I can help you with the Castings," Bertie offered. "I've gotten much better with those."

Finn, again taking charge, broke in impatiently. "When you've released everyone in the dungeons, split up and see what you can do to free the Caomhnóir and Apprentices. Jess, you said the Caomhnóir are being held in the barracks, right?"

I nodded. "That's what Carrick said."

"Right, then," Finn began. "Bertie and Savvy, go to the barracks with some of the teachers. Bring Carrick with you, if you can—he likely knows more about the Caomhnóir quarters than any of us. Annabelle, you bring the others up to the bedrooms where the Apprentices are being held and release them, too."

Annabelle took a deep breath. "Okay. And if we *do* manage to do all of that? Then what?"

"Head for the central courtyard," Finn instructed. "We'll need all the help we can get, I expect."

"And what are you going to do?" Savvy asked.

"Jess, Milo, and I will head straight for the courtyard. We need to show Hannah that Jess is alive, and we need to release the spirits from that Torch before someone puts out the flame. Milo, we need you at full strength. Disappear until we call for you, but stay close."

"And if Hannah reverses the Gateway before we can stop her? What'll we do then, mate?" Savvy asked.

Every head turned to me. "Let's hope it doesn't come to that," I answered. This was a dodge on my part, and we all knew it. The real answer was that if the Gateway were reversed, I would Walk. And if I Walked, I might... I shuddered inwardly. Frankly put, Walking might be the last thing I ever did, and we all knew it.

"It won't," Finn muttered. More forcefully, he added, "It won't come to that."

I couldn't say all the things I wanted to say to Finn, so I swallowed these thoughts—along with the bulk of my fear. There would be time for all of that later. I hoped.

Dropping us brutally back into the reality of the moment, a spirit, wailing like an injured animal, flew directly over our heads.

"Wait at the edge of the trees for me," Finn instructed. "I'll release the Elemental and meet you there. We'll split up when we get to the castle."

We all looked at each other. It was the flimsiest of plans, but what else could we do? We had no idea what was coming, and therefore no way of planning for it. Bertie was right after all: We'd just have to wing it—and hope for a miracle.

Finn dashed off back toward the *príosún* while the rest of us, bathed in the light of the moon, sprinted for the trees. From behind a large knobbly oak, we watched as the spirits flew toward the castle. As they drew closer to the courtyard, they were swept into a sort of cyclone, which whipped them around and around before sucking them out of sight below the ramparts. An eerie glow emanated from the spot where I knew the *Geatgrima* stood. The light was tinged with purple; even as I looked at it, I felt a desperate, half-formed desire to follow the light, to see where it might lead...

"Don't look at it," Annabelle said firmly. We all tore our eyes from the glow and turned to her. "The Gateway is open. It will draw you in. Don't you feel it?"

"Yeah," I said with a shiver. I reached into the mental space around me for Milo and sensed him there, reassuringly close, still resisting the pull.

"Stay close, Milo, okay?" I said aloud. I felt, rather than heard, his answer: He wasn't going anywhere.

"Oi! Look at the Wraiths," Savvy cried, pointing. "It's like they're immune to it."

She was right. The Wraiths, which dotted Fairhaven's grounds, hung motionless in the air— or else continued their slow, steady pacing. All were blind and deaf to everything but the instructions housed inside them.

"The Gateway is calling, but there's no one left in them to answer," I said. "They're already empty."

With a great and overwhelming rush, suddenly the forest itself seemed to laugh. Every leaf, every tree, broke into a mad cackle. The grass sang with the sound, the air vibrated with it; it was an evil chortle, silver and shivery, a terrible delight expressed in aural form. Footsteps came pounding through the underbrush behind us; we turned just in time to see Finn throw himself to the ground beside us, panting and coughing.

"Here it comes," he said, completely unnecessarily.

And come the Elemental did, in the form of a billowing winged creature with a gaping maw and eyes like fire. Flapping tentacles of stolen emotion streamed out behind it, like tails on a nightmare kite.

We—all of us—completely forgot for a moment that we were supposed to be following the Elemental, but instead sat frozen in crippling fascination as the beast swooped like a bat over the lawns. As the Elemental passed over a nearby Wraith, its tentacles shot out like whips, wrapping around the helpless Wraith. The Wraith, still as a stone, didn't protest or cry out in pain, but sank, utterly senseless, to the ground like a fallen leaf. The Elemental seemed to swell with pleasure; in its laughter, I could hear its many voices.

"Ah, the freedom! To fly, to feed, to gorge!"

"Such a glorious feast!"

The tentacles unfurled in every direction, entwining with Wraith after Wraith, sucking them dry of every hateful thought they'd been weaponized with.

The Necromancers who guarded the lawns were scattering like insects, confusedly shouting into their walkie-talkies for backup as they ran. Then a tentacle lashed out and caught the first Necromancer, wrapping him in the most parasitic of embraces. The Elemental's voices rose in enthrallment.

"We feed! We feed!"

"Fear us! Fear us!"

The Necromancer did indeed fear, if his screams of terror were any indication. He sank to his knees. Within half a moment, he was cowered in the fetal position, with arms over his head, begging for mercy.

"Now! Move!" Finn shouted. "Stay close to me!"

We pelted out across the lawn, staying to the tree line until we had to break across the open space to shelter behind the Elemental. We were all tensed for an attack, but none came. No being, living or dead, had so much as a glance to spare for us. The Elemental cleared our path for us, smiting all within reach; those who had yet to fall were fleeing in terror—some even leapt over walls or hedges in their desperation to escape.

A Wraith nearby spotted us. It flew forward, screeching like an alarm bell, but was cut down by the Elemental before it had gone even a few yards. I ran for all I was worth toward the castle, with my breath stabbing at my lungs as I tried to keep close behind Finn. On all sides, Necromancers fell as if they were being struck by lightning.

As we rounded the central fountain, one of the Necromancers lay crumpled only a few feet away. When he saw us, rather than trying to attack, he reached a supplicating hand out to us, moaning as the Elemental's snakelike appendage lashed at him again.

As I watched this man suffer, I knew the anguish he was experiencing. Maybe his suffering should've triggered some empathy in me, but it didn't.

The castle loomed before us. Although I'd walked in and out of Fairhaven Hall a hundred times before, I felt very much as if we were running into the mouth of a strange beast, sacrificing ourselves. We reached the massive front doors and crouched in the entryway; we peered back in horrified fascination. The Elemental hung over the fountain, with its tentacles waving and snaking beneath its enormous winged body, like a many-legged sea monster swimming in the dark water of the sky.

As more and more Necromancers appeared, the Elemental ensnared each one with serpentine flicks of its many tails. The arriving Necromancers did not overwhelm it; in fact, the Elemental only strengthened further as it glutted itself.

"We have to stop it, Finn," I cried. "You've got to send it back to the *príosún*."

"I say we leave it here," Savvy said. She was staring in awed fascination as yet another Necromancer fell screaming to his knees. "It's cutting 'em all down without breaking a sweat. Let's just open the doors and let it in the castle, yeah? The fight'll be over before it starts!"

Finn hesitated, and I knew why. It *was* tempting. Honestly, nothing gave me quite so much satisfaction as the thought of unleashing the Elemental on Neil.

But Finn pointed to an unfamiliar rune carved above the door. "The Elemental can't go in—it can't cross this threshold. And we can't leave it out here unchecked. It's growing too powerful! Who's to say it won't begin attacking us, or the people we've come to free?

Savvy furrowed her brow as if she was trying to come up with a plausible argument, but it was Annabelle who spoke. "It's done what we needed it to do. It got us to the castle. This needs to end now."

Even as she spoke, six Necromancers ran out of a door a few yards to our left. One of them carried a candle, another was scattering pieces of quartz onto the gravel walkway. They began chanting in Gaelic while creating a Circle in salt, but all was in vain. The Elemental spotted them and let loose a raucous peal of laughter that rang between the trees and reverberated through the ground beneath our feet. Its neck elongated so that its face, a constantly morphing kaleidoscope of horrific images, shot toward them.

The nearest Necromancer, paralyzed with fear, dropped his candle. The Elemental's head hovered just inches from his; each expression that flashed across the Elemental's face was at once inquisitive, curious, even amused. Then the Elemental closed the last inches between them and kissed the Necromancer. The man stiffened and began to shake, crying and pleading for mercy in a muffled rasp. But the Elemental only lingered, sucking the mounting terror from its victim's lips like blood from a wound.

"Enough," Finn muttered. "No. Enough." He pulled the crumpled Casting notes from his pocket, bolted forward, and raised his arms as he began the expulsion.

The Elemental released the Necromancer from its poisonous kiss; the man dropped like a stone to the ground. He did not move again.

"We have only just begun."

"It wants to stop us, to banish us again."

"But it cannot. We have only just begun. We are not sated."

"We are never sated."

Even as it continued to feed, the Elemental flew toward us; its wild, flickering eyes full of bestial greed.

I couldn't move—nor, it seemed, could anyone else. Our collective fear turned us to stone as we watched this nightmare being shot toward us. Even if he hadn't been stunned into submission, there was no way Finn would've been able to complete the Casting quickly enough—in seconds, we would all become victims of the Elemental's insatiable appetite.

A pearly form shot out through the castle's door, blocking the Elemental's path. The form moved so quickly that it was blurry, but as it stationed itself at attention I realized who it was.

"Carrick! No! Get away from it!" I cried.

He didn't answer. He didn't turn to me. Carrick just stood in front of us like a statue, blocking the Elemental's path. Surely the Elemental could have gone around him, or even through him, but it didn't. Instead, the Elemental inhaled a slow, deep breath and sighed longingly for what it sensed in Carrick.

"Ah, the delicious grief!"

"Such exquisite sadness!"

Carrick proved too tempting; rather than attacking us, the Elemental latched onto Carrick, whose twenty years of shame and regret had created a fathomless darkness within. All that I had learned of Carrick's love for my mother, of their forbidden relationship, of Hannah's and my birth—every particle of it was steeped in loss and pain. Carrick must have been the most tempting morsel the Elemental had ever come across.

"No, stop! Stop it!" I cried. "Finn, do something!"

But Finn was already performing the Casting. I watched as he raised a small silver knife into the air and swung it sharply down, driving it into the earth at his feet. The Elemental was expelled backward as if it were a pellet launched from a slingshot. As it flew through the air, the Elemental's many feeding tentacles released their victims and curled up against its body like the legs of a dying spider.

The Elemental's scream became the air itself. The sound reverberated against the stone walls of the castle so fiercely that many of the windows above us exploded in a shower of glass needles; we threw ourselves to the ground and covered our heads as the shards rained down.

I raised my face just in time to see the trees of the forest part like jaws and swallow the flailing, shrieking form of the Elemental. The screams died away, leaving a lingering ringing in our ears and heaps of motionless bodies littering the grass.

"Carrick! Carrick! Are you okay?" I cried, crawling toward his form; he was floating, supine, just a few inches above the ground.

Carrick—shuddering and alarmingly faint—managed to nod his head. "Did it... attack you?"

"No," I replied. "No, you stopped it long enough for Finn to expel it and send it back to the *príosún*. It's gone now."

Carrick actually managed a small smile. "Good."

"I... thank you." What else could I say?

"Jess! We need to move! Now!" Finn shouted as he raised himself up from the ground.

"Will you be alright, Carrick?" I asked.

"Don't worry about me," he replied.

"Just tell me you'll be fine, or I won't be able to go in there," I said. "Lie to me if you have to."

"I'll be fine."

I accepted Carrick's words because that was the only reaction my brain would allow. He would be fine. Everything would be fine. Because it had to be.

Finn reached out and pulled me to my feet. We left Carrick hovering feebly behind us as we wrenched open the doors and entered the castle.

"Look after him!" I called back to Annabelle and Savvy.

"And yourselves!" Finn shouted. "Bertie, remember: You are a member of the proud Caomhnóir brotherhood!"

The entrance hall was barely recognizable. The hall's beautiful tapestries, draperies, and paintings had all been removed. In their place were the strangest of relics—ancient armor, a giant gong, an immense drum, and black ceremonial robes adorned the walls. The black robes drooped on the wall like grim reapers—reapers who were backdropped by my own massive and gruesome Prophecy mural.

Finn was tensed for combat, but not a soul, living or dead, remained to confront us; all had fled out into the waiting arms of the Elemental.

"The most direct route to the courtyard is through the Council Room," Finn said. "And we need to know if the Torch is still there."

"Let's go," I replied, with my heart beating so fast that it seemed to be humming.

I felt for Milo again, grateful that his being Bound meant that he could follow me into the castle's Warded areas. "Milo prepare to manifest," I told him quietly. "When we find her, Hannah will need to see you just as much as she'll need to see me."

I felt Milo's flare, his glowing little "*yes.*"

Keeping to the shadowy areas under the galleries that ran along the entrance hall's perimeter, we approached the Grand Council Room's enormous wooden doors as silently as we could. One of the doors was slightly ajar. Finn peered carefully into the room.

"Empty," he announced. He started forward.

"Wait," I said, and fumbled in my pocket for one of the Soul Catchers Flavia had made for me. I tied it clumsily around my wrist.

Finn glared at the Soul Catcher like he wanted to tear it into a thousand pieces and light every single one of them on fire. "You're not going to need that," he grumbled.

"Just in case," I said.

He didn't answer. We crept across the Grand Council Room, again keeping to the walls for safety. We climbed behind the upended Council benches, using them as cover, until we reached the place in the back wall that had crumbled away in the fire. It opened onto the central courtyard.

I peered into the courtyard and knew we were too late. I knew it because I'd seen it before, scrawled in ash and my own life's blood.

The Prophecy had come to pass.

24

SPIRIT PROPHECY

HANNAH STOOD IN SILHOUETTE before the towering, glowing *Geatgrima*, with her arms outstretched and her hair whipping around in the fierce wind-born vortex of spirit energy. I threw my hands up, shielding my eyes from the brightness and my soul from the nearly unbearable pull of the Gateway. Above us, spirits were being tossed and blown around in the storm of power emanating jointly from Hannah and the *Geatgrima* itself. The ground under my feet vibrated and pulsated, and yet—despite the chaos and devastation—the courtyard was utterly and impenetrably silent.

Beside me, Milo flickered into sight, his face aghast.

"Hannah!" our voices cried out together as one as I rushed forward. Our cry was swallowed in the eerie vacuum.

"Jess, no! Wait!" Finn shouted.

Finn lunged forward to stop me. He managed to grab my shirt, but I wrenched it out of his grip—tearing the sleeve right off. I broke into the open just in time: Two Necromancers leapt from the shadows and grabbed Finn, pinning him to the ground.

I started running back toward Finn. I had no idea what I was going to do, but I couldn't let him fall to the Necromancers. Panicking, I picked up a jagged rock and swung it back behind my head, preparing to throw it.

"I really wouldn't do that, if I were you."

I dropped the rock in shock as I spun on the spot. Neil stepped out from the darkness on the far side of the *Geatgrima*. His face wore a smug, satisfied expression.

"Hannah? Sweetness? Can you hear me?" came Milo's voice.

Milo shot toward Hannah, who—in her trance—hadn't given any sign that she'd noticed us. But before Milo could make contact with her, he was thrown backward by a violent force. He slowed to a stop halfway across the courtyard, floating just above the ground, utterly motionless.

"Milo! What's happened?" I cried. He didn't answer, but continued to float as though unconscious; his form became so faint that he was barely solid enough to be seen.

Neil made no move to stop me as I took a few cautious steps toward Hannah. I was afraid to get too close to her, or to get between her and the *Geatgrima*. Her face was pointed toward the sky; her eyes stared beyond the vortex before her, fixed unblinkingly on something I couldn't see. A strange, cold power emanated from her in waves that made me dizzy. Perhaps I could touch her, even if Milo couldn't? I reached a tentative hand toward her, but pulled it back at once as a current like electricity shot through my fingers.

"Well, well, well, Miss Ballard. I must say I'm surprised to see you. I had it on very good authority that you were dead. However did you manage to return to us?"

"I took a page out of Lucida's book," I answered, as boldly as I could manage. My hands contracted convulsively into fists at my sides. I clenched my teeth tightly as I answered, in an effort to keep the tremble out of my voice. "Playing dead worked for her—although I notice it didn't keep her out of the dungeons. Not that I'm complaining, but why did you lock her up?"

"She had... outlived her usefulness," Neil replied with a casual shrug. "I didn't think she could be trusted to cooperate if there was any possibility of your sister being harmed. As it turns out, Lucida harbored an inconvenient spark of affection for her little protégé."

"She had a funny way of showing it," I shot back. Behind me, I could hear Finn grunting as he struggled against his attackers. I turned just in time to see one of them deal Finn a savage blow across the face. He crumbled back to the ground, stirring only feebly.

"It's been quite a while since we've seen each other. Outside of David Pierce's office this past spring, if I'm not mistaken, wasn't it?"

I saw red. His audacity. His gall. Using Pierce's murder—an in-cold-blood murder committed by Neil's very hand—to mock me. Was it possible that Neil was even more manipulative than the Elemental? Because I'd already played that game...

The mention of Pierce—and all he'd done for me—obliterated

all fear from my body. "Don't you dare say his name," I growled. "Don't you dare."

"I do regret what happened to him," Neil said with a theatrical sigh. "He needn't have died. I gave him countless opportunities to give me the information I needed, but he was a very obstinate man."

I swiped angrily at the hot tears that had sprung into my eyes. "Fuck you," I spat.

"Tut, tut, Miss Ballard. Language," said Neil, clicking his tongue disapprovingly. "As I was saying, I thought we would've located you sooner, but you've been rather more adept than I expected at keeping yourself hidden. I applaud you, truly. Your Guardian was obviously well chosen, although," he laughed delicately, gesturing toward Finn, "he doesn't look as if he'll be of much use to you now."

I would have given practically anything to have the power to protect Finn the way he had always protected me, to possess the strength and skills needed to tear to shreds the men holding him. But I didn't. Finn was trapped. Milo was unconscious. I was alone.

The Soul Catcher suddenly seemed to weigh a hundred pounds on my wrist. As if she might assuage my utter despair, I called to my sister.

"HANNAH!"

"She cannot hear you. She's far beyond where you can reach her now," Neil said smugly.

"Stop this!" I demanded.

"I couldn't even if I wanted to," Neil replied. His long black robe made no sound as it trailed behind him. "You're too late. The reversal has begun."

Even as he said it, I could feel the energy from the *Geatgrima* shifting and morphing. Soon, I knew, the pull would become a push, and unknown horrors would come bursting into our world.

I tore my eyes from the *Geatgrima*, afraid it might lure me forward somehow; as I did, my gaze fell on a shape crumpled at the base of the *Geatgrima's* dais.

"Finvarra!"

She was lying slumped against the bottommost step, with her long silver hair spread over her like a death shroud, obscuring her face. "What have you done to her?"

"We needed her to unlock the *Geatgrima*," Neil explained,

speaking to me as if I was a child, as if sacrificing the High Priestess was a natural and obvious part of the reversal process. "Only the High Priestess of a given clan has the ability to activate a *Geatgrima*. There are only a handful of places on the earth where the fabric between the worlds has worn thin enough to make the reversal possible—it was always inevitable that we would need to find a way in. If the Northern Clans had been willing, even for a moment, to entertain the possibility of our return, they would surely have fortified this place against us. But their hubris was their fatal flaw, as in every great tragedy. And, most conveniently, Finvarra's own Council had already locked her up for us. It was rather like finding her gift wrapped, bow and all."

I glanced down at Finvarra again. I couldn't tell if she was breathing. With a jolt of horror and guilt, I realized that Carrick, determined to protect me as we unleashed the Elemental, had most likely left Finvarra alone to come after me. I piled this guilt onto the teetering stack of things that I just couldn't deal with now—a stack that threatened to topple and crush me at any moment.

"I searched for you for so long," Neil said. In the moment when I had shifted my gaze to Finvarra, he'd edged closer to me. "I knew you must be out there; all of the signs pointed to it." He cocked his head to one side as he examined me. "The Northern Clans themselves were on high alert from the moment your mother disappeared. You can't imagine how carefully we hunted, how patiently we waited in the shadows for the right moment to make our move." Here Neil paused, and laughed derisively. "Across all these centuries, finding you and your sister may have been the one goal the Necromancers and the Durupinen ever shared—even if we had very different motivations."

I didn't answer. My throat had gone dry as my panic began to rise again.

"Naturally, I had to know for sure what you were. I arranged to meet you, through our mutual friend Pierce. I corresponded with him for weeks, waiting for the chance to see for myself what you could do. It was I who appealed to the college's board to allow the library investigation—they were highly persuadable, once I had donated enough money. I was also the one who planted the spirit in the library to prove what you were."

My mind flew immediately to Evan, for whom I hadn't been able

318

to spare a thought in weeks. It couldn't be. It wasn't possible. How could Evan and Neil be connected? But then my eyes fell on Neil's long black robe, and it clicked.

"William—that ghost who tried to Cross through me—wasn't really from the Swords Brotherhood, was he?"

"Very astute, Miss Ballard. You've seen by now how we can control the spirits. A simple Casting in a quiet corner of the library... William truly believed he'd been sacrificed by the Brotherhood—and provided me with all the proof I needed of your powers. And, of course, we had found Hannah only months earlier by following the Northern Clan's Trackers. When I had ascertained you were indeed the pair we had been waiting so long for, I contacted Lucida. She tricked your High Priestess into sending her to Boston immediately."

I could feel the anger splashing itself across my cheeks. Neil had been playing puppet master practically since the moment my mother died; I was hit with a wave of hatred so intense that it sickened me.

"We had to bide our time, though," he went on, sighing. "We had to give you both the chance to hone your abilities. We needed to determine which of you was the Caller—and therefore which of you we required. We were lucky your sister's powers were so very well developed, so impressive in scope. We knew in a matter of weeks she was the one we needed to capture; you were the one we needed to destroy."

I chanced a glance at Hannah. She hadn't moved, but the energy coming from her now seemed more intense, more focused, somehow.

"This day is our destiny. You know that, don't you?" Neil asked, rubbing his hands together like a villain in an old-fashioned melodrama. The gesture was so stereotyped that I very nearly let out a laugh. "Despite all the Durupinen bravado, they never truly succeeded in vanquishing us. When we were first torn down, at the height of our power, we rebuilt again almost immediately. But we learn from our mistakes, unlike your precious sisterhood. We chose to rise again slowly, cautiously, protected by dark Castings unknown to the Durupinen. We knew that to gain our rightful power, we could not seize it back outright. We waited. We steadied our hand and bided our time, knowing this day of Necromancer glory would come, for it was foretold that it would."

"Yes," I said, and felt my wrist twitch beneath the Soul Catcher. "I'm just sorry that it's not going to work out like you've planned."

Neil laughed; the sound was slightly mad. "Is that so? I must admit, you've come much further than I ever thought possible. Using the Elemental to enter the castle was inspired. Truly, I applaud you. But the fact remains you are too late. The moments during which you could've convinced Hannah to turn back have come and gone. You cannot stop her now. She will emerge from this trance only when the reversal is complete. And in fact, it is I that must thank you: Your supposed death was the linchpin that finally convinced her to reverse the Gateway."

Neil paused, then reached around the far side of the dais and pulled the Spirit Torch into view. He lifted it high above his head. "We've been up to our own tricks too, though. What do you think of my Wraith army?"

"They're an abomination, and you're a sick, twisted lunatic." I practically vomited the words at him.

Neil laughed as though I'd told a hilarious joke. "You don't mince words, do you? You must broaden your mind, Miss Ballard. Your sister did. With a little persuasion, she came to see the potential in our experiments. It was she who Called the spirits to Fairhaven, and it was she who trapped them in here," and he waved the Torch back and forth, feeding the flame so that it sparked up into the night. "We won't need these insignificant Wraiths soon, of course. When the reversal is complete, we will have countless, more powerful, Wraiths at our command."

He tossed the Spirit Torch aside; it landed on the stones in a shower of golden sparks. I started toward it, afraid the Torch would go out, but the flame continued to burn. As I watched it flicker there, faint voices floated up with the sparks, crying out for help.

I turned away from Neil—and his maddeningly vainglorious expression—and tried to talk to Hannah. Surprisingly, Neil didn't try to stop me.

"Hannah? It's me. It's Jess. I'm here. I'm alive and on this side of the Gateway with you. You need to stop this now." Neil began laughing maniacally at my attempts to reach through Hannah's trance. I didn't care: I let him laugh.

I reached down for Hannah's hand. A force so strong that it felt like a solid wall deflected my outstretched fingers, which then buzzed and tingled with the energy. I tried again, but it was useless; I couldn't touch her.

"Hannah, listen I'm here." I began again. "Milo's here. Everything Neil and Lucida told you was a lie." Hannah gave not the slightest sign that she could hear me, but continued to concentrate, transfixed, on the *Geatgrima*. Her arms, I realized, were smooth and unblemished; the many scars that had once marked her wrists and forearms had vanished. Those reminders of horrors past were gone, swallowed up by the spirit energy emanating from the *Geatgrima*. In fact, everything about Hannah's appearance had altered subtly but dramatically. Even in her unearthly trance, I could see that her complexion was flawless, her hair voluminous. Intentionally or not, she had Leeched back some of what the spirit world had stolen from her; she was barely recognizable.

Neil's voice cut through my shock. "Let's be fair, Miss Ballard, it wasn't all a lie. I may have manipulated a few facts in my favor, but I think I was more than generous with the truth. Your sister has been badly used by the Durupinen. She deserves her revenge, and we are only too happy to help her achieve it. The Durupinen have been powerful, but that power was painfully limited; it made them weak. They never dared to explore their power, never dared to ask what it could become. They accepted their mortality and their drudgery to the spirit world. They lacked the vision that ought to accompany such power. But the Necromancer Brotherhood, we saw beyond that. We saw infinite possibility—and we weren't afraid to reach out and take it! When the Gateway has reversed, we will at last be able to learn what lies beyond. We will unlock the great mysteries that have spawned religions and confounded philosophers! We will no longer have to answer to unnamed forces that determine whether we live or die. We will be gods, Miss Ballard. Gods on earth."

"We're not weak," I said defiantly. I felt the weight, the significance of that "we." I was a Durupinen, and it was time to live up to everything a Durupinen should be—even if centuries of others before me had not. "We have a calling and we have risen to it. You are the weak ones. You can't resist the temptation. That's why the Gateways have never been entrusted to you, and that's why you're going to fail."

The energy shifted. Above us, the spirits that had been swirling into the eye of the vortex slowed to a stop, forming a great motionless canopy of the dead. Slowly at first, but then faster and faster, they began to spin in the other direction, breaking the heavy silence with a deafening cacophony of screams. They reached, with a thousand desperate outstretched arms, down toward the *Geatgrima*. The glow of the *Geatgrima* intensified, seeping into every crack and crevice of the dais, illuminating every tiny gap between the worlds. Finvarra wailed and convulsed wildly in pain.

"It begins!" Neil shouted, and his expression was sheer maniacal glee as the light from the *Geatgrima* illuminated his features. "Fail, shall we? You will see now what the Necromancers are capable of!"

I opened my mouth to retort, but I was blasted off of my feet as a tidal wave of energy exploded out of the *Geatgrima*. I sailed through the air and slammed into what remained of the castle wall behind me. Pain sliced through my skull: My vision went white, then black, then red. I put a hand to the back of my head and held my fingers up before my eyes; they were soaked in my own warm, scarlet blood. In my panic, I rolled over and found myself staring into a pair of wide, petrified eyes very like my own.

"Jess! What are you... I don't understand!"

Hannah lay a few feet away, having been thrown to the ground by the force of her own power. She stared at me through features so altered by the energy coursing through her that I could barely believe it was her. The only thing more striking than Hannah's beauty in that moment was the haunted, terrified look in her eyes.

"You're here! You're alive! But..."

"Yes, I'm here." I crawled painfully across the ground and reached out for her hand. She clutched for me, and when our skin connected a wild pulse of something shot through me. I felt the pain in the back of my head recede, felt a new strength flow through me; Hannah had healed me.

"But you were dead! They told me you were dead!" she exclaimed as she began touching my face to make sure I was real.

"No. They lied to you. It was all a lie."

I watched the truth sink in, as the realization—a panicked gleam of absolute unadulterated horror—come alive in her eyes.

"What have I done?" she whispered.

We turned as one to the chaos she had unleashed. The flood of purple light began to swell like fire, and instinctively I knew that the *Geatgrima's* gaping archway would soon begin disgorging essence-less spirits—the Wraiths Neil so desperately wanted for his army. The light, like the ultimate force of nature, roiled across the courtyard and up the castle walls, threatening to burst open and release its sea of trapped, distorted faces and clawing limbs.

The explosion of energy had rolled Finvarra and Milo across the ground like ragdolls. It had sent Finn's attackers crashing through a stained glass window. Finn was now army-crawling across toward us, mouthing words I couldn't hear over the howling spirits. Only Neil remained on his feet; he clung to the stones of the *Geatgrima*, which shook beneath his hands.

The time had come. I had only a mere moment, no more than a heartbeat, to decide what to do.

I looked at Finn, and whatever he saw on my face froze him.

"No!" I could hardly hear Finn's cry over the din, but I watched as his mouth formed the word; it couldn't have struck me more deeply if he had screamed it in my ear.

"I'm sorry, I have to," I shouted. "It's my job, Finn! My duty!"

I turned to Hannah. "Call me back."

"What are you talking about?"

"No time to explain. But I can fix this Hannah, all of it—it's there in the Prophecy if you know how to read it." I squeezed her hand reassuringly. "And don't be scared by what you'll see next. But I need your trust to fix this, I need your love; I need my sister. Just Call me back. You can do it. I have faith in you. Call me back."

Before Hannah could respond, before Finn could do more than reach a hand out toward me, I jumped to my feet and pelted toward the rift between this world and the next. As I ran, I reached down and snatched up the still-burning Torch, alive with the essence of a thousand trapped souls. As I clutched it in my hand, its solidness gave me courage—something real to hold onto. I skidded to a halt at the base of the steps; with a mighty heave, I threw the Spirit Torch deep into the heart of the blinding, violet light.

The *Geatgrima*, which had seemed to open wider as I approached, gaped before me—as if it had been ready for me all along. Hannah and Finn may have been calling after me, but I would never know for sure. The *Geatgrima's* lure blotted everything else out. It wanted me. It welcomed me.

It had always been waiting for me.

I sprinted up the steps of the dais, afraid that if I slowed down—if I hesitated for even a moment—I would never again find the courage to do what I knew I must.

I raised my arm, with the Soul Catcher glinting in the purple glow. With a single swipe, I would fly freely through the portal. But as I raised my arm, a hand closed around my wrist and spun me around violently.

I was face-to-face with Neil Caddigan; his silvery eyes blazed mere inches from my own. He swung at me, trying to shove me off of the dais.

But Hannah hadn't just healed me. She'd given me a strength beyond my own physical abilities, a fierce new power. I called on this strength now as I gripped Neil by the arm, wrenched free of his grip, and shoved him into the *Geatgrima* itself.

Despite the steady outflux of spirits, the vortex opened to receive him; the Gateway could not resist taking another into its depths.

And it was about to take one more in, too.

I recited the words that allowed me to Walk. Then I clenched the Soul Catcher between my teeth, ripped it apart, and soared upward. With a thrilling terror, I envisioned myself on the other side of the Gateway. I plunged headlong through it and into the Aether.

A gloomy, nebulous space greeted me. The Aether itself was thick and weighed heavily on my spirit form; I felt it compressing me, almost as if I were trying to pass through a solid object. This realm seemed composed entirely of sloughed-off human emotions. Fear and loss, joy and love, mourning, celebration, and a hundred other feelings—none of them my own—pricked at me simultaneously, all trying to anchor me to this place.

But no. It would not trap me. I focused on the rift into which the spirit energy was flooding. There, I found the door to the other side—the human side—and, with every particle of strength I possessed, willed it shut.

Everything went still.

25

SPIRIT ASCENDANCY

I OPENED MY EYES AND SAW THE STARS. Thousands upon thousands of them.

The stars were just as I remembered them—randomly scattered yet at once perfectly ordered—as they stretched across the night sky.

I looked at the heavens for what felt like a long time, gleaning comfort from the familiarity of the constellations and allowing the sprawling vastness to wash over me, awe me. My spirit form felt different somehow; I could at once feel my body as if I was back in it, but at the same time I was freed from the heaviness of physicality—as if I was weightless, as if I could only feel the best parts about having a physical form.

I turned my head and looked to my right. The broad, barren Arizona landscape stretched out around me, bathed in starlight. A dusty and abandoned stretch of highway snaked off into the distance between two plateaus. The windshield of the Green Monster curved beneath me, cool and firm against my back.

I knew who I would see if I turned my head the other way. My heartbeat rose to a violent gallop as I looked.

My mother was gazing up at the same stars, her expression childlike in its wonder. Her always-bright eyes seemed a hundred times brighter with the light of countless stars reflected in them. Her hair fanned out around her head, giving a temporary order to her usually untamable mass of curls. A single freckle darkened the hollow of her cheek; I reached out to touch it with a tremulous finger.

"Don't rub too hard or it might come off," she said—an old but never-tired joke that had never stopped me from stroking her cheek, not even once. As I touched her familiar freckle, I felt a long-tightened knot loosen in my chest.

325

"You're here," I whispered.

"Of course I'm here. Where else would I be?"

"I don't know."

A shooting star blazed across the great expanse of the sky; we both fell silent as we watched it.

"Did you make a wish?" she asked me.

"No."

"Why not?"

"I couldn't think of anything to wish for just now."

"Yes. I know just what you mean," said my mother. *My* mother, with me.

Her breath, her familiar scent, was like pure oxygen to me. I groped across the dusty old hood of the Green Monster until I found her slender fingers, and wove my own through them. They fit together like puzzle pieces.

There was something I needed to tell her. What was it? Something important. But I couldn't remember, the thought wouldn't coalesce; an absence expanded in my mind. Then I felt a sort of ache in my other hand, an emptiness, and I suddenly knew the absence wasn't merely in my mind. I realized who should have been there with us, from the very beginning.

"I found her," I said.

"I know. I'm so glad."

"She's beautiful. And fragile. But strong, too. And so much more like you than I ever was."

My mother squeezed my hand. "I know that, too."

As I spoke of Hannah, a distant echo pressed faintly in my ears. I turned away from my mother and looked down the highway, straining my eyes against the distance.

A shape darkened the horizon there. It might have been a door.

"What's that?" I asked.

"That's your way back," my mother answered.

I looked at the shape again. A sound emanated from it, reverberating softly along the bends in the road. It might have been music. It might have been a voice. It was so hard to tell... and I didn't want to think too much about it just now.

"I can hear something," I said. "There's a voice."

"Is there?"

"Yes. Can't you hear it?" I asked.

"No. I can only hear the stars."

We listened, together, to the quiet mystery of the stars stretched out and singing above us.

"This is the night I always think of when I think of us," I said.

My mother turned to me; her eyes filled with a glistening hope that plucked at the very strings holding me together. "Do you mean that?" she asked gently, tenderly.

"Yes. I mean it."

"Because there were a lot of other nights..."

"Forget about them. They don't matter. Just this night, Mom. Let this be the night."

"I love you, Jess."

"I know that, now more than ever. I love you, too."

"And Hannah, too. And tell her... she decided for me. Three days old, I had to leave one of you. You cried. But she looked me in the eyes, quiet and strong—so much stronger than any soul I'd ever met. I knew then. An impossible choice, but Hannah made it for me."

"I'll make sure she knows it. She'll understand, I know she will. She'll forgive you... she's so strong, Mom. And I know she'll love you, too, in time."

My mother squeezed my hand again. I closed my eyes for a moment, drinking in the smell of her. When I opened my eyes again, we'd been transported inside the Green Monster. The car seemed to come alive as it jetted deep into the vast space of the Arizona night.

We soared through the air with our hair fluttering out of the open windows. I shielded my eyes against the sudden, blinding brightness of the stars—stars now so candescent that they seemed to be trying to imitate our own sun. My mother sang one of her made-up songs, gentle as a lullaby, as we swept through the sky. I watched the asphalt flash past us below. It was just as I had imagined when I was a kid—not driving, but flying like birds.

Then I noticed a small, smudged face staring at me from the rearview mirror.

"Mary!"

"Yes, I am here too."

I turned to look directly at her, but the battered back seat was empty. I could only see her in the mirror. I was suddenly full of hot, bubbling guilt.

"Mary, I'm sorry. I brought you here," I said.

"I *should* be here," she replied.

"It should've been your choice to Cross. You, and all those other trapped spirits. But if I didn't do something, I was afraid the Torch would go out—that you'd never be at rest."

"We were enslaved—the choice was already taken from us," said Mary. "You freed us. I know that. We all know it. You saved us, truly."

"Did I?"

"See for yourself," she said, as she and the backseat vanished from the mirror. The image in the mirror morphed into that of a darkened room. I leaned forward for a better look, and the mirror gaped and swallowed me, pitching me into blackness; I tumbled through the dark until...

To my right, a brick wall. To my left, a jagged row of book spines. I was crouched in a dark, dusty corner between the two. The familiar smell of mildewed, neglected pages was sharp in my nostrils.

"Don't spook them. Whatever you do, don't spook them away, or I'll never invite you on one of these investigations again!"

I looked around for the source of the voice—this familiar, eager voice full of comforting inquisitiveness—but I could see nothing. I couldn't pin the voice down to any one place: First it was hissing from behind me; then it was echoing as if coming through stereo speakers; then it was right beside me.

"Who said that?" I whispered.

"I did. I said that. Who the hell else would it be? Now be quiet before you screw this up, Ballard."

"Pierce!" I cried as recognition hit me. "Where are you?"

"Where am I? I'm right here! Get your head out of your ass, Ballard."

I looked around and spotted him smirking at me from the cover of a battered old volume on the history shelf.

"What the hell? What are you doing here?" I asked.

"Me? I'm dead! I'm supposed to be here! Shouldn't I be asking you that question?"

I glared at Pierce, not just because I hated the idea of his being dead, but even more so because he had the nerve to joke about it.

I sat in silence for several minutes, waiting for something to happen. The library was utterly still but for the ticking of a clock and the dull clunking of a nearby radiator.

"What, exactly, are we waiting for?" I hissed finally.

From the cover of the book, Pierce rolled his eyes at me. "The door. Look at it."

I followed his gaze and saw the door for the first time, way at the end of the longest row of books I'd ever seen. Surely no library was that big.

"I see it," I said. "What about it?"

"It's the focus of the investigation!" Pierce whispered, and suddenly he was no longer plastered on the book's cover, but kneeling beside me. His eyes were trained on the screen of a thermal camera.

"What are we looking for?" I asked. I stared down at the little glowing screen in his hands, but all I saw was the same impossibly long passage ending in a closed door.

"You tell me, Ballard. You're the ghost girl."

I stared down at the door. It was old and battered, but otherwise looked completely ordinary. And yet...

"I think I hear something."

"What is it? What do you hear?" Pierce whispered excitedly as he pulled one of his recorders from his pocket and held it up to my face.

"It's difficult to tell. It's really faint. A voice, I think."

"Concentrate really hard, Ballard. Can you tell what it's saying?"

I listened for a moment, and while I did, Pierce held absolutely still. Little red glimmers, reflections from the recorder's light, danced in the dark hair of his beard. He was beaming like a kid in the glint of his own birthday candles, as if he were making a wish he knew would come true.

The voice was repeating something, over and over again. There was a lull to it; it tugged at something inside me. "I think it's a song... or a chant..."

"Is it a male voice or a female voice?" Pierce asked.

It was soft. Gentle. Tearful. A forlorn, heartsick, yet somehow expectant, sound.

"It's a girl. She's really sad."

"But you can't make out the words?"

"No."

Pierce clicked the button on the recorder, and the tiny red light went out—along with all of the lights in the library. I yelled as we were plunged into darkness, but silenced myself almost at once as a desk lamp beside my elbow popped on, illuminating Pierce's cluttered office.

"Let's examine the evidence," he said. He elbowed a stack of books onto the floor to make room for the recorder on his desk. He slid into his rickety chair and pulled it up to the desk until he was crouched so closely that his nose was barely an inch from the little device. He looked up and rolled his eyes at me. "How do you expect to hear anything all the way over there? Get over here and listen!"

"You're so bossy," I grumbled. Pierce grinned at me as I clambered up off of his threadbare sofa. We bent our heads together; his breath smelled of strong coffee. Pierce pushed the "play" button.

The voice began again, but it wasn't coming from the recorder; it was coming from somewhere outside. I maneuvered around the boxes and stacks of junk to the window, where the queen of England stared primly up at me from the nearest pile of books. I pushed the dusty old ficus tree to one side and peered out into the courtyard.

It wasn't the courtyard of St. Matt's; it was Fairhaven's courtyard. An unkindness of ravens, shadowy and silent, swept through the moonlit sky.

"Where are we?" I asked.

No one answered. I turned around. I was alone in the office. The books on Pierce's shelves had been replaced with teapots, ceramic figurines, and bobblehead dolls of the royal family.

I rubbed at the grimy window with the sleeve of my shirt and looked out again. A tiny figure facing an ancient stone arch was standing in a Circle made of cobblestones. She looked disquietingly familiar. I still couldn't hear what she was chanting, but her song was so alluring that I half wanted to leap from the window to follow the call of it.

The call of it. The Call of it. Calling. The figure was Calling me. But... but... who was she?

I turned and ran out of the office. In the hallway, Anca pointed me toward a steep, winding staircase.

"Walk home carefully," she warned me. But before I could ask her what she meant, Anca disappeared.

I ran down the staircase as fast as I could. A few steps from the bottom, I lost my footing and stumbled forward. I thrust my arms out in front of me to break my fall.

My arms plunged wrist-deep into cold, fluffy snow.

I looked around. Before me was an unfamiliar brick building. All of the windows were illuminated, and figures moved back and forth in some of the rooms. I could hear raucous laughter and the rhythmic thudding of music.

The snow was soft under my hands, like a bed of down. So soft I thought that if I lay down, I could fall asleep on it. I pressed my cheek to the snow and stretched myself out. It was cool and comforting. Then I waited to hear his voice, because I knew I would.

"Hey there."

"Hi, Evan."

I rolled over. He lay beside me, looking at me with those same warm, friendly eyes; his face was alight with that same heart-stopping smile.

"Nice fall."

I groaned. "You saw that?"

He winked. "Maybe."

"I am the epitome of grace," I said, blushing. "I'm well known for it."

"What took you so long?" he asked.

"I don't know."

Evan took my hand, causing my heart to leap with giddy excitement into my throat.

"How did you get here?" he asked after a moment.

"I don't remember. I came out here looking for something."

"What was it?"

"I don't remember," I said again.

We lay in silence for a long while. The snow beneath my head seemed to be leeching my already-waning memories away, leaving me in a pleasant, happy haze. It was lovely not having to think, to worry, to fight. It was so easy, just being here with him.

"Tell me something," I said. It was almost a question, a request.

"What do you want to hear?" Evan asked.

"I don't know. Anything. Just your voice."

He laughed, a carefree sound. It was musical, in perfect harmony with the rhythm floating down from the nearest window.

"Anything, huh? Okay, let's see." He cleared his throat theatrically, and we both laughed. Then he began, "She abides with darkness."

331

I jolted upright. "What did you say?"
He smiled.

"She abides with darkness.
It clings to her like ash,
From the tips of her eyelashes to the soles of her feet,
Darkness wraps about her, a soft gossamer shroud,
Shielding the world from the shining heat of her eyes.
If I could brush this ash, like stardust,
Away from the constellations of her cheeks,
And see beyond her caliginous veil,
To the blossoming sorrow beneath—
What mightn't I give to be so blinded?
All within me, surely, the pulse of every cell,
For a single brush of lip upon lip."

I stared at him. Those weren't Evan's words. They belonged to someone else. To someone I needed. But who?

"You didn't like it?" Evan asked as his brow furrowed.

"Why did you say that?" I replied, confused.

"You told me to say anything I wanted," he answered, with big, sad, puppy-dog eyes. Puppy-dog eyes almost as alluring as his smile.

"I know but... of all the things you could've recited, why did you choose that?"

Evan shrugged casually, turning his eyes back up to the sky above us. "It just seemed like something you should hear."

I stared up at the sky, too. It was vast and starry, like the sky my mother and I had sat beneath when we stargazed all those years ago... Or was it a few minutes ago?—Wait, where was I?

"How do you know that poem?" I asked.

"I read it somewhere," Evan replied with a contented sigh.

"Where?"

"In this."

He pulled a small, battered black book from his back pocket and tossed it into the snowy space between us.

Finn's notebook. I remembered. They were Finn's words.

I slid my hand out of Evan's and reached for the book. In the moment I let go of him and touched the notebook, I knew I couldn't stay here.

332

Where the brick building had stood just a moment before, there was now a door—an old and crumbling door carved all over with faded runes. The door stood ajar, bathed in a purplish glow; if I squinted, I could just make out a tiny shadowy figure standing deep in the heart of it.

"Hannah."

"Yes, you found her, I knew you would," Evan said.

"No, I mean it's Hannah. She's Calling me."

Evan frowned. "I don't hear anything."

"You aren't supposed to. It's just for me."

I had to go. I knew that now.

I turned for one last look at him. Evan smiled at me—a smile so captivating it almost convinced me to stay. Almost. He was beautiful. He was perfect. And I had to let him go. Again.

I wasn't ready. I wasn't ready to go, to be gone from him. But this world wasn't for me, not yet anyway. Hannah had reminded me. She Called me and reminded me where I belonged, just as I knew she would. And I would answer.

I strode, without looking back, to the threshold of the door. I stood upon it as though poised for flight. Then I leapt onto the current of Hannah's Calling and rode it back home. The door closed firmly behind me.

§

I sat up and sucked in that first, dizzying breath as I connected once again to my body, but almost immediately, all of that air was knocked clean out of me; Hannah had tackled me with a hug so fierce that she knocked me down flat.

"It worked! Oh, it worked! Oh, Jess, thank God, thank GOD!" she sobbed.

I wrapped an arm around her. "I never doubted you. I knew you could do it."

"I didn't. I thought you were gone," she gasped.

"I'm not going anywhere. I'm not leaving you." I brushed her mane of hair away from my eyes and saw Finn smiling at me, his face glazed with tears.

"Are you alright?" I asked him.

Finn actually threw back his head and laughed. "You literally came back from the dead, yet you ask me if I'm alright?"

I laughed too, a little sheepishly. I could feel myself blushing under the intensity of his gaze; I hastily looked away just in time to see Milo flying at me.

"Gah! Stop! Back away!" I cried as he attempted a ghost version of a hug. But far from being warm and welcoming, his spectral embrace left me freezing cold and tingling uncomfortably.

"I can't help it! I'm having a proud Spirit Guide moment over here!" he said. "My two girls! That was the most badass thing I've ever seen!"

"If you say so," I said. Then I gasped as I caught sight of the *Geatgrima* behind him.

Or rather, at what had been the *Geatgrima*; it had crumbled into a pile of rubble upon its dais. Stunned, I gazed at the dais for a moment before looking around the courtyard. Figures were gathered all around its perimeter, just visible through the still-settling dust. Savvy and Annabelle stood arm in arm—with Bertie just behind them—near the Council Room's entrance.

The three of them had obviously been successful in freeing all the prisoners. To their right, Celeste and Fiona were helping Finvarra rise shakily to her feet. Students, teachers, Caomhnóir, and Council members alike, all with awed expressions on their faces, filled the courtyard; I felt myself turn even redder under their gazes. I dropped my eyes and found myself staring at Neil's motionless figure, which was sprawled on the far side of the dais.

"Neil?" I asked.

Hannah shook her head. "The part of him that could follow you into the Gateway did. It didn't come back out again."

I stared at Neil's body a moment. I did that. I killed him. I'd battled foes and spirits and monsters; death had surrounded me and chased me across two continents; I'd witnessed cruelties so harsh they still seemed like nightmares; but this life—Neil's life—had left this world by my own hand. Someday, I knew, I would feel guilty about this. But not today.

I pushed the reality of that thought away and allowed the intense relief bubbling up inside of me to wash over everything. It was really over. For the first time in more months than I cared to count, no disaster loomed on the horizon, no enemies lurked around each corner, no duplicity was luring us into danger. The Wraiths were gone, the Gateway was closed, the Necromancers were defeated, I had my sister back, and we were all safe.

"Jess, I don't know how to... I'm just so sorry," Hannah said. "I was so stupid. They told me... I mean, they made it sound like—"

I cupped her face between my hands. "Look at me. Don't apologize to me. Not for this. Not ever," I said. "I'll explain later, but I know all about how they manipulated you, what they did to you. You have nothing to apologize for. We ended this together. That's all that counts here, no matter what anyone else says. You understand me?"

My sister's face broke into a watery smile. And from her lips came that one little word, "Yes."

A little word, reclaimed. I smiled back.

I started to climb to my feet, but before I could do more than slide one awkwardly bent leg out from under me, Finn was at my side; he wrapped one arm around my waist while holding his free hand out to help me up. Jess from a few days ago would have slapped him away. But that Jess hadn't seen what I'd seen.

"Thank you," I said, accepting his help and leaning on him as I regained my bearings.

"You're welcome."

I let Finn accept my thanks without his really understanding exactly what I was thanking him for. I wondered if I would ever tell him how close I'd come to giving in to the pull of the next world, to staying behind and ignoring the Call that brought us back together. I wondered if I would ever tell him that it was his words—the words he'd woven together so beautifully—that had rebirthed the memory of this world in my soul, that had spun the net which held me back long enough to answer Hannah's Call. Without knowing it, Finn had pulled me back before I'd been irretrievably lost. I thought, perhaps, I *would* tell him... someday.

I held tightly to Finn's hand long after I'd managed to stand on my own two feet again.

EPILOGUE

"**I** CAN'T BELIEVE WE'RE PACKING AGAIN. Doesn't it feel like we just did this?" Hannah sighed.

"I guess so," I said breathlessly as I dragged my suitcase over to the stack of luggage by the door of our room. "But then again, we haven't been here very long in the grand scheme of things, even though a hell of a lot has happened since we got here. In some ways, Boston was a lifetime ago."

Many lifetimes ago, and none of them our own.

Hannah nodded. "You're right. I don't even know how I feel about going back."

Nearly a week had passed, but Hannah's features still reflected the transformative beauty that the power of the reversal had left upon them. It was unsettling to look at, so I kept my eyes on my luggage as I answered.

"I do—I'm voluntarily getting back on a plane. That should give you a fair idea of how I feel about it."

Hannah smiled a little sadly and looked out the window. I didn't share her reluctance to leave Fairhaven and everything it stood for. Because we *were* leaving. That was certain—even if nothing else was.

"If I were you, Jess, I'd leave all that luggage here. You need a whole new wardrobe anyway. It's like you're allergic to color," Milo quipped from his perch on the fireplace's mantel, where he had been lording over the packing process like a self-proclaimed monarch.

I sighed. I couldn't even be annoyed with him; it was just too damn good to have Milo back to his old, fashion-obsessed self. I even let myself laugh, just a little.

"What time is it?" I asked.

Hannah glanced at the delicate silver watch on her wrist. "Nearly time. Should we go down?"

"*They* should be coming up *here*. When I think of them having the nerve to summon you anywhere..." Milo shook his head, apparently lost for words dire enough to express his opinion of

337

the Council and its members. And when Milo lacked the ability to bitch someone out, the circumstances were indeed extreme.

"They aren't summoning us," Hannah said patiently. "Not like that, anyway."

"Yeah well, I still say they should be groveling," Milo grumbled.

"Let's get this over with," I said. I took a last look around the room. It really *was* beautiful, with its wood paneling, antique furniture, and lush draperies—like something out of an Austen novel; my own personal slice of Pemberley. But despite the low fire crackling warmly away in the fireplace, all I felt when I looked at the room was coldness; I'd take the industrial cinder blocks and poster-plastered walls of my dorm room at St. Matt's any day.

As we walked down the hallway, some of the other Apprentices watched unabashedly through the open doors of their own rooms. They weren't pelting us with exactly the same kinds of stares and whispers as when we'd first arrived; there was a subtle shift in tone. Their hostility had diminished into a fearful sort of awe, and their superiority had melted into wariness. We were no longer ostracized, but we were still outsiders—now more than ever.

The trip down to the Grand Council Room was much quieter and less eventful than walking through the halls of Fairhaven used to be. Most of the spirits that had escaped being transformed into Wraiths had Crossed through the open *Geatgrima*.

As we reached the staircase, I swallowed back a terrible, guilt-ridden something that had risen in my throat; although Mary had seemed at peace, I would always wonder about my decision to thrust the Spirit Torch through the Gateway. Surely, the spirits belonged on the other side, yet they hadn't made that choice for themselves. But Finn had reassured me that Mary had been right; I wasn't the one who took the choice away from the spirits in the first place, and a fate on the other side was far better than what would've happened to them if the Torch had been extinguished.

"Are you okay? You look troubled," Hannah asked, watching me.

"I'm just anxious to get out of here," I lied. There was no point bringing up the Spirit Torch. My guilt couldn't even begin to compare to Hannah's own; she had spent days apologizing to me—even though I didn't blame her for a damn thing.

Karen was waiting for us at the bottom of the stairs with her tan trench coat thrown over her arm and a black, carry-on suitcase at her feet. She'd arrived back at Fairhaven less than twelve hours after the ordeal had ended, and she'd been doing damage control and advocating for us ever since. She'd already met with the Council once, and—as she'd marched into their chamber—I knew, just from watching her stance, that she was in true mama-bear mode. I had heard her shouting before the doors had even fully shut behind her.

Karen had that same protective gleam in her eye as we reached the bottom of the stairs. The entrance hall had been restored to its former glory; the Necromancer's paraphernalia had been removed, and all traces of my Muse-created mural had been meticulously scrubbed away. As much as the mural had terrified me, it felt wrong to see it gone—almost as though the Durupinen were once again sweeping the unsavory details of their history under the rug.

"Ready?" Karen asked as we arrived beside her. She dropped her cell phone into her pocket.

"Yes," I said, and then pointed to the pocket into which her phone had just vanished. "Any word from Annabelle?"

"Yes," Karen said. "I've put her in touch with a friend of mine. She's a real estate lawyer. The insurance situation is a bit of a mess, but I think Annabelle will be able to reopen her shop when it's all cleared up. She's very glad to hear you'll be stateside again soon."

Someone cleared his throat. A Caomhnóir stood waiting to bring us before the Council. He was tapping his foot impatiently.

"They're waiting for you," Karen said, gesturing in the direction of the Grand Council Room.

I took a deep breath. "Are we sure they're not going to try to lock us in the dungeons again?"

"Oh, I don't think you need to worry about that," Karen answered, with the shadow of a smile forming around her mouth.

"Are we leaving soon?" Hannah asked.

"Very soon. Our flight departs in five hours." She, too, seemed to have a hard time looking Hannah in the eye, although I think part of Karen's squeamishness was because Hannah's resemblance to our mother was even more pronounced now. "So whatever the Council has to say to you, they'll need to say it quickly. You aren't bringing a lot of souvenirs home with you, are you? We won't have a lot of extra room in the car on the ride home."

"No souvenirs," I said with a snort. "I looked everywhere, but they don't sell 'I SURVIVED THE SPIRIT APOCALYPSE' T-shirts."

No one laughed. Not even Milo, who had materialized beside us.

"What, too soon?" I asked, widening my eyes innocently. "Aw, c'mon kids. If we don't laugh, we'll cry." I nudged Hannah in the ribs; she gave me a grudging, tight-lipped smile. I turned back to Karen. "What do we need the extra room in the car for?"

Karen smiled. "Tia. Her flight gets in just after ours. We're giving her a ride back to the city and she's going to stay with us for a few days before you head back to St. Matt's."

"Tia's coming back!" I cried. "Why didn't you tell me?"

"I just did!" said Karen, winking. "I wanted to surprise you."

"Tia's great, you're going to love her," I told Hannah. "She likes her stuff almost as organized as you do."

"And you don't think she'll mind living with me?" Hannah asked anxiously.

"Are you kidding? She spent half of our freshman year looking for you! Of course she won't mind! You, on the other hand," I said, smiling at Milo, "are going to take some serious getting used to."

Milo batted his eyelashes. "What are you talking about? I'm delightful."

"We'll talk more about all the college arrangements on the way to the airport, especially yours, Hannah, since you'll be coming in as a new student. But for now..." Karen gestured to the Council Room's doors again, "After you girls."

The scene in the Grand Council Room was fairly identical to the day we had learned of the Prophecy. The Council all sat on their benches, silent and waiting. Other Senior Durupinen, and even a few Apprentices, sat in chairs along the interior wall. The floor's Triskele inlay had been polished to a high shine; it now gleamed as if ash and soot had never marred it. Finvarra had been reinstated as High Priestess; she sat on her throne with the Durupinen amulet shining around her neck, and Carrick stood at attention beside her. I didn't know if her relationship with Carrick would ever be quite the same again, but it was good to see them together. Carrick caught my eye as we entered; he nodded respectfully but looked quickly away again.

Hannah knew the truth about Carrick now; he'd had a long talk with her after he'd recovered from the Elemental's attack. But there was still so much that remained unsaid between the three of us. I didn't see how we could ever have a meaningful relationship with his being Bound to someone who lived on another continent, but I was leaving that door open—just in case any of us wanted to walk through it one day.

Although much in the Council Room looked the same, a few glaring differences reminded us all that much had changed. The back wall was nearly rebuilt, but a few feet of gray morning sky peeked through an opening where a stained-glass window had yet to be replaced. The tapestries that once adorned the walls were gone—burned in the fire—and much of the furniture had yet to be replaced. Catriona sat in the crowd, looking strangely incomplete without Lucida beside her—Lucida was being held in a new, modern-day *príosún* until an international committee of clan leaders could be assembled to try her as a traitor. Bertie sat to the left of the Council: As a reward for his service—and, I suspected, to offer him a position for which he was better suited—Finvarra had created a new Caomhnóir position for him as the Council's Official Recorder. Bertie had taken to the role with alacrity; he sat, poised and almost confident, behind his steno machine.

Marion was gone. She'd been voted off of the Council and—if the rumors were true—would also face the international committee to answer for her attempted coup. Marion's crimes were so severe that her own clan could even be stripped of its Gateway—or at least that's what Mackie had whispered to us the previous night as a very subdued Peyton had passed us in the hallway. The Council members who had been closest to Marion sat stiffly in their seats, perhaps worried about their own continued status on the Council.

"Thank you for coming," Finvarra said.

I nodded. I hadn't really felt that we'd had a choice. Perhaps Finvarra had felt differently.

"I thought it important that we meet with you before you go," she went on. "Much has transpired."

Milo laughed softly behind me. I could almost hear him through our connection, or perhaps we just knew each other really well now. *"Hello? Understatement of the century."*

"I have called the members of our community here because I wanted to make things as clear as I can. The events of the past few weeks have been complicated in the extreme, and only time

341

will bring to light the many layers and factors that brought us to this moment. But the important thing to know is that these factors cannot be reduced to black and white, or to right and wrong."

The room went so still it felt as though the collective group of us had stopped breathing. Hannah began trembling beside me. Karen was standing very stiffly, doing her very best not to fly off the handle; her hands were clenching and unclenching at her sides.

"Countless errors of judgment were made, some of them my own. In many ways, we, the leaders of the Northern Clans, brought about our own near destruction. History, no doubt, will judge us for it, for we are surely leaving behind a complicated and troubling legacy."

Agitated stirring swept through the benches like the flapping wings of nervous birds.

"Hannah," Finvarra said, and although she had addressed my sister quite gently, Hannah jumped beside me. I reached out and grabbed her hand, squeezing it tightly, as Finvarra continued. "I want to make it perfectly clear to you, and to the others assembled here, that you are not to blame for what has come to pass. It was the Necromancers alone, with their machinations and manipulations, who brought about the Prophecy. If we had done more to protect you, to earn your trust, you would not have been left in such a vulnerable position."

I couldn't help but notice that many faces did not reflect this attitude. Indeed, there were nearly as many disgruntled expressions on the Council benches as there were contented ones. Finvarra's pronouncement had obviously been far from a unanimous decision. But Hannah's eyes were locked on Finvarra; my twin stared at her with a pronounced relief splashed across her features.

Finvarra turned to face me. "Jessica, we owe you a great debt of gratitude. You risked your very life to close the *Geatgrima* when it seemed all would be lost. Our order survives because of you. Quite possibly, our world survives because of you. I promise you that, as long as I am High Priestess, we will not squander this second chance we have been granted by your actions."

Blood rushed to my face. I had no idea what to say to any of this. I nodded again—it seemed the most solid response I could give.

"That is why our first order of business is to invite your family to rejoin our Council," Finvarra declared grandly.

A ringing silence met her words.

"What are you saying?" I asked when I found my voice.

"Marion's position on the Council is now open, a position that was held by your clan for many years. Your family has rendered a great service to the Durupinen, and so it seems only fitting to offer the Council seat to you. Your input and opinions would be greatly valued here."

"You want us on the Council?" I asked blankly.

"Indeed. What do you say? Shall Clan Sassanaigh sit amongst the ruling clans once more?" Finvarra asked, with her arms raised in welcome.

Karen turned to us. Her mouth was open, but it was empty of words. My eyes sought Hannah's: In what was perhaps our first telepathic twin moment, we said not a word but understood each other perfectly.

"No," I said firmly; the cavernous hall added an emphatic echo.

Finvarra dropped her arms along with her warm expression. "No?"

"No, thank you," said Hannah, with a tone and words that were far more polite than my own, but just as resounding.

"But this is a great honor," Finvarra said, as the room began to buzz like a hive with reactions to our refusal. "Surely you must see that. This is your chance to establish your clan's position once again. Perhaps you do not understand what you're walking away from."

Perhaps it was Celeste's approving nod or Fiona's amused chortle. Perhaps it was Savvy's defiant voice somewhere to my left exclaiming "A right gutting, that!" Or perhaps it was simply Finvarra's casual use of the word *walking*—a word which would surely never hold the same meaning for me again. Whatever the inspiration, I drew myself up with more confidence than I'd ever felt in that room before.

"We understand exactly what we're walking away from."

§

Finn was waiting by the car, with a duffel bag slung over his shoulder and something very like a smile on his face. He was coming with us, of course: Where the Gateway goes, its Guardian must follow. There was a time when I would've felt both guilty and angry about that, but now...

"Well, they let you leave. You didn't have to burn the place down. That's an improvement," he said as we loaded our luggage.

"Was that a joke?" I asked. "An actual joke?"

"I guess so, yes," he said with a shrug.

"There's hope for you yet, Finn," I said, punching him playfully on the arm. "Are you sure you're ready for this move?"

"As ready as I'll ever be, yeah."

"Are you sure you can handle it? I'm all kinds of trouble, you know." I tried to keep a straight face as I said it, but a mischievous smile snaked traitorously across my lips.

"Proper trouble. I know."

Karen snatched the keys from the waiting Novitiate. "We'll drive ourselves, thank you," she said, as she slipped herself behind the wheel of the car. Karen was so smooth, the poor kid never stood a chance.

"Oi, OI!" Savvy called from the window above. "You're not skiving off without proper cheers, are ya?"

"Of course not!" I yelled up to her. "Here's to ya, Sav." And with that, I opened my top and flashed her.

Savvy's cackle echoed through the air as we piled into the back seat—Finn, now slightly mortified, sat on one side of me, Hannah on the other. Milo yelled "Shotgun!" at the top of his lungs before stretching out luxuriously in the front seat, as if he needed a physical space in the car.

A small black book peeked out from Finn's pocket. I grabbed it and tucked it into my own.

"Hey, why are you pickpocketing me?" he asked, scowling a bit.

"I need something to read on the plane. I've heard this is pretty great. You don't mind, do you?"

Finn tried to maintain his frown, but couldn't. "No, I suppose I don't."

The car hummed to life. We crunched along the gravel drive and through the castle gates before heading out onto the open road. I turned and watched Fairhaven Hall shrinking into the heavy English-morning mist as the cradling arms of the valley enfolded the castle. I was glad to see it go. I told myself I would never see Fairhaven again.

344

I was wrong, of course. But that, as they say, is another story entirely.

The following pages contain a sample chapter from *Whispers of the Walker: The Gateway Trackers Book 1*, a continuation of *The Gateway Trilogy*.

SAMPLE CHAPTER FROM "WHISPERS OF THE WALKER: THE GATEWAY TRACKERS BOOK 1"

I KNEW SHE WAS WATCHING ME BEFORE I GLANCED UP. I could feel the waves of animosity—sheer negative energy—radiating down toward me from the window two stories above. My fingers twitched inside the pocket of my jacket, itching to draw a face I had not yet seen. I balled my fingers into a fist and calmed them with my familiar mantra:

"Patience, now. Art will follow."

I bounced on the balls of my feet, trying in vain to keep warm, as I stood outside on the sidewalk. On general principle, I'd refused to break out my winter coat in early October—I was still mourning the warmth of summer. As a result, I was now freezing my ass off. I yanked the collar of my sweater up to my chin, and watched my breath turn to damp swirling clouds around my head.

A smart, two-door sports car rolled up beside me and slipped deftly into a very narrow parking space. A short, harried looking woman jumped out; I watched as she shut the car door with her foot while hastily twisting her hair into a messy bun.

"Are you Jessica?" she asked.

"Yes. Tanya? Nice to meet you," I said, holding out a hand.

Tanya was so preoccupied with trying to extract a set of keys from her pocket that she didn't notice my offer of a handshake. After a few awkward seconds, I lowered my hand and thrust it back into my pocket—where it could at least stay warm.

"So, um, this is it, obviously," said Tanya, gesturing vaguely over her shoulder at the house. It was one of the boxy old Colonials which crowded the historic district of Salem; the houses stood shoulder-to-shoulder along the block as if they were all vying for position. A tiny, grassless strip of a yard stood before each, adding even more uniformity. The house looked stately from across the street, but up close I could see that its yellow paint was starting to peel, and its windows looked warped in their black-shuttered frames. A tarnished plaque next to the front door read: "The Samuel Harner House, 1704."

"It looks really cool," I said truthfully. "I'm a sucker for historic houses."

"Yeah, me too," Tanya replied, although she sounded rueful rather than enthusiastic. "That's why I bought it in the first place." She thrust a sheaf of papers at me. "These are all the details about the apartment, which you might've seen online. Is that how you found it?"

"Yes," I said, but I didn't look at the papers. A movement had caught my eye; a lacy white curtain was fluttering in a window high above.

"It's the third-floor unit... Although," and she laughed a little hysterically, "I can now offer you the first or second floor as well, if either would suit you better."

"No, no, the third floor is fine," I said, smiling at her. "I'd rather not have the noise of upstairs neighbors."

"Although neighbors might not be the trouble," I added in a whisper to myself. The curtain above us twitched again.

We stood staring at each other for a moment. The keys jingled agitatedly in Tanya's hand as she gnawed on a fingernail; it was already bitten to the quick.

"So... can I see it?" I asked finally.

Tanya opened her mouth as though to tell me something, but shut it again and nodded. Then she turned without another word and marched to the door. I stood quietly beside her while she fumbled with the keys, then attempted to jam one of them into the lock with her shaking fingers.

"What site did you find the listing on?" she asked me, to break the awkward silence as she struggled with the keys. "I like to ask, so I know which of my advertising methods works the best."

"Oh, uh... Craigslist, I think?"

"Mmm-hmm. Okay, great." Her response was perfunctory; she wasn't listening to me at all.

And that was good, because I hadn't found the apartment on Craigslist. In fact, I didn't even know if the apartment had been posted on Craigslist, although it seemed a pretty safe bet. No, I'd learned of the apartment while I was working at a nearby coffee shop.

Two students, both girls, had been swept into the Juniper Breeze Café by a biting, bitter wind two days earlier. Their faces were pink and raw; their scarves were yanked up around their ears. They had stumbled over to the counter, hopping up and down to warm themselves, and ordered skinny lattes before sliding into an empty table in front of the pastry display.

I had half-listened as they debated between ordering a Danish over a scone, but then perked up my ears as one checked her phone with a groan.

"Oh, God. That other place isn't going to be available until next Thursday."

"The one on Halifax?"

"Yeah."

"Shit. I really liked that one."

"What are we going to do now? I'm not spending another night in that apartment."

"Neither am I. I'll text Katie and let her know we'll be crashing for the next week."

"Yeah, but what about all our stuff? And our security deposit?"

"I don't know. At this point, I just want to say, 'Screw it.' Oh my God, this is such a mess."

I set the two lattes carefully down on the table in front of them. "Sorry, but I couldn't help overhearing. You're moving out of your apartment? Is it local? I'm looking for a new place, and I'm sort of in a hurry."

The girls exchanged an uncomfortable look before one of them shook her long, wavy blonde bangs out of her eyes and said, "Uh, yeah, it's only a couple of blocks from here on Brimfield Street, but... well, trust me, you don't want to live there."

"Oh, really? Why's that?" I asked.

They looked at each other again, clearly unsure of how they should answer.

"Loud neighbors?" I suggested.

The second girl, who had short, dark hair, gave a harsh laugh; it was just possible to detect a note of hysteria in it.

"You could say that," the other answered. Her face was turning the same shade of red as her scarf.

"Well, I don't mind a little noise. What's the address?" I asked, pulling a pen from my apron.

The blonde girl sized me up, then said, "112 Brimfield Street. Unit C."

All trace of laughter fled from the brunette's face. She whacked her friend on the arm before hissing, "You can't just tell her that!"

"Why not?" the blonde murmured back. "If we find a new tenant, we might have a prayer of getting our deposit back."

"But you can't let her... that's not right!"

"You heard her, she said she doesn't mind some noise," the blonde said, glancing at me again. Her eyes lingered in a familiar way on my hair, my clothes, and my elaborate, recently acquired tattoo. I repressed a sardonic grin and tried to look politely puzzled.

The brunette threw a disgusted look at her friend before turning back to me. "Look, just take our word for it, okay? You really don't want to live in that apartment."

"Why?" I pressed. "I really need a place."

Then, ignoring a glare from her roommate, the brunette unleashed the entire story—not a solitary detail of which deterred me in the least.

§

"Come out, come out, wherever you are," I sang under my breath.

Tanya looked up from her struggle with her keys. "What did you say?"

"Oh, nothing. Just humming to myself," I replied, watching her hand tremble violently as she tried another key. "Is everything okay?"

"It's fine. It's just... it's been a hell of a week, if you'll pardon my language," Tanya said, and the laugh that bubbled out of her could have been a precursor to tears. Just as she finally managed to fit the key into the lock, it shot out from between her fingers and landed noisily on the front step.

We both stared at the key for a moment. Then I bent down, picked it up, and offered it back to her. "We all have weeks like that. It'll get better," I said.

Tanya forced a smile that clearly said, "You don't know what you're talking about." She didn't take the key from me.

"I'll get it," I said, and thrust the key into the lock. It turned easily, and I pushed the door open.

"Thanks," muttered Tanya, as she pulled the key from the lock and stepped over the threshold. Her expression looked as though she were expecting an imminent lightning bolt to the head. When nothing happened, she exhaled a long-held breath and began trudging up the stairs, cocking her head for me to follow.

"The house is old, obviously," she said as she climbed, "but the heating system was replaced five years ago, and the whole house has been deleaded. I redid all the kitchens when I bought it, so the appliances are less than three years old."

"Great," I replied, since she seemed to expect a response. I was barely listening, though. New heating system or not, there was a definite chill in the air that deepened as we ascended the stairs. Every cell in my body tingled with a familiar sensation, a latent sensitivity to the presence of someone who belonged in another world entirely. By the time we reached the top of the staircase, my breath was visible and chugging out of me like puffs from a tiny locomotive.

"So... I'm guessing that new heating system isn't actually on right now?"

Tanya turned to look at me. "Yeah, uh... I didn't expect it to be so cold so soon," she said with yet another slightly wild laugh. I knew she was lying. She was a New Englander; the area was notorious for its unpredictable—and often freezing—weather. The poor woman was in panic mode, however desperately she was trying to hide it. I nearly took pity on her and told her the truth about why I was here, but since I didn't know exactly what I was dealing with yet, I decided to keep my mouth shut.

Tanya pushed open the door to the third-floor apartment and flicked on the light. We stepped inside the entry hall. The hostile presence I felt was so powerful that I could taste the sour acidity of it on my tongue. Tanya could feel it too, I realized, although how she perceived it—apart from the cold—I couldn't tell. But her body language told me all I needed to know; she knit her brow ferociously and seemed to withdraw into herself. Perhaps the cold was causing her to anticipate the manifestation of something she couldn't understand, something that had perhaps appeared to her before.

"So... um, this is it," she said so weakly that I almost couldn't hear her. Her whispers hung in the air, like little hovering cumulus clouds of fear.

"Nice!" I replied brightly as I began walking briskly around the apartment; the unit contained a huge brick fireplace and several large built-in bookcases.

I stepped into the kitchen, which was a fair size. "Oh, yeah, I can see the appliances are newer," I said encouragingly.

A blast of cold pulsed from the living room and into the kitchen, causing Tanya to gasp and my hair to blow back from my face.

"These old places are pretty drafty, huh?" I said, trying to keep my tone light. "You should think about replacement windows, eventually." I couldn't hide a small shiver.

Tanya blinked and forced a smile. "Uh, yeah. It's on the wish list."

I opened the nearest cabinet, then ran my hand over the counter near the sink. "It seems really clean. Can't say that about many of the places I've seen."

"Yes, I had a service come in after... uh, before I started showing it," came Tanya's shaky response.

"So this is the half bath?" I asked cheerfully, pretending I had missed the hesitation in her answer. I poked my head into a small bathroom off of the kitchen. As I glanced inside, the antique mirror over the sink fogged over as though someone were breathing all over it. Then two slender-fingered handprints appeared on the mirror's cloudy surface. The tiniest of whimpers escaped Tanya. I turned quickly to face the kitchen, as though I'd seen nothing unusual.

"I could totally see us living here," I said. "Can I check out the bedrooms?"

"Of—of course," replied Tanya, with the faintest trace of hopefulness in her voice. She took a deep breath and followed me.

The apartment's three bedrooms were directly off of the living room. I poked my head into the first bedroom. It was small but cozy, with a wall of exposed brick and lots of shelf space for books; I could almost see Hannah curled up in a chair in the corner, lost in her latest library loot.

Almost. It was kind of hard to picture Hannah sitting there, while also staring into a very angry set of eyes.

"Ah, so there you are," I said quietly.

The spirit looked young, maybe twenty-five. Her jet-black hair was braided back from her face, and she had a goth look that made my own penchant for black look tame. She was wearing a decorative lace corset cinched over a long, trailing dress; a pentagram and other mystical charms hung from silver chains around her neck. As I stared at her, she extended her arm towards the nearest item—a vase of fake flowers on the windowsill—and, with a sweeping gesture, caused it to fall to the floor.

Tanya screamed, dropping her last vestiges of pretense. I turned to her.

"It's okay!" I said with a gentle nudge. "It was just a vase. You're jumpy, huh?"

"I... I just... what?" Tanya stammered.

"This vase fell over," I said, trotting over to it and picking it up. "Might have been the draft when we came in. These old houses can have crazy cross-breezes sometimes." I was really putting on a show; this was some first-class improv.

If Tanya looked confused, it was nothing compared to how the spirit now looked. She gazed around for something else to scare me off with. Then, with a smirk, she reached toward the lamp in the corner. As she opened and closed her hand, the light bulb began to flash on and off.

I looked at the lamp and chuckled. "Old wiring, huh? I'll be sure to bring some surge protectors," I said, speaking half to Tanya, half to the spirit.

Tanya had reached her limit: She dropped her face into her hands and started to cry. I took advantage of her momentary distraction and looked the spirit straight in the eye. She stared back at me, wide-eyed, and dropped her hand to her side.

"What the hell?" I heard her mutter.

"I can see you," I whispered. "And your little poltergeist tricks won't work on me, honey—You can chill with the antics."

The spirit's expression turned into a mix of shock and fear. She vanished. I walked back over to Tanya and placed an arm around her shaking shoulders.

"Hey. It's alright."

"No it's not," she sobbed. "It's not alright. It will never be alright!"

"Why not? It's okay, I've already decided that I'll take it."

"You'll...what?"

"I'll take it. I want the apartment."

353

Tanya shook her head violently. "No. No, I can't let you. It's... it's haunted, okay? I'm sorry I didn't tell you, but I haven't been able to rent this place out for longer than a month or so before the tenants leave. I sank all of my savings into this house, and now..."

"It's okay. Tanya, look at me." I grabbed her gently by the shoulders, shaking them slightly so that she raised her head and looked me in the eyes. "I know it's haunted. I knew it before I walked in the door."

Tanya blinked at me. "You did? How could you possibly have known that?"

"I can just tell. It's one of my most interesting and annoying traits. And you don't need to worry about renting this place to me. I'm telling you I can handle it. In fact, if I have some time here, I can probably get the spirit to leave."

"Oh my God, do you really think so? I've tried everything! Three different priests, a psychic, and I even had a neo-pagan grad student teach me about cleansing and sage-burning. I was actually walking around with this smoking bunch of herbs, coughing my head off! But nothing worked. I'm completely at the end of my rope! You have no idea!"

"I do. I really do. Give me a month in this house. You'll be ghost-free in no time."

"This is so bizarre. I don't even believe in ghosts. At least, I never have," Tanya whispered, shaking her head.

"I know that most of the time when people say this, it's bullshit—but I *do* know exactly how you feel," I replied gently. "So what do you say? Do I get the apartment? Can we move in next week?"

Tanya still looked torn. "I guess so, but I just don't understand why you'd want to live with a ghost!"

I smiled grimly as my new roommate shimmered into view in the corner, with her arms crossed and her eyes looking daggers at me.

"I know Tanya, it must seem strange to you. But actually, I'm not sure I know how to live *without* ghosts anymore."

E.E. Holmes is a writer, teacher, and actor living in central Massachusetts with her husband, two children, and a small, but surprisingly loud, dog. When not writing, she enjoys performing, watching unhealthy amounts of British television, and reading with her children.

To learn more about E.E. Holmes and *The World of the Gateway*, please visit www.eeholmes.com

Made in the USA
Middletown, DE
07 June 2021